moth
to a

CAMBRIA HEBERT

moth
to a
flame

The faint smell of chlorine lingered, underscoring the other scents of mold, grime… and death. Chlorine and death didn't go together. The combination made me think I was sitting in a hospital that specialized in killing their patients, not saving them.

I guess, really, it wasn't far off.

I wasn't in a hospital, but this place definitely wasn't going to save me. I was going to have to do that myself.

Hopelessness so thick and putrid lodged in my throat, and tears burned the backs of my dry, tired eyes. I had no idea how I had any tears left to cry, how there was anything left of me at all. I felt like a mere hollow shell of who I used to be. A casing of skin and bone containing nothing but a woman sentenced to death.

I had no idea how I got here.

The memory of the hours I spent before opening my eyes to this hellfest were so hidden by my mind I actually believed they would never be retrieved.

It's for the best was what I told myself about those missing links because anything that ended with me being here wasn't anything I wanted to know. Right?

No.

Not knowing was just more torture in the already grim situation in which I found myself trapped. Maybe if I could remember, I could think of a way to escape. Or, at the very least, understand what I did that would result in my murder.

Scratch, scratch. The faint sound might as well have been a gunshot because it scared me just as much. Huddling closer to the grimy tile I would never have touched before, my shaking, weak arms wrapped around my knees as dirty, matted hair fell across my face.

Rattling chain made me freeze, regretting instantly the movements I made to protect myself.

Now he would know I was awake.

With bated breath, I waited, trying desperately to calm the way my body quaked as I listened for him to come closer.

Scratch, scratch.

With my eyes squeezed closed, the sound continued to taunt me.

Scratch, scratch.

I didn't know how long I waited, but finally, I realized he wasn't here. The sound was something else. It was coming from someone else.

Biting down on my lip until the metallic taste of blood spilled over my tongue, painstakingly, I lifted my eyes to peer around the protection of my hair. It was so dark in here… would be pitch black if it weren't for the random spotlights erected around the space.

Pitch black would probably have been less ominous because there wouldn't be any shadows in complete darkness.

The sound was coming from there.

A place I intensely didn't want to look.

Scratch, scratch.

A thought occurred to me and, with it, the first inkling of hope I'd had in what felt like centuries. If he wasn't here making that sound, then maybe I wasn't as alone as I thought.

Whimpering and lowering my arms from around my legs, I sat up straight and gazed into the place I swore I'd never look again.

"Hello?" The sound scraped out of my raw throat.

"A-are y-you…?" The words wobbled, but I managed to get them out anyway. "A-a-alive?"

Scratch, scratch.

My heart jumped, causing me to sit forward to peer into the shadowy corner. That was an answer, right? Maybe the only one she could give, maybe all she had the energy for.

A sob built in my throat, the pressure of it hurting so much it felt like I might choke. "I'm here!" I said, scooting forward. The back of my thigh caught on a jagged piece of broken tile, and my skin tore.

I ignored it.

"You aren't alone," I whimpered, relieved because it meant I wasn't alone anymore either.

I'd thought she was dead. All that blood…

Pushing away the gruesome thought, I focused on her telling me she was alive.

"We're going to get out of here." I promised, tears streaking down my dirty, cold cheeks.

I waited for another scratching sound. Anything to show she heard me, anything to know I had an ally.

No more sound came. Instead, she turned her head.

Forgetting all about being quiet, I started to scream.

He was coming.

Something no one ever needed to announce. The second he drew near, the very air within a twenty-yard radius around him changed. Almost like it was sucked out of everything and everyone. As if everything, even the most inanimate of objects, waited with bated breath for his striking good looks and charming smile to christen the room with a gulp of fresh air.

The crew in the trailer began scrambling around, suddenly wide awake even though it was still hours until the sun would rise. Hair was fluffed, boobs were pushed up, and Carson (our resident diva) actually adjusted the junk beneath his jeans.

Hiding a smile, I picked up the travel mug of hot tea I'd brought from home and sipped at the honey-laced brew, enjoying the show. It was never a dull day in show business.

Being around celebrities wasn't new for any of us. Normally, we didn't bat an eye at their presence. But there were a few that still seemed to create a buzz in the air.

Nick Preston was one of those celebrities.

Currently, he was the number one actor in the country, recently coined the "Sexiest Man Alive," and had the top two movies in the box office.

Nick's newest movie, *Tom Ford*, was number one for the second week in a row and was the first movie in what I knew was going to be a successful chain of films based on a US Marshall who turned bad but still always came out the hero. *Code Blue* was number two for the second week in a row (only bumped out of the number one spot by *Tom Ford*) and was about the heroic acts of an emergency responder who was one of the first on a scene in a natural disaster.

Both films were action packed, filled with kickass graphics and suspense, and left the audience breathless. They had some romance elements to them as well, but truthfully, it wouldn't matter if they did. Women would still flock to see his films because he just had that kind of on-screen presence. And the men went because the guy could seriously kick ass in a fight.

The sound of booted footfalls outside the trailer made my stomach flutter a little. What? I wasn't immune to his charm either. I was just better at hiding it.

After all, I had a lot of experience with hiding.

Nick's wide shoulders and narrow waist filled the trailer door, and beside me, Carson squealed beneath his breath. I elbowed him in the side, and he gave me a look like he knew I wanted to fangirl too. It was hard, but I resisted the urge to stick out my tongue at him, something I might not have bothered fighting if there wasn't a chance I'd get stuck making some awful face when Mr. Handsome himself showed up.

Speaking of… Nick ducked into the space, moving farther into our temporary quarters. The second he did, the entire room took a collective breath around him. His hair was longer now than it was in his previous movie. The sides were trimmed close, but the top could be styled into that messy, sticking-up look everyone loved so much these days. Currently, the strands were chaotic, not in the styled way, but in a way that said he hadn't bothered to touch it before coming here. He probably preferred it short. Most guys did because then they didn't have to comb it.

His jaw was shadowed with stubble, the same in-between color as the hair on his head. Nick's hair wasn't blond, but it wasn't brown either. It was sort of a golden shade, or maybe it was just brown that had been expertly highlighted to appear multidimensional.

"Morning," he said in his signature deep baritone. "I'd have brought donuts, but not even the donut makers are up this early." White teeth flashed as he spoke. "Besides, I can't eat them anyway. Watching you eat them would only make me question my career choice."

Even though I knew Nick was joking, Carson, who was still beside me, made a low sound of distress. Out of the corner of my eye, I glanced over and almost spit out the tea I was sipping. In his hand was a round pink-iced donut with sprinkles. He'd already taken a bite out of it.

I watched, totally amused, as he stealthily took another huge bite, then nonchalantly dropped it in the trash behind him. Chewing super slow, he caught my eye. "Not a word, girl." He warned.

I winked.

"Have a seat, Mr. Preston," Laura said, bursting into action and motioning toward a swivel makeup chair in front of a lit-up mirror. It was the closest to the door.

If she wanted to work on Nick this morning, it was okay by me. Based on the daggers flinging out of Carson's eyes, I would wager he wasn't as okay with it, but he didn't say anything.

"Nick," he corrected, glancing at Laura.

"Can I get you a coffee, Nick?" Carson said, hustling toward him, flinging out a hand like he was a waiter and not an uber-talented stylist. "Anything at all from Craft Services?" He was dressed in a pair of khaki shorts that hugged his self-proclaimed "bubble butt" and a black polo shirt with a pink animal logo on the left breast. The polo was tucked in, and for a belt, he had on a fanny pack. Yes… a fanny pack. It was 80s hot pink and looked like he'd dug it out of his mom's basement. Carson wore pink a lot. He said it looked good with his chocolate-colored skin. I couldn't really disagree with him.

Craft Services was the huge setup of food and drinks for the entire crew and actors. It was filled with almost anything you could imagine. Somedays, it made me feel guilty when I looked at it because sometimes it felt as if those tables had more available than most third world countries.

I remembered what it was like to be so hungry it felt as though your insides were shriveling up in contractions of pain.

"Nah, thanks," Nick said, smiling at Carson. "My assistant will be in with my trainer-approved meal." His eyes slipped to me, then went right back to Carson. A smile lit his features. "In other words, my plate of sadness."

Carson tipped his head back and laughed like it was the funniest joke he'd ever heard. Maybe it was funny to him, the taste of icing and sprinkles still in his teeth.

Laura made a sound and motioned to her chair. Nick's mossy gaze swung around. "Actually, Laura, I'm working with Zoey today."

Laura's face fell, but he didn't see because he was already swiveling in my direction. Jolting up from the table I was leaning against, I could have sworn I was hearing things.

He knew my name.

The deer-in-headlights look I must have plastered all over my face made Nick frown. "Unless you planned to work with some of the other cast today? Landen?"

"Landen…" I wondered out loud.

Nick's lips pulled up into a ghost of a smile. "The bad guy."

"Oh!" I gasped, and Carson threw his hands up into the air behind Nick, shaking his head. Nick was talking about his adversary in the movie they were filming. Duh.

"Um, no, I'm free. Laura can work on Landen. Right, Laura?"

I glanced around Nick to the other artist who was watching us. She was dressed in a pair of navy-blue leggings and a large white T-shirt with the words "No Comment" written across the chest. Because the shirt was oversized, she had it tied up at her waist. Her long blond hair was pulled up into a high ponytail, and her flawless face was makeup free.

This morning's call time was three a.m. I didn't even consider the hour morning, but the middle of the night. I'd bet half my paycheck ninety percent of the crew was probably still in bed, snoozing away until the very last second, then would roll out of bed, pull on some clothes, and climb into their cars.

They'd show up wrinkled, yawning, and sleepy-eyed. Most of them would have on hats and be guzzling coffee. It didn't matter. In fact, it was pretty much perfectly acceptable, even for Hollywood.

You see, behind the glitz and glam of movies and TV, behind the luxury and perfectly put-together "reality" everyone saw, stood entire teams who were anything but. We were the people who made Hollywood what it was, because without us, the celebrities and stars everyone envied for their beauty and status would look exactly the way the rest of us did… average.

Now before you go getting your panties in a bunch, average is not an insult. In fact, average, for me, was something to aspire to. But let's face it. Not everyone— hell, most of us—looked like Halle Berry, Jennifer Lawrence, or Chris Evans.

A lot of the people who worked with me said we were like the moms who rolled up in the car line at school in our minivans filled with Cheerios, dressed in mismatched pajamas with coffee and jam stains, hair in ratty buns, and slippers on instead of shoes. We were all ten-point hot messes, but when the doors opened and our kids stepped out, they looked like an ad for GAP.

We put all our energy into everyone else instead of us. It's just what we did, and we were paid very well for it.

"Umm, sure." Laura nodded. I knew she wasn't happy, but it wasn't as if I were trying to poach her client. We were all working on the same set.

Nick's long legs carried him closer to me at the end of the row. "This your chair?" he asked, gesturing to the black one on the end.

I nodded, and he slid right by me into the seat. The soft fabric of his sweats brushed against my wide-leg jersey pants as he moved. He was a good height. A strange thought, I know. But when a girl is nearly six feet tall herself, a man with impressive height is something that doesn't go unnoticed.

After plopping down in the seat, he swiveled around to face me, his back to the rest of the room. The weight of a million stares hit me in that moment. Well, a million might be an exaggeration. It was more like three, but the sharpness of each gaze made it feel like way more.

Clearing my throat, I decided to ignore the stares and get down to what I did best: faking it. "Let's just start with the base." I began studying his face, then reached for his uncombed strands to run my fingers through it. It was soft and silky. "And get the hair fixed up."

Side note: I had a cool job, yes? I could run my fingers through the sexiest man alive's hair and claim it was for work.

"You know, it doesn't matter if I'm on my death bed in a scene, good hair is a must," he quipped.

I snort-laughed. "Well, this is Hollywood."

He smiled but didn't say anything. I tugged my fingers out of his hair, which actually didn't look highlighted, feeling slightly on the spot because his mossy eyes remained on me.

Turning away to set down my tea and grasp my rolling cart of supplies, I asked, "Do you have any notes from the director on the scene or how you need to look for today's shoot?"

Movies weren't often filmed in sequential order, so every day was different. Any given shoot could range from normal hair and makeup to something extreme. It also depended on the movie. This one required less in terms of makeup and special effects because it was an action flick, not something like zombies or historical. It was a welcome job, though. I was tired. The last two movies I worked on had me on the other side of the country and on two different continents. For months, I worked very long hours, and my eyes basically crossed at the amount of detail and work that went into the makeup and costumes.

It had been worth it, though. Some even said those two films put me on top of the list of go-to makeup artists.

Maybe they were right. Maybe those successes were what got me this cushy job where I could stay in L.A. for the majority of the shoot, working with A-listers like Nick Preston and Josh Landen.

I didn't like to balance where I stood now on the success of only two jobs. The floor under my feet—the entire life I had today—wasn't just because of two jobs. It was a culmination of the last seven years.

Seven long years of sacrifice, pain, hard work, and yes… lies.

Although, could a lie (or many) still be considered such if it had become my truth? The lines blurred together for me now. Most of the time the falsehood felt like me, and I didn't wonder about who I had become.

But I still clearly remembered who I'd been.

That girl… she would be forever embedded beneath my skin. Hell, beneath my makeup.

"Hardcore," Nick replied, reminding me that I was actually supposed to be having a conversation instead of an inner monologue.

"What?" I turned around, confused.

He seemed amused I hadn't been paying attention to him. That actually earned him some points in my book. Thank goodness he didn't seem to think he was God's gift to women. I admit I expected him to be that way. So far, Nick seemed pretty down to earth.

"Today is the big boating scene. The fight scene. You know, the big showdown toward the end of the movie."

"Ah, so you need to look extra dashing?" I said it with flourish, waiving a makeup brush out like a wand.

His white teeth flashed, and I swore one of them sparkled and a little angelic sound floated over his head. "More like extra beaten up and ugly."

The makeup brush flopped against the outside of my leg when I dropped my hands. "Why do you seem excited about this?"

The deep vibration that was his chuckle rattled my chest. I straightened and took a small step back. His eyes locked on my movement.

"It's easy to look good all the time. I like the challenge of looking like crap."

I couldn't help but feel a little jealous tug deep in my gut. I wished it was easy for me to look good all the time. I brushed off his words and smiled. "Well, I think the challenge is mine. Making you look anything but handsome, even with a beat-up face, is no easy feat."

"Exactly why I wanted to work with you today. Your talent precedes you. You do the best gory, best scars, and best busted-up face work I've seen in a long time."

Because I knew exactly what those things looked like in real life.

The door to the trailer opened. The wind outside blew the door out of the incomer's hand, and it banged against the side, rattling everything. I jolted a little with the loud crack, then chastised myself for being such a fool.

Nick's chair rotated quickly, spinning away from me to face the front. From where I stood behind him, I noted the tension in his shoulders and neck. The large hands wrapped around the armrests were also rigid, as if he were ready to spring up out of the chair at a second's notice.

Maybe being an action hero taught him fast reflexes.

"Sorry!" someone called from outside as a small group of people entered the trailer. One of them was Jessica Blaine, Nick's love interest in the movie. She was gorgeous, with long platinum hair, porcelain skin, and blue eyes.

"I should have known," Nick muttered. Then his body relaxed.

"Morning, Nick," Jessica chirped, slipping into Carson's chair, which was beside the one Nick was seated in.

"Hey, Jess," he replied warmly.

Carson started fussing over her hair and makeup and pulling out fifty products. He was a good friend—okay, my only friend—but when he got into work mode, he made me feel like a slacker.

"Mr. Preston," a young woman said, rushing toward us. She had a container of food in one hand, a coffee or some type of drink balanced on top, a pen behind her ear, and a stack of papers shoved under her arm. "Sorry I'm late. I was taking notes from the director on your look."

"No problem, Callie," Nick said patiently. Leaning forward out of the chair, he snatched the cup, which was teetering on the food container, and then snagged that out of her grip as well.

"Coffee, black with just a dash of cream. No sugar," she said, nearly tripping to a stop beside him. If he hadn't taken that coffee when he did, he would likely have been wearing it. Pointing to the container of what I assumed was his "plate of sadness," she said, "White fish, light seasoning, no salt, and a side of steamed spinach."

Oh. That was sad.

I took a sip of my honey tea to make myself feel better.

Nick drank his coffee and jerked back with a grimace. "You sure that was cream you put in this coffee, Callie?"

Horror broke over her features. "Not again!" she wailed. Shuffling from foot to foot, she lifted her hands to ring them. The movement caused the papers under her arm to slide to the floor and scatter everywhere.

"Oh no!" she groaned and dropped to her knees, frantically trying to pick them up.

Nick swung around and gave me a wink, holding out his food and drink. I took them and watched as he got down on the floor with her to pick up what looked like his script.

"I'm so sorry, Mr. Preston. I really don't try to be such a klutz."

"It's just paper," he told her as they both leaned forward to retrieve the remaining loose sheet.

I winced when they knocked heads.

"Ow!" they hollered at the same time. Nick sat back, rubbing at his forehead.

Poor Callie looked like she was ready to cry. "I'm—"

"I know." Nick sighed. Carefully watching Callie like she might have a gun, he slid up and back into the chair. I bit the inside of my lip to keep from laughing.

"Silverware?" he asked.

The assistant gasped. "It must have blown off the tray when I was bringing it over."

Nick sighed. "Would you mind getting me some more?"

"Of course!" She jumped up. "Right away." As she was hurrying off, he called her name. She glanced back.

"Maybe some coffee that has cream in it instead of gravy."

Gravy?

Callie's face flamed red, and she hurried off.

Nick's eyes found mine, his lips twitching. There was a red spot on his forehead where he'd hit it.

"Gravy?" I asked, lifting an eyebrow.

He laughed. "God, she is the worst assistant ever."

"She tries hard, though," I said, gazing after her.

"Yes, she does." He sighed. "Too hard."

"You haven't fired her, though," I pointed out, watching him even though he was busy putting all the papers in his lap back in order.

Glancing up, he said, "Don't have the heart to do it. Besides, she makes up for her lack of assistance in other areas."

I didn't know why, but those words twisted inside me like a knife. The perusal of his profile and strong shoulders ended there, and I snapped around to my work station.

Maybe Mr. Movie Star wasn't as down to earth as I thought he was.

"We should get started. Can I see the notes from the director?" Holding out my hand for the notes, I avoided his gaze. Glancing over the paper and knowing how long filming was slated to last today, I heaved a mental sigh. This was going to be an exhausting day.

Turning to look at Laura, thinking maybe I could somehow pawn Nick off on her, I noted Landen was already sitting in her chair.

Bummer.

Poor me, stuck with a famous, good-looking client for the day. *Get a grip, Zoey. Things could be way worse, and you know it,* I told myself.

The trailer door banged open yet again, and Callie appeared, carrying a new cup of coffee and a packet of silverware. Her short blond hair bounced around her shoulders as she walked, making her seem extra energetic. "Here you go," she said, handing both over to Nick. "I promise I stayed far away from the breakfast table with your coffee."

Nick took a sip, not even a hint of apprehension in his mannerism (I guess being an actor came in handy), glanced up at her, and smiled. "Just the way I like it."

Callie let out a huge sigh of relief. This girl couldn't be an actress if her life depended on it. Her face was far too open and expressive. It was kind of endearing.

"Now that you have me all set up for a while, Callie, why don't you get yourself some coffee and breakfast?" Nick told her.

"You're sure?"

"Positive."

She nodded precisely. "Will do. Then I'll be right back to oversee your look and go through some scheduling."

"Don't worry about the look," I told her, wanting to take something off her plate. She seemed kind of frazzled. "I got it covered."

Callie looked over. "Great! Just basic for now, a little swelling around the left eye, windswept hair. Then you can come out on set and get your station set up to work on the rest between takes."

Working on set wasn't my favorite thing. I preferred the trailer, but it was necessary sometimes. And if it was what the director wanted, then I would do it. Besides, sometimes I could get even better effects done on set with the right lighting and watching the takes because then I would know exactly how to make the injuries look.

Someone else poked their head in through the trailer doorway. He was wearing a headset over his head with a small mic in front of his lips. Using the clipboard in his hand, he blocked the mic and yelled to the entire room, "Thirty minutes. Then everyone on set!"

Nick glanced at Callie. "Better get that coffee now."

She jumped into action and scurried away. His green eyes glittered, making it hard to look away when he said, "Once she has a coffee or two, she'll be a lot less clumsy. She tends to be worse in the very early morning."

"You seem to know an awful lot about your assistant's early-morning habits," I said before I could stop the words from literally exploding out of my dumb mouth.

Nick raised an eyebrow.

Despite the makeup I was wearing, I knew my face turned about twenty thousand shades of red. Hell, I probably just invented a new shade.

Instead of apologizing, I picked up my tea and took a sip.

"Well," he drawled as if he decided he wasn't going to call me out on my rude commentary. "We keep having these early call times, by the end of the month, I'll know a lot about your early-morning habits too."

I forced a laugh, but deep down, I wasn't amused.

Nick Preston would never know about my early-morning habits.

No one ever would.

I was drawn in.

I wished I wasn't.

She embodied everything in this business I'd spent about eighty-five percent of my life in, except for one thing. Her signature scent.

Yes, I know. Don't even go there with me.

I already knew her signature scent. If I were anyone other than Nick Preston, movie star and sexiest man alive, knowing that would put me on the top ten list of creepy stalkers.

But I wasn't a creepy stalker. I was a movie star. That made my attention to detail romantic.

I tried to ignore it, to be indifferent. My nostrils overruled my attempts, though, and I couldn't help but notice her light, fresh scent whenever she was nearby.

It's why I was drawn in, because despite the fact she was pretty much Hollywood at its core, she didn't smell like it. Kind of like a breath of clean mountain air in the middle of all the L.A. smog.

This business had a way of leaking into every aspect of a man's life. To the point he almost became the character… Less human, more fiction.

I loved my job, but even in love, a man still had to breathe.

It wasn't her air I wanted in my lungs, though, no matter how purely fresh it felt filtering from my chest and into my bloodstream. I wanted something—someone—that wasn't a reminder of my life. The sad meals I ate, the long flights, the photographers, and the need to be "on" almost every single moment of every single day.

It was exhausting, even for a charming guy like me.

I wanted a reprieve. Something real in a world where so much was bogus. I wasn't fooling myself, though. I worked in movies. In make-believe. A land where producers and writers controlled the script, where they basically bent characters' lives to their will. The odds of me finding something "normal" in the middle of the life I led was nearly impossible. It would only happen if it was written into a script and I got to play the role for a few months.

Besides her scent, I couldn't quite figure out why my eyes kept finding her when she was around. She was beautiful, sure, but that wasn't it. Beauty was practically a given in Hollywood. I barely even noticed it anymore. In my eyes, it would take something a lot more than perfectly sculpted eyebrows, full lips, and flawless skin to earn and keep my attention longer than a passing glance.

I told her the reason I sat down in her makeup chair this morning was because she was the best and I wanted to look as roughed up as I could for this fight scene. I loved giving raw, gritty performances when it looked like I was truly going to lose a battle. The kind where the audience had been rooting for me the entire movie and they thought I would be on top… but then I fell.

I loved the dimension of a strong character who didn't always win. Or at the very least, almost died getting back to the top.

Zoey's work in this business was getting around. Her attention to detail and the realism in the way she did special effects was earning her quite the reputation. It was a no-brainer I would want to work with her on set, even though the other makeup girl consistently managed to snag me the second I walked in the door.

Not today, Laura. Not today.

Zoey's talent wasn't the only reason I sat in her chair today, though. I was annoyed with her. Annoyed I was so intrigued and couldn't figure out why.

"So how long have you been doing this?" I asked as she took a sponge and started patting it over my skin.

Dude makeup. It was a thing in movies. I'd made my peace with it.

Without pausing or looking away from what she was doing, Zoey replied, "Seven years."

"That's a long time," I replied, wondering how old she was. She didn't look very old, but there was something about her demeanor that spoke of wisdom.

She paused for a split second, then went back to patting. "Not really in makeup. It changes pretty quickly, so it still feels new."

I liked that answer, which just annoyed me more.

What was it about her? What was it about this seemingly typical Hollywood girl that got under my skin?

I was getting the side eye.

Women everywhere—hell, even men—knew the side eye. The half-sneering, half-critical, definitely all-hateful look that was not so discreetly laser beamed out of the side of a woman's line of vision in a way she could pretend she wasn't actually trying to strike you where you stood, but if I happened to die on the spot, they wouldn't be wounded.

And who was I getting it from?

The starlet herself, Jessica Blaine, America's sweetheart. Such a shocker she didn't appear to actually be a sweetheart.

Did I say shocker? I meant the opposite.

She was actually a good actress, but since we'd started filming, I noticed she might not be as good of a person.

I'm being nice here. Let me just say it. The girl had a head the size of Shamu, and she expected everyone to fawn all over her.

And if they didn't?

They got the side eye.

I should mention to the director if he was looking for someone to fill a psycho role, she would be perfect.

Standing behind a makeup chair, as well as other life events, taught me how to read people. And let me tell you, Jessica's book was super interesting.

Not.

She was snooty, entitled, and didn't like me. Why? Because I had the audacity to come to work and not look like complete shit. A fact she didn't really care about until Nick Preston sat in my chair. Guess that meant she hoped the on-screen kisses she was getting from him would turn into off-screen ones as well.

I should probably note that I wasn't one of those aforementioned moms in the car line or one of the crew who rolled out of bed at the very last second. I wanted to be, so much so sometimes I daydreamed about it.

Ironic, isn't it? Those women probably daydreamed about looking pulled together, and I wished I was able to roll around looking like I didn't care.

I had to care about the way I looked. For more than one reason.

When I first started in the industry, I got asked quite a lot why I always came to work fully "done." Most makeup artists were too busy doing their clients to bother with themselves. It was sort of like being a chef and spending all day in the kitchen, cooking up a storm. By the time they got home, cooking themselves some gourmet meal was the last thing they wanted to do, so they ended up eating PB&J.

The questions and almost strange looks I got for it had made me uncomfortable at first. It was odd that an industry that basically coveted beauty and glamour would frown upon me coming to work in anything less. Just goes to show how freaking judge-y people were, no matter where a person lived.

My answer became standard. I'd laugh and smile and say I loved my job so much it didn't seem fair only the stars had all the fun. Then in a more professional tone, I would add that doing myself up on a daily basis was a way for me to try out new products and test new techniques so I would know how they worked when I was on set and needed to save time.

Everyone accepted the answers. Why wouldn't they? I knew some of the cattiest women whispered and gossiped behind the scenes that I was just beyond vain, but I let them talk. I'd rather they gossiped about my vanity than about the truth.

"Nick!" one of the stagehands bellowed into the half-open door. "You're needed on set!"

"That was not thirty minutes." I sniffed. I would be offended, but I was used to this. When they said thirty minutes, they really meant fifteen and some change.

"Take your time. I'll tell them it was my fault I was late."

Pressing some powder against his cheek, I was slightly offended. I was perfectly capable of taking care of myself. "No need," I rebuffed lightly. "I'm just about finished."

Pulling back, I studied my handiwork. With a quick nod, I stepped out from in front of him so he could look into the mirror.

His eyes widened. "You're finished."

"What do you think?" I mused, enjoying his faint surprise.

"It's great," he answered, still looking at himself. "What about the hair?"

I made a small sound, dropped the makeup brush in my hand, and stepped up to him, slipping between him and the mirror. I don't know how, but I'd nearly forgotten about his hair.

Guess I'd been too distracted with the rest of him.

Both hands delved into the long strands on top of his head to finger-comb them. Our feet bumped when I moved slightly closer so I could reach better.

He cleared his throat, and my eyes shot to his. Hands still tangled in his hair, my eyes bounced between his green ones, suddenly feeling shy.

"I'm not really used to anyone being taller than me."

"Should I sit down?" His deep voice was low, sort of like it was meant just for me, and I fought a shiver working its way up my spine.

"No need," I answered briskly and returned to adjusting his hair with my fingers. Quickly stepping back, I grabbed a giant can of hairspray and attacked his head.

He coughed dramatically. "This isn't an eighties movie."

I sprayed him again, not because he needed it, but because I could.

I set aside the can and reached up once more. At the same time, he waved away the nonexistent cloud in front of his face. The swiping motion knocked into my outstretched arms and made me slip back. Proving yet again he had lightning-fast reflexes, Nick caught me around the waist before I could fall into the mirror. Automatically, my hands fell onto his shoulders, gripping the broad muscles.

"Sorry," he murmured, and I swore his hands tightened around me.

Jolting back, I came up against the mirror, pushing his body away from mine. "I just need to—ah—" Gesturing to his hair, I completely ignored the little current of excitement zinging through me.

Clearing his throat, he lowered his chin to oblige.

Quickly, I adjusted the strands, and he lifted his face.

Nodding once, I gestured for him to go. "That should be good until I get out on set."

"Do you need help getting your stuff out there?"

"No, I've got it. You go ahead. They're waiting."

He watched me for another split second, then turned, nearly colliding with Callie. She squeaked and doubled back, almost falling, but Nick caught her too.

Guess he was a real knight in shining armor, stopping women everywhere from busting their asses.

"I was just coming to get you," she said as he righted her.

"Lead the way." He motioned, turning back to me. "See you out there."

I nodded but didn't breathe until he was nearly out of the trailer.

"Gurrl," Carson drawled, coming up close beside me. "I think I just saw some sparks."

"I think you're on a sugar high from that donut."

"I only had two bites," he refuted, glancing longingly at the trash can, then at the door Nick just left through. "It was worth it."

I giggled.

"I wouldn't read too much into it," Jessica said from Carson's chair. "Nick has sparks with everyone. It's his job."

Carson gave me a look, then sauntered back over to finish his work on the starlet.

I didn't say anything at all as I packed up my cart. It was going to be a long day.

"Cut!" the director yelled, and my body relaxed. Instantly, all the blood drained down into my head.

"We'll have you down in two shakes of a dog's tale, Mr. Preston!" one of the hands called out.

"Take your time," I called as my body swayed like a pendulum. "I'm not going anywhere." Chuckles from around the set erupted and so did the familiar constant click of a camera.

Just another day on the job, you know. Hanging upside down, "caught" on the sail of a boat while battling the bad guys.

"Special effects!" the director yelled.

Even though I was woozy and dangling, I gazed around for Zoey, instead seeing a camera crew gathered close to the large tank of water. Jessica was standing there in full glamour, smiling and answering the questions the woman with the mic was asking.

I recognized her instantly. Candace Grimes, face of *Hollywood Access*, the top news outlet for celebrities. I use the term *news* lightly because mostly it was gossip with just enough truth and entertainment coverage to qualify as legit.

Feeling my gaze, Jessica turned her baby blues to where I was strung up and waved. Of course, everyone standing there with her turned to me as well. I delivered a devilish smile that made my job look fun and daring.

Beep, beep, beep…

Ear piercing, high-pitched noise shrouded everything as a large machine pulled right up to the side of the giant tank. Mechanical arms extended and a platform slid under me. One of the stagehands appeared, and I was lowered until I was sitting on it with the harness and ropes still attached around me.

"We're just going to leave you hooked in," the man beside me explained, holding out a bottle of water. "Soon as the makeup people do their thing, we'll finish shooting this scene."

As I sipped, there was a bit of commotion nearby, drawing my attention. The crew from *Hollywood Access* split, and Zoey stepped through. Her face was downturned, so I could only see the top of her dark head. Her shoulders were hunched in a bit as if she were trying to make herself look small. Noticing the kit both her hands wrapped around, I figured it was probably heavy.

Portable stairs were leaned against the tank, and she climbed them. Arriving at the top, she paused, glancing at the beam she had to walk across to get to the platform where I sat. After glancing over her shoulder at the camera crew, then quickly back, her shoulders tensed and the grip around the kit's handle tightened.

"Filming resumes in ten!" someone from down below yelled.

Her chin came up, and our eyes collided briefly, long enough for me to see the flash of panic in hers before she gazed down at the beam once more.

Setting aside the water, I pushed up to my feet, ignoring the wash of dizziness over me as my blood went back to all the places it belonged. The harness was tight, and the long rope tangled around my feet when I moved forward.

"You should stay there," the stagehand advised, reaching down to move some of the rope.

Ignoring him, I stepped onto the beam and held out my hand. "Give me the kit," I said.

Zoey's eyes widened. Sucking her lower lip into her mouth, she started across, seeming woefully unsteady.

"Are you afraid of heights?" I asked, trying to keep my voice as low as I could for privacy's sake.

Yes. Privacy was sort of a joke with all the cameras pointed at me, but I still tried.

"No," she said, extending the kit.

I took it and handed it to the stagehand. Turning back, I noticed the way she wobbled on her way across, even though the beam was wide enough for her to walk across. Her feet shuffled a bit, almost like she was dragging them.

"Give me your hand," I told her, extending mine.

Her throat worked when she swallowed, hesitation clear in her face.

"Are you getting this?" Candace said from the other side of the tank, and I practically felt the spotlight on the camera aimed at us intensify.

Sheer panic burst across Zoey's face. Lines around her mouth formed, and her balance seemed to get worse.

Instead of waiting, I took a couple more steps and wrapped my hand around hers, giving it a reassuring squeeze. "Want me to call for Carson or Laura?" I whispered.

Her eyes slid in the direction of the camera crew, but she didn't turn around. A slight shake of her head was all the answer I got before she was clutching my fingers like I was her lifeline and moving the rest of the way across the beam.

Her eyes gripped mine as if I were the only person in the room, as if I were the sole reason she was still upright. A sense of trust and responsibility dropped over me like a heavy blanket, but it wasn't uncomfortable. If anything, it made me feel stronger.

The toe of her sneaker tangled in the ropes around me, making her pitch forward. Alarm flashed over her features, and she squeezed her eyes shut so tight that wrinkles formed at the corners. Despite being slightly unsteady from hanging upside down for so long, I caught her.

All six feet of Zoey tumbled right into my torso. Her arms reflexively pulled into her chest in a protective gesture. We rocked back slightly against the force of her tumble, but I recovered almost instantly to keep us upright.

The click of camera shutters and buzz of voices seemed miles away, mere background noise to whatever was happening between us.

Hands still fisted against her, my arms adjusted, taking her weight more comfortably. Then I gazed down. Slowly, she lifted her face, her lashes fluttering open as bright-pink spots bloomed across her cheeks.

Wary brown irises fixed on mine, her lips pressing into a thin line. "I'm sorry."

"First time on a platform like this?" I asked, keeping my voice light.

She swallowed and pushed off my chest. "No." Straightening and flipping her hair behind her shoulders, she steadied herself quickly. "I'm okay now. You can let go."

When our physical contact continued, her stare flashed up. The brown was beautiful… but it just didn't feel right.

I shook my head. Her eye color didn't feel right? Hanging upside was clearly messing with my brain.

Her indignant little sound snapped me out of the thought. I smiled. "You're the one holding on to me," I informed her, pointedly gazing down at where her hand clutched the sleeve of my shirt.

She snatched her hand back as if I were on fire. "Time is limited." Her words were brisk and businesslike.

Taking the kit from the assistant's hand, she kneeled down with it, opening it up. "Can you sit?" she asked, not looking up.

I did, lifting the water and taking another long sip. "So," I mused as she began working on my face, "if you aren't afraid of heights and have been on a platform like this before, what's got you spooked?"

"I'm not spooked," she said, not even pausing in her work.

"Liar," I whispered.

"I need a spray bottle. We should wet your hair down and some of your clothes. It's unrealistic for you to be so dry." She started to get up, but I caught her wrist, keeping her at my side.

"Can you go grab that for us?" I asked the stagehand.

"Sure thing," he said, going off instantly.

I felt her gaze when I turned back. Lifting my face, I motioned to it.

Without another word, she started working again. "They want me to add a gash to your forearm," she said when my face was done.

Dropping back onto her butt, one foot pressed against the inside of her thigh while the other leg stretched across the floor. "Arm," she instructed like she was a doctor that needed a tool.

I held out my arm.

"Other one."

Making a sound beneath my breath and pulling back, I had to turn around and slide closer to her, offering up the skin she wanted.

"This okay?"

Rotating a little so her knee bumped against my body, she grasped my forearm with both hands and placed it across her lap.

The sound of her rummaging through the kit beside us affected me like heavy rain on the roof in the middle of the night. Soothing, relaxing… something I didn't want to fall asleep and miss.

When her hands were on me, I noted the slight tremble and frowned. She hadn't been trembling earlier in the trailer.

"You sure everything's okay?" I whispered so low I wondered if she would be able to hear.

"I'm sure," she answered, her tone matching mine.

How the hell we managed to create such an intimate, private space in the middle of a bustling and noisy movie set, I didn't understand. It was a reprieve I didn't realize I needed.

She avoided my stare when my eyes sought her face. Could she feel it too? Was this one-sided?

"You almost done?" Admittedly, the words came out harsher than I intended, but sitting here, realizing how drawn to her I was, annoyed me. Especially when she seemed entirely unaffected by me.

What about the tremble in her hands? What about the way she clung to you like a lifeline?

The thoughts confused me, making regret rise in the back of my throat.

Zoey glanced up, then back down at her work. "Almost."

The platform wobbled, and her fingers momentarily gripped my arm.

"Here it is." The assistant burst into our little world, thrusting a large spray bottle between us.

"Thank you." I took the bottle and held it while she finished.

"What do you think?" she asked, eyeing her art. "Think that's gruesome enough?"

I studied my arm, which still rested over her lap. The skin appeared to be ripped and draped open, revealing a bloody red gash. It was slightly shiny, oozing and uneven, just the way my arm would really look if the rope I was tangled in rubbed it raw.

"Looks nasty," I observed. With a grin, I met her eyes. "I love it."

"Oh, wait!" she mused, pulling my arm back when I started to move away.

My leg brushed against her when I sank back down. Her hands felt cool on my skin. Producing a pair of tweezers, she leaned over me, grasping some of the rope.

I watched her add a few fibers to the wound, making it look even more realistic.

"There." Satisfaction filled her tone.

"Wet him down," the assistant instructed.

I pushed to my feet as she repacked the kit. Then without thinking, I reached down to help tow her to her feet.

Clearing her throat, she took the bottle and began spraying my hair, running her hands through it. The mist was fine and floated around my head, clinging to my cheeks and ears.

The director called out a few notes while she sprayed down my shirt and neck. Even though I was having a conversation with someone else, all my attention was focused on her. Especially when she took her palm and rubbed it across the side of my neck.

Like a moth to a flame, my eyes fluttered to her. Sensing the change, her tentative gaze lifted to mine.

My stomach dropped, sort of like I was on a rollercoaster, compensating for the sudden imbalance inside me. My heart began to pound.

"Finished," she announced, stepping back.

"Hold the frame!" someone yelled.

I wasn't the number one action hero in Hollywood for my looks alone. I had skills too. So even though my brain wasn't working, my body went on autopilot. Turning for the camera, I stood still, allowing them to zoom in with the cameras, and all the people who needed to check out my appearance gathered around the monitors.

"Good to go!" the director yelled, signaling with a thumbs-up. "Positions!"

"I'll help you across," I said, reaching for her kit.

"Over here, Mr. Preston." The assistant motioned for me.

"Nick," I corrected without thinking but didn't move toward him.

Zoey pulled the kit back, denying me. "You have work to do. I'm fine."

"You sure?"

She nodded and moved away.

My name was called again, so I turned to take my place, readying to be strung upside down once more.

Seconds later, someone shouted, the loud grinding of gears filled the set, and chaos erupted.

I said it was going to be a long day, didn't I?

Understatement of the century.

I should have known the second Nick Preston plopped his tall, handsome ass in my chair this morning and rabid laser beams from Laura's and Jessica's eyes nearly burned a hole in my face that my cushy, "simple" job on set would become a living nightmare.

And I would know. I am well qualified in nightmares.

That's what makes a nightmare so horrifying, though. You can't know when they're coming, what form they will take, or how bad it might change everything.

Being well qualified in nightmares didn't stop them from coming… It only made you live in fear.

I was well versed in that too.

For a split second, I didn't pay attention. For a split second, I glanced at the camera crew as I turned to leave the platform.

The ear-splitting grinding of gears pulled my attention back, but it was too late. A bone-chilling, aggressive blast of water so cold it felt like tiny knives punched into me.

The kit fell to the floor as I raised my hands to block the spray that was so strong it felt like a fire hydrant exploding in my face. Not only was the breath robbed from my lungs, but the unexpected onslaught knocked me back. Scrambling to get away from the explosion, I stumbled, unable to see or hear a thing.

I was falling.

Plummeting over the side of the small platform with nothing but air to protect me… and air was a lousy shield.

My stomach bottomed out, and a crippling sense of panic stole what little thought I had before my back slammed into the surface of the water below, the waves sucking me under like a vacuum and swallowing me whole.

So much turbulence. There was so much violence in the water despite it being a mere tank. It was as if I really had plunged into the ocean during a hurricane. I felt like a rag doll being tossed around without any clarity of what I needed to do to save myself.

This wasn't the first time in my life I'd stared into the face of death. It taught me no matter how many times a woman was about to die, it never became less scary.

Water rushed up my nose, burning my throat as I struggled to see which way was up. It felt like I was being shoved deeper toward the bottom, and the light in the water began to fade, becoming dim, as though the sun were setting at the end of a long day.

It had been a long life… far longer than my twenty-six years would suggest.

Suddenly, the water seemed to calm, almost as if it knew the battle was over and it was victorious. My eyes opened, focusing immediately on a large dark figure plunging through the water, making the waves I'd just fought against appear painfully week.

The figure grew closer and closer until blue eyes pierced through the darkness dragging me down. My body glided toward him the second he wrapped his hand around mine, his arms and legs closing around me like a vise.

It felt as though the water expelled us, forcing us out of a place we didn't belong. I began coughing and gasping for air before I even realized I hadn't drowned. My limbs were heavy, and everything beneath my ribs burned intensely.

Large hands pulled me up, holding my boneless body away from whatever was wrapped around me. I tried to grab it back, but I was too weak, too out of it.

"Zoey!" The insistent calling of my name brought me back.

My head bobbed when I was shaken, making me groan.

"Zoey, are you okay?"

Fisting my hands in the saturated material of his shirt, I collapsed against him again, one arm thrown around his neck as more coughing racked my waterlogged frame.

He wasn't gentle as he patted me on the back, but I didn't care. If it weren't for him, I wouldn't be breathing at all.

The realization made me gasp, and I clutched at him even more.

"It's okay." Nick soothed, lowering his lips against my ear. "I got you."

Shuddering, I pressed a little closer. Nightmares aren't as scary when you aren't alone.

Sensing the desperate need I had for comfort, Nick wrapped both arms around me, holding me tight. Water splashed up my back, and I realized we were still in the giant water tank.

"Don't let go," I said, shivering. "Please, hold on."

One of his hands went to the back of my head, holding me against him. "I'm not going anywhere." He vowed, his voice utterly calm and confident.

The worst panic in me slipped away, defeated in one blow by his assurance. Starting to relax, awareness of my current situation plowed in.

Around us, bedlam reigned. People shouted, lights flooded the surface of the water, and the furious buzz of people talking pressed in on me.

I'd fallen off the platform on set, knocked into the tank by a blast of water of some kind.

I gasped so forcefully it brought on another coughing attack.

"Whoa," Nick said, easing back to look down.

"No!" I panicked, burying my face into his shoulder and arm.

Briefly, he paused, then tried to pull me away from him to look down again.

"Please don't look at me."

"What?" he asked, lowering his head closer to me.

"Don't look," I repeated, my voice still muffled against his chest.

"Are you seriously worrying about the way you look right now?" he asked, a disgusted tone coming into his words.

I had to. I had to think about it every minute of every day.

When I didn't reply or pull back, he made a rude sound and proceeded to peel me away from his chest. I wasn't a match for his strength. He clearly worked out, he was clearly comfortable in the water, and he wasn't currently a shivering drowned rat.

The second he forced me off, I suctioned back against him like the tentacle of an octopus. Winding both my arms around his shoulders, I buried my face in his neck and clamped one of my legs around his waist.

"That's enough," he spat, gripping me again. "I know there's a TV show here and you're one of those L.A. girls, but this is a bit much."

Oh my God, *Hollywood Access*!

Turning my head so my face was tucked against his, I whispered, "Are they still here?"

"Who?"

"The TV show?"

I felt him gaze around. "Of course. We'll probably be the top story on tonight's show."

A painful shudder moved through me.

"We're going to tow you up now!" someone yelled from above.

Nick lifted his face to holler up, but I grabbed his cheek, splaying my hand over it to stop him.

"Wait." I felt him pause, so I plunged on, trying not to think too much about what I was about to do. "Please help me."

A humorless laugh rolled through his chest. "Pretty sure I just did."

Shaking my head against him, still holding on, I lifted my chin to whisper in his ear. "If you won't help me now, you should have just let me drown."

His body stilled.

At that moment, my shoe floated past us. It wasn't just a sneaker, though. It represented something important to me… something I'd just lost.

I began shivering uncontrollably.

"Zoey?" Nick whispered, all the disdain in his voice gone.

"Turn around," I whispered.

"What?"

"Turn us so you're blocking me from the cameras."

He did it, rotating us in the water with power and ease. I realized he was still wearing his stunt harness that allowed him to hold me without having to tread water.

Before he could ask anything else or tell me how shallow I was, my fingers sank into his shoulders. Slowly, I pushed back, easing away from the protective shield of his body, keeping my chin against my chest.

Long wet strands hung around my face like a curtain, providing me with some protection.

A frustrated sound broke out of him, and the rope around him tugged. We were being towed up.

"Wait!" he yelled up. Instantly, the rope went slack.

People called out to us, but we were in our own little world… Well, actually, the world I'd painstakingly built for myself shattered, shard by shard.

Taking a deep breath, I did something I never, ever wanted to do.

I showed him who I really was.

I was holding my breath, but I didn't understand why. All the annoyance I'd been feeling drained away, leaving me with an ominous sense of anticipation.

Something was happening right now… something I felt I had to protect.

What was it about this woman—?

All thought ceased.

Her eyes fixed on mine. But it wasn't the same stare I'd been gazing into just minutes ago. Well, one was. One brown eye that just hadn't seemed quite right.

The other?

It was blue. It was right.

"Your eyes," I whispered, bouncing between the different-color orbs.

Her shivering intensified. Instinctively, my arms tightened, shoulders curling in, trying to surround her.

Her chin lifted a little bit more, but my eyes never left hers as she reached up and pushed some of her saturated hair back just a little.

"Look," she beckoned quietly. I didn't realize so much pain could be in such a simple word.

Tearing my eyes from her multi-colored ones, I scanned the rest of her face.

I was an actor and, like I told you, a good one. But nothing could have prepared me for what I saw. Schooling my reaction to such a reveal was just not possible.

My breath faltered. Shock stiffened my limbs.

The left side of her face was… damaged. Scarred. Burned. A roadmap of pain I couldn't even comprehend.

She only let me look a second. Long enough to register there was so much more to this woman than I ever would have suspected.

"Ah, Zo," I whispered, lifting a hand to cup the side of her face.

She winced and turned away from the touch.

"Please," she whispered. "Please help me get back to the trailer without everyone seeing."

Keeping her close against my chest, I wrapped both arms around her, swallowing up as much of her body as I could.

"Pull us up!" I yelled.

I didn't say anything to try and reassure her. What the fuck could a man say? I couldn't process everything I was thinking and feeling right now. All I could do was pull us through this until we were somewhere safe.

I don't know how I realized Zoey wasn't safe out here like this. Exposed and vulnerable like a lamb in a field of coyotes.

But I did.

The protective lion she'd awoken within me roared to life and took control.

The second we were lowered onto the platform, I started issuing orders. "I need a blanket! Get me my jacket! Turn off those spotlights!"

Everyone scrambled to do as I demanded because I was Nick-fucking-Preston—usually an amiable and easy guy. However, I knew how to command a room. It's what made me so good at my job.

Zoey continued to shiver, plastered so tight against me I could feel every inch of her long, thin frame along my front. Keeping her secured in my arms and shielding her from prying eyes, I stayed still while the guys unhooked me from the harness.

"Step back, ma'am," one of them said, trying to reach between us.

Her fingernails dug into my back, and I gave the handsy guy a dark look. He pulled back instantly.

"She's fine where she is," I told him, shifting so I could reach between us myself and pull off the rest of what they needed.

A blanket appeared, and I draped it over her head and back completely.

"All right now," I whispered, pulling back enough to tuck the blanket closed around her.

Her hand fisted in the front of my shirt, silently asking me to stay close.

"C'mon," I said, tucking her beneath my arm and leading her toward the beam. I noticed her limping but didn't call attention to it because getting out of here was more important.

That's when the whispering started.

Her foot…

What was wrong with her foot?

I stopped walking and gave the whispering man closest to me a piercing look. He pointed at her feet like there was something I should see.

A moment passed while my brain processed what I saw, because at first, nothing looked amiss. Her sneaker came off in the water. Big deal.

Then I felt her fingers tightening, felt her shrink closer against me.

I looked again.

Five toes. Flesh-colored and shaped just like anyone's foot would be… but it wasn't.

Her foot wasn't real. It was a prosthetic.

Zoey was missing one of her feet.

Bending without a word, I lifted her into my arms and forged ahead, carrying her across the beam, down the steps, and across the set.

Of course Candace appeared, wide-eyed and practically drooling at the scoop she thought she was getting. Despite the blanket being tucked around Zoey's head and face, I cupped my hand around her head, shielding her with my arm.

"Nick! Nick, can you say a few words about what just happened up there?" Candace pounced. "Do set accidents like this happen often?"

Setting my jaw, I pushed forward, refusing to acknowledge her.

"Nick! My God! You could have been seriously hurt!" Jessica gasped, running alongside me like the ever-concerned costar she was.

I knew our agencies wanted us to act like there might be love blooming behind the cameras, but I wasn't in the mood. The fact she was acting like I was the hurt one and not the woman who was knocked into the tank with no harness, no warning at all, pissed me off.

"Excuse me," I said, pushing through the camera crews swarming us.

"How well do you know the woman you leapt in the water after?" Candace questioned, shoving a mic close. "Is she hurt? Should we call 9-1-1?"

"Security!" I bellowed.

Breaking away from everyone, I rushed off set and went to the trailer where Carson was standing at the door, looking like a dear in headlights.

"Heavens!" He gasped. "What happened?"

"Grab the door," I barked.

Carson snapped up like a soldier, pulling open the door so I could sweep through.

"I need the room," I announced, making everyone look up.

Mouths dropped, and the other makeup artist, Laura, came rushing over. "Is that Zoey? What happened? Let me help you."

Under the blankets, Zoey made a small sound.

"Out!"

Everyone rushed out, with Carson standing in the still-open door.

"Don't let anyone in here," I demanded. Outside, I could hear Callie rushing over, calling out my name. "Not even my assistant."

Carson saluted and pulled the door around, the fanny pack spinning on his waist with the movement.

Carefully, I set Zoey down in a makeup chair and sank down in front of her. She huddled back, gripping the blanket around her, keeping her face buried inside.

"Are you hurt?" I asked, resting a hand on each armrest. "Do you need the paramedics?" We always had some on standby.

"No," she said quickly. The blanket slipped a little with the definitive shake of her head.

I couldn't help it. I glanced down at her foot. Her pants were soaking wet and sticking to her. A mechanical-looking ankle rose out of the foot, and from this angle, I could see the limb was really just like a shell or case for more metal.

Flexing my fingers around the chair, I forced my eyes up and reached for the ends of the blanket to pull them back.

She jerked away the second I moved, practically cowering inside the cover. "Let me help you."

"I want to be alone."

"Zoey—"

"Just go."

I sat there debating but, in the end, conceded. Going to a nearby cabinet, I pulled out a few towels and carried them over. Laying them in her lap gently, I stepped back out of her personal space.

She looked small hiding in the folds of the blanket, and I knew she was still trembling. There were so many things I wanted to say. So many things I wanted to ask.

"Please go," she whispered again, her voice hoarse and weak.

Embarrassment washed through me because it probably seemed to her I was standing here staring, trying to get another look at everything she'd been hiding.

Aren't you? A voice heckled me.

As I reached for the handle on the door, I noticed for the first time that I was drenched as well. I needed to—

"Nick?"

I spun around. Any thought I had of myself was silenced by my name on her lips.

"Yes?"

"I-I need my shoe."

"It's probably soaked. I'll get you some dry ones."

"I need that one."

I glanced down at her exposed foot again. Emotion welled up within, but I didn't know how to identify what it was. "Just wait. I'll get it for you."

"Thank you."

Those two words were spoken about a million times a day. They were common, often said automatically without the proper sentiment behind them.

Not this time. This time it felt like I was hearing them for the very first time. Like I finally understood what it was to have someone be truly thankful for something I'd done.

It made me feel small but strangely filled up inside.

I left the trailer with the sole mission of getting that shoe, knowing I would go to the ends of the earth to achieve it.

7

I was indeed alone.

My companion, most definitely dead.

The scratch, scratch, scratching I heard? The movement I thought was her head turning toward my voice?

The sliver of hope that offered me a slice of life here in this pit of death?

A rat.

A large, beady-eyed thing that decided a corpse made a promising meal.

Skittering back against the wall, my fist jammed against my mouth as I shuddered and shook. It had taken all my courage to look over there, but now I couldn't tear my gaze away.

What a hideous way to die. To lie there in pain while blood seeped from your body, saturating the old, crusty tile, streaking it like some sort of abstract work of art. Knowing you would never get up again and the last sound you would hear was the life sliding out of you and dripping down the drain in the floor.

The rat moved again, making me whimper. It paused and looked in my direction, then turned back and started pawing at her face like its claws were a fork.

"Stop!" The scream burst out of me, and I lunged forward. Anger overpowered my fear in those moments as I watched a young life reduced to rat food. I was so enraged at the rodent's audacity that all I could think about was stopping it.

The rat gave a squeal and rushed off. I sprang forward, hand outstretched. Maybe I would have caught it.

If not for the chain.

It yanked me back, a grim reminder that I was not free. That I was not unlike the dead body rotting away so close by. My ankle ached, and pain radiated up my leg.

I collapsed, weeping. The inhuman sounds ripping from my own soul were something I never would have thought I could make. Something sticky and thick coated my hand, squishing between my fingers, making me go quiet.

Lifting my head, I stared at the blood dripping down my wrist. It was cold. Not mine.

My eyes drifted to the corpse.

Backpedaling to my corner, I ignored the way my legs tangled in the chain keeping me prisoner, furiously wiping my hand down the wall to rid myself of the blood. Seeing the streaks down the wall, seeing the red still discoloring my hand, a thought occurred. I could wipe every last drop of this away, but I would still be stained forever.

"Help!" I screamed as loud as I possibly could. I didn't even care if he heard. "Help!"

The plea echoed through the giant room, rising out of the vacant, abandoned pool. I cried and screamed until I couldn't anymore. Finally collapsing against the cold wall, I gazed through swollen eyes at the way the floor sloped up toward the shallow end.

I imagined the pool filling with water, rinsing away the blood and death, offering some kind of fresh start. It wouldn't even matter if I was still chained. If I drowned down here. Drowning would be better than this.

* * *

I needed to get up. To put myself back together and find some dry clothes. Makeup. I needed makeup. I needed my kit so I could cover up.

Oh God, how many people saw?

All these years, I'd painstakingly made sure no one ever saw, that no one ever knew. Was all that ruined now? Ruined by some freak accident on set? Had my perfect cover become a terrifying reveal?

Tightness squeezed my chest, and a noxious feeling squirmed around just below my diaphragm. The urge to get up and escape, to run away without looking back, was so strong my entire body tensed, readying to spring out of the chair.

But I didn't move.

Despite needing to get away, despite the clawing desperation climbing up my throat and scratching at every nerve ending in my body, I couldn't run.

Instead, I cowered in the chair, shrinking, wishing that if I became smaller, the panic and anxiety tearing me up inside might become smaller too.

Shaking so much my teeth began to clatter, I forced my jaw still, but it hurt too much to hold and I wound up chattering again.

Goose bumps rose along my arms and legs. I could feel the way they prickled the surface of my skin. My mind was everywhere, yet it was scarily blank. There was just too much to process to even form a sensible thought. Instead, I slumped there beneath the blanket, my body overrun by the panic my mind refused to acknowledge.

This wasn't my first panic attack. It wouldn't be my last.

But every single one felt like the first time.

It didn't matter if I tried to reassure myself that this too would pass, if I whispered promises that I was safe and fine. It didn't matter. The adrenaline was already shooting through my body. My system was already in shock and fighting against all the threats it perceived.

I was so tense my body ached. My fingers stung cold, and the wet ends of my hair dripped down my back.

I just wanted this to stop.

The flashbacks. The memories. The reminders. I didn't want to be drained by panic attacks and embarrassment at my lack of self-control.

I felt like a robot, like someone who didn't even have control of her own body, when I stiffly pushed up in the chair. Clutching the blanket while my teeth still chattered, I glanced around at my bag hanging over by my station. I needed the meds inside. I hated those pills, but they would bring this down. I would be left feeling like a wrung-out dishrag, but at least I would be able to think. Be able to function.

The towels Nick had placed in my lap fell onto the floor as I scooted forward. The blanket tangled around my legs, and my foot got caught in the bar at the bottom of the chair. I fell forward, unable to catch myself on my hands because they were tucked inside the fabric. My cheek smacked on the concrete floor, but it didn't hurt.

I couldn't feel anything just then but panic and nausea. Instead of scrambling up, I pressed my face against the floor. The cold temperature felt good against my feverish skin, and my eyes slid closed.

Commotion outside the trailer reminded me of the situation. Shoving up, I stumbled to my bag, ripping it off the hook and delving my hand inside, searching desperately for the small bottle I always carried.

The second my hand closed around it, I dropped everything else. It hit my foot, but I didn't feel it because there was no feeling there. My foot was not real.

The cap on the bottle made loud clicking sounds as I turned it around and around.

A sob ripped from between my lips when despair washed over me. "Open, dammit!" I wailed, squeezing the bottle in my fist.

With a shuddering breath, I calmed myself and tried once more. The lid unscrewed, and with it came relief. My palm trembled while I shook out what I needed into my hand, the pills in the bottle rattling around from my unsteady grasp.

The door shoved open, and the bottle went flying. Shrieking, I dropped to the floor, huddling beneath the blanket as if it had some kind of invisibility magic.

"It's me, Zoey. Nick." His voice broke into my dull thoughts.

He cursed. The sound of his footsteps coming closer seemed like loud gunshots in a quiet night.

"I didn't mean to scare you," he said softly, feeling him kneel close to me. "I didn't knock because I didn't want to dally around in front of the door. There's, ah, quite a crowd out there."

I didn't say anything. He cleared his throat.

"The paramedics are there. Should I let them in?"

I shook my head but had no idea if he would know I did.

"I got your shoe. It was, ah, still in the tank."

My teeth started chattering again. My body ached, and I was so cold I wasn't sure how much longer I could endure.

"You were getting some pills?" he asked, his voice very calm and almost conversational. I envied that amount of control, that amount of serenity. "Do you still need to take some?"

I nodded.

I felt him get up and move away. Disappointment made me tense more. A second later, he was back, lifting a corner of the blanket and setting an uncapped water bottle on the floor. "How many do you need?"

"T-two."

His hand slipped beneath the blanket and, with it, a sliver of light from the room. Two white pills lay in the center of his very large palm. Again, I was moved by the steadiness in his hand, by the calmness in his presence.

My fingers brushed against him when I picked up the medication. He didn't wince or seem surprised by the icy feel of my skin. I swallowed down the pills gratefully, and when he nudged the water closer, I lifted it and took a drink.

I heard him picking up the scattered pills, dropping them back into the bottle one by one. The familiar sound of the lid clicking into place registered and so did his colorful curse. "It'd be easier to see the devil's tits than it is closing this fucking bottle."

A giggle bubbled out of me.

Wet sneakers stepped close. So close the drenched toes nudged beneath the blanket. Squatting in front of me, Nick expelled a breath.

He was just as wet as I was. I wondered why he hadn't changed clothes yet.

"My mom takes those. They work pretty fast. You'll be okay in just a few more minutes."

His mom took the same kind of pills I did?

"She's been on them for years. I took one once because I'm a nosy bastard and wondered what it would feel like."

The sound of his voice was comforting. Before, all I could think about was being alone, but now all I wanted was for him to keep talking.

"I was pretty disappointed. They didn't do anything for me. I felt the same as I always do… didn't even get a little bit of a high."

I made a sound.

"They must do something, though, huh? Otherwise, y'all wouldn't take them."

"They don't make you high," I heard myself saying. "They calm you down."

"Maybe that's why my parents have been married for so long," he mused.

I don't know how, but I laughed. It bubbled right up past all the angst inside me, filling up the space beneath the blanket.

The sound was shocking. How could I laugh at a time like this? My whole life could be over. Everything could be ruined.

"Cold, huh?" Nick observed. Clearly, the sound of my chattering teeth was audible.

"I grabbed some extra sweats out of my trailer. They're dry and warm. I'll leave them here so you can change." His throat cleared. "Take your time, all right? I'll occupy the press, keep them away."

The toes of his sneakers disappeared from beneath the blanket.

Panic clawed at me anew.

"Wait," I said, my voice tainted with desperation.

Silence filled the room, and neither of us moved. In the span of several heartbeats and the painful drag of a few ragged breaths, his shoes appeared again.

The brush of his fingers over my back made me stiffen. He froze. I froze. His hand stayed where it was.

My lower lip wobbled.

His hand curled a little farther around me.

I sniffled.

He duckwalked closer, and then I was in his arms, both of them wrapped around me while I curled into his chest. Despite his drenched state, he was warm. I was cold. He was solid. I was evaporating.

A sob built up in my throat, straining to get out, burning because I held it in. His hand lifted, then fell back against me. Again and again, the motion repeated. He was patting my back, gently loosening the sob trapped inside.

"It's okay." He promised, the whisper almost like a gentle breeze.

It dislodged.

All the pain I'd been holding in. All the fear and trauma. The panic attack I'd been stuffing down rushed to the surface and broke free.

I started to cry.

He didn't move. Like a tree with ancient, unfailing roots, he stayed in place, holding me calmly, warming me selflessly while a storm that would never fully pass raged inside me.

He saw my face. He saw my scars.

He wasn't asking about them or running away. He just held me while I cried.

I ignored the constant ringing of my cell phone. My number was supposed to be private, but let's be real here. Privacy in Hollywood, in life, would be harder to obtain than milking a buffalo.

The little mishap on set today? You'd think a small country had been bombed for all the media coverage it was getting.

It was a load of horse shit. But it was good for business.

It cost the studio quite a bit of change because afterward, production shut down for the rest of the day. But no one was mad. The money lost on production would be gained in media coverage and publicity.

Example headlines:

"Action hero, Nick Preston, Saves Damsel in Distress!"

"Hero on screen… and off!"

So far, social media was flooded with photos of me diving into the water after Zoey. There was also one of the blast of water slamming into her just before she fell backward.

The water hid her face, something I knew she was probably worried about.

Plucking the still-ringing phone out of my pants, I started to call her. I didn't have her number. I didn't know anything about her except her name.

And what she looked like underneath her makeup.

Fuck, I'd been a dick. Calling her an L.A. girl, making assumptions that she was just like every other Hollywood dweller I knew. It annoyed me how drawn to her I was when I'd made up my mind a long time ago. I wanted something, someone, different than the norm in my private life.

The expression in her eyes when she commanded me to look at her in the pool haunted me. The sound of her crying echoed in my ears. I couldn't untie the knot she tangled in me when her hands clutched my shirt like I was the only thing keeping her from spinning away.

"Callie," I called roughly. My assistant jerked around, splashing water on the front of her blouse.

"Yes?"

"I need Zoey's phone number."

Her eyes went round as though she didn't understand at first.

Holding on to what very little patience I had left, I sighed. "Find it. Please."

"Right away!" she chirped, jumping into action.

My phone rang again. It was another reporter. I powered off the device and tucked it back in my pocket.

I wondered if she was still wearing the sweats I'd given her or if she'd changed out of them the second she arrived home. I'd distracted the press while she snuck away with the oversized hood pulled over her head and a pair of large black sunglasses covering her face.

Carson escorted her off the lot, and by escort, I mean she allowed him to trail behind her to "cover" her retreat.

I didn't bother to point out she was taller than Carson, so he wouldn't be able to block her from sight. Plus, dude really liked hot pink. Not exactly a blending in kind of color. She seemed more comfortable with him than anyone else, though, and that seemed more important at the time.

Thinking of the makeup artist, I spun around, looking for him. He would know how to contact Zoey.

I spotted him going into the trailer and jogged across the lot. The staff that had yet to leave for the day were all gathered around a small flat-screen propped on a portable table against the wall.

Laura waved me over the second she saw me. "*Hollywood Access* is going live. You're the headlining story!"

I'd rather pluck my eyeballs out with plyers found in a bucket of piss before watching that pile of crap, but today was going to have to be an exception.

Zoey was worried about this broadcast. About all the media coverage.

Please. Please, help me get back to the trailer without everyone seeing.

I shielded her as best I could, but I didn't know how good of a job I'd done. I knew better than most that the prying eyes of a camera and journalist wanting a scoop were a formidable opponent.

The crew made some space when I came forward, just as Candace's face filled the screen.

"We're starting off tonight's broadcast with some exclusive footage and eyewitness accounts of the shocking on-set accident of this summer's most anticipated movie. I was behind the scenes of *Triple Impact* earlier today, having been granted special backstage access…"

She wouldn't be Candace if she didn't let everyone know she was invited to do things the other kids weren't.

Classy.

"Nick Preston, along with the hardworking crew, was shooting an incredible action scene, and I was interviewing the heroine—and rumored girlfriend of Nick himself—when tragedy struck!"

I just gagged in the back of my throat.

Maybe she should be an actress, because this one was full of drama.

"As you can see from the clip, Nick was up on a platform while one of the makeup artists was preparing him for shooting."

I was no stranger to seeing myself on screen, but this was somehow different. Personal. The stunt assistant was standing over us while Zoey and I were on the floor. Lifting my face, I said something to him, and he went off. The camera zoomed in the second I was alone up there with her, and a noticeable current went through me as I watched us interacting.

We did nothing out of the ordinary, but there was something. Something in the way we sat so close. The way she tucked my arm in her lap. Then I saw it.

I saw it and knew instantly how this entire story was going to play out.

Fuuuck.

The video clip paused and, by the magic of TV, zoomed in on the captured image. Schooling my reaction, I did nothing but stare dryly at the screen.

I felt several sets of eyes glance my way, and I suppressed the sigh building in my lungs.

"As I mentioned before, Nick's costar, Jessica Blaine, is this sexiest man alive's rumored lady. But we couldn't help but notice that look. The smolder Nick is so famous for on screen. They aren't filming right now, though, and the recipient of those eyes is not Jessica. It's an industry makeup artist we were able to confirm is Zoey Halston. You know here at *Hollywood Access*, we're suckers for details, so of course we noticed the way he looks at her. But we might not have mentioned it if not for what happens next."

Ah, the smolder. I've won awards for it. Been cast in roles solely because of it. Lots of women (and men) have been the recipient. I always controlled it.

Until today.

In that moment up there on the platform with Zoey, it controlled me.

When she hit the water, it felt like I had too. My torso stung with the impact, and adrenaline coursed through me in warp speed. I didn't think about it. All I did was feel. The safety harness was still attached, but even if it hadn't been, I would have done the same.

Beneath the surface of the churning water (due to yet another malfunction), I saw her struggle. Zoey clearly wasn't a strong swimmer, and seeing her vulnerable but still fighting affected me in ways I didn't really realize until thinking back.

"Without hesitation, Nick dove into the water, pulling the woman to safety, even going as far as supporting her weight in the water as well as his. Quick to come to their aide, the crew started to pull them up. But Nick stopped them. You can see the pair exchange a moment, one that clearly belongs on the big screen.

"When the star and crew were finally pulled to safety, the woman hid under a blanket and was shielded by our heroic leading man. Was she embarrassed? Or was there something more to the accident?

"Several eyewitnesses came to me after to report catching brief glimpses of the makeup artist as they were being hauled from the water. You know *Hollywood Access* doesn't report rumors—"

I laughed, making everyone snicker.

"But I admit we are intrigued. People who work regularly with this woman were shocked to see a completely different face than they usually saw. What's more is this woman lost her shoe in the fray, which prompted my crew to notice something else about her."

I muttered darkly, practically growling at the TV. She wouldn't dare.

"A prosthetic. It appears that Nick's current makeup artist has a prosthetic leg."

Laura gasped. Her ponytail whipped around when she turned toward Carson. "Did you know that?"

"Why you looking at me?" He tsked and averted his gaze. I could tell by his reaction that he hadn't known, and being in the dark hurt his feelings.

"Let's check in with some of our viewers who are already weighing in on this breaking story."

"LUCKY B@TCH! I WISH NICK PRESTON WOULD SAVE ME!"
-@THE_FUTURE_MRSP

"UHH GUYS... WHO IS THIS WOMAN? THEY LOOK REALLY CLOSE."
-@NICKPRESTONFAN

"JESSICA BLAINE WHO?"
-@CELEBRELATIONSHIPS

"As you can see, people are already wondering what the relationship is between Nick and this makeup artist. You can be sure that *Hollywood Access* will stay on top of this possibly developing—"

"Turn that trash off!" I snapped, spinning away from the TV.

I swear, did that show have no kind of conscience at all? Why would they broadcast those so-called "fan comments?" What if Zoey saw this?

#Damagedgoods

I should sue.

"Callie!"

My assistant came rushing in, tripping over her untied shoelace. I caught her before she faceplanted.

"Did you get the number?" I asked, righting her.

"The crew manager went home—"

"Carson." I interrupted, turning around.

"At your service." He flourished, bowing.

"Do you have Zoey's number?"

Straightening, he pressed his lips together. "She's my bestie."

Gesturing with my chin, I said, "Call her."

"What? Now?"

I nodded, considering his reaction. "Best friend code, right? No giving out her number to strange men."

"You're hardly strange."

"So don't give it to me. Just dial the number and hand me your phone."

His mouth formed a little O. "You want to use my phone?"

I smiled. "Would that be okay?"

"Well, I guess it would be okay." He reasoned, pulling the phone out of his fanny pack. "You just want to see if she made it home okay?"

I nodded.

Carson hit the screen, and faint ringing filled the area between us. "I can ask her—"

Plucking the phone out of his hand, I grinned. "Thanks, Carson. I'll bring you a pink donut tomorrow to make up for the one you threw away this morning."

His eyes widened. "You saw?"

I winked, and he started fanning his face.

The phone kept ringing, and the knot inside me tightened. Just when I thought maybe she wasn't going to answer at all, her voice filled my ear.

"Am I fired?"

Relief poured through me, and the grip I had on the cell relaxed. Then my brain registered what she said.

"Why would you be fired?" I intoned.

There was a pause in which I imagined her pulling the phone away from her ear to stare at it like it grew legs. It was entertaining as hell.

"You aren't Carson," she said, cautious.

"Figured if I called, you wouldn't pick up."

"You don't have my number to call."

She knew who it was.

"So you would have answered?"

"What do you want?"

I'd just take that as a yes. Glancing up, I noted the interested audience who wasn't even trying to pretend not to be listening. I'd give them points for that. At least they were honest.

I wasn't going to reward that honesty by giving them a front row seat to the rest of my conversation, so I turned and went to the other side of the room, lowering my voice. "Did you make it home okay?"

"Well, since I'm not screaming in your ear, I would say so."

False bravado. Her voice was filled with it.

It pissed me off. "Don't be fake."

She sputtered.

"Did you watch?"

I could almost hear all that bravado slip away. The way her shaky breath expelled made my palm hit the wall.

"They released my name," she answered, hoarse.

"The footage didn't show much of your face," I said low.

"I didn't want this."

"It'll blow over. It seems like a big deal now, but by next week, someone else will have done something juicier."

"Next week." Her voice was stricken as though I'd just sentenced her to something that would last forever and wasn't temporary.

"Zo—"

"I have to go."

"Wait!" I said, pushing off the wall, my voice rising.

She was quiet so long I thought she'd hung up. Swearing beneath my breath, I began to lower the phone.

"What?"

Jamming the phone against my ear, I said, "You're not fired."

She didn't say anything.

"You're coming to set tomorrow, right?"

The desperation I felt was entirely new to me. I never had to work to see anyone. I never feared they might disappear. I never cared enough even if they did.

I wanted to see Zoey again. My instincts told me this was a girl who would run and never look back. Not even at Nick Preston.

"You have to come to work."

"Why?"

I faltered. Why did she have to come? "We're in the middle of shooting a scene. If you don't do my makeup, it will look off and I'll have to reshoot everything."

"I'll think about it."

I started to say more, but she hung up.

No one had ever hung up on me before.

I wanted to disappear.

Disappearing would make me look suspicious. Like I had something to hide.

I did, but that wasn't really the point. The point was to make it look like I wasn't hiding anything. Of course, wasn't this all a moot point anyway?

Everyone knew I was hiding something, thanks to *Hollywood Access* and all the blabbermouths on set.

"It could be worse," I told myself for the thousandth time. And it could. Really, it was all rumor and speculation. There were no actual photos of me with my real face exposed. And those claiming to see it wouldn't have gotten a very good look because Nick had done so well covering me. So even if people did think I had some scarring, no one would really ever dream it would be as bad as it was.

I'd have to acknowledge the foot. People saw, and if I didn't concede the fact I had a prosthesis, it would just make people more curious. Usually, the best way to get in front of a rumor was to confront it.

I could do that. It might even work in my favor.

Did I actually believe that? More or less. It felt like I was trying to convince myself.

Glancing at the TV as pictures flashed across the muted screen, my heart squeezed. That report scared me. In so many ways. Grabbing the remote, I shut it off and stared around the room, numb.

Without thinking, I pushed up off the couch. Then I realized I didn't have my prosthesis on. I couldn't just pace across the room the way I wanted.

I'd have to hop.

Hopping and pacing were very different movements.

Blowing out a breath, my chin dropped against my chest. Strands of dark hair fell over my shoulders, and my bangs caught in my eyelashes, making me blink furiously.

Forgetting all about my hair, I lifted my arms, gazing down at myself. When did I put this on?

The second I got home from the studio, I took off the sweats Nick had given me, tossing them right on the couch. I'd forgotten about them while I showered, changed, and did my best to dry off my prosthesis, which was currently upside down in my bedroom. I hadn't been submerged enough to do any serious damage, but getting it wet like that wasn't advised. It wasn't something I could swim in. Those kinds of prosthetics had to be specially made.

The foot shell was a different matter. I'd spent quite a bit of time taking it apart so I could dry it out. It was currently still disassembled, so I was going to have to get out my spare when I went to work tomorrow.

Was I going to work tomorrow?

Again, I looked down at the sweatshirt I was wearing. Nick's hoodie. I didn't even realize I put it on. I must have subconsciously reached for it and put it on while watching the *Hollywood Access* broadcast.

"Why?" I asked myself out loud. "Why would I do that?"

A feeling I didn't like squirmed around in me, and I made a face. "I was probably cold. It was there. Watching that trash on TV was enough to make anyone feel cold inside."

Frustrated, I grabbed the hem, pulling the fabric up over my head. With the shirt partially inside out, my face buried in the ultra-soft fabric, I paused.

Dropping my arms, the shirt fell back into place, and I flopped back down on the sofa. Scratching my forehead through my bangs, I gazed at the phone lying beside me.

You're coming to set tomorrow, right?

A rude noise burst from my throat. He just wanted me to come so he could gawk at me, just like everyone else would. The thought made me shrink into the cushions of the couch, and my lower lip puffed out.

I hated when people stared with that look in their eye.

Like they were dying of curiosity, but they knew it was rude to ask. So they just looked and stared in a way they thought was noninvasive. It was. It always was.

And the pity.

Don't even get me started on the pity.

But you know what?

I could live with those things. I had for many years. It was the feelings that arose inside me when those looks were levelled at me. It reminded me of things I didn't want to remember and brought back memories I already battled to keep at bay.

Those were things I hated most of all. The things people stirred up unknowingly… things people couldn't even fathom.

Absentmindedly rubbing my palm over my middle, I glanced down once more. Where the hell did he get this shirt? Shangri-La? It felt like it was spun from clouds and beamed down from heaven.

Seriously.

Tugging it off, I looked at the tag. My look turned into a gaping stare.

It was designer. This one shirt probably cost more than an entire month's rent. Folding it carefully, I set it aside with the matching pants. I'd take it back to him tomorrow.

Guess that meant I was going to work. Just thinking of it made me nauseous. What else could I do? Run? Hide? Let one mishap at work ruin everything I'd built for the last seven years? There really was no reason to run, was there? The cops didn't think so.

He can't hurt you anymore.

My head told me this constantly, so why did my heart struggle to believe?

"You know you can't do that," I said, rubbing my temples. The sun wasn't even up yet, and this day was already dragging.

"Just who do you think you're talking to, mister?"

"I'm sorry I didn't call you back last night, Mom. It was insensitive, and you have every right to be upset." I wasn't just saying that to pacify her. I actually meant it. I should have called. She probably hadn't slept a wink, something that was proven when my phone rang ten minutes ago.

"Well, if you aren't hurt, why didn't you call?" she demanded.

I watched a few raindrops slide down the outside of the window. It was raining. It hardly ever rained in L.A. "I was distracted," I mumbled.

I had been distracted. Fuck, I still was.

I couldn't stop thinking about Zoey and if she would show up to work today.

"Well, I guess that's understandable given what you went through. You're sure you aren't hurt?"

Groaning, I looked away from the rainfall. "I told you I wasn't the one who fell. I just dove in the help since I was wearing a harness."

"I want the name of the set director. These things are inexcusable."

"Shit happens."

"I'll be there after the sun rises. I—"

"Mom!" I said, strengthening my voice. I tried to play the indulgent son, but I'd had enough. "You know you can't just show up to the studio like that. It will cause commotion."

"Maybe if I did more drop-ins, things like this wouldn't happen. Set safety is of utmost importance."

"Everyone agrees with you on that. I'm telling you I'm fine. No one was hurt. If you show up, it will only incite more press and publicity."

She sniffed. "Well, that would make the director happy."

"The woman who fell doesn't want the attention."

"This is Hollywood. Everyone wants that kind of attention."

"She doesn't," I deadpanned. I felt Callie glance at me from across the seat.

Lowering the phone from my mouth, I whispered, "Pink donuts."

Her eyes widened, and she leaned up behind our driver to instruct him to make a stop.

"I'll come see you after we finish shooting tonight, okay?"

"I'll have dinner prepared."

"I have no idea what time shooting will go to. Yesterday was cut short."

"I'll have something in the fridge you can heat up." After a pause, she added, "Something good."

"Don't tell my trainer," I whispered.

"Please be careful," she said after a light laugh. "If anything happens to—"

"I know." I cut her off gently. "I'm going to be fine. I promise."

When the call ended, I leaned my head back with a breath of relief. A few minutes later, the car pulled up to the door of a local donut shop.

"Make sure they have sprinkles." I reminded Callie. "And are pink."

She nodded.

"Carl, you want anything?" I called up to the driver.

He held up a plastic shaker, half full of his morning protein shake, and declined.

"Should I get you a coffee with cream?" Callie asked.

"Please."

After watching her fumble with the door handle for a few minutes, I reached up and hit the lock button so she could get out.

Wincing, she glanced at me. "Maybe I should get a coffee too."

"A big one." I agreed.

As expected, the press was gathered outside the gates leading onto the lot. The amount of security buzzing staff through was doubled, and the second our car paused, it was swarmed with reporters, flashing cameras, and incessant knocking on the windows.

My driver barely had to lower the window for the guard to wave us through. A few sleuth-y reporters tried to slip beyond the gates with the car, but they were caught and escorted back. They would camp out there all day, waiting and hoping to get a glimpse of anything they could print or put on TV that would fuel the already-swirling rumors.

Gazing at the cars as we passed, I realized I was looking for Zoey's, but I didn't even know what she drove. If she drove.

Could she drive?

What if she didn't show up?

Panic met me with that last thought. She had to come to work today.

I wanted to see her.

"Here's fine," I called.

My driver slowed, glancing into the back. "You usually go to your trailer first."

"I don't need to this morning." I held up my coffee like it was some kind of proof. Holding a hand out to Callie, I said, "Donuts."

"I'll carry them for you."

I shook my head, gesturing for the box in her lap. "I need you to get my script for the day and find out what hair and makeup needs to do first."

"Right." She handed it over, a bit of confusion in her eyes.

I smiled. "Don't tell me I've been so spoiled that you're shocked I'm carrying a box of donuts on my own."

"Of course not." She scoffed, then scratched behind her ear. The short blond hair was left sticking out when she pulled her hand away.

"Thanks for the coffee. It's one of the best you've made me."

"That's because I didn't make it," she muttered.

"I know." I snickered and let myself out of the car.

Nerves knotted high in my stomach as I pulled open the hair and makeup door. I felt everyone's eyes turn toward me, but I didn't meet any of them, scanning the space for only one face, only one person I genuinely wanted to see.

She wasn't here.

Swallowing down the stark disappointment, I went over to where Carson stood, extending the box of donuts. "Pink. With sprinkles."

His dark eyes rounded. "You didn't!"

"I told you I would."

Leaving the box balanced in my hand, he pulled the lid up to look inside. He squealed, then pressed his fingers against his mouth. "How can I eat these?" His words were muffled by his fingers.

"Preferably over there." I motioned across the room. "So I don't have to watch."

Carson made a stricken sound and snatched the box, holding it against him like it was precious. "I'll never forget this."

"That's because those fried puffs of pastry will attach themselves to your ass for the next ten years," Laura called out.

He gasped. "Honey, don't you know that everyone needs a little extra junk in their trunk?" To prove it, he rotated and stuck out his khaki short-covered rump and smacked it. He glanced back at me and winked. "Men love a booty, isn't that right, Nick?"

"Where's Zoey?" I asked, avoiding all talk of booty.

Straightening, he flipped back the lid on the box to snatch a donut. Taking a bite, he turned, glancing at the door leading into the bathroom at the far side of the room.

As if on cue, it opened, and she stepped into the space.

I scanned her like I would the page of a script, trying to commit even the smallest details to memory.

If I hadn't seen her myself yesterday, held her while she sobbed in this very room, I probably wouldn't believe it had happened. She was completely put together, the L.A. girl I'd thought she was.

Her tall, thin frame was draped with wide-leg, high-waist jeans, the hems skimming the floor with every step she took. She wasn't wearing the shoes she had on yesterday, the one I had to dive back into the tank to retrieve. I wondered if they were ruined after all or if maybe they were still wet.

She had on a loose, long-sleeved white T-shirt, the hem tucked into the waistband of her jeans. Long dark hair fell over her shoulders, layers resting against her face almost like armor and the dark curtain of bangs over her eyebrows, nearly into her brown eyes.

They weren't supposed to be brown.

My stare latched onto her face, remembering the glimpse she let me have yesterday and marveling at how well hidden it all was now.

Her eyes flicked to me, then away quickly. Shoulders tensing, she walked to her station and picked up a tumbler with the string of a tea bag hanging over the side.

Carson cleared his throat. "Who wants a donut?" he announced, moving past.

I noticed then how quiet the room grew when she walked in. How charged and mildly uncomfortable the atmosphere became.

Carson chattered on about donuts and some new line of sunglasses by his favorite designer launching later today. His attempt at restoring the normalcy to this room was admirable even if it only half worked.

Zoey watched the room as she took a sip of her drink, her eyes shuttered. Pulling it down in front of her, she walked toward the center of the room, not having to ask for everyone's attention because she already had it.

"I have a transtibial prosthesis, which means from below the knee, all the way down, I am missing my leg and foot." I watched her chest expand a bit when she pulled in a deep breath. Lifting up her jeans, she showed a glimpse of the prosthetic. "I was in an accident when I was young. I'm sorry if you felt like I lied. It's not something I like to talk about. I… I'm embarrassed about yesterday, about how it came out. I hope we can all just go back to the way we worked together before."

When she finished talking, it was me who swallowed thickly as if I were the one who said those heavy words, as if I were the one who felt the eyes of the room.

I wanted to speak up, to be the first to just move on with the day and make it so what she wanted could happen seamlessly. I couldn't find the words.

"Having a prosthetic is no big deal," Landen said, walking farther into the room. I hadn't even noticed him inside the door before. "Ooh, carbs," he said, snagging a donut out of Carson's box. Taking a big bite and chewing obnoxiously, he wandered over toward Zoey, powdered sugar on his lips. "No reason to be embarrassed either. We're all friends here."

Zoey's cheeks pinkened a bit, then she smiled gratefully at the actor. "Thanks."

"Come make me look good for the camera." He beckoned, plopping down in her chair. "And don't tell my trainer about this," he held up the donut before shoving the rest in his mouth. A blissful sound erupted from his throat. "So good."

Zoey laughed lightly, the sound making me jealous.

That was my laugh. Not Landen's.

Just like that, the crew started up again. People started eating donuts, Carson made a bunch of noise about who knows what, and Jessica came into the trailer for hair and makeup.

Zoey grabbed her cart, wheeling toward Landen.

"Landen," I said, moving to stand over him. "You're with Laura today."

Laura made a sound. "I can work with you, Nick, since Josh is already with Zoey."

"He's not with Zoey. I am," I declared.

Zoey's cart stopped rolling. Laura's eyes widened.

Landen grinned lazily.

I cut off whatever comment he was about to make. "We were in the middle of a scene yesterday. I need her to do the same thing on me so we don't have a bunch of reshoots."

Landen shrugged, then held his fist out to Zoey. "Catch ya later, robo-girl."

Startled, she looked between his fist and smiling face.

My hand shot out, bunching in the fabric at his shoulder, partially tugging him out of the makeup chair. "What did you just call her?"

"Robo-girl," he said like it was nothing. "You know, 'cause of her…" He gestured toward his own leg.

The hand at my side fisted, and I was two seconds from giving him a black eye makeup wouldn't need to fabricate.

But she laughed. Zoey giggled, the sound beckoning all of our attention.

Landen relaxed, even though I was still grabbing him, still debating on clobbering his face. "What's the point in having a fake leg if you can't get a cool nickname out of it?"

"I guess it beats feeling insecure about it," she mused.

He made a sound, offering his fist again. Zoey pounded it out with him.

Landen turned toward me, looking pointedly between his shirt and my hand. I let go, but I still wanted to punch him.

Swinging an arm around Laura's shoulders, he steered her toward their makeup setup. Carson was already working on Jessica, but I knew he was really watching what was happening over here.

"It might be better if you work with Laura," Zoey said quietly. "I'd really rather not come out onto set today."

I shook my head. "I'll come back here when changes are needed. Just stay in the trailer."

"That will waste time."

"So will reshoots if the makeup isn't right."

After a moment of deliberation, she gestured toward the vacant chair. I took a sip of coffee while watching her pull out her supplies. "You know…" I began, speaking quietly. "If you don't like Landen calling you that, just say the word."

Her hand paused in reaching for a brush. "Please don't make a big deal out of it," she whispered.

I let it go.

A few minutes after starting on my face, her fingers tipped my chin up, angling me so she could see better. Our eyes fused. The setting of the entire room fell away.

She was so close I heard her swallow. Then she whispered, "Thank you for yesterday. For what you did."

"I'd do it again."

Another heartbeat passed, and Zoey straightened, breaking whatever spell had just been cast.

You know what coming to work got me?

A big ol' pile of paperwork.

An apology was attached to that paperwork as well, and it became even more sincere after I signed all the stuff promising I wouldn't sue the studio for negligence.

I also had to promise I wouldn't go on TV and let the world know I'd found myself half drowned and the subject of exciting headlines because one of the set directors fell asleep at the equipment and hit a few buttons he wasn't supposed to.

That's all it took. One tired man to totally threaten my cover and reveal all the things I didn't want people to know. Obviously, the higher-ups in the studio and the people in HR knew I had a disability.

I hated that word. Disability. Like I was somehow not whole.

You aren't, I reminded myself. Sometimes parts of me were really cruel.

I thought of it like a side effect from everything I'd been through.

I felt like I was slapped with a permanent warning label even though I desperately tried to appear unchanged. It was too late for that. Everyone knew about my leg now. Hopefully, the whispers about everything else would stop because I gave them something definite to gossip about.

The door to the trailer was open. The wind must have kept it from closing and no one noticed. My hand closed around the handle to bring it around when I went inside, but the murmur of voices stopped me.

"'Hollywood royalty and a makeup artist.'" Laura scoffed. "What kind of headline is that anyway?"

"One that sells," Jessica answered, her voice bored.

"Do you think that's why she always comes in here all done up, without a hair out of place? She's trying to make up for all the things she's missing?"

Glancing up toward the sky, I tried not to let Laura's words pierce me. The truth shouldn't hurt, right? Well, it did. Especially when it felt like my truth was being used against me.

"It must be hard showing up on a set filled with actors who are perfect when you never will be. At least Nick knows now. I've seen the way she looks at him. This is just a little reminder that he's way out of her league." Jessica surmised, her voice smug and uncaring.

Tears burned the backs of my eyes as I blinked furiously and stared upward so none managed to streak my cheeks.

"The headlines coming out today are all frothing with the possibility that someone like her could snag someone like him."

"Of course they are. Everyone loves an underdog. A real Cinderella story. But that's all this is. A story to sell papers… and movie tickets."

Letting go of the door handle, I backed away slowly before turning around and walking off. I wasn't a coward. I was someone who picked my battles. Though it hurt, petty things like gossip and rumors were a waste of my time and energy. Besides, hadn't I just been hoping people would talk about something other than the whispers regarding my face?

Truthfully, I felt fragile today. A feeling that, yeah, left me to wonder if perhaps I was a coward after all, hiding under clothes and makeup and lies.

There was a fine line between cowardly and protecting oneself. I wasn't really sure on which side of that line I stood. So maybe I liked to tell myself I was just choosing my battles when really what I was doing was walking away before I could admit defeat.

I wouldn't let those barracudas see me cry. No way.

What the hell was Jessica flapping her Botoxed lips about anyway? The way I looked at Nick. A light scoffing sound filled the space around me. I didn't look at him any way other than an artist studying her canvas.

Rounding the row of trailers, my hair blew back with a gust of wind. The rain from this morning stopped a while ago, but the sky still seemed heavy, as if it were about to downpour again at any given moment.

The light sound of scuffling feet and a sense of foreboding rolled over me like the thunder suddenly rumbling through the sky. Without looking behind me, I fought to keep my pace normal so as not to show I was suspicious.

Unexpectedly, something unforgiving and strong clamped down around my wrist, snatching me off balance.

Stumbling into the narrow space between two trailers, I would have fallen if not for the body that pinned me intimately against the wall. A scream bubbled up inside me, but it was stifled by a large hand pressing fully against my mouth.

The flashback hit me hard and fast, knocking reality away and transporting me back into the past… back to that day.

* * *

It was the perfect day. The weather was warm, but not hot. The masterclass I was taking let out early, and later, I was meeting friends for a thank-God-it's-Friday dinner.

"Look what I have!" a bubbly voice bounced near.

Forgetting about the lipstick in my hand, I spun with a wide smile. "It came in already!" I squealed, rushing forward to take the small package from her hand.

"We always get the new releases about a week early so we can stock everything for launch day."

Excitedly, I tugged open the top of the box and pulled out the newest, most anticipated foundation the beauty industry was buzzing about. Even the instructor at the masterclass I was taking mentioned it.

"Oh my God, it's gorgeous," I breathed out like it was something holy.

To a makeup artist like me, it was.

"I know." Samantha sighed. "Don't tell anyone I showed you!" she said, sternly pointing her finger at me.

Laughing, I agreed. "But I can have this, right?"

Teeth sank into her lower lip. "I don't know… If my boss finds out…" She trailed off.

I flashed puppy dog eyes.

Defeated, she groaned. "If those baby blues work on me, I can't imagine how many guys fall at your feet."

Pleased, I lunged forward and hugged her. "Thanks, Sam! I won't tell. Cross my heart!"

She waved me off. "Yeah, yeah."

"Having a best friend working at the top beauty supply in town is the smartest thing I ever did."

"I feel used," she bickered sullenly.

"I'll buy you a drink tonight," I sang.

"Make it a big one."

"Deal!"

She laughed and dragged me toward another new product I'd yet to swatch.

I spent most of my afternoon browsing the aisles until there was only an hour until we were supposed to meet up for dinner. "I'm going, Sam!" I called to her on my way out. "I need to change. I'll see you at dinner!"

"See you soon!" she hollered.

The sun was just slipping low in the sky as I sipped at the iced coffee while strolling down the sidewalk. I was already planning the look I wanted to create with my new items and how the pictures would be a great addition to my portfolio.

A prickly feeling fingered the back of my neck when a gentle wind blew. Shivering slightly in the denim jacket I wore, I reached up, making sure my hair wasn't caught on the collar.

I'd been so deep in my own creative thinking that I hadn't realized how empty the street seemed, how eerily quiet everything was for a Friday night. Another wave of uneasiness washed over me, and my fingers tightened around the small sack in my hand.

The wind blew again. Strands of blond hair brushed across my cheeks, momentarily blinding me. As I raised my hand to wipe them away, something clamped around my wrist.

The coffee hit the sidewalk with a splatter. The sound of the cup rolling away was strangely loud.

Panic jolted my system, shocking me numb for long seconds.

My shoes made a scuffing sound against the concrete as I was dragged into a dark alleyway beside my apartment building.

My nostrils flared, lungs seizing, when a hot, heavy hand slammed over my nose and mouth. The brick of the building dug into my back, rasping against the jacket. The man holding me shoved my face to the side, my cheek scraping against the rough surface. I tried to scream and fight.

He used his entire body like a bulldozer, slamming into me, pinning me with his weight.

"No!" I yelled, though it was muffled against his hand. "No!"

I squirmed, trying to see who was assaulting me, my foot connecting with his knee. A low sound tore from him, and I shot forward, only to be slammed back into the brick. Dizziness overcame me, my vision blurring. The bag in my hand was ripped away and my fingers pinned over my head.

A rough hand grabbed my chin, and I felt him studying my face.

"Please, no," I begged, my lower lip trembling.

I couldn't believe this was happening. This wasn't happening.

He was wearing a hood pulled low to conceal his features. Squirming, I tried to see beyond the fabric, to get a look at the man who was trying to hurt me.

Shockingly, he lifted his head.

An ear-piercing scream ripped open my throat and burst from my lips. But it was caught too, trapped by a thick white rag covered in liquid that smelled astonishingly foul.

I tried not to breathe, but my lungs demanded it. And then I was falling… falling… gone…

My vision was blurred, entire body trembling and limp, and I was still pinned. The warmth of a palm cupped the back of my clammy neck and slid up to caress the side of my face. Sucking in a breath, I heard someone talking from far away, but I couldn't understand his words. My heart was pounding, and I knew the clock was ticking.

I had to get away.

Using every bit of strength and clarity I could muster, I threw my weight into the man restraining me, knocking him off balance. I jolted away, but my legs betrayed me.

Just when I would have hit the pavement, I was caught, pulled up and around to stare at the man with no face… Except he did have a face.

Even though my eyes were blurry and my mind muddled, I took in his features. That brief recognition was the very last thing my mind and body allowed before my entire system shut down.

"Maybe we should call someone." Callie fretted near the door.

Zoey would hate it if I called someone in here. The more people that knew, the more chance there was of this hitting the news.

Even knowing that, my resolve was wavering. How could it not be? She looked colorless and frail lying against the couch, as if she weren't even a match for the fluff-filled cushions cradling her.

Fuck, I hadn't meant to scare her. I was trying to protect her.

Fine job you've done of that, Preston. Maybe next time you want to protect someone, you just don't.

No. I'd do the same thing again. The current situation was better than the one we could have been in.

"Nick." Callie's worried voice disrupted my thoughts. My gaze swung around to meet hers. "I'll get one of the medics, bring him here. We can swear him to secrecy."

Glancing back down at Zoey's white face, I gave the nod.

Callie jerked upright, spinning around to leave.

Zoey groaned.

"Wait!" I called out, dropping beside the couch. "Zoey, can you hear me?"

Her eyes squeezed closed as if I were trying to wake her from peaceful sleep. The action would have been cute if she was asleep and hadn't just wiped out in my arms.

Her head tilted toward the sound of my voice. Callie hovered over my shoulder as I gently slid my hand beneath Zoey's head to lift it off the pillow.

"Zo…" I cajoled. "Open your eyes."

Slowly, her lashes fluttered until a sliver of her brown gaze could be seen. Her eyes were hazy, pupils slightly dilated and unfocused.

Still cradling her head, I used my free hand to brush away some of the strands stuck to her clammy cheeks and forehead. "Can you hear me?"

"Nick?" she whispered.

I nodded. "You passed out. I brought you—"

Her eyes shot all the way open, and though they still seemed fuzzy, her body jackknifed up, arms gripping the couch as if she suddenly remembered she was trying to escape.

"Whoa, whoa…" I soothed, staying where I was, not reaching for her. "You're safe. We're still on the lot. I brought you into my trailer so no one would see what happened."

"Can I get you some water?" Callie asked.

Zoey's eyes snapped to my assistant, realizing she was there. Her body plastered back against the sofa, but her eyes relaxed a little. She nodded, and Callie quickly went to the fridge.

A bottle of Voss water appeared over my shoulder. I accepted it before Zoey could, uncapped it, then held it out.

She took it, the tremble in her hands obvious.

"Callie," I said, slowly pivoting around to stand. "Can you go to the makeup trailer and get Zoey's bag? She probably needs it."

"Sure thing."

Callie was partially out the door when Zoey called out. "Can you get my makeup kit sitting beside it? And the small bag that's there too."

When Callie was gone, Zoey glanced up at me. "I can just do your makeup in here, right?"

The last thing I was worried about was my makeup.

Squatting beside of the sofa again, my eyes swept over her face. "You collapsed."

She took another sip of the water, avoiding my gaze. "Did anyone else see?"

"No. I managed to get you in here before anyone could."

Her shoulders slumped with obvious relief. "Thank you."

"I scared you."

She nodded.

"I'm sorry."

"It's not your fault. I—" Her words faltered, and a shudder moved through her. "I just need a minute."

Carefully, I moved to sit near her on the couch, the cushions sinking beneath my weight. Zoey sat sideways, her body turned toward where I sat, her cheek pillowed on the back cushions. She clutched the water against her chest like it was either a shield or a comforting stuffed toy.

Neither of us said anything. We just sat there in silence, and I listened to her uneven breathing. Feeling helpless, I snagged a blanket off the nearby chair. "You seem cold," I said, spreading it over her, tucking it beneath her chin.

She started to say something when the trailer door opened, making her jump. The blanket fell when her hand shot out, tightly grabbing my forearm.

"It's Callie," I told her, not flinching away from the way her fingers strangled my arm.

Her grip lessened, but she didn't pull away. I stood, taking the stuff Callie was carrying and setting it aside.

"Can you tell the director I need a few extra minutes to prepare for the scene?"

"On it." Callie nodded. Her eyes strayed to Zoey. "Do you need a doctor?"

"No," she said instantly, confirming my instincts. "I just need a minute. I, ah… missed lunch."

"Low blood sugar." My assistant nodded gravely. "It happens to me too."

Suppressing a smile, I shooed her out, then locked the door behind her.

"Low blood sugar, huh?" I kept my tone teasing.

She didn't seem to notice. "Just another lie among many."

I frowned, picked up her bag, and held it out. "Do you need anything in here?"

Shyly, she took the bag without a word and pulled out the familiar bottle of pills. Guilt encompassed me as I watched her swallow two.

"What happened?" she asked, lowering the water from her lips.

"I was coming back from set to find you." When she looked up, I motioned to my face so she knew I meant it was work related. "There were two reporters trailing you. They must have snuck onto the lot. So I slipped between some trailers, and when you passed—"

"You pulled me in." She finished, leaning her cheek against the cushions again.

"You started to scream, so I covered your mouth. I thought you knew it was me. You looked right at me, but then you sort of…" I searched for a way to describe how she sort of left her body like a ghost.

"Went lights out?"

I half smiled. "Yeah."

"I had a panic attack," she said, once again refusing to look at me.

"Because I grabbed you?"

She hesitated, then spoke. "I've been a little on edge since yesterday."

"I was honestly just trying to keep the press away from you."

She nodded. "Did they see us?"

"No. I called security after I brought you in here. They're gone by now."

She took another sip of the water, pulled the bottle back, and glanced at it. "You even drink fancy water."

I felt my brows rise. "I do?"

"Like you don't know."

"Callie is the one that stocks it, not me."

She rolled her eyes. "That's something fancy people say."

I chuckled.

"Come on," she said, sitting forward. "You need makeup." Her movements were a little too fast, and she dipped back, dizzy.

"Whoa." I put an arm across her back, keeping her upright.

Gazing up, her eyes met mine. That same feeling I had this morning electrocuted me, making my insides buzz.

"Take your time," I whispered, shifting so my body was closer and more of me was there to support her weight.

She relaxed into me for the span of a single heartbeat. It didn't matter it was a fleeting second because it was more than enough time for satisfaction to hum across my skin.

Jolting up, her body left mine and she slid until she was just perched on the edge of the couch, sending a clear message of the boundaries she wanted to keep between us. "Let's get to work."

"If you still need a minute—"

"I don't." She cut me off. "Makeup is sort of my happy place."

I was glad she had something to give her peace.

But I was jealous too.

Jealous the thing giving her peace wasn't me.

I learned something today. Passing out for a while did not count as a nap. Kind of a shame, wasn't it? I mean, couldn't something good come out of nearly face planting on the pavement in front of the actual sexiest man alive?

Guess not, because I was bone tired. My muscles were tight, my neck stiff, and I couldn't wait to get home and stretch out. I needed it. My hamstrings needed it. The last thing I wanted or needed was a contracture that made it hard to walk.

I was trying to avoid drawing attention, constantly reminding people I was missing part of my leg.

Overhearing Jessica and Laura still circulated in the back of my mind even though it had been hours ago. As much as I tried to ignore the whispers, it wasn't easy. Especially when I was mentally exhausted.

Everyone stayed late to make up for the lost time yesterday, but I was still one of the last to leave. Hoping to avoid the press waiting for us all to leave, I stayed behind to clean makeup brushes.

Once they were clean and drying for the night, I grabbed my bag, pausing beside the one I'd forgotten about. Nick's sweats. If I'd been thinking clearly earlier, I could have had Callie grab them and put them back in his trailer.

But I wasn't thinking clearly. They were too expensive to just leave lying out, so I looped the handles around my wrist and left.

The filming lot was a little creepy at this time of night. Okay, it was a lot creepy right now. What was usually bustling with noise and crew was eerily quiet and dark. Streetlights created bright spots on the pavement that gave way to shadowy patches.

Basically, the set looked like a giant parking lot filled with trailers, buildings that looked like warehouses, and a bunch of other heavy equipment. My sneakers were quiet as I walked past a few dark trailers and a row of parked golf carts.

The back of my neck prickled with caution, and the flashback from earlier today resurfaced in my mind. Drawing in a deep breath and pressing my palm to my pounding chest, I continued on. Briefly, I thought about going back into the makeup trailer and calling for security to walk me to my car, but I was already halfway there and I was being ridiculous.

I was at work. On a gated set with security and cameras everywhere.

The shrill sound of metal rubbing against metal brought me up short. *Bang!* Alarmed, I jumped about a foot in the air. Pain clenched around the back of my upper leg, making me stumble. Leaning over, I grabbed the back of my thigh, sucking in a breath while adrenaline surged through my limbs.

Pain still squeezing my leg, I forced myself upright, favoring my right foot. The bag hanging from my wrist banged against my side when I spun, glancing around for the source of the noises.

Deep in the back of the lot was a set that looked like a busy street in the middle of a city. The buildings were tall, the sidewalks looked real, and when it was all lit up and bustling with extras, a person might actually believe they were in Chicago or New York City.

Right now, it appeared abandoned. Like a ghost town evacuated in the midst of an emergency. The street was shadowy, the buildings hollow. The only sign of life was the disturbing sounds from a moment ago.

It was all too easy to feel like I was walking home at night, alone on the streets, being stalked from one of those dark windows above…

A large piece of equipment started up and drove out from behind one of the buildings, going straight down the middle of the street. Headlights lit up everything, including the large pile of wood it was transporting.

The man driving yelled something, and someone shouted in return.

Relief made me shoulders sag. Starting forward again, I winced at the tightness in the back of my leg, the muscles cramping with pain.

I was too tired for this.

Since no one was around, I allowed myself to limp a little and take some weight off the constricting hamstring.

My car came into view, so I straightened, forcing myself to walk normally now that I was in a place where

I knew other people could be. Not far from where I parked was the tall fence line blocking off our sets from the street. Moving forward, my eyes scanned for reporters or any other busybodies that might be hanging around.

It seemed they'd all gone home for the day, which made my staying longer well worth it even if I was tired and cramping up.

Pulling my bag in front of me, I started digging around for my keys. You know how it is. The keys are always somehow crammed at the very bottom of the bag, buried underneath all the stuff you carried around because you just might need it.

Just as my hand closed around them, commotion broke out around me.

"There she is!" someone yelled.

Rushing feet and excited voices filled the quiet of the parking area. I glanced up, only to recoil when harsh, bright light shone right into my eyes, nearly blinding me.

Throwing my arm up to shield my eyes, my keys made a jangling sound as they dangled from my fingers.

"Miss Halston?" someone shouted. "Zoey!"

I was surrounded in a matter of seconds. The lack of time they gave me to escape was actually scarily impressive.

"Zoey Halston, can you give us a comment on what happened on set yesterday?"

"Were you hurt in the accident?"

"What was it like being saved by Nick Preston himself?"

My head swam with the onslaught of questions, and I didn't know how to react. Keeping my arm up to shelter my face, I turned toward my car, wanting nothing more than to escape.

I was surrounded. How had I not seen these people? How did they get onto the lot?

Why wouldn't they go away?

I tried to push through, but they pushed back, preventing me from fleeing.

"Please, just a few words," someone yelled from behind the blinding light.

"No comment!" I said, my voice sounding a lot less powerful than I intended.

"Are you dating Nick Preston?"

"What's your relationship with the sexiest man alive?"

Dizziness washed over me, making my world tilt sideways. Lowering my hand, I blinked profusely, trying to right the universe again.

"Please lower the light," I said, squinting, swaying on my feet. "It's so bright."

The cameraman angled the light down slightly, barely enough to do anything except make my eyes stop watering.

Just as I turned to run, someone grabbed my arm, spinning me back. I cried out, my car keys falling out of my grip. The sound of them slapping on the pavement was an ominous blow.

Breathing became something I had to think about, something no longer natural. The light came back full force, and I shied away like I was being struck by fists and not overwhelming sensations.

"Everyone, step back!" a familiar voice yelled. "Give her some space!"

Blinking, I glanced up, my vision still showing double.

A smiling woman appeared, but she wasn't friendly. It was Candace Grimes. The woman who started all this in the first place. Anger lit me up inside, blissfully pushing back some of the panic and unsteadiness overcoming me.

"You," I spat.

"Nice to see you again, Zoey." Candace smiled, serene. "I'd very much like to get a statement from you. Or maybe even an exclusive interview on *Hollywood Access*."

A few other vultures started yelling their own offers and vying for my attention.

I didn't look away from Candace and her smirking expression. She knew I didn't want to talk, but she didn't care. Dislike swelled up inside me so swiftly it made my stomach roll.

Swallowing back the rising bile, I glanced around for my keys. Spots swam before my eyes and everything was still fuzzy, but I looked anyway, desperate to get out of here.

"Looking for these?"

Lifting my eyes, I saw my keys in the palm of Candace's hand. I started for them, but her fingers closed around them and she pulled her arm back. "The statement first."

"Security!" I shrieked, angling my face toward the gates where the guards were posted. Glancing back at her, I narrowed my eyes. "Give me my keys."

"What is your relationship with Nick Preston?"

My upper lip curled. "There isn't one."

I reached for the keys.

"What happened to your leg?"

I froze.

Sensing she'd taken me off guard, she advanced. "People on set yesterday say they saw a glimpse of your face. That it looked different."

A sound ripped from my throat, and I lunged for my keys. My hamstring clenched, making me stumble and cry out. The bag hanging around my wrist hit the ground and tumbled over. Palming the back of my leg, I began to wilt under defeat.

The chaos assaulting me was suddenly obscured. Warm strength encompassed me like a shield protecting me from deadly blows or an umbrella concealing me from the rain. Arms slid around me, supporting my weight, making it so I could stand tall. One large palm buried itself against the back of my head, pushing my face into the protection of a wide, unforgiving chest.

I breathed in deep, recognizing the scent, comforted by it.

Nick.

Bedlam erupted. The people crowding around pressed in. I felt their energy clawing at me, trying to attack. It didn't matter. It didn't matter how close they came because they wouldn't get past my defense.

They wouldn't get past Nick. He wouldn't let them. I didn't know anything else in that fleeting second, but I did know that.

More bright light beamed. Question after question was thrown at us like daggers at a target.

The arms around me strengthened as if he drew strength from their battle and couldn't possibly be drained. Winding my arms around his lean waist, I hugged him as tight as my limbs would allow. He felt me shifting onto my right foot and shifted himself, adjusting so more of my weight was his to bear.

My stomach burned and tumbled. The anxiety overwhelming me was pushed away by something entirely different.

"This is below you, Candace," I heard him rumble, the sound of his voice making my toes curl in my sneaker.

I don't know what she said, what anyone else said, because he was here and it didn't matter. My eyes slipped closed; my body felt heavy.

Once again, Nick was protecting me, shielding me from a storm he probably didn't even understand. I clung to him as strangers tried to close in, believing he would guard me even if it meant taking a few hits himself.

No one else had done that for me before. I'd never dream of asking, but I didn't have to, did I? Nick was here all on his own.

Nick, my rooted tree, my unlikely hero.

The man who had somehow become something more than a stranger.

"Can you walk?" I asked quietly right beside her ear.

I felt her brief nod against my chest, but honestly, I had my doubts. I saw her stagger when I pushed through the crowd. Even now, she favored her right side, making me worry about her left.

Security pounded across the pavement, shouting and blowing whistles. What a freaking clusterfuck this was. Ignoring it all, I bent, scooping up the bag she dropped and her along with it.

She gasped but didn't fight to get away. Instead, her arms looped around my neck and she buried her face close.

The press, of course, ate it up. Internally, I cringed but refused to show it. My publicist was going to shit a brick. Candace stood in the center of everyone, untouched by the storm of reporters and security. Our

"Don't." She gasped, trying to pull away when my hands slipped under her legs to pull her around, facing me.

Her attempts were simple to avoid. The moment my hands wrapped around her leg, breath hissed from between her lips.

Kneading my fingers into the tight, knotted muscles, I made a tsking sound. "Why'd you let it get like this?"

"I was busy," she snapped.

Ignoring her foul and noisy temper, I massaged a little deeper.

Zoey melted against the seat, her arms going slack. The anger and alarm pouring out of her just seconds ago was gone. A sound of appreciation vibrated her throat, making me glance up. Her eyes were half closed, lips relaxed.

"Feel good?" I asked, making her tense anew. "Calm down," I murmured, continuing my ministrations.

She settled once more, slumping into the seat, a virtual puddle in my hands. She felt small despite her long frame, and I couldn't help but worry how she would have driven home if I hadn't showed up when I did.

After a few minutes of me working the tight muscles, I felt her shuttered gaze. Unable to resist the call, I glanced up, our stares colliding.

The pull I felt toward her was physically demanding, as though we were two magnets with irresistible force. We were alone here in this public space, night closing around us. The hum of L.A. in the backdrop created a rhythm that the adrenaline she made me feel buzzed to.

The way I was touching her wasn't sexual. It wasn't even for pleasure, but out of necessity.

The heat was undeniable. Desire scorched my fingertips, burned my hands, and spread through my limbs until my stomach felt full of need. I felt like some kind of premium race car whenever she was near. Usually a pretty even-keel man, I went from zero to sixty in two seconds flat when she looked at me like that.

"It feels better now." The rocky quality of her voice was like a poker to the fire already rampant inside me.

She felt it too.

She didn't want it, but our bodies seemed to have a will of their own when we were close.

Easing my hands back, allowing them to rest on my knees, I raked one lingering look over her. "I'll drive you home."

I was already to my feet, preparing to close the door, when her voice floated up to me. "How will you get home?"

Unable to resist, I leaned back down, crowding into her space. "You worrying about me?"

Her eyes averted, aptly avoiding my gaze. "The press saw us drive off together."

"I'm used to the press." I closed the door. On my way around, I dialed Callie. "What's your address?" I asked Zoey, sitting behind the wheel.

She gave me her address, and I asked Callie to meet me nearby with my Range Rover.

I felt her anxiety almost as clearly as I felt the chemistry between us. "Don't worry," I said, dropping my cell in the cup holder between us. "I'll meet her a couple streets over. No one will know."

She nodded, absentmindedly rubbing her leg.

"You should put some heat on that when you get home."

She made a sound, staring out the window as I drove.

of me, and even if my eyes weren't on her, the rest of me was. It was enough.

Traveling my hand up, I felt the hood pulled over her head, shielding her face.

"You scared me tonight," I told her, keeping my promise, keeping my eyes closed.

"How did you know something was wrong?"

"It was just a feeling."

She didn't say anything, and anxious emotion started to spark inside me again. Perhaps it wasn't enough. Maybe I needed to see it too.

Letting go of her hand, unwinding my arm from around her body, I grappled for her face. Sinking my fingers under the hoodie, I reached for her.

She flinched away, nearly falling backward.

I caught her around the waist, keeping her upright. "Are you hurt?"

"No."

"I need to see you now, angel."

"Why are you calling me that?"

"Because in my dream, that's exactly what you looked like."

"Dream?" she echoed, confusion in her tone.

"I'm opening my eyes."

"No!" She pulled away, her movement like a hop.

Her leg.

"Zoey." It was a command.

Her hand found my arm, holding on for support. "My crutches are beside the couch."

"You don't have your…" My words faltered. I wasn't sure how to say it. I didn't want to sound insensitive, but could speaking a question or the obvious truth be just that?

That awkwardness I'd battled back before came galloping forward.

This time it was her who slayed it.

"That's right. I'm not wearing my prosthetic right now. I don't sleep with it on."

My hand clenched into a fist. Someone broke in here while she was sleeping, while she was vulnerable in bed. It slammed into me how ill-equipped she was to protect herself.

How could she run if she needed to?

A nauseous feeling churned below my ribs. It was getting harder and harder to keep my eyes closed.

"Turn away." My voice was gruff.

"What?"

"If you don't want me to see your face, turn away."

Her hand lifted, and disappointment washed over me. "You can trust me," I told her, wanting her to do just that, wanting her to stay right here in front of me.

"You can open them now," she said a moment later, her voice still close, making my heart thump with anticipation.

So I did.

Rage and panic gave me strength, and I swung with the crutch, putting all the force I had into the swing. It connected with his body, knocking him sideways.

He stumbled, falling onto one knee, and I raised it up, swinging down again. He rolled out of the way, leaping up in a way that made me jealous. Pulling the crutch down, I used it to rush after him as he scrambled through my apartment.

"Give me the camera!" I roared.

In response, he turned back and took another photo. I ran into a small table, knocking things to the floor. It was a slap in the face that he went to the door for escape instead of using the window again.

His laugh taunted me as he stopped to unlock the door and turn the handle. I made it to him, my hand closing around the back of his shirt just as he slipped outside.

I let out a cry, trying to pull him back into the apartment, reaching for the camera strap, but I was too late. He jerked, and I toppled over, unbalanced, falling onto the floor as he slammed the door in my face and ran away.

I lay there facedown, dividing my stare between the piece of cut glass beneath the window and the closed apartment door. The sound of the chain lock swaying against the frame taunted me, reminding me of everything I couldn't do.

Despite how defeated I felt, I got up, moving to the window. The screen was sliced open, pulled out of the frame and lying outside. I shut and locked the window even though, yes, there was a hole neatly cut into the pane.

Leaning against the wall, I waited for my heart rate to return to normal and the tears slipping down my cheeks to dry.

Next, I got the lost crutch and taped the cut glass back onto the window with some duct tape. As I did, I kept seeing the flash of the camera, breath coming in short gasps.

When I turned from the window, I saw all the things I'd knocked to the floor as I tried to run after the man assaulting me.

I sank onto the floor and scooted into the corner of the room, leaving the crutches where they fell.

Pulling my knees up against my chest, I wrapped my arms around them tightly, never once noticing the fact that one of my legs wasn't there to wrap my arm around.

I allowed the shakes to overcome me. The panic and the worry.

I should call the police.

Really, it would likely be too late.

That man got what he came here for. I was going to have to brace myself for what came next. All the convincing I'd done to get myself to believe this home was my safe space turned into wasted effort.

Bowing my head into my lap, I wondered if I would truly feel safe anywhere ever again.

With a sigh, she slipped into the bed, rolling away, keeping her back to me. Sliding in beside her, I spooned against her body, slipping my arm around her waist.

I felt her reach up to tug the hood closer around her face, but then her hand slid over the one holding her.

"You can go to sleep, angel." I promised softly. "I won't take advantage and look at you while you sleep."

She believed me. Not much later, she slept.

I shouldn't have been able to sleep. Not after the break-in. After the panic attacks. Not with Nick lying in my bed.

I slept anyway, drifting off quicker than I had in seven years. When I woke, light from the sun outlined the closed curtains, and I was still in the exact same position I'd been in before I shut my eyes.

For a girl who didn't surprise easily, I was amazed.

I felt rested despite all the restlessness in my life.

Refreshed despite being drained.

Nick's arm was still thrown over me, my body perfectly tucked along his. We were so close I felt the even rise and fall of his chest against my back, heard his soft snore against the pillow.

If he hadn't shown up here last night, you'd probably still be shivering in the corner.

Most of all…

What was this, a pro/con list all about Nick?

He promised not to look, and he didn't.

I made a scoffing sound, scrubbing my arms a little too vigorously. "How do you know? He probably studied every inch while you were sleeping like a fool."

He didn't look, and you know it.

Grabbing the handgrip on the wall, I let the spray pelt me. I did know. Even though I had no proof, I knew Nick hadn't looked.

And that right there was why I was in so much trouble.

After my shower, I pulled on my clothes and stood staring at the closed door. "Please be gone," I whispered.

Tentatively, I opened the bathroom door, peeking around the wood. When the coast was clear, I pulled it open farther and glanced across the room to the bed.

It was empty.

A giant sigh of relief escaped me, and I moved out into the bedroom.

"I made tea," an abrupt, unexpected voice announced.

I screamed, one of the crutches falling to the floor.

"We really need to work on your jumpiness," Nick said, appearing soundlessly to pick up the crutch.

I turned sideways so he couldn't see me. "I thought you left."

"Aren't you glad I didn't?"

"No," I told him. "Go home."

"I will after you pack your stuff."

"What?"

"You said you couldn't stay here anymore."

"That didn't mean I wanted to go home with you!" I nearly choked on the words. What the hell was he thinking? "Are you on drugs?"

"Despite ample opportunity, no," he mused like this conversation was fun for him.

I flung out my arm behind me. "Give me my crutch."

Instead of placing it in my outstretched hand, his own curled around mine. My stomach dipped and rolled unexpectedly, making me feel like I'd just gotten off a roller coaster.

"What are you doing?" I said, sounding embarrassingly breathless.

"Giving you this back," he explained. His voice was close, and his body stepped closer. His heat brushed against me, his chest rubbing against my shoulder. The hand holding mine lifted my arm to gently place the crutch beneath it.

Still holding my hand, he guided it down to the handle, where he showed my fingers how to grasp on.

As if I didn't already know.

I couldn't say that, though. Sarcasm just wasn't something I was capable of in the moment. No words were. My heart somehow jumped into my throat, leaving my chest hollow but my neck unexpectedly full.

My stomach wouldn't stop flipping, and my skin was starting to tingle.

"I need to get ready," I said, hoping he didn't hear the unsteadiness in my voice.

Finally, his hand lifted off mine, and some of the tension relented. It didn't last, though. More skyrocketed through me when that same hand smoothed over the side of my head, pressing against the red-hooded robe I was wearing.

"I like my hoodie better," he told me before turning and leaving the bedroom.

The second he was gone, I deflated like a balloon with a sudden puncture. If it wasn't for the crutches, I'd be in a puddle on the floor.

I was so vulnerable to him in so many different ways. It frightened me so much that my fingers shook with it.

"Why the hell don't you have any coffee?" he yelled from the kitchen.

A laugh bubbled up inside me.

"I don't drink it," I yelled back, going to sit at my vanity. It was covered in everything I needed to disguise who I really was and make me into the woman I let everyone see. I'd gotten quite skilled at the process, and something that used to take me quite a while, I could do now in about an hour.

Water dripped from the ends of my damp hair, sliding down my back beneath the robe. I squirmed uncomfortably, wanting to drop the hood so I could pull out the damp ends and let the robe soak up the drips.

Just as I was about to pull it down, Nick appeared once more.

Ducking, I stared at my lap so he couldn't see me in the reflection of the mirror. "You should leave."

"There are reporters staking out the front."

I gasped. "Again?"

"They were here yesterday?"

"They've been here almost every day since *Hollywood Access* aired," I replied, picking at a string on the robe.

He cleared his throat. It sounded ominous to me.

I sighed heavily. "What?"

"Pretty sure they know that's my SUV out front."

I buried my face in my hands.

"I should have parked a couple blocks over. I wasn't thinking too clearly last night."

I groaned.

"Here," he said. The clink of a mug against the top of my vanity made me glance between my fingers.

"You made me tea."

"I told you that earlier," he muttered. "I don't know how you drink it."

"Black with honey," I answered offhand. "What are we going to do about the press?"

He left the bedroom, reappearing with a bear-shaped container of golden honey. Had he gone through all my kitchen cabinets? "Really made yourself at home," I muttered, annoyed.

He chuckled like he was proud of himself before uncapping the bear, holding it in front of me. I stared at how small that honey bear looked clutched in his large hand.

Taking my inaction for something else, he cleared his throat. "I won't look."

I added the correct amount of honey to my tea and used the spoon he also provided to stir it in. "Thank you."

"You really don't have any coffee?" he asked, hopeful.

I giggled. "Sorry."

"Savage," he muttered. After a deep sigh, he said, "I'll get rid of the press."

"How are you going to do that?"

"I have people."

"Shut the door," I called as he walked out.

"I won't look."

"Shut it!"

The latch shut with a definite click.

Flipping the hood off my head, I picked up the tea for a sip. Just the way I liked it. Stealing a glance over my shoulder at the closed bedroom door, I couldn't help but smile.

The bedroom door opened soundlessly, and her dark head peeked out. "Are they gone?" she whispered as though I'd invited the press inside for a meal.

A meal that did not include coffee. Seriously, who the fuck didn't have coffee?

Chuckling because she looked so cute peering at me, I rose from the sofa. "For now. But we should go before they come back."

Stepping into my full line of sight, I got my first good look at her since yesterday. She was dressed in a pair of distressed denim overalls and a snug white shirt with sleeves that went to her elbows. The hem of the jeans was frayed and nearly touched the floor.

Her long dark hair fell over her shoulders, the layers all styled to fall against her face. A curtain of bangs brought focus to her eyes, beautiful blue orbs that were hidden behind brown contacts.

Why would she hide such beautiful eyes?

"Don't you think you're going to get hot in that?" I asked.

She glanced down the length of her body. "No. I like this outfit. It has lots of pockets for makeup brushes." She grinned at the fact that her cute outfit was also functional.

Suppressing a smile, I said, "Why not a tank top beneath it?"

The sunny look on her face faded, and her hand lifted to rub lightly at her left bicep. Feeling guilty for something I wasn't sure of, I closed the distance between us. Taking her hand from her arm and wrapping my fingers around hers, I tugged her gently toward the couch.

When she was sitting, I lowered onto the coffee table in front of her and reached for her thigh.

She gasped, lifting up her right knee defensively. "What are you doing?"

"How's your leg?" I asked, slowly pressing down the knee between us.

"My leg?" she echoed.

I liked having her eyes on me, even when she was staring at me with suspicion and wariness. I would like it if she looked at me a lot, no matter her expression.

"The cramps." I reminded her, focusing again on her left thigh.

"Oh." Her body was still tense. "I'm fine now."

The jeans were soft and worn beneath my fingers, and I began massaging the back of her leg. "Feel good?"

"You don't need to do that," she said, shy.

"It's going to be another long day on set. I don't want that happening again."

"I can take care of myself." Her hand covered mine, stopping the ministrations.

Lightly, I lifted her hand, moving it back into her lap. "I know you can." I went back to massaging, and her body relaxed.

We sat quietly for a few minutes as she allowed me to work the tight muscles in the back of her leg, slowly moving down toward her knee.

"That's good." Her voice was abrupt, as was her movement to sit up straight.

Letting my hands fall away, I sat back to regard her. "Where's your stuff?"

"What stuff?"

"The bag I told you to pack."

Her brow arched, disappearing beneath her bangs. "I don't need to pack a bag."

"You can't stay here, Zo. Not after last night. Not after the press got my plate numbers this morning."

"Zo-ey," she enunciated, making me smirk. "And I know that. I'll come back and get my stuff later."

"Just get it now. I'll take it to my place."

"I'm not staying with you."

Crossing my arms over my chest, I gave her a squinty-eyed look, which she returned.

Sighing heavily, I said, "Where you gonna stay, then? A hotel where press can come and go all night long?"

Her eyes slid away as though she hadn't considered that.

"Do you have family in L.A.?" I pressed.

"No." Her chin stuck out stubbornly. "I'll stay with Carson."

Mild surprise shot through me. "Carson knows about…" My words faded, but Zoey's attention on me was opaque. Lifting my hand to her face, I said, "He's seen your face?"

Just before I could stroke her skin, she pulled back, eyes alarmed. Pulling up both knees between us like a shield, her sneakers rested on the cushions.

She was wearing the shoe I had to go back into the water tank for.

"He hasn't. No one has," she said quietly.

"Does he know you cover it up?"

"I'm sure he's heard the rumors now."

"So you're going to let him see?" I demanded, temper in my words.

"That's up to me!" she spat, jumping up from the couch. The narrow space unbalanced her as she tried to rush away, making her stumble back.

I caught her around the waist just as she fell in my lap. The back of her head dropped against my shoulder, and she gazed up, surprised. "I'm sorry."

Linking my arms around her, I smiled. "You're clumsy."

"Am not!" she argued. "I work really hard not to be!"

"I like it," I teased softly.

Her brow furrowed. "What?"

"The clumsier you are, the more I get to touch you."

She tried to scramble up, but I wasn't about to let her go. It was pure hell lying in that bed all night beside her. Knowing if I reached out, she would panic.

She fell silent, and her struggle to get away ceased.

"You're better off with me, angel." I spoke softly. "I live in a gated community with state-of-the-art security and a private piece of property. You'll have your own

146

bathroom, your own bedroom, and you won't have to stress about trying to hide."

"Why are you doing this?" Her voice was weary.

"The press wouldn't be hounding you if it weren't for me."

"I thought it was going to be okay. But now I'm not so confident."

Apprehension corded the muscles in the back of my neck. "What do you mean?"

This time when she tried to get up, I let her go. Zoey went to the window, lifting the curtain to look at the window she'd covered in tape. Anger bunched inside me anew, making me wish I'd been there when that asshole broke in.

"What did he take?" I asked.

"Something personal," she whispered, still gazing at the tape.

"We need to call the cops." I began.

Her eyes slid toward the corner of the room, making mine follow. I got a funny feeling in my stomach, though the corner of the room was empty and we both stared at open space.

"The cops can't do anything."

"We can file a report. Maybe they can find whatever was taken. You can get it back."

"I can't get back what he took from me." Her voice sounded hollow, far away, and sort of strange.

The hair on the back of my neck lifted, creating a chill around me that L.A. never had before.

Moving across the room, I took the curtain out of her hands, letting it fall back into place, covering the broken glass. She was still staring into the corner of the room.

Wrapping my hand around her thin wrist, I pulled her around toward me. "Zoey."

"He took my picture."

Confusion filled my head. "What?"

"He had a camera. He took photos of me… of my face."

Rage burned my veins. My hand gripped her wrist, making her cry out.

"I'm sorry." I relented, letting go instantly. She didn't move away, making me feel like she understood I'd been angry on her behalf. "What do you mean he took your photo?"

"I mean right now, everyone is interested in me because of you. But if that man releases those photos, there will be an entirely new level of attention."

The definitive fear in her voice chilled me to the bone. Shifting closer, I said, "All the more reason for you to stay with me."

"Distance yourself now, Nick." A staunch warning laced her words. "This isn't something you should be involved in."

"Ange—"

She spun at me, angry. "Stop!" She pulled back, disengaging the hold I didn't even realize I had on her arm. "This isn't some action movie. You aren't the hero here. This is real life with no stunt doubles, fake sets, or scripts. You can't even imagine the kind of hell this could unleash."

So she was supposed to walk through it alone?

I didn't realize I'd posed the question out loud until she answered, "I did it before. I'll do it again."

"Girl, your face is whiter than the blow I saw those models doing in the club bathroom last night," Carson drawled, waving his fork around in my general direction.

I made a face. "You need to find a new club."

Pushing the hot-pink Ray Bans onto his head, he gave me a *yeah right* look. "Pssh, you know damn well every club around here has treats."

"Long as you aren't doing tricks to get them." I smirked.

"Please, honey. This body is a temple, and I must treat it as such."

"Sprinkled donuts must do a temple good," I quipped, putting down my chopsticks to sip the ice water in front of me.

Carson and I had escaped set for lunch at our favorite ramen shop. At first, I'd been nervous we would be followed, but we rode in his car. Since the incident on set last night, security had been doubled, which meant we got away without issue.

It was nice to be here, doing something normal like eating with a friend. I didn't get out much, for obvious reasons, so when I had the chance to do something other than work and go home, it was always a treat.

And by treat, I don't mean cocaine.

Did I mention the Hollywood scene was filled with money, beauty, and drugs?

I probably didn't need to mention that, right? It's probably obvious.

"I would have invited you out last night, but I don't like rejection," Carson said, dabbing the corners of his lips with a napkin. He was so extra. I really loved him for it.

I loved that he could be whoever he was with no apologies. It was so cool to just see him be all in with himself and his own life. I envied that.

He also looked better than me in pink.

"I'm sure you had a ton of groupies without me," I teased.

Adjusting the collar of his electric-blue polo shirt so it was perfectly flipped up, he nodded. "You gonna tell me why you look like Casper and seem jumpier than a frog on a lily pad?"

"Someone broke into my place last night."

His fork dropped into the ramen, splashing everything with broth. He squealed, making a few people turn around, but he didn't notice. Pressing his hand to his lips, his eyes doubled in size, and then he began fanning himself with a fresh napkin. "Tell me everything."

"There isn't much to tell. He broke in, and I chased him out."

"Did you call those sexy men in blue?"

He meant the police.

"No. He didn't take anything before he ran off, so I didn't bother."

He made a tsking sound. "The press sure isn't making it easy. You almost drowned, and they're acting like it's the hottest scoop since Brendan Marx got caught with his pants down!"

"I saw that headline," I noted, using a spoon to sip some broth.

"Poor guy. Did you see his underwear? If he's going to be going around dropping his pants, he should at least let his stylist choose something photograph worthy."

I laughed. "Maybe you should slide into his DMs and offer your shopping expertise."

"Girl, you know I already did."

I laughed some more. He gave me a level look. "I wasn't joking."

"That's why I'm laughing."

Shaking his head, he sighed. Carefully unfolding a large white cloth napkin, he draped it over the top of his bowl, signaling he was done.

"Well, you'll just have to come stay with me," he offered. "We can carpool to the set every day."

I hesitated, thinking back to my conversation with Nick this morning. I told him I would stay with Carson, but now that the offer was truly out there, I faltered.

"What's the look on your face?" Carson asked, instantly smelling gossip.

Setting aside my food, I answered, "Nick asked me to stay at his place."

"I'm schvitzing," he announced, reaching into his fanny pack (blue to match his shirt) to pull out a portable fan and switch it on.

"I said no, of course." I continued.

"What?" he shrieked, the fan landing on the table, blowing all the napkins and straw papers all over the floor.

I reached over and switched off the fan, then brushed my bangs back down where they belonged. "Keep your schvitzing to a minimum," I muttered.

"Call him up right now and tell him you had a brain fart and you do want to stay with him."

"I can't do that."

"Well, why not?"

"He just feels responsible for the press bothering me."

"Well, he does have some responsibility." Carson leaned across the table, resting his elbows on top. "I saw the headlining story last night on Candace's show. Nick rushed into a crowd of hungry tigers to protect you! Then he whisked you off on his black stallion."

"It was my four-door Camry," I muttered. Though, I couldn't correct him about the press because they did act like a bunch of tigers. Wincing, I got back to the subject. "That was on last night?"

"Haven't you looked online at all?"

"Busy being robbed, remember?"

"That's no excuse for not checking the news."

News to Carson was the celebrity headlines.

"Speaking of, I haven't had the chance to look since my morning latte." His cell appeared out of his fanny pack, and I smiled at the rainbow-colored case on the back. In the center was the PopSocket that looked like a diamond that I'd given him for his last birthday.

"So anyway," I said, picking up the chopsticks, "if the offer is still good, maybe I will stay with you for a couple days, just 'til things die down."

He didn't answer. I didn't even think he was listening. He was totally engrossed in whatever headline filled his screen.

"Earth to Carson," I said, snapping my fingers in front of him.

His face snapped up. "Zoey," he whispered, gripping the phone like it was a bomb.

"What is it? Did someone wear plaid with polka dots again?" I guessed.

His eyes actually shimmered with what looked like tears but clung to my face, almost as if he was searching for something... like he was trying to see past my makeup.

My stomach collapsed into my feet, and dread spread out over me like blood draining out of a dead body.

"Oh, Zoey," he crooned, shaking his head. "It's too much."

"What's too much?" I asked, my voice already hoarse.

Holding his phone across the table, I took it, turning the screen so I could see.

Makeup Artist or Monster?

Explosive secret photos reveal all!

My heart began to pound so fast that my head swam and the headline on the screen blurred into one giant letter. Collapsing back into the chair, I blinked about a thousand times, trying to make my vision clear so I could convince myself that what I saw was a trick of my imagination.

My arms and legs started to vibrate, the palms of my hands sweating. A thick, inescapable net of panic tossed over me, vowing to keep me prisoner.

I didn't know how long I sat there trembling like a leaf in the bitter winter wind, but eventually, my desperation beat out the blurry vision. Focusing back on the phone, I scrolled past the headline, praying to God I wouldn't see what I was terrified I would.

They wouldn't. It couldn't possibly be the photos from last night.

It was.

Right there in grainy, dim color were two photographs of me in all my honesty. No makeup. No hood. No leg.

Nothing but surprise in my eyes.

An odd keening sound filled the restaurant, and I found it annoying and disruptive.

Carson appeared beside me, draping his arms around my shoulders. "Shh, c'mon now. We should probably go."

The sound continued, and my head began to hurt.

"Zoey, stop making that sound. They're going to call the paramedics," Carson hissed.

That awful sound was me. It was the sound of my world imploding.

Pressing my lips together, I quieted down.

"It's not the food." Carson assured everyone. "We just got some heinous news."

The phone screen had gone dark, and I held it out for him to scan his fingerprint. "Maybe we should—"

"Do it," I insisted, shoving the phone closer.

He did, and we both stared down at the photos. They weren't great. The color quality sucked because he'd used the flash wrong. They were slightly blurry because he'd been running and I was chasing him.

But you could still see.

You could tell there was something wrong with my face. That I was damaged. You could see it was the left side, and my left side was also where the bottom half of my leg was missing.

Even though the photos weren't good, they were enough. Enough to ruin everything I'd built. Enough to turn my life into a constant battle of looking over my shoulder and reliving the worst time of my life.

"Is that really you?" my best friend asked, his face close to mine.

A tear streaked down my cheek as I bowed my head.

Making a sound, he patted my shoulder. "It doesn't matter, okay? Uncle Carson doesn't care. This is just trashy tabloid filth."

When he pried the phone out of my hand, the images onscreen left my stare, but I didn't need that phone to see those images. They would be burned in my mind forever, just like the rest of my scars.

"Cut!" the director yelled.

Landen and I unlocked from the "fight" we were in and fist-bumped a job well done. "Want to grab some lunch?" he asked.

"Let's take thirty and then get Jessica on set with Nick."

I pointed in the direction from which those commands were just hollered. "I think I have to go to makeup and get ready for the next scene."

"Later," Landen said, patting me on the shoulder and turning away. "Whoa," he swore, his body lurching out of the way as Callie came rushing toward me.

"Sorry!" she called as she hurried, nearly plowing into me too.

Catching her around the shoulders, I held her back and looked down. "What's the rush?"

"There's something I thought you would want to see." She panted, holding out a phone that was not mine.

"This your phone?" I asked, taking it.

She nodded, pushing it up in front of my face.

The headline caught my attention, making me feel like someone just dropkicked me in the nuts. Thumbing past the article I didn't bother to read, I went right to the photos.

My eyes closed, and a filthy word dropped out of my lips.

"Is that Zoey?" Callie asked, her voice quiet.

Quickly, I hit the side button on her phone, darkening the screen. "Don't look at that again," I ordered, handing it back to her.

"O-of course," Callie stuttered.

"Where's my phone?" I barked.

She held it out, and I tapped the screen. Motherfucking shitbag. It was trending.

Even if my people managed to pull it down, the screenshots, reposts, and gossip would never go away. The internet was a black fucking hole. Scrolling through the pages of coverage, I avoided looking at the photo every time it came up on my feed.

Until I scrolled past one.

I stopped.

I stared.

I got angry.

It was a split screen image. A photo of me from the "Sexiest Man Alive" shoot on one side and the grainy, unflattering photo of Zoey on the other. The headline read: *Beauty and the Beast.*

A harsh sound ripped out of my throat, echoing up into the rafters overhead. Backing out of that shit, I found the original article that Callie brought to my attention. It had been published for two hours.

In only two hours, this one article, these two photos taken without consent, obtained by breaking and entering and taking a scared, innocent woman off guard, spread to every corner of the web.

She was going to be crushed.

My head shot up. *Zoey.*

The unnatural quiet of the set made me gaze around. Everyone was standing there staring at their phones, whispering and stealing glances in my direction.

"No one look at that!" I raged, going around and pushing everyone's phones down to their sides before rushing off set toward the makeup trailer.

On my way, I dialed a familiar number, not even pausing when they answered. "I need extra security with me for the foreseeable future. I need it now. Send some men to set."

As soon as the man on the other end agreed, I disconnected the call and stormed into the trailer. The people sitting around glanced up from their phones the minute I appeared. I knew just by looking at them what they were so acutely entertained by.

"Where's Zoey?" I demanded.

Jessica turned around in the makeup chair. "She's not here."

"Where is she?" I asked, barely holding on to my patience.

"She went to lunch with Carson," Laura told me.

I glanced at Callie, who'd been running alongside me since showing me the article. "Craft services," I said, starting off.

"She's not there." Laura called me back.

I glanced around.

"They went off the lot to eat today."

My blood turned to ice. She was out in public right now? Away from the security guarding this lot?

"Where?" I yelled.

Laura's eyes widened, and Jessica's mouth fell open.

"Nick—" Jessica started, but I cut her off.

"Where did they go?"

"I don't know," Laura answered.

Callie's footsteps were frantic as she ran, trying to keep up with my much longer stride. Rushing toward the parking lot, I dialed Zoey's number and waited while it rang. And rang. And rang.

Hanging up, I tried again, getting the same result.

"Where are you going?" Callie asked, her breath coming in short gasps.

Her car was here, parked in the same spot it was the night before. Right near the place she'd been assaulted by the press.

My God, what would they do to her now?

I was about to run off toward my Rover when a red Prius drove into the lot.

"There's Carson," Callie called, pointing.

As I jogged toward the car, Carson had no choice but to roll to a stop right there in the middle of the asphalt. With the car still running, his door popped open and he got out, adjusting the neon shades over his eyes. "Now's not really a good time," he called, looking a little frayed around the edges.

Ignoring him, I bolted around to the passenger side, staring through the window where Zoey sat. She appeared shell-shocked and pale.

Wrenching the door open, I bent low, just the way I had last night when I massaged her leg. I wanted so much to reach out and grab her. To pull her into me. The way she sat staring off at nothing kept my hands off at first. She probably already felt betrayed and violated. I didn't want to make it worse.

"Zoey," I said, imploring her to look at me.

She didn't. I wondered if she even knew I was there.

The phone gripped in her hand began to ring. The sound jolted her, and she glanced down. A laugh bubbled up in her throat. "It's the press."

I grabbed the phone and chucked it off in the distance. The sound of it shattering was dull.

Carson and Callie stood at the hood of the car, watching us through the windshield, but it didn't matter.

"Angel," I whispered, this time sliding my hand over hers clasped in the center of her lap. Her skin was icy, but she looked at me, a flicker of life sparking in her gaze.

"Did you see?" she asked, gravelly.

"I didn't look." I promised.

"Don't lie."

"I saw the article, and I know there are pictures, but I didn't look at you. I swear."

Her chin wobbled, and my heart constricted. I held out my arms. She leaned in. A dull roaring filled my head as she allowed me to hug her close. One of her hands slid up around the back of my neck, clutching me closer. The sound of her sniffling against me made my eyes flutter closed.

"I'm sorry," I whispered.

Over and over again, I whispered apologies, until eventually, she pulled back just enough to say, "It's not your fault."

Swiping gently at a tear falling down her right cheek, I said, "I'm sorry anyway."

Curling back into my chest, a quake shook her body. The vulnerability I felt from her did not match the conviction in her words.

"It's not your fault," she said again. "It's his."

I felt the draw once more. The undeniable pull of a moth to a flame, of an editor tidying up the plot holes in a story.

Seven years I'd been waiting for the flicker of fire. Seven years of slumber about to come to an end.

As I stared down at the photo lying in the palm of my hand, the warm feeling of joy made me smile.

How lovely.

The chance to finally film our sequel.

"Quiet on set!"

I used the director's command as an excuse to slink back into the shadows of the set, so grateful for the respite.

Yep, I was back on the job.

But there was no tank of water or any big action sequence happening, so as long as I stayed out of the way, I'd be fine. As if it could get any worse.

A cold chill scraped down my spine like a dry branch on a windowpane. Shivering, I regretted the thought immediately. I knew things could get worse.

I had firsthand knowledge of hell, of things people in the movie business couldn't even conceive.

I didn't want to go back there. So I came to set instead. I could have asked Carson to come in my place and stayed in the trailer, but there was more than one reason I didn't:

1) I could work here on set. Work would keep me busy. Busy was good.

2) The set had an extra layer of security because they were filming and needed no interruptions.

3) No one would be staring at me in light of the fabulous news coverage because phones weren't allowed here.

Just in case you didn't get my sarcasm: fabulous news = loathsome.

And one more reason:

4) I was closer to Nick.

Like a brick through a window, those now viral pictures shattered any peace I'd gained over the years. They took away something so precious to me, leaving me raw and afraid. We'd barely escaped the press at the ramen shop. How those vultures figured out where I was so fast, I would never understand.

Maybe they smelled the blood from all my reopened wounds and they'd come to feast on what was left of my carcass.

Carson drove his Prius like it was a race car, weaving that little red bullet through the cameras and traffic and bringing us back to the relative safety of the filming lot.

Even his quick thinking and friendship didn't make me feel better.

The first glimpse of relief I knew was Nick bolting around the car. The second he flung open the door, his reassuring presence wrapped around me.

How had this happened? How was it that when he opened up his arms to me, I went into them automatically?

It wasn't much, but a few of those shattered pieces inside me were glued back together when he appeared at my side. When he threw my phone, breaking it into a million pieces, more of the fragments inside me fit back together.

I knew later I would regret all this. Regret letting him comfort me and sticking close to his side afterward. I couldn't bring myself to worry about it just then. There were bigger worries pushing down that fear. I would take things step by step at least until work was over for the day and I could fall apart in private.

I definitely couldn't go home now.

Going home with Carson probably wasn't the smartest idea either, considering the amount of press that saw us escaping from the ramen shop together. They found my place in a matter of hours. By now, they probably already had his address too.

Leaving town was a good option. Probably the best one I had.

"Zoey," Laura hissed, her hand reaching into the shadows to grab my wrist.

Startled, I jumped back, knocking into the makeup kit at my feet. People around us turned to look, making me shrink back even farther.

"Come on. They need us," she said, ignoring the way I recoiled.

Realizing they were waiting for us to do our jobs, I hustled forward toward Nick and Jessica. Laura got to work on her instantly, and I stepped under the lights toward him. The focus of his green stare was entirely on me, equal parts reassuring and discomforting.

"Make me look good for my close-up," he teased, a twinkle lighting up the jade.

Frankly, he didn't need anyone to make him look good, but I didn't tell him that. The guy already had a fan club big enough to fill a European country. There was no point in feeding his ego more.

I worked quietly, then grabbed my kit and slid back into the shadows behind the crew.

He looked sort of like a god under the bright lights on set, his golden hair glowing like a halo, his perfect complexion seemingly kissed by the sun. The white shirt he wore skimmed his body, draping off his shoulders like a caress, like even the fabric touching his body knew how fucking lucky it was.

When he smiled, a dimple was revealed, the corners of his eyes crinkled, and the Cupid's bow in the center of his lips deepened.

He was indeed the master of the smolder. Something the press never forgot to mention. The weight of Nick's stare was heavy but never a burden. He had this way of making someone feel like the only one, as if nothing had ever captured his attention the way they could.

It would be so easy to fall for a man like him.

"You came for me." Jessica's breathless voice filled the quiet of the set. "How did you know where I was?"

Nick moved forward, capturing her elbows in his palms, drawing her into his space. "I have a built-in GPS when it comes to you," he replied, sliding down one of her forearms to press her palm against his heart. "I'll always find you, no matter where you go."

The set lights glistened off a tear that fell delicately from the corner of her eye, trailing along her perfectly made-up cheek in a single stroke of emotion.

They made a striking couple bathed in light, standing in the center of a battle zone, but looking like they'd finally found peace.

Cameras moved soundlessly around them, capturing the moment from every angle, and people in front of me pressed hands to their chests like their hearts were fluttering.

My heart was not fluttering.

My stomach was nauseous, and all those broken shards inside me were stabbing me anew.

Jessica lifted her chin, all her perfect blond hair falling behind her like a waterfall. Gently, Nick palmed her jaws, stroking his thumb over her cheekbone while eating her alive with that smoldering green gaze.

My hand balled into a fist, squeezing until my knuckles ached. Backing away from the set, I went deeper into the darkness. I didn't want to see this. I couldn't look away.

"I love you," he whispered.

A collective breath released from all the people standing around, and his lips were on hers, his mouth firmly claiming hers.

Chest squeezing, my eyes fell to the floor. The kiss seemed to go on and on… and on. I stood there averting my gaze until the director called cut and everyone seemed to come back to life.

Bending down, I arranged some things in my kit, trying to ignore the prickly way I felt. Tears burned the backs of my eyes, and it horrified me.

Now was not the time to cry about everything that had happened today.

You aren't crying because of everything that happened today. You want to cry because of one thing only.

"Can you touch me up?"

I jerked around, nearly falling back onto my butt at the sound of the chipper voice.

"Jessica."

She smiled. "I need a touchup. My lipstick wore off." Using a perfectly manicured finger, she pointed at her lips.

The lipstick was indeed smeared.

My stomach revolted.

"Sure thing," I said, forcing myself to sound normal. I was good at that. I'd been doing it a very long time.

Lifting the kit, I carried it over to a rolling cart, set it down, and looked around for the right shade.

"Maybe I should get the exact color from Laura," I said, wondering why she hadn't just gone to her in the first place.

"Whatever you have is fine," she said, moving to stand beside me. The silk blouse she wore brushed against my arm. "Oh!" she said, reaching into my kit. "It's this one."

Taking it, I grabbed a lip brush and uncapped the product.

"How did we look?" she asked, parting her lips.

"Pardon?"

"Nick and me? How did the scene look?"

Swallow. "Ah, it was beautiful. I think it will look really great on film."

She smiled while I brushed the color onto her lips. "You know," she said, making me lift the brush so she could speak. "The casting director was so thrilled with our pairing. He said we have chemistry like he hasn't seen before."

"You both are very talented actors," I murmured, going back to work.

Lightly, her fingers pressed against my wrist, once again pausing my work. "Oh, it's more than just acting. You can't fake this kind of chemistry." Leaning in, she whispered, "I think soon, we will be Hollywood's royal couple."

I sincerely thought about accidentally painting lipstick on her teeth, but then she'd have to come back over here so I could fix it for the camera.

"There you go," I said, pulling back and forcing a smile. "Looks perfect. Like you never even kissed."

"Guess I'll just have to have him mess it up again," she said, winking.

I turned back to my kit. My throat felt tight, and the ramen I'd eaten wasn't settling properly.

I thought she would walk away.

She was still there when I turned back around.

"Powder?" she inquired.

I grabbed the correct one and dutifully powdered her face.

"Let's run through that again!" the director called.

Jessica perked up. "Gotta go! To think, most women dream of kissing Nick Preston, and here I am going back for seconds."

"Have fun," I said, waving at her with the powder brush.

When she was gone, I felt drained and climbed onto a nearby chair, letting the back support my weight. Purposely, I stared into my lap, not wanting to watch them kiss again.

Those eyes, though. That smolder. It beckoned me even when I actively tried to avoid it. Reluctantly, I lifted my gaze, not even having to seek out what was summoning me. Briefly, our stares collided, his unreadable but intense.

I looked away almost immediately, unwilling to even try and understand what it was he wanted to silently convey.

What the fuck was this, everyone talk to Zoey day?

It was getting on my damn nerves.

I was a good actor, but my ability to pretend was fading fast. She was avoiding me, something I wasn't used to. Usually, I was the one avoiding other people, trying to slip past them without a big production or signing an autograph. Or twelve.

She'd allowed me to hold her for a few minutes. She clutched me like she wanted to climb beneath my skin. I thought for sure she'd be unreachable the rest of the day.

It's not your fault. It's his, she'd whispered to me.

And then a switch inside her flipped.

I'd never seen anything like it. Not even among the country's best actors. Zoey shoved down all the pain and whatever else was going on inside her, pulled away from me, and went back to work.

She didn't acknowledge it, and it was almost as if she dared anyone else to either.

The only time I felt the self-imposed force field around her slip was when we were on set... when I was kissing Jessica.

I wanted to talk to her, but there were too many watchful eyes and too much work I had to do. Finally, filming was done for the day, and what did I find?

Josh Landen sitting in her makeup chair like it was his own personal throne.

I didn't like it.

Carson was leaning against the counter, one leg crossed over the other, his hands waving around like he was signaling a plane. But really, he was just talking.

Zoey was bent down close to Landen, the back of his head blocking her face from view.

"I really appreciate this, robo-girl," he was saying. "Since filming ran late, me showing up to the shoot already in hair and makeup is a huge lifesaver."

"Anytime," she answered, straightening up.

The sponge in her hand paused. Her stare flicked to me immediately, sensing my presence. Spotted, I prowled farther into the room. Her attention slipped away almost as fast as it arrived. Turning back toward her cart, she grabbed something else and leaned back toward Landen.

"I haven't seen anyone wear these since elementary school," he teased, tugging on one of the straps on her overalls.

His action made her giggle, and jealousy bit into me like razor-sharp teeth. A bitter, tangy sensation washed over my tongue.

"You're still working?" I stopped just behind Landen's chair, towering over him, but directing my words and eyes at Zoey.

Glancing around, Landen seemed surprised to see me. "I thought you left for the day."

"I'm waiting for Zoey."

Carson made a sound, and Landen's eyes widened.

Looking back at Zoey, he said, "You should have told me you had plans. I could have had Carson fix me up."

"We don't have plans," she said, directing the words to me.

I really wasn't in the mood for this. "My car is right in front of the trailer."

"I am not going home with you."

"Zoey!" Carson hissed like a mother scolding her kid at the grocery store. Glancing at me, he smiled. "She's had a long day."

"You said I could stay with you." Her eyes turned on her friend.

"Why on earth would you want to stay with me when you could stay—"

"Why do you need somewhere to stay?" Landen interrupted.

Zoey began packing up her tools. "The press has been staking my apartment... and someone broke in last night."

"While you were there?" Landen asked, concern darkening his tone.

I stepped forward, a silent reminder he didn't need to be worried for her.

"It's probably best if I don't stay there for a while. Especially after this afternoon..."

"I wasn't going to bring that up," Landen said.

"The press saw you with Carson earlier. They're probably already watching his place."

Carson pressed a hand to his chest like he was shocked. Then, with flair, he spun toward the mirror. "I better make sure I'm ready for the cameras!"

Zoey rolled her eyes.

Landen spun the chair to look at me. "And you said she could stay with you?"

"It's my fault the press is hounding her, and I've got good security."

"The last thing I want to do is give the press more reason to think we're… linked somehow," she said.

We are linked. I can feel it.

"Stay with me." Landen dropped the words into the center of the conversation like an earthquake.

We all reacted at the same time in three very different ways.

Carson: Dude swooned against the counter like he might fall to the ground.

Zoey: "What?" Shocked surprise.

Me: "Hell no!"

Landen seemed to like my reaction best of all, settling his gaze on me for a brief moment before smirking and looking away.

"I have good security too, and the press wouldn't suspect you being with me."

Taking a threatening step toward him, I intoned, "What the fuck are—"

Landen slapped a hand on my shoulder, interrupting my words. "What do you say, Zoey? Want to stay with me?"

Her mouth worked, but no sounds came out. The sudden urge to grab her by the arm and drag her away was so strong I took another step. The hand on my shoulder squeezed. My eyes slanted to Landen.

The look on his face stopped me.

—I'd like to insert here that it was not because I was intimidated.—

"I, ah… I'll go to a hotel."

Landen made a sound. "Probably not the best idea. Most of the employees at those places have side deals with tabloids for information and photos." He shook his head regrettably. "Can't trust anyone these days."

Zoey blinked. I could see the weariness in her eyes, the tired set of her shoulders. All the anger and jealousy drained out of me, replaced with honest worry.

Shaking off the hand on my shoulder, I angled so Zoey was blocked from everyone's view but mine.

"I've already doubled my security. Let's go." The words were quiet as I reached for her kit, hefting it at my side.

"Who's it going to be?" Landen stepped forward.

Her stare bounced between us, but strangely, I was confident. There's no way she'd pick him over me. Not after last night. Not after I slept beside her and kept my word not to look.

Landen knew it too. He might not know that we'd spent time outside of this set together, but he could sense Zoey trusted me more than him. Her wariness was something palpable. Out of the corner of my eye, I stared at him. Did he offer up his place to nudge her toward mine?

Zoey took a small step toward me, and victory was mine.

"If you change your mind, my door is open," Landen said, sincerity in his voice.

She smiled. "Thank you."

Palming the small of her back, nudging her, I said, "Get your bag."

Carson had it ready, handing it over before she could even step away. "Take care of my girl," he said.

The second we approached the door, two bodyguards moved into action, one heading outside first and the other waiting at the door for his word. The second he gave it, we stepped out of the trailer and right into the back seat of a black SUV with windows so dark no one could see inside.

"They opened a back gate on the lot," one of the security guards informed me. "No one knows about it yet, so we should be able to leave tonight without anyone seeing."

"Good."

"Straight to the house?" the driver asked.

"My bags," Zoey said, sitting up.

Gently, I pushed her back. "They're already at my place."

The SUV drove forward, and she glared. "I told you I wasn't staying with you."

"Then why didn't you go with Landen?" I countered.

Falling silent, she turned to stare out the window.

Because even if you don't want to admit it yet, you trust me.

26

The distinct sound of the spotlights flipping on made my eyes pop open. There was no such thing as restful sleep here. There was only the body and mind giving out just enough so it could wake to fight all over again.

He was here.

His footsteps were silent, his breath barely there. But the shadow he cast in the bright beam of light seemed unnaturally large.

Whenever he stood like that, hovering somewhere above, close enough to present his shadow but far enough to stay out of sight, a fear unlike anything I'd ever known roused inside me, silencing nearly all my humanity and making me question if I was already dead.

My eyes strayed toward the body, the smell so putrid and thick one would think I wouldn't even need to look.

There was no way anything alive could smell that way, but still, his presence made me doubt.

As if he were the devil himself, come to rouse his handmade demon, I expected to see that decaying, rat-ravaged corpse rising to meet her master, joining him in whatever depraved deed was next.

As if she were a puppet, he was the master, and soon, I would also be on his strings.

Despite the filthy, urine-drenched state I was in, my fist found its way into my mouth. I knew it didn't matter how quiet I was, but still, I made a valiant effort.

Those bright spotlights filled the wooden rafters with shadow and highlighted the thick dust swimming in the air. Seeing it float so lazily in the light made me want to cough and gag, but I averted my gaze and pretended it was snow flurrying down on a fresh winter's night, cleansing the air instead of crowding my lungs.

Exposed wires draped from the ceiling. Cracked tiles had fallen off the walls. The plaster shaping the pool was chipped and jagged. Puddles of stagnant green water with floating debris occupied a couple corners and the center of the uneven deep end.

I'd thought about drowning myself in those puddles every day since I'd been down here. Seven days of hell. Seven days of torment.

It didn't seem like very long in the grand scheme of time.

But, oh… these past seven days had completely changed what had taken me nineteen years to become. How quickly everything could be eradicated. How quickly someone who previously loved life could wish to die.

Drowning wasn't an option for me. He'd made sure my shackles didn't allow me to go that far. It was another form of torture, wasn't it? Knowing there was an escape right there, staring at it every second of every day, but it being just out of reach.

The prone shadow shifted, and everything inside me went on high alert. I might sit down here and wish to die, but never at his hands. I would die a thousand deaths if a thousand of them could be granted by anyone but him.

Trembling against the wall, the shadow shifted and changed. A long shape seemed to grow right out of his arm, lengthening down toward the ground, the end wide and thick, the handle extending into his hand.

He swung it like a pendulum, my time running out.

His footsteps echoed when he stepped near. Fear closed my throat. Through unsteady, blurry eyes, I watched and waited. The shadow disappeared, but the man creating it came close. Leaping from the side of the pool, he landed on both feet, one catching the edge of the nasty water, splashing it across my skin.

I knew it was cold, but my skin was colder. I knew it was dirty, but I was filthier. I was dehydrated and it was wet, so prying my hand out of my mouth, I rubbed in the few splatters, hoping my skin would soak it in.

Unfolding from the position he'd landed in, he straightened to his full height. His shoulders were wide, his body stocky. The boots he wore were made for hiking, and the hood pulled over his head concealed his face.

The hammer in his hand made my stomach knot. Unhurriedly, my captor came forward, walking to me like he was taking a midday stroll. I had no way of knowing what time it was. If it was night. If it was day.

Hell didn't have a clock because in hell, every minute was the same.

When he lifted the hammer above him, I shielded my head, cowering in the abandoned pool, anticipating the blow. Rearing back, he brought the weapon crashing down. My piercing scream stopped him. Inches from my face, the wide, rusty hammer halted, and his head tilted.

"Please," I begged. "Let me go."

His head tilted in the other direction as he lowered to one knee before me. I whimpered, recoiled, but there was nowhere to go.

Reaching out with a gloved hand, he stroked the side of my head like I was some kind of beloved pet. I shivered, peering into the hood, trying to see his face.

Sensing my curiosity, his fingers knotted in my hair. I cried out when he yanked my head back and it cracked off the unforgiving concrete wall.

It took a moment for my vision to clear, but the pain still throbbed. I wondered if when he finally pulled his hand away, he would have a chunk of my hair in it.

The hammer thudded onto the floor, and his other hand grabbed the side of my face. The chain shackled around my ankle rattled and shook when he dragged me forward, my bare toes cutting open on the shoddy floor.

My hands dug into his arms, and I struggled to stand up, not completely under his command.

When he shoved me down, I fell backward, expecting a blow.

Instead, he reached into the black leather coat, withdrawing a folded white cloth. He held it almost lovingly, caressing the frilly old-fashioned-looking material and holding it out to me like I was being bestowed a gift.

When I didn't take it, he kicked me, the hiking boot cracking at least one rib. Wheezing, I folded in on myself as pain rattled my middle. Holding up one thick finger, he waved it at me like he was scolding a very bad child.

He came forward. I skittered back.

His hands were rough when they ripped the clothes off my body. The harsh sound of his breathing made me think he was excited as he ripped every last scrap of cotton from my limbs.

I screamed and cried, fighting against him to no avail. Soon, I was lying at his feet, a naked, shivering mess. "Please," I begged. "No."

He reached into his jacket again, pulling out something long and black. It looked familiar, but before I could think it through, he brought out a small blowtorch and new horror dawned.

Despite being chained, I scrambled up and away until the chain forced me back and I fell on my knees. Then I tried again.

Behind me, the sounds of the blowtorch firing up kept me clambering away. Glancing over my shoulder, I saw him hold out the long black thing in the center of the blue flame.

No, no, no…

I ran again, throwing myself at the green puddle, but my fingers were just out of reach. Out of desperation, I rushed back, diving at the hammer he'd almost beat me with. When my hand closed around the handle, I cried out with glee.

Finally. Finally, I could help myself.

My forehead bounced off the floor when he shoved my head down. I bucked, but he straddled me, sitting on my body. My naked torso pressed against the plaster, scraping open and stinging with pain. His hand forced my head back down, the flesh above my eyebrow ripping open. Blood welled in my eye. His body anchored mine.

White-hot, surging pain made me squeal. My God, it was so intense I wondered how in the world no one heard me howl.

The scent of burning flesh and singed hair masked that of the decaying body.

I couldn't have told you which was worse.

I wailed until my voice gave out. And even then, I wailed silently. He pinned me down, branding me with whatever it was he held until the red-hot metal melted my flesh, robbed my voice, and finally turned cold.

My skin tore farther when he finally pulled the iron off my body. I lay there half conscious, my own vomit a pillow, and a sticky burning sensation at my back.

I wished I was all the way unconscious.

Not because of the pain, but because if I had been, I wouldn't have heard his whispered words.

"I own you."

* * *

Woo-o-woo-o-woo!

The brash siren cut through the memory, waking me from the dream state I was in and forcing me back to reality in a cruel way.

In the midst of running, I spun, trying to make sense of my surroundings when I tripped and fell onto my hands and knees.

It was dark and everything was foreign. Still struggling in the web of dreamlike reality, trying to grasp anything else was virtuously impossible.

Woo-o-woo-o-woo!

The sound was so disruptive and loud. Slapping my hands over my ears, I struggled to rise to my feet. On my knees, I looked up, seeing a dark figure rush toward me.

"No!" I cried, slamming my eyes shut and tumbling back onto the ground.

"Zoey!" A voice that didn't scare me cut through the chaos. Nick dropped to his knees beside me, his warm hands covering mine where they pressed against my ears.

"Turn that fucking thing off!" he mouthed to people I didn't see.

His hands were warm, and mine felt so cold.

The piercing noise cut off, leaving behind only the sound of my breathing and the pounding of my heart.

Prying my hands away from my ears, Nick took my hands in his. "What happened? What's wrong?"

"Where—" I gasped, but then I remembered.

I was at his house. Nick's. Where it was supposed to be safe.

His big body surrounded mine when he lifted me up into his chest. Cradling against him, I heard the timbre of his voice speaking to people around us, but I kept my face hidden in his neck.

Oh God. My face.

I whimpered, and his arm came up around my head, shielding me.

"Make sure the place is secure just in case." It wasn't his words that soothed me. It was the sound of his voice.

I felt like I was floating when he carried me away. The muscles in his chest and arms rippled as he walked, my clammy skin sticking to his.

We went into a room that had no light, but he moved around with utter familiarity and confidence I found soothing.

Cool sheets hit my back and legs, the crispness of the cloth surprisingly enjoyable. Nick stepped back, the night swallowing him whole.

I called out to him. Anxiousness made my hands curl into the blankets.

"I'm right here." He promised, nothing but steadiness in his tone.

The opening and closing of a drawer was brief, and then he was back, sliding an arm beneath my back, helping me sit up.

"Put this on," he murmured, holding out some clothes.

Slapping myself in the chest, I gasped, realizing I wasn't wearing a shirt, just a bralette and a pair of shorts. "Where the hell is my shirt?"

"It wasn't me," he said, mild humor in his voice.

Sighing, I picked up the shirt he offered. It was a lightweight tee, but it had a hood.

It had a *hood*.

The gesture—probably something he hadn't even thought of—hit me right in my most vulnerable place. I was already shredded open from that dream, and now here he was offering me some dignity, offering me some shield.

A sob caught in my throat.

Weepy and still shaken, I sat in the center of the bed, doing everything I could to hold it all in. Gently, he reached out, making sure the hem was tugged down and then lifted the hood over my head.

The sob I'd been fighting broke free, filling the room with sorrow.

"All right now," he murmured, sitting close and wrapping an arm around my frame.

He wasn't wearing a shirt, and his skin was smooth beneath my cheek.

"Do you sleepwalk often?" he asked, not letting me go.

"No, I can't really run off..." I sat up and looked down, remembering I'd gone to bed with the prosthetic in place. Bowing my head, I stared at my leg through the dark. "I was having a nightmare."

Realizing the chaos I caused, I reached for his hand, giving it a squeeze. Since I didn't want to look at him, this was the next best option.

"I'm sorry."

He made a soft, amused sound. "It keeps the guards on their toes."

The guards. "That was who I saw running toward me," I mused.

"You opened the back door, set off the alarm. He was afraid you were going to fall into the pool."

The mention of a pool made me shudder violently.

"Hey," he said, then gentled his voice. "Hey…"

"This is why I shouldn't stay here," I said, pain masking my voice. "I do better with familiar surroundings, places I can trust."

"What about familiar people?"

Forgetting about my face, I lifted my head. When I remembered, I flinched and lifted my hands. But he wasn't looking. His face was turned away.

I whispered, "What did you say?"

"Are familiar people just as good as places?"

"I-I don't know," I said honestly. "No one's ever—" I stopped there before I could sound any more pathetic.

"C'mon, lie down," he urged, sliding me back against some cloudlike pillows.

"Where am I?" I said, realizing this wasn't the room I'd gone to sleep in.

"My bed."

Stiffening, I sat up. His palms caught my shoulders, stopping me from running away. "You're safe here, angel. Just lie down."

I relented, lying back once more, the scent of him rising around me in a fragrant cloud.

"I thought you didn't sleep with this on?" I felt him looking at my leg.

"I wanted to tonight."

Walking around to the opposite side, Nick slipped beneath the covers, bringing his body close to mine.

"Do you want to talk about your nightmare?"

"No."

Settling onto his back, one arm reached for me. "Come here."

Rolling onto my side, I stared. He stayed where he was, open and waiting. Timidly, I scooted forward. Only then did he fold his arm to bring me right against his side.

"No more nightmares tonight, angel." He spoke like his words held the power to banish all the bad. "The guards are watching the house, and though it's unfamiliar, I'm not."

"You're not?" I echoed.

I felt him shake his head, his hand palming mine. "I'm right here."

I wanted so badly to rest my cheek on his chest, but I didn't want him to feel the texture of my skin.

After a few minutes of lying in quiet, I slid closer, lifting my head and pulling the hood around so it was a barrier between my skin and his. The moment I settled, a deep sigh went through me like a strong gust of wind.

Even though there was fabric between us, he was still closer to me than anyone had ever been.

It was true I did better with familiar surroundings, in an environment I could trust.

Did that apply to people?

As my eyelids grew heavy and my body wondrously calmed, I found the answer.

Yes. Apparently, it applied to people... or at the very least, to Nick.

She was so familiar to me. From the first moment I saw her, something inside me recognized her. I couldn't understand why or how. We'd never met previously, but it didn't matter.

We were connected in some way. The more time I spent with her, the more I was sure.

What was it that drew me to her?

How could I feel so connected to someone I'd just met?

"You really need to make a decision soon," said a voice I didn't recognize.

"I've already turned this down. Twice," declared a voice I was much more acquainted with. The stubborn frustration he spoke with? Not so much.

Leaning a little more against the wall, I settled in to eavesdrop.

What? A girl could be curious.

In fact, as I stood there listening to the hum of voices going on in Nick's kitchen, I realized I didn't know much about him at all. Every time we had a conversation, it was about me. Or the movie.

"That's a kneejerk reaction, and you know it. This movie will be huge."

"I said no!" Nick yelled, his anger silencing everything else.

Stiffening, my shoulder blades pressed against the wall, tension tightening my muscles.

"It really fucking offends me, Rick, that you come here and bring this up again. We've worked together a long time. I thought by now you would think of me as more than just a goddamn paycheck."

"This isn't about money."

Nick made a crude sound. "You sure about that?"

"I keep bringing this up because I know you. I don't want you to have regrets when this releases. And it's going to whether or not you're involved. That's a guarantee. Frankly, if you were anyone else, the studio would have already told you to shove it and started filming. But your family—"

"My family has suffered enough."

"Which is why you need to do this. Make sure this is accurate. Make sure the world sees what this did to your family. Use this as a chance to—"

"And what should I tell my mother?" Nick's voice was strained.

"You haven't talked to her about this yet?"

Nick was silent, which was a clear denial.

The man sighed heavily. "The studio is going to reach out. All the more reason for you to involve yourself. You can be a buffer, the representative of your family. Minimize her role."

A strangled laugh erupted out of him, making my fingers curl against my palms. "Minimize? They'll want to drag up everything she went through and ask for personal details the press doesn't know."

What in the world were they talking about? Was someone trying to make a movie about Nick's family? Why? Was his mother famous too?

Preston. I searched my brain for any kind of scandal I could recall involving the Preston family, but I couldn't think of a single thing.

"It's happening, Nick. With or without you. Get in front of it. Put it all to bed once and for all."

Nick said nothing, but the atmosphere was charged. I could tell he was upset without even being able to see him. Guilt crept up on me, making me feel like a dirty sleaze for listening to what was quite clearly a private and painful conversation.

Nick didn't deserve this from me. He'd been nothing but a pillar of strength, going as far as giving me enough peace to actually sleep well two nights in a row.

When I woke up this morning, everything was foreign, his room a completely new place for my eyes to take in. I didn't panic. I found myself gathering the blankets and holding them up beneath my chin. They smelled like him. Somehow, Nick's scent had become a source of comfort, and though everything was pretty much a wreckity-wreck these days, the storm inside me was calm.

Straightening away from the wall, I stepped around the corner, clearing my throat. Nick was turned away from me, both his palms flat on the marble island. The width of his shoulders seemed imposing.

Hearing me, his surprised eyes glanced around, almost as if he'd forgotten I was here.

Funny. I'd always worked so hard to be forgettable. Seeing that look on his face now made me bitter.

"You're up." His voice was far different than it was when he'd been conversing with the man standing across from him.

"I can, um, come back later," I said, gesturing back the way I'd come.

"No." When he came toward me, the fierceness in his body and spirit made me falter.

I was a brave woman. While often afraid, I was very good at looking fear in the face and moving forward. And Nick didn't scare me. He never had.

Intimidate? Maybe. I mean, he was the sexiest man alive, for crying out loud. But since I'd spent a little bit of time with him, I couldn't even say that.

This was a new side to him, though, one I didn't know.

Sensing my urge to retreat, Nick stopped in front of me, spreading his legs a bit to lower his body to match my height. I felt the man behind him watching us, but I couldn't look away from Nick's piercing green gaze.

"I want you to stay." His voice was soft. "Come on. There's tea. And the chef made you breakfast."

Whoa. "You have a chef?" I echoed, wonder in my tone.

He half smiled. "Who else do you think cooks my plates of sadness?"

I grimaced.

Grasping my chin between his forefinger and thumb, he gave me a little shake and chuckled. "Ah, don't freak out. I told him to make you something that actually tasted good."

His hair was slightly damp, the golden strands a little darker than usual. It was all pushed back off his face, falling over to one side of his head. The T-shirt he wore was white and slim fitting. His biceps seemed to challenge his sleeves. Lowering my eyes, I noted the gray sweat shorts with white drawstring and his bare feet.

I wrinkled my nose. "How long have you been up?"

"Long enough to be tortured by my trainer, shower, and have a meeting."

"Did you get any sleep at all?" I wondered as his palm settled at the small of my back to propel me farther into the kitchen.

Leading me to the stove where there was a hot kettle of water already waiting, he stopped at my back, caging me in with his frame to reach for a mug out of one of the cupboards above me.

After placing the mug in front of me, his fingers dragged across my arm as he pulled away. So close to my ear, he whispered, "It wasn't easy getting out of bed with you lying between the sheets."

I sucked in a breath, shocked he would say such a thing in front of some man!

Chuckling low, he turned away. "Rick."

"Tell me that's not the makeup artist burning up the Internet," the man named Rick entreated.

"Her name's Zoey." Nick corrected.

He groaned. "Are you trying to make my life hell? What the hell are you thinking spending the night with her?"

After putting a tea bag into the hot water, I turned. Rick gave me a squinty-eyed look and rubbed a hand over his forehead.

"She's staying here for a while." Nick delivered the news like he was talking about a stale piece of bread.

Rick gawked while Nick helped himself to a mug of coffee, setting it down to step up to a massive fridge to get some cream.

A high-pitched laugh erupted from the man, and he smacked the counter with his hand. "Good one, Nick. Good one."

"I'm not joking. The press broke into her place."

Rick sputtered, then groaned. "No. Absolutely not."

Lowering the mug from his lips, Nick raised an eyebrow.

"Do you have any idea what a shit show this will be if the media finds out she's here? When I said we needed press for the new movie, this was not what I meant!"

"No one needs to know she's here."

Rick laughed again. "That's rich. You know what bloodsuckers they are. They'll know by dinnertime."

Nick made a sound. "You plan on telling them?"

My God, these two were like bickering fourth graders!

"Um, who are you?" I asked, trying to sound polite but probably failing miserably.

Rick pointed to himself like I'd offended him. Lowering his finger, he answered, "I'm the guy who is going to have to clean up this mess!"

Nick turned to me. "This is Rick. He's my manager-slash-agent."

Closing the space between us, I offered my hand over the marble-topped island. "I'm Zoey Halston, makeup artist on the set of—"

"I know who you are," he deadpanned. "Everyone knows who you are."

I gulped, nervous energy surging down my spine.

Still feeling his scrutiny, I looked back.

He squinted. "I thought your face was damaged." He waved a finger toward me.

The blood drained from my head.

"What the fuck?" Nick burst into the conversation, somehow putting himself between me, the island, and his manager. "We're friends, Rick, but I have my limits."

"I didn't mean it like that," he sputtered. "I apologize if that came out insensitively."

Poking my head around Nick, I asked, "Is there a polite way to ask someone where they are disfigured?"

"The pictures!" he proclaimed, tossing his hands up. "The pictures online. The gossip all over the net… They all say—"

"We all know what they say." Nick's voice was dangerously low.

Rick fell silent for a moment. "What's going on here? I need to know so I can be ready with damage control."

"Meeting's over," Nick proclaimed. "Thanks for stopping by. I'll call you later." He began ushering him out of the kitchen.

"We haven't finished…" Whatever else he said trailed away as Nick pushed him toward the front of the house.

Blowing out a shaky breath, I went back to the tea to cradle the warm mug between my palms.

A few seconds later, Nick reappeared. "He's an asshole. I'm sorry."

"If you spent all your time apologizing for the assholes of this world, you'd never do anything else."

He barked a laugh.

Instead of stopping beside his coffee, he kept walking, closing the distance between us and raising my awareness of him by one thousand percent. My breathing stopped when his toes bumped mine. I stared, frozen, when he leaned close, holding my gaze hostage with his. Thought seemed to flee my mind, and all I could do was stand there as currents of unnamed energy coursed through my limbs, tingling my fingers.

Just before the tip of his nose brushed the side of my cheek, he straightened, reaching into the cabinet above my head. A golden honey bear appeared in front of me.

I blinked, my mind so hazy from his closeness I could barely understand what was happening.

"Don't you want this?" he asked, his voice like sandpaper.

Fingers tightening on the mug, I nodded but didn't reach out.

Amusement sparkled in his already gorgeous eyes, giving him a playful air. Pulling back, he popped the top and added some to my mug.

"Tell me when," he whispered.

"When," I whispered back after he'd added some of the sweet syrup.

I held my breath again, anticipating his coming close to put the bear away. Instead, he set it aside and moved across the room, giving me ample space.

Disappointment befell me.

"Eat up," he said, gesturing toward a plate with a large silver dome covering it that I hadn't even noticed before.

"I don't normally eat breakfast."

"Eat."

Raising an eyebrow, I challenged. "If I don't?"

"Think of it as punishment for eavesdropping."

I gasped. "You knew?"

"I'm a lot of things, Zo. But stupid ain't one of them."

"I never said you were stupid," I muttered.

Pulling the dome off my plate, he crooked a finger at me. I found that little beckon quite sexy, and the bottom fell out of my stomach.

What the hell was wrong with me?

Nick seemed not to realize his affect, or rather… it seemed that my plate was doing to him what he managed to do to me.

"I miss bacon." He sighed sadly.

Picking up his mug, he moved away from the plate to lean against the counter.

The dish was filled with scrambled eggs, bacon, and some kind of vegetable hash that looked pretty good. Lifting the fork, I tried a bite and was impressed.

"What did you eat?" I asked, taking another bite.

"Fish and steamed vegetables."

I made a face.

"At least I still have coffee." He hugged the mug.

I snickered into my food.

"Aren't you going to ask me?" he said after a few quiet minutes.

"Ask you what?"

"About what you heard?"

"Am I allowed?"

Cocking his head to the side, he gave it a heartbeat of thought. "You can ask me anything you want, angel."

My stomach dipped again. Butterflies erupted to life inside me, making me forget all about the food. "You aren't mad I was listening?"

He shook his head.

"Why?" I blurted. He was totally knocking me off balance. I worked so hard to maintain that balance. How come it was so easy for him to make me wobble?

"It's just a feeling I have," he said, vague.

"This isn't some cheesy soap opera. That's not an answer."

His mug made a clinking sound on the white countertop, and his hands slid into the pockets of his sweats. Strolling forward, he tried again. "Because I want you to trust me. Because there's something between us, and I want to know what it is. Because when the alarm went off last night, all I could think about was if you were okay."

By this time, he was right beside me, his body heat brushing my front and his size making me feel small.

He reached for me, and I felt time reduce to slow motion. Nervous energy sprang up as I anticipated his hands. Afraid of what he was making me feel, I turned toward my plate, shoving an entire piece of bacon into my mouth.

The abrupt change in direction didn't deter him. As he caught my shoulders, pulling me around, my eyes squeezed closed.

I stood like a statue, ignoring the bacon hanging out of my lips, pretending to ignore his closeness, hoping he would go away.

Nothing happened.

Eventually, one eye cracked open, and I gazed up.

He was staring at me, patient amusement clearly on his handsome face. Cracking open my other eye, I focused on him, slowly taking a step back.

Hands back in his pockets, he bent swiftly, like a lion going in for the kill.

Holy shit, he's going to kiss—

His lips closed over the end of the bacon hanging out of my mouth. I felt his teeth tug the strip, slicing it clean through. Pulling back, he chewed, his eyes slipping closed.

"So fucking good." He moaned.

My heart was pounding as though I'd just run twenty miles. My hands were trembling, and all I could do was stare at his lips, which were slick with bacon grease.

"You're going to pay for that!"

"How's that?" he asked, still chewing.

Grabbing the hem of his white shirt, I yanked it up. He gasped, and I cackled because finally, I'd caught him off guard.

A choked sound stopped my glee.

Dear Lord in heaven. His abs.

Sad food sure did a body good.

Still holding up his shirt, dividing my gaze between his chiseled abs and face, I stuttered. "I was going to say there goes your perfect abs," I said, glancing back at them. I wanted to run my fingertips over all those ridges. "But they're still there."

"Maybe you should check again," he teased.

Gasping, I dropped his shirt and stepped away.

Chuckling, Nick pushed up onto the counter to sit, motioning with his chin. "Eat. It's going to be cold."

I picked up the fork, avoiding him. I really needed to stop. Clearly, having my eyes anywhere on him was very dangerous. I mean, I thought he was going to kiss me just a minute ago!

Get a grip, Zoey!

"Your agent wants you to do a movie you aren't interested in?" I asked, wanting to distract myself.

He made a sound. "It's not just any movie. And it's based on true events."

I forgot I wasn't supposed to be looking at him. "It has something to do with your family? Your mom?"

His voice was quiet. "Not just my mom."

I didn't want to press, so I waited until he was ready to tell me.

Eventually, he answered, "It's about my grandmother's murder."

She didn't know?

Shock transformed her movements into wooden, automatic gestures. Slowly, the fork lowered from her mouth until it jangled onto the plate, forgotten.

"Y-your grandmother was murdered?" Her voice was incredulous.

"You really didn't know?"

Her brow wrinkled. "Why would I?"

"My family is pretty well known in Hollywood."

Her eyes turned down, and I could practically see her searching her memory for anything she might know. Still confused, her eyes swung back to mine. "Preston?" she questioned. "The only other Preston I know of is a director, a man."

Ah, so it was the name throwing her off. "David Preston is my father." I agreed.

Slowly, she nodded. "I think I have heard that before."

Having a famous director for a father wasn't what my family was famous for, though. "But it's my mother's side that's well known."

Coming around the island, Zoey hopped up onto the counter as I had moments before. Her sneakers swung gently as they dangled over the floor while we faced each other.

"My grandmother is… was Deborah Ascott."

Zoey repeated the name to herself, eyebrows coming together beneath the fringe of her bangs. Recognition dawned. "The famous actress from the eighties?"

"She was famous in the seventies too." I informed her.

"Right!" She pointed into the air, recalling. "She did that iconic cult favorite slasher movie!" Snapping her fingers, she murmured, "What was that called again…?"

"*Moth to A Flame*," I told her.

Hands falling into her lap, a funny look crossed her features. "Right." Her voice was hollow.

"Zoey?"

She didn't seem to hear me call out to her as she stared off into space, raising her hand to grasp her upper arm and rub up and down.

Hopping off the counter, I went to her, crowding into her space and settling my hands on either of her hips. "Zoey."

She blinked, awareness filling her eyes. "Oh, sorry."

"What happened?" I demanded, pointedly looking at where she was still rubbing. "Are you hurting somewhere?" I reached out to touch the spot.

Flinching back, she nearly fell over trying to get away. Obviously, she didn't want me to touch her. I did anyway. Wrapping my arm around her, I bent forward to scoop her up. Her cheek bounced off my chest, my fingers tangling in her hair.

"Be careful." I warned. A shuddering breath rippled her chest, and even though I didn't want to, I pulled back. "What happened?"

She shook her head, refusing to meet my gaze. "Nothing. I just remembered…"

Instinctively, I shifted closer. Even though I knew she was perfectly safe, I felt I had to make sure. "Remembered what?"

A few seconds passed, making me frown.

Her throat cleared. "What I heard about your grandmother."

"I never met her. My mom was only twelve when she was killed."

Sympathy filled her eyes, and her fingers slid over my cheek, cupping the side of my face. "How awful."

Her sympathy didn't make me uncomfortable. I liked it. It made her touch me.

"They say I take after her," I confessed quietly. "She's where I got all my acting talent."

"She was a legend." Zoey stated. "Right up until—" Her eyes rounded.

"Until she was murdered." I finished, stepping back. "The way she died made her even more famous."

It was the kind of famous no one wanted to have. To be remembered for your slaughter and not all the success that came before it.

"It was on a movie set right?"

I nodded. "She was filming the sequel to *Moth to A Flame*."

Clasping her hands in her lap, she asked, "Is it really true what they say happened?"

Leaning back into the counter, I crossed my arms over my chest. "They were filming the final scene of the movie. Everyone was there. The cameras were rolling." I began, feeling myself slip into that day as if I were there. As if I hadn't been told this story a thousand times, but I'd been a witness instead.

* * *

Giant cocoon-shaped objects hung from the ceiling, swaying back and forth very slightly as if a gentle breeze carried through the dark house.

Moonlight cast upon the light-colored objects, but it was too dark to know what was inside. Her nightgown brushed against her ankles, either urging her on or warning her to run away.

She couldn't run anymore.

Too many people had died. He would keep coming to her, just as he promised. Like a moth drawn to a flame—until the moth was burned up or the flame went out.

Out in the hallway, the creaking of the stairs proved she was right. Her heart accelerated to the point of pain, her feet quickening farther into the bedroom until she bounced off one of the hanging bundles.

Grabbing it for balance, she turned and looked.

A bloodcurdling scream rattled the darkness, piercing the entire night.

"Ahhhhh!" she screamed, shoving away the cocoon and backing away slowly. The bundle swung toward her, providing an ample view of the corpse wrapped inside.

Her eyes were open, her face frozen in horror. Blood soaked her cheeks, and her blond hair was tangled in the plastic wound around her mutilated body.

Another shriek filled the night, and she tripped over her nightgown, falling onto the floor. Rolling over, she crawled, bile rising up her throat and tears streaking her cheeks. She crawled until something hit her back.

Squealing, she leapt up, only to come face to face with another wrapped corpse. Her boyfriend. And there was a knife still stuck in his skull.

Her feet pounded over the sound of her whimper as she weaved through the other dead bodies, rushing for the door. Out in the hall, she stopped, coming face to face with the killer who was obsessively drawn to her.

"You should have died!" She raged. "I killed you before! You should have stayed dead!"

His faceless, expressionless head tilted to the side. He had no hair. No skin. Nothing but shiny pale rubber coating everything above his neck. The shirt beneath the open zip hoodie was ripped and bloodied. The hem was burned from a fire he'd somehow survived.

The hiking boots he wore left bloody prints on the carpet as he strolled close, promising another gift of death downstairs. She backed away, feet tangling in the gown, thinking of all the bodies he'd hung in her room and wondering why he couldn't just die.

He came closer.

She stepped back.

Moonlight bathed her outline from behind, and her shoulder blades hit the cold windowpane.

"Stay back!" she screamed, holding out a hand to ward him off.

He came so close she could feel his chest with every breath he took. Bending low so they were eye to eye, he stared at her without saying a thing.

Fumbling with the curtain, she grasped the knife hidden inside. Moonlight glinted off the shining, silver blade when she lifted it high above her head.

"Die!" she ordered, consumed with all the rage of the people he'd killed before her.

His hand caught her wrist just before the blade could penetrate his skull. The sound of her bones cracking and the way she crumbled to the floor was shockingly real.

"What are you doing?" she screeched.

The knife clattered onto the hardwood, and he released her wrist to wrap a large hand around her throat. She choked and gagged, grabbing at his hand, her eyes bulging.

"What's happening?"

A few whispers floated from the set.

"Steven," our heroine croaked, reaching toward the dark.

"It's good. Keep rolling!" the director called.

The killer lifted her anew, sliding her up the window and pinning her as she fought.

"Help!" She gagged. "Help!"

He pulled a knife from inside his hoodie, plunging it right into her middle.

She gurgled and slumped, would have crumpled if he hadn't still been gripping her neck.

"Cut!" the director yelled. "What the fuck was that? You know she doesn't die—"

The killer turned, bringing her body with him like a rag doll. The blood-drenched knife dripped onto the floor when he pointed the blade at the director.

"What's going on?" he said, his voice suddenly confused and scared.

He plunged the knife back into the heroine, directly into her heart. The sound of her sternum cracking with the trauma made everyone scream. Pulling the blade out like it had been speared into butter, he stabbed her again and then again.

Her body fell at his feet, her white gown now stained with crimson. Her surprised, glassy eyes matched those of the bodies hanging in the other room, but hers were more lifelike… because hers were real.

Before anyone knew what was happening, the killer dropped the knife by the body and jumped out the window, plunging himself right through the glass.

People ran after him, gazing down into the yard below.

He was gone.

Never to be seen again.

And the heroine who was supposed to burn the moth with her flame? In the end, it was her flame that went out.

* * *

"They said it was some crazed fan who somehow managed to get onto the closed set. The actor who was originally playing The Moth was found knocked out and tied up in a closet," I said quietly, feeling hoarse from recalling that day. "He killed her right there. Everyone stood by watching because they thought it was part of the scene…"

Gentle arms sliding around my torso made me jolt. Grabbing her by the shoulders, I looked down, blinking when I saw her gazing back. Relenting instantly, my arms fell at my sides, and she leaned into my chest. Her hand rose and fell against the center of my back in a soothing repetitive way.

"Your family must have been absolutely devastated."

I nodded. "It was my grandfather who took it the hardest. Watching his wife murdered right in front of him."

Zoey pulled back, though her hands remained on my waist. "He was there?"

"He was the one directing the film. The one who told them to keep going with the scene."

Her hand covered her mouth, eyes shining with disbelief. "He was the director?"

"Steven Price. Famous director of eighties horror who eventually became part of the worlds he created."

"I-I didn't know that."

"My mother lost both her parents that day. One to death. One to madness."

"He went mad?"

"You don't know?" I asked, partially surprised.

She shook her head. "No. It was so long ago... before my time in Hollywood."

"But you know my grandmother?"

She nodded. "Of course. I've used some of her looks for reference when doing films and camera work."

"My grandfather killed himself six months after that day," I told her somberly.

"Suicide?" she echoed.

"He left behind a note saying he would never un-see the way her eyes stared at him in death because he'd stood there and watched her murder."

"He didn't know!" Zoey said fiercely.

"No," I said, cupping the back of her head and bringing her into my chest. "He didn't. No one realized until it was too late."

Her arms hugged me tight, and I couldn't help but feel like it was the first time she was offering comfort, not just allowing me to give it.

After a few minutes, she eased back, lifting her eyes to mine. "They're making a movie about this?"

A sound of agreement vibrated my throat. "They've tried in the past, but my parents always managed to block it."

"Can't they block it again?"

"Not this time." I rubbed the back of my neck. "The studio producing it wants me to be involved. They say they want to be accurate, not just sensational." A rude noise erupted from me. "In the same breath, they offered to create a role for me—a detective investigating the case."

"It's okay to say no," she said, astoundingly astute.

"That's not what everyone else is saying."

"Your agent? The movie execs?" Crossing her arms over her chest, she made a face. "Screw them."

I chuckled.

"I'm serious!" She flung out her arms. "You shouldn't do anything you don't want to do. They shouldn't even ask you to relive such a painful memory!"

The passion in her voice made me feel like she was talking about more than just this movie. "Technically, it's not my memory. But it is my mother's."

Zoey hesitated, then asked, "Is that why she takes the same kind of pills I do?"

I nodded.

"No wonder you're so good with trauma," she murmured, speaking to herself.

"What trauma do you have, angel?"

Her head shot up. Fear flashed in her eyes like lightning. She retreated from me faster than the speed of light.

"Hey, you know what?" I hurried to say, pretending to glance at the clock on the microwave. "If we don't head out, we're going to be late."

"I have to get my bag," she announced, rushing out of the room.

I stared after her, wondering when she was finally going to trust me.

"Where do you think you're going?"

Nick's voice stopped me from rushing out of the house, fleeing toward my car. Stopping like I was caught fleeing the scene of a crime, I turned back. "To work."

"We'll go out through the garage. They're waiting for us."

They? Shaking my head, I turned him down. "My car is out front." I stepped outside, stopping cold. "Where's my car?"

"It's in the garage, away from prying eyes."

I sniffed. "I thought this was private property."

"That doesn't mean we should be careless."

Making a face, I came back inside and waited while he locked the front door and set the alarm.

"Come on," he murmured, putting his hand at the small of my back.

Electricity sizzled my nerve endings, skittering along my spine. He guided me this way a lot. It was just a harmless touch.

But for a person who avoided physical touch with anyone, it didn't seem harmless.

"This way." His voice was quiet, sort of cajoling. Or maybe just the sudden intimacy I felt made it seem that way. This was bad for me. Staying here wasn't a good idea.

Sidestepping his touch, I hurried along in front of him even though I had no idea where we were going. At the bottom of a wide, iron-trimmed staircase, I rushed on.

"Woah," Nick swore, grabbing my hand and pulling me back around. My hair swung around me like a curtain as I clutched the bag at my shoulder. "Wrong way."

"This is a big house," I muttered, embarrassed.

"You should have let me give you a tour."

"It was late last night." I countered. "Besides, I won't be here long enough to need to know my way around."

Without a word, he pulled open the door leading into a "garage" that looked more like a showroom. Sucking in a breath, I stared at him.

"I like cars," he said, shrugging off my awe.

"I've only ever seen you drive the Range Rover."

"You don't like the Rover?"

Waving my hand in apology, I hurried to say, "No, no. I like it fine." It dawned on me I was apologizing for no reason. Backtracking, I said, "Like it matters. It's your car."

Laughing beneath his breath, he hit a button, and one of the doors began to slide up soundlessly. A large black SUV was waiting, engine running and windows so dark it was impossible to see inside.

"I can just take my car if you tell me where you put it."

"Driving your car out of the gate of my property? I know you're smarter than that," he drawled, tapping on the side of my head with a finger.

I smacked it away. "You've already done enough for me."

"We're going to the same place."

I stewed for a minute, then relented. "Whatever," I muttered as he started toward the giant ride. A shining red sports car caught my attention, and I paused beside it. "Why you wouldn't want that to drive this is beyond me," I grumbled. "Ah!" I exclaimed seconds later when I ran right into his back, bouncing off and nearly falling on my butt. "What are you doing?"

One minute he was walking and the next he was a statue!

"You like the Viper, do you?"

My mind went blank. "The Viper?"

He gestured with his chin.

My lips formed an O, and I pointed to it. "That's a Viper?"

"You don't know?"

"I like its shiny red color." And the black racing stripe was hot. (I didn't tell him that part. His ego was giant enough.)

His teeth flashed with his laughter. Lifting a finger, he started walking backward. "Hang on."

I watched him jog toward the SUV as a window rolled down to meet him. He said a few words, gestured toward the garage, then jogged off. Snatching a pair of keys out of a box on the wall, he tossed them up into the air, catching them easily.

"Come on." The lights blinked on the Viper when he clicked the remote in his hand.

"No. I—"

Wrapping his fingers around my wrist, he towed me around to the passenger side. "In you go," he instructed.

I couldn't help but notice the way he put his hand on the side of the roof while he stuffed me inside. Making sure I didn't hit my head.

The garage door in front of the sports car slid up, and he climbed behind the wheel. He looked commanding and big in the driver's seat, but not cramped. If anything, the black leather interior seemed to wrap around his body like a caress.

Teeth sinking into my lower lip, I averted my eyes to everything but him.

The sound of the engine purring to life vibrated my chest, the power injecting right into my body.

"We should just ride with them," I said, reaching for the handle. "Your driver already came to pick us up."

The automatic locks clicked, keeping me in the car. "Hey!"

"Don't worry about them. They're following us in."

My hand fell from the handle. "They are? How come?"

"Should I ask the bodyguards to sit in the trunk?" he teased.

"Bodyguards," I echoed. Worry expelled the thoughts of not looking at him. "Did something happen? Did someone threaten you?"

When he leaned across the already close quarters, his nose became level with mine. "Why? Are you worrying about me?"

"Of course not!" I said, moving back. Then, because I actually was, I said, "You've never had bodyguards on set before... Something must have happened."

"Ahh." He understood. "You think they're for me."

"Well, who else would they be for?"

Keeping his stare level on me, he raised an eyebrow. Slowly, it dawned. Incredulous, I pointed at myself. He nodded.

"Uh-uh!" I disagreed. "No way!"

"Put your seatbelt on," he instructed, ignoring my staunch denials.

"Nick!" I bellowed. "Why would you sic bodyguards on me?"

"The press is harassing you. Your apartment was vandalized. You can't even go to lunch without being mobbed. If I hadn't been there the other night, you might not even have been able to drive yourself home."

"I'm not your problem," I said through gritted teeth.

"You're right. You aren't a problem."

Collapsing into the buttery soft seat, I turned away. "Nick..."

Clearly, he didn't understand that I was exhausted and overwhelmed. If he had, he would have stayed in his seat. Instead, he leaned closer, practically hanging over my lap.

"I told you to put this on." He scolded me, but in a gentle tone. His arm brushed against me as he pulled the strap across my chest. Holding my breath and turning my face away, I waited for the belt to click into place.

When it did, I let out a shuddering sigh, thinking I was safe.

I was anything but.

Instead of pulling back like I prayed to God he would, Nick's fingers slid beneath the strap, brushing against my collarbone. Jolting from the touch, I gripped the sides of the seat tight. "It's twisted," he whispered, leaning even closer to adjust the strap.

I was damn near hyperventilating when he finally pulled away.

The dark SUV backed up, making room for him to pull the sports car out into the driveway, and we sat waiting for the garage doors to close. In the rearview mirror, I could see the men ready to follow.

"Hey." He beckoned. When I looked up, he tugged the end of my hair. "Just let them shadow you for a few days, okay? I'm worried."

"Why would you be worried?" I blurted out, forgetting to conceal my thoughts as I fell into his mossy stare.

"Because I care," he said simply, rocking my world.

I started to stutter, but he just smiled wide.

"Hold on." He warned.

Before I could ask why, the Viper launched forward.

She taunted me with her cleverness. I could almost hear her laughing. Right under my nose. She'd been right under my nose all these years.

She knew our sequel wasn't finished; our movie wasn't over. If it was, why hide? Why play cat and mouse games?

I found you. You thought I wouldn't, but here I am.

Still, something wasn't right. *She* wasn't right.

We couldn't finish this sequel until I knew for sure. Once I did, I could set things right again, and the show could go on.

Hovering in the darkness, peering through a small opening, anticipation coursed through me.

Watching.

Planning.

Waiting.

I'm coming. This time you won't get away.

"Resuming in five!" the director hollered.

"Where the hell is Callie?" I muttered, glancing around. "Did she go to France to get the damn coffee?"

Zoey giggled, drawing my eyes and making me forget about coffee. The corner of my mouth lifting, I hitched my chin at her. "You think this is funny?"

Her fingers clasped my chin. "Hold still."

She was close. So close the scent of her skin filled my senses. "You smell like me," I whispered.

The sponge she was using paused, and her brown gaze shot to mine. "W-what?"

"The soap you use." I amended. "It's the same one I do."

She was so close I felt her indrawn breath, felt the nerves skittering along her skin. Turning toward her makeup kit, she said, "I ran out this morning, and that one was in the shower…"

I felt her retreating. I didn't want that. I wanted her to move in the opposite direction of retreat. Circling her wrist, I tugged her around.

Her eyes fell to where I held her and then up.

"I like it," I said low. "Use it anytime you want."

Her pulse beat rapidly against my fingers, almost to the point that I wanted to look down at her vein. It excited me to know I could affect her this way, that I wasn't the only one whose heart went wild when we were close.

"I'm sorry!" Callie exclaimed, interrupting the moment we were lost in. "They were out of coffee, and I had to wait—*ah*!"

Her foot caught in one of the many cords on the floor, and she pitched forward. The chair I was in scraped back with an earsplitting sound as I lurched up, wrapping myself around Zoey and spinning.

Callie crashed into my back, the lid popping off the cup and coffee exploding all over me. Zoey's hands gripped my forearms, hugging me close as she hunched in on herself.

The hot liquid made my back sting and burn, but I didn't let her go.

"You okay?" I asked, still folded around her from behind. "Did you get burned?"

She turned her face to glance at me from the corner of her eye. Confusion made her blink. "What?"

Gently, I asked her again, "Are you okay?"

She nodded.

"Nick!" Callie fretted, grabbing my arm and pulling me around. "Oh my God, Nick! Are you burned? Hurry, get this off!"

Straightening away from Zoey and shaking off my stellar assistant's help, I peeled the drenched shirt off my body.

"Nick!" Jessica gasped, appearing. "Your back is beet red! Let me see." Her hands felt cool against my back, offering a little relief from the stinging.

"I'm fine," I said, pulling away. "It's not serious."

Jessica tugged the ruined shirt from my grip and spun on Callie. "You have got to be the world's worst assistant! What the hell were you thinking? What would you have done if Nick had been scarred?"

"I-I…" Callie shrank back, tears swimming in her eyes.

"That's enough, Jessica."

"He's a huge celebrity. He's the sexiest man alive, for Christ's sake! He can't have scars. Scars are not sexy!"

Even though I was turned away, I felt Zoey's silent reaction to my costar's thoughtless words. I knew Zoey had scars. Lots of them.

"Enough!" I roared. Everyone on set looked at me.

"I don't know how you treat your assistant, but you aren't allowed to treat mine like this." I turned to Callie, who was swiping rapidly at the falling tears, trying to be discreet about it. "It was an accident. I'm fine. No harm done."

"I'm so sorry." She started toward me.

I held out my hand, stopping her. "How about you just get me another coffee?"

"I'm not fired?"

I laughed. "No."

The director was standing close by, watching the unfolding events. "I'm going to wardrobe to get a new shirt."

"Of course." He agreed. Then gesturing to the spilled coffee, he told someone, "Clean this up!"

Callie excused herself, carefully stepping over every cord, and Jessica shot lasers from her eyes as she went.

"Hey," I said, grasping Jess's arm. "It's fine. Don't give her a hard time."

She made a face. "I don't know why you put up with her."

"Your lipstick is smudged."

Horror overcame her features, and she covered her mouth with her hand. "Carson!" she yelled, rushing off.

Using the shirt, I mopped up some coffee that was dripping down my arm, then started toward wardrobe.

A small hand curled around the space just above my elbow, not strong enough to pull me back, but it didn't need to be.

By the way my body hummed, I knew who it was the second we came into contact.

Stopping, I turned back, but not enough so her hold on me would be dislodged. I didn't say anything, just waited for her.

"I can wipe off your back," she offered, pulling her hand away. "There's still coffee all over you."

I nodded.

Pulling open the bottom drawer of her large kit, Zoey produced a pack of wipes. Pulling a few free, she motioned for me to turn around.

I flinched when she first made contact.

Her hand grasped the side of my waist. "Does it hurt?" She worried.

"It's cold," I complained.

Her light laugh floated over my shoulder. "Don't be a baby."

Falling silent, I held myself still as she gently wiped away the mess. Occasionally, the pads of her fingertips would brush against my skin, and I had to school myself to not react.

Leaning over my shoulder, she said. "Are you sure you aren't burned?"

Shaking my head, I answered, "Does it look burned?"

"I don't think so." The words were followed by a caress over a patch of still-stinging skin. "It's red right here."

My jaw clenched, and I lowered my chin because I was worried people might catch a glimpse of that smolder. "I'm fine." My voice was raspy.

Her fingers paused. "I think I got it all," she said, pulling away.

"I'll be back."

"Nick?"

My patience was wearing so thin. My name on her lips… Her fingers on my bare skin… "Yeah?"

"That should have spilled on me."

That drew me around to look into her eyes.

"Thank you."

Damn it all to hell. This woman was going to steal my heart.

I think I needed to see a doctor. My heart wouldn't beat regularly. Breathing was no longer involuntary.

What is wrong with me?

Sneaking a glance at Nick's retreating shirtless back, I knew. The ailment affecting my heart and lungs was him.

"Zoey!" Carson hollered from across the set. "I need your number fifty. Mine broke."

Digging around in my makeup kit, I found the lipstick he needed.

"I'm back, without making a mess again," Callie announced, making me glance up. Looking around, she asked, "Where's Nick?"

"Wardrobe. He'll be right back."

She sighed. "I seriously wonder why he hasn't fired me yet."

"Maybe he likes you." The words popped out before I could even think twice.

Callie jolted in surprise and pointed to herself. "Definitely not."

I recalled the day when Nick told me Callie might not be a good assistant, but she was good for other things.

Yeah. So? Maybe I still thought about that. Maybe it made me a little jealous… Maybe I wanted to know Callie's exact relationship with her boss.

"Why not?" I answered, closing my hand around the lipstick. "You're beautiful, and you spend more time with him than anyone."

Leaning in, the steaming cup of coffee between us, Callie whispered, "Actually, it's you who sees him the most."

"Zoey!" Carson hollered.

"Duty calls," I sang, holding the lipstick up between us. "Nick will be back in a sec."

Callie nodded, and I headed across set. People milled around, adjusting lighting, checking sound, and getting everything in place for the filming to resume.

If Nick hadn't reacted so fast, I'd have been the one covered in hot coffee. My shirt would have been drenched through. *It would have burned.*

The thought made me shudder. It was the kind of pain a person couldn't forget.

The sound of a match striking echoed through my head, and the flicker of a flame flashed in my mind. Stumbling over my own foot, I straightened, glancing around to make sure no one noticed.

"Girl!" Carson called. "Are you walking a turtle?"

Trying to rid myself of the unpleasant thoughts assailing me, I hurried forward. The skin on my shoulder and upper arm tingled, but I resisted the urge to rub it.

Jessica was tapping her toes on the floor, looking really annoyed that she had to wait for me to bring over what she needed. I recalled the way she fawned over Nick, touching his back and laying into Callie. It made me want to walk even slower.

Thunderous sound rumbled overhead, making me tilt my head. Barely a second later, ear-splitting screeching made everyone wince.

"Watch out!" someone yelled.

I looked up in time to see a large metal hook and sandbag plummeting right toward me. Flinging my arms up over my head, I cried out and launched forward.

The force with which that thing fell was greater than the force I used to escape.

The weight of the sandbag slammed into me, knocking all the wind out of my body and pounding me into the ground. Pain ripped through my wrist, and my arm gave out, my cheek smacking against the floor.

I lay there sprawled out on my stomach, cheek throbbing and wrist screaming with ache.

"Oh my God!" Carson exclaimed. "Get it off! Zoey!" He rushed forward, but the sound of more screeching gears above made everyone falter.

"Is something else going to fall?" Jessica exclaimed, totally freaking out.

I could feel the chain attached to the sandbag pinning me wobble. "Stay back," I told Carson, my voice breathless and weak.

"Get that lifted!" a man yelled, probably the director.

Cranking sounds filled the set, and the bag on top of me trembled as it was hefted up, much slower than it had crashed down. My chest felt stiff from being pressed into the floor, and when I tried to lift onto my hands and knees, my wrist screamed in pain.

"It's lifting!" Carson said, wringing his hands.

I took a deep breath, feeling some of the crushing pressure start to ease, but it was instantly replaced with a new sensation.

As the chain was lifted… so was I.

"Wait!" I cried, but my raspy voice wasn't loud enough.

Up, up I went until I was off the ground, hanging like the bag, caught on whatever it was lifting me.

"Whoa! Whoa!" the director yelled, everyone noticing I was literally being dragged up off the floor like a rag doll.

The ripping sound was likely very low, but it was louder than a gunshot to me. As I hung there suspended, the place where my shirt was caught tore.

With a lurch, the chain started moving me up again, taking me farther away from the ground.

"No! Stop!" I yelled, struggling to get free as I felt the fabric of my clothing give way. "Stop!" I screeched.

But it was too late.

My shirt tore open, the fabric ripping completely. I hit the ground with another hard smack, the rush of cold air brushing over my newly exposed skin.

There were a few gasps.

Goose bumps prickled my body.

Oh my God, everyone will see… everyone will know…

Tears and panic came at once, overwhelming me the way the air did my back.

Roll over, Zoey! Roll over!

Body obeying my insistent mind, I started to roll. Searing pain ripped into my wrist, and I collapsed again onto my stomach.

A wrenching sob built in my throat, threatening to explode.

Something warm and solid covered me, sheltering me from prying eyes. Nick's chin brushed my shoulder, and his voice filled my ear. "I'm here, okay?"

I whispered his name, and his weight shifted a little more firmly over me.

One of his arms slipped between me and the floor, his hand curling around my waist. "Let's get up now."

Clutching his forearm, I said, "Don't let me go."

"I won't ever." He swore.

His balance was great enough for both of us. We stood without him loosening his grip even the slightest bit. Keeping my back plastered against his chest, I clutched at his arm with both hands, feeling jittery and sore all at once.

"My shirt," I said, cowering into him even more. "People will see."

"No one's gonna see." His voice was so quiet my ears had to strain to hear.

But I did, and I believed him.

He walked with me until we were at the edge of set, positioning himself in front of me so no one else would see.

Quickly, I turned around, putting my back to everyone, including Nick.

Shivering, I looked up, afraid of what I would see on his face.

It wasn't what I expected. Tenderness was definitely not even on my radar, but it was exactly what I was getting.

"I leave you alone for five minutes," he muttered. "You're almost as bad as Callie."

My shirt was shredded in the back, falling off my shoulders, and would have hit the floor if it wasn't for me clutching it over my chest.

Sighing heavily, he pulled off the shirt he'd just gone to get. "C'mon," he urged, holding it out for me.

"Th-that's yours."

"You got a better idea?"

I peeked around him, noting everyone—and I mean everyone—staring. Shoulders slumping, I shook my head.

Flinging the cotton over his shoulder, he peeled what was left of my shirt off my body, allowing it to flutter between our feet.

"Arms," he instructed after he put the shirt over my head.

He held the hem while I peeled my arms away from my chest and stuffed them through. Once the T-shirt fell around me, I breathed a sigh of relief.

Perching his hands on his hips, he scowled. "What the hell happened?"

"Something fell and ripped my clothes—"

Staring up toward the ceiling, I saw the sandbag with the hook rocking back and forth, a torn piece of my shirt still attached. An eerie, surreal feeling overwhelmed me, and I shuddered.

The hairs on the back of my neck stood up, making me feel vulnerable and afraid. Sliding my hand around my shoulder, I rubbed at the spot and then continued rubbing down the back of my arm.

Instinctively, I spun, glancing over my shoulder into the darkness beyond set.

Something felt creepy… *off*.

Everyone swarmed us, and I was swept away by the medics, the director, and a fussing Carson.

Even though there were tons of people all around, the urge to glance back into the shadows haunted me.

34

She could change her appearance. She could change her name. There was one thing, though, that never would. She belonged to me.

35

Her screams echoed through the house, pounding into my closed bedroom door like a madman trying to break in.

Or maybe the pounding was my heart thumping so hard it was trying to break free so it could run to her.

My heart didn't have to go alone, though. The rest of me was just as anxious to be there. The door smacked against the doorstop, making the wall shudder and the wood bounce back. It didn't hit me, though. I was already running through the house.

Turning the corner, I saw a man in black reaching for her doorknob.

My vision went dark, and all the fight training I'd had over the years kicked in without hesitation. The flying kick knocked the man sideways, his body hitting the floor with a satisfying smack. Leaping up almost instantly, he came back for me, but all I heard was Zoey screaming and no one was going to keep me away.

A swift uppercut to the man's jaw and then a few jabs to his ribs knocked him back. I dove, grabbing him by the front of his clothing, hauling up his limp body between my legs. My fist was on the way down when I saw who it was.

One of my bodyguards.

His suit was black, but the shirt under it was white.

I dropped him, his body hitting against the floor, and he rolled to sit up.

"Fuck, I'm sorry," I said, rough. "I thought—"

"Go to h-her." He waved me off, motioning to the door.

I didn't even think twice, turning my back on the man to throw open her bedroom door. Her screaming reduced to whimpers and cries.

She was alone.

No one was attacking her.

She writhed and clutched the blankets in the center of a bed that seemed to swallow her whole. Dark hair thrashed across a white pillow as I climbed onto the bed.

"Zoey," I called. "Zoey, you're having a bad dream."

"Please, no," she whimpered. "It hurts… I don't want to die."

A lump the size of a planet formed in my throat, nearly choking me. Forcing it down, I slipped my arm under her shoulders, lifting her upper body off the mattress.

"Wake up."

Her eyes fluttered open. Even in the dark, I could see the tears bathing her cheeks.

"Nick?" she whispered.

Nodding, I wiped at her cheek. "I'm here. You're okay."

A sob filled the room, and I no longer had to hold her up. She pressed tightly against me, her hands clutching at my back.

The sound of her weeping made my heart hurt, and the feel of her tears running down my chest left me helpless. I didn't know what to do. I didn't know how to comfort this woman, even though it was all I wanted to do.

Her sobs quieted, her body collapsed into mine, and I continued to hold her, stroking the length of her hair while her breathing evened.

"You were having a nightmare," I whispered.

Her voice was hoarse. "I'm sorry I woke you."

"Don't be sorry. I'm glad I was here."

Pulling away, she started to look up, then abruptly stopped, ducking her face. When I reached out, she pulled back slightly, as if afraid. I didn't stop, though. I just moved slower to give her time to get used to the movement.

"You're sleeping in my hoodie," I observed.

"It's comfortable."

Fingers clasping the hood, I lifted it gently so it offered more coverage for her face.

A face I intently wanted to look upon.

Once the hood was in place, I eased back. "Want to tell me about your nightmare?"

Her head shook.

"It might help."

"It won't."

"How about I stay with you for a while?"

She didn't say anything for a few minutes, but then she grasped the hood to pull it tighter around her. "You don't need to."

I wasn't going to give up this easily. Not tonight. Not after today on set. Not after everything.

Pushing to my knees, I moved around her on the bed.

She stiffened, glancing around. "What are you doing?" her voice was wary.

"Getting comfortable," I replied, slipping between her and the pillows at her back. Opening my legs, I pushed them beneath the covers on either side of her hips. Our bodies brushed together, and she stiffened, instantly starting to move away.

"It's fine." I assured her, wrapping one arm around her shoulders.

"I-I don't have it on."

Ah, she was worried I would feel. "Your prosthetic?"

She nodded, trying to scoot away.

Winding both arms around her waist, I pulled her into my body, my front colliding with her back. "It's okay, angel."

She was shaking.

I was pushing too much. She'd just had some hideous dream, and even though I was trying to comfort her, it seemed I was doing the opposite.

"I'm sorry," I whispered, feeling bereft because I craved closeness with her but knew it was probably too much too soon.

She caught my hands just as they were letting her go. Everything inside me stilled, even my heartbeat gently offering her the lead. Not breathing, I waited to see what she would do.

Tentative fingers wrapped around mine, tugging my arms back around her waist. "Stay."

I hadn't felt like this since I was in high school and my crush let me hold her hand at the movies. Back before I was famous, when I had to work to make someone like me… when I liked someone purely because they made my stomach wobble.

It was unsettling, foreign, and… addictive.

Everything under my skin buzzed with awareness, and excitement soared through my veins. Gathering her close again, I settled my chin on her shoulder and smiled.

She tugged the blankets up to her waist, fluttering her hands afterward like she wasn't quite sure where to put them.

She's nervous too. Probably more than me.

Covering both of hers with one of mine, I brought them to her waist so I could hold them, along with the rest of her.

This wasn't enough. I might have been holding her body, but what I really wanted was her heart.

Her trust.

"I was sort of annoyed with you when we first met," I admitted.

She made a sound. "You were mean."

"I wasn't!" I argued.

"You called me an L.A. girl."

Gently rubbing my chin against her shoulder, I thought for a moment. "I was really drawn to you. Whenever I saw you on set or in the trailer, this weird tugging sensation made me want to be near you."

"You didn't like it."

"I was intrigued by it. By you." Pausing for a moment, I smiled into the side of her neck. "And yeah, maybe it kinda pissed me off."

She didn't laugh or say anything at all, mentally making me wince. "This talking stuff is hard," I muttered to myself.

"There's no script to refer to, huh?" Her voice was light and teasing, which put me at ease.

"I guess it's easier to talk about your feelings when you're pretending to be someone else."

A small sound of agreement filled the room. "Yeah, I get that."

Settling a little closer against her, I confessed, "I couldn't understand why. Why I was so lured by you. You looked like everyone else here in L.A.... but you didn't feel like them."

"It's a lot of work for me to look like those L.A. girls you seem to dislike so much."

"I don't dislike them. Hell, I've dated my fair share. But I want something different, something real."

"Everyone wants real until reality sets in," she mused.

"In my world, you learn just how fake everything can be. Everyone wears a mask, puts on an act. It's appearances for appearances' sake. It's like wading through a river of bullshit, searching for a shred of genuineness."

"I don't alter my appearance because I want to look perfect," she murmured.

"I know. I've known it since that day you fell into the water."

"How much of me did you see that day?" Her voice was timid. "And again today?"

"Some." I hedged, not wanting her to pull away.

"Enough to understand why I hide myself."

"You aren't hiding, angel." I corrected. "You're protecting yourself."

"You're just curious," she told me. "You probably have a million questions you're dying to ask."

"I do," I admitted, not shying away from any truth. If I wanted her to trust me, then I had to be transparent.

Her body puffed up with her indrawn breath. "Go ahead. Ask. I'll answer."

Bravado. Strength. Resignation. I heard all these things in her voice. She thought once my curiosity was satisfied, I would walk away.

She was wrong.

"How lonely have you been, keeping people away? Did you cry a lot in the beginning? Was anyone there to dry your tears?"

Her body elongated as I spoke, sitting up in fascination.

"Does it still hurt? Do your muscles contract a lot? How many times have you woken up screaming in the middle of the night?"

"Nick," she whispered, her body turning toward mine.

"When you look in the mirror, are you reminded of all the bad things that have happened, or has anyone told you that it's all just proof of how strong you are?"

"Stop." Her voice caught, fingers tightening around my hand.

"You told me to ask. You said you would answer."

"That's not—" she stuttered. "This isn't what I thought you would ask."

"You thought I would want a firsthand account of your accident. You thought I would want to marvel at your scars, ask about your missing limb, and be fascinated by your trauma."

She rotated just a little bit more. Even though I stared right at her, the hood still protected her face. "Aren't you?"

I nodded. "I want to know those things, but not because of morbid fascination. Because it's part of who you are. More than anything, though, I just want to be able to look at you."

"Why?"

"I want see your scars. I want to see how many times you needed me and I wasn't there."

Her chest rose and fell rapidly, and her body trembled finely. Bowing her head, she said nothing, but the sound of her uneven breathing filled the room. "Please don't play games with me," she whispered, her voice heartbreakingly defenseless.

"Nothing about you is a game to me."

Pulling her hands from under mine and smoothing them over the blankets, she released a shuddering breath.

"Turn around, angel." I cajoled. "Let me see the you I always felt but haven't gotten to see."

She hesitated so long I thought I failed in getting through to her. This woman's wall was so high and so thick I was beginning to see nothing would ever be able to break through.

The only way someone would ever get beyond her defenses was if she opened a secret door and invited them in.

"It's okay." I relented. Cupping her covered head, I leaned in, pressing a kiss against the hood. "I'm going back to bed."

Her hand hit my thigh, stopping me from pulling back. Glancing down, I looked at her pale, slim fingers lying against my leg.

Zoey's fingers slipped away, and her body began to turn, rotating between my thighs, settling with her hands tucked into her lap.

Her head was bowed, the fabric of my hoodie still robbing me of the sight I wanted most. Nervous as hell, I took a chance. Curling my fingers around the edges of the fabric, I slowly peeled it back.

I was going to be sick. I'd long ago passed the sensation of butterflies gently filling my middle, giving me a giddy sense of excitement.

No, this was way different than that.

The butterflies turned into dragons. Fire-breathing ones with razor-sharp wings.

I wanted to throw up. The desire to catapult off this bed and flee into the darkness, into a new town, a new life, was so strong my teeth ground against each other.

His words held me in place. They were the only thing I'd ever met that rivaled my extreme fear of getting close to anyone.

I was so scared to trust him. So scared not to.

Nick surprised me again and again. I was off balance with him, and as much as I wanted to run… I also wanted to stay still.

And so I was here.

Sitting within the protection of his body. Shaking like the last leaf clinging to a bare tree in winter. Feeling the warmth of his skin and the sincerity in the way he eased away the very hood he'd provided.

I had no idea what was going to happen next. This was uncharted territory for me—a destination I never ever planned to visit.

Gulping back the nausea roiling inside me, I pressed a hand to my stomach.

One more inch, just another slight tilt, and he would be able to see it all. My lips shook, tears swimming in the depths of my eyes.

If only he knew how hard this was. If only he knew what this moment cost.

"Look at me."

I did.

Neck slightly arched, chin tilted up, no hood to hide behind. My eyes clung to his, seeking out his true response. More scared than I think I'd ever been in my entire life.

He held my gaze for only a moment. The warmth in his eyes did not reassure me. I watched him look at me. I watched his mossy green irises scan my features, taking in the thick scar slicing through my eyebrow, the uneven texture left behind by the burns. Even though the room was dark, he would be able to see the discoloration, the pigment of damaged skin. Another scar ran along my jawline, reaching up toward my cheek. Beneath my bangs was more of the same—the edges of mutilation, the mottled, raised scar tissue denoting more burns.

As he looked, my eyes could hold no more sorrow, and a fat, heavy tear slid free, streaking down my cheek.

He moved to brush it away. I flinched, and he stopped. Unreadable eyes met mine before again raking over my face.

The hand that had been trying to wipe away my sorrow changed direction, lowering toward my shoulders to brush back the hair falling around me.

Unable to help it, my eyes drifted closed when the pads of his fingers brushed the sides of my neck.

"Look at me."

Obeying, I watched him watch me, my hand still pressed against my middle, still swallowing the vomit threatening to spew. His gaze was everywhere, as though he was reading a map or trying to solve some kind of puzzle.

Another tear fell, but this time, he ignored it. My hands were shaking now, my fingertips icy and numb. Slowly, he reached up again, meeting my eyes as if asking for my trust as his fingers lowered to brush away the bangs.

I allowed him to touch me this time. To reveal the rest of my damage. There was no turning back. Not sitting in his lap like this, not feeling so exposed and utterly sick.

All I could do was watch him and wait. Watch him and pray to God this wasn't a mistake.

"Nice to meet you," he whispered, letting his hands fall between us.

A sob echoed in my throat. It physically hurt.

I tried to look away, but he grasped my chin, keeping me in place.

"Please trust me," he whispered again. There wasn't a hint of anything other than acceptance in the way he looked at me. In the sound of his voice. He was solid while I sat and shook.

God help me. "I do."

More tears dripped down my face. I allowed him to brush away the wetness on my cheek.

"Does it hurt?" he asked, once again looking over my scars.

"Not anymore."

"I wish I'd been there."

"I'm glad you weren't."

The pad of his thumb brushed lightly over my cheekbone, soothing the severity of my fear.

"Blue eyes suit you," he whispered, his stare bouncing between them.

"It's too dark in here for you to know that," I argued, trying desperately to hold on to any footing I had left.

He shook his head slightly. "I know."

I was too far gone to say anything else. There was just no room left inside me for words, emotion overcoming even the most basic of thoughts.

"Angel?"

"Hmm?"

"Now that I've finally met you, there's something else I want."

Weariness assailed me. "There's nothing left."

"I think there is."

"What?" I asked.

Before I could protest, his hands were cupping my face. Both sides. My stomach clenched anew and started to heave.

"Easy," he murmured, rubbing slow circles on either jaw with his thumbs.

"I don't want you to touch it."

He shook his head. "I'm not touching it. I'm touching *you.*"

More tears filled my eyes. Dear sweet Lord, I was a freaking mess. I couldn't handle this. Him.

"I've held back so many times," he confessed, still drawing slow circles over my skin. "But now you're here. You're close." Pausing, he smiled. "I'm not going to hold back anymore."

This was Nick holding back? What the hell was he holding back? "Wha—" I started to ask, but I didn't have to.

His lips descended onto mine.

The brush of our lips.

Once.

Twice.

Again.

If I had been drawn to her before, now I was consumed. Swallowed whole by desire, eaten alive by intimacy. It was just a kiss… but it was far more.

Heaviness settled inside me, anchoring me to the bed. I'd wanted to tell her she was beautiful, but I thought they would sound like token words. I didn't want to give her words she would struggle to believe. I wanted to give her feelings that were impossible to ignore.

Gently nibbling on her lips, I tasted her lightly until the hand pressed against her stomach pressed into mine instead. If I'd been wearing a shirt, she'd have clutched the fabric, but I wasn't, so the pads of her fingers flexed against my skin.

When I eased back, her lower lip followed mine as if we'd fused together. Her lashes fluttered open, the blue of her irises startling. We stared at each other for the span of a few heartbeats, neither of us saying a thing.

This time, I covered her mouth with mine, not nibbling, not teasing or tasting. This time, I drank her in. Not separating from her for a single second. Rubbing my lips over hers full on. Reveling in the pillow-soft fullness rising up to meet me.

My fingers tightened as they cradled her face. Her body swayed toward me, so I wrapped an arm tightly around her, supporting her weight as I made love to her mouth the best way I knew how.

I let her feel how moved by her I was, let her be touched by not only my kiss, but the tenderness only she evoked within me.

The sound of our lips pulling apart made my stomach dip. When she tried to duck her chin, I grasped her face and held it. I wasn't done yet. I wasn't done telling her how much she meant to me. I wasn't ready to let this moment become a memory.

As I stroked my tongue across hers, her intake of breath made me pause.

Cracking open my eyes only enough to glance at hers, I let her see my desire. Watching her watch me, I licked against her once more.

The fingers lying against my stomach flexed.

Her lips parted. My tongue slid inside. She was soft and warm. Accepting but hesitant. Her reaction made me want to give her everything I had. It made me want to pluck the moon from the sky and give it to her as a gift.

Never in my life… Never had I ever been so moved by someone, by a single kiss.

Sitting in the center of this bed with this woman in my arms and the slight tang of salty tears mingling with the sweetness of our first kiss, I succumbed.

I knew she probably felt like she'd surrendered to me. That she'd given up a portion of herself she'd never planned to part with.

But I'd just done the same. She reached into me with those blue eyes, with her honest touch, and claimed a piece of me I hadn't even known was there.

I kissed the tip of her nose before pulling back, leaving an arm tucked around her waist.

"Okay?" I asked.

She nodded.

"C'mon," I instructed, gesturing for her to lie down beneath the covers. "Go back to sleep now."

"Will you stay?"

My chest swelled up with pride. "Try and make me go."

Her dark hair fanned out across the pillow, a small smile playing on her lips.

Sliding next to her, I tucked the blankets around us before hooking an arm around her, gazing into her face.

Her eyes looked everywhere but at me, denoting the uneasiness she still felt at allowing me to look at her.

"Thank you," I whispered.

Her eyes moved to mine. "Thank you?"

"For showing me the real you."

"No one else has ever…" Her words trailed away.

Surprise rippled through me. I knew she was guarded, but no one? Ever? "No one?"

"Just the doctors."

The rush of emotions robbed my voice. Instead, I lowered, pressing kisses to her cheek, her forehead, and her chin. Gently turning her face toward me, the worst of her scars came into view. As I lowered again, she sucked in a breath.

I kept going, pushing past her defenses to rest my lips upon the raised and damaged skin. Lying on my back, I pulled her into my side, cheek pillowing on my chest.

As I stared up into the darkened ceiling, I smiled. *Finally.* Finally, I'd earned her trust.

The sun was streaming through the windows when I cracked open my eyes. Groaning against the intrusion, I rolled, burying my head beneath a pillow.

Something bounced onto the bed, making me groan again. Cool air brushed over me when the blankets lifted and someone climbed beneath them.

The attack of wriggling fingers to my side made me squeal and squirm. "Nick!" I yelled, trying to get away.

The pillow on my head ripped away. The sound of it hitting the floor somewhere nearby was nearly drowned out by the pounding of my heart.

Nick stared down at me, golden sleep-mussed hair hanging into his playful green eyes. He looked ornery and mischievous, a smirk on his lips.

Lips I kissed just last night.

Holy crap. I kissed Nick Preston.

Squealing, I covered my face with my hands, turning away.

"Oh no you don't," he said, straddling my hips and pulling me around. His hands covered mine. and I knew he was going to try and pull them away.

So he could look at me.

In the new light of day.

"Wait!" I gasped, pressing harder against my face.

His hands lifted immediately, but he stayed on top of my body.

"Zoey." He warned.

"Why did you open the blinds?"

"Because it's daytime."

I gasped, realizing the sun was much brighter than it usually was when I got up for work. "We're late!"

"My call time wasn't 'til later. I called and told Carson you'd be in with me. He's covering for you."

Opening up my fingers, I glared at him through the crack. "Why'd you do that?"

"Because I wanted to stay in bed with you."

"I need to get ready for work."

He lifted an eyebrow. "We have a few minutes."

"Don't you have your own room?"

"This whole house is my room."

I scowled, but he couldn't see because I was covering my face.

Leaning closer, he teased, "Are you being shy?"

I swallowed thickly.

A serious note crept into his eyes, the corner of his lips turning down. "Why are you hiding from me?"

"It's bright in here."

"You think my reaction will be different than last night."

I peeked again through a crack in my fingers.

Shaking his head, he confirmed. "That's not going to happen."

"It might."

"It won't."

We sat there at a stalemate for long minutes.

Eventually, his fingers curled around my wrists. "I'm not going anywhere until you lift your hands."

"Please?"

"How am I supposed to kiss you good morning if I can't find your lips?"

My stomach flopped over. Oh God. He kissed so well. "You can't kiss me anymore."

He laughed. Then laughed some more.

Scowling, I looked between my fingers again.

"Move your hands, angel."

"No."

His fingers jabbed into my ribs and started to tickle. I squealed and tried to buck him off. All his boring, sad meals had made him strong, and he stayed right where he was.

Automatically, my hands came down to grab his, trying to get him to stop the attack.

Gasping, I realized what I'd done and tried to cover up again.

Nick stopped me. Catching my wrists, he pinned my arms above my head.

Well and truly caught, I went stock still, squeezing my eyes closed. I felt him staring. I felt his weight firmly on mine.

My skin tingled everywhere, his full attention making me itch.

A full minute later, his hands left mine. Sitting up, he released my arms but stayed straddling my hips.

Confused, I blinked up, our gazes colliding.

"Just right," he murmured. "Those blue eyes are just right for you."

Teeth sinking into my lower lip, I waited for what else he would do. But it was definitely not what I expected.

His chest nearly collided with mine when he leaned in, pressing butterfly kisses all over my face. The last one he gave was to my eyebrow, or rather, the thick scar that ran in the center of it.

"Nick," I whispered, my voice shaky.

Pulling back enough for us to see each other, he smiled. "You're so beautiful," he whispered. "I know you might not believe it, but I really wanted to say it out loud."

Everything in me recoiled from those words. I wanted to reject them almost the second they came out because there was no way anyone could think the way I looked was beautiful.

My heart wanted to believe him. The look deep in his eyes made me second-guess my mind.

Everything inside me felt unsteady when the palms of his hands dragged up my forearms and over my wrists, sliding against mine.

Our fingers closed around each other's, and his head dipped low. I lay completely still, allowing him to kiss me, but not kissing him back.

If he noticed, he gave no indication, instead tightening his fingers and changing the direction of the kiss.

This time, I moved under him. This time, my lips parted to meet his. He was a little more aggressive than he'd been last night in the dark. His lips more demanding, the sound of his breathing more labored.

Lifting my chin, I met his request. A split second of surprise made him falter, but then his tongue swept against mine and a low groan vibrated his throat.

"Good morning," he rasped when he finally set my lips free.

"Hi," I said, shy, turning so my good side was more visible than the bad.

He shook his head, untangling our hands, bringing my face back around. "Don't do that," he requested. "Don't ever hide from me."

"I don't scare you?" Just asking him that made my belly clench.

"No," he said simply, honesty ringing in the single word. "What does scare me is what you went through that left you like this."

I averted my gaze.

"About that…" he said, wariness in his tone.

I braced myself for the question, wondering just how in the hell I would answer.

"Did I scare you yesterday?"

Surprise made me look up at him. "What?"

"In the Viper. Did I scare you?"

Wrinkling my nose, I tried to understand. "Why would you have scared me?"

"I was driving pretty fast. I didn't think about it at the time…" His voice trailed off so he could clear his throat. "I realized later, last night in bed after you woke up screaming. You had a car accident, right?"

I blinked. "A car accident," I echoed.

He nodded. "That day at work, you told everyone about your leg. You said you had an accident years before…"

Oh. He thought I was like this because of a car accident. "I wish," I muttered to myself.

"What?"

"Oh, I—"

His eyes were so earnest and concerned. It pierced my heart that he thought anything he could do would bring up the horror of what I'd gone through.

I need no reminder. I never forget.

"It wasn't a car accident."

"It wasn't?"

I shook my head.

I could see the wheels. I knew he was asking himself if it wasn't that, then how was I like this.

He didn't ask.

"So I didn't scare you, then?"

I smiled. He was so incredibly sweet. "No. I like your car."

"What about me?" he teased. "You like me?"

I shrugged. "You're okay."

He tickled me again, and we ended up in a wrestling match in the center of the mattress with the blankets tangling around us.

"I **like you enough** for both of us," he confessed when we were breathing hard.

His face was incredibly close. His jade eyes were intensely sincere. The rise and fall of his naked torso against my upper body was short-circuiting my system.

"You don't have to," I confided, cupping his cheek with my hand. "I've got my part covered."

He groaned, burying his face in the side of my neck. "You're killing me."

"I need to take a shower."

His head popped up. "Need some help?"

"No!"

His chuckle filled the room as he rolled away. "Fine. When you're ready, come out to the kitchen. I want to introduce you to your new bodyguards."

"New bodyguards!" I exclaimed, sitting up. "What happened to the ones I had yesterday?"

"I fired them."

"What?"

Turning back to the bed, his eyes flashed, the square jaw everyone loved so much hardening. "You nearly got crushed by that sandbag."

I gasped. "It was an accident!"

"That's why I hired them. They should have had you out of the way before you were hit."

"It happened so fast."

"Then they should have lifted the bag off instantly."

"The director told everyone to stay back… The chain was faulty."

"All the more reason for them to intervene!" he yelled.

I sat back, not wanting to be alarmed by his outburst, but alarmed just the same. Glancing down and tucking my hands into my lap, I went quiet.

Nick cursed, his weight causing the mattress to dip.

"I'm gonna yell sometimes. And cuss. And get pissed off. Don't ever be scared of me. Don't ever back down. I will do a lot of things… but I will never hurt you."

Looking up, I whispered, "You speak like we're going to be around each other for a long time."

"We are."

"The movie is almost done filming."

His eyebrows rose into his forehead. "You think when the movie is done, we will be too?"

Confusion and hesitation hit me. Of course I thought that. Didn't he? What else was I supposed to think. I didn't have permanent relationships with people, aside from Carson, whom I also held at arm's length.

You didn't hold Nick at arm's length last night.

"Okay." He cajoled, somehow sensing the alarms going off inside me. "Take it easy. We'll talk about this later."

What was there to talk about?

"Just get ready and come meet the guards, okay?"

"I don't need bodyguards."

"I need you to have them."

Was that supposed to make me relent? It wouldn't. *It will.*

"My trainer is waiting," he said, cupping my head, leaning down to kiss the top.

When he was gone, I let out a shuddering breath. Reaching up to finger my scars, then staring at the indent his head left in the pillow next to mine, I felt the shift inside me.

I wasn't sure what it meant, but I knew nothing between us was going to be the same.

"Your phone is ringing," I told Zoey as I pulled the Viper into the production lot.

Wrinkling her nose, she glanced at me. "It's yours."

Lifting mine up, I showed her the black screen.

Surprise flashed over her features. "The only one that has my number is Carson and people for work…" Glancing at the screen, she said, "It's Carson."

"You gonna answer it?" I asked, amused.

Zoey was a conundrum. Wise, obviously, with pain and heartbreak but surprisingly innocent with so much.

"Carson?" she said, cutting off the ringtone. "I'm in the parking lot."

I could hear him erupt into a flurry of words I couldn't understand. Zoey gasped, her face screwing up into an odd expression.

"Wait, what?"

Again, I heard him talking, and Zoey fumbled around for the door handle. "I'm coming right now!"

"Zoey?" I called as she rushed out of the car. She didn't answer, so I jumped out and sprinted after her. "What's wrong?"

"Something happened," she said, not slowing her pace.

The black SUV with the bodyguards pulled up, and I signaled to them to follow.

The door to the makeup trailer was wide open, the weird atmosphere inside spilling out into the lot.

"Zoey!" I yelled, grasping her around the upper arm, stopping her from rushing inside.

"What?" She was exasperated.

"You can't just run in there."

Yanking her arm free, her eyes glinted. "I have to."

Like hell. I caught her again, holding her back until the bodyguards dashed in around her. Only then did I let her go.

She glared like I was in trouble, but I didn't care. I'd rather have her mad than in danger.

"Can I go now?" she snapped.

"I'll go first." I decided and went ahead.

She muttered something behind my back, but I didn't hear because the second I stepped inside, all my attention shifted.

Everyone was standing around Zoey's section near the back of the trailer. The two bodyguards had their backs turned, diligently checking out the room.

"What's going on?" Zoey asked, rushing past me.

The group of people parted, and her steps faltered. "Oh my God!" she exclaimed, rushing forward.

The bodyguard closest to her held out an arm, keeping her from walking into the middle of the mess.

And there was a mess.

A big one.

"That's my stuff!" she cried, pointing over his outstretched arm. "Let me pass."

"Let us check it out first, ma'am."

She made a sound and spun to me.

"Give them a second."

A strangled noise erupted from her, and she put her back to all of us, looking at Carson. "What happened?"

"We all came in from set, unlocked the trailer… and found this," he said, pressing a hand to his lips. "I just can't even…"

Zoey turned back to her station. All her supplies, her giant makeup kit… even the smaller box she often carried around was destroyed. It looked like a hurricane had ripped through.

The rolling cart was turned on its side. Every drawer was pulled out and dumped. Makeup scattered the floor. Mirrors were broken. Powder of all different colors dusted everything.

A few bottles of foundation were shattered, the thick liquid creating small puddles and splatters everywhere.

A strangled sound erupted from her as she stared at it all. Pushing past the bodyguard, she fell to her knees next to some of the shattered items and a broken lipstick. "It's all ruined."

Nearby, her smaller kit lay on its side, and she made her way to it, righting the box and opening the lid. There was nothing left. It was all busted and scattered all over the floor.

Even the chair we all sat in for her to work on us was covered in powder and creams.

Dropping a cracked lipstick on the floor, Zoey spun to look at Carson and then Laura. "Your stuff? Is it all ruined too?"

An awkward silence descended. She hadn't realized.

"Honey…" Carson began.

Zoey jumped up, moving around everyone toward Carson's station. It was untouched. Same with Laura's. In fact, the entire makeup trailer was in complete order—except for everything Zoey owned.

She took a moment to digest what she was seeing, then turned back to her destroyed belongings.

"It's just me," she murmured. Her sneakers crunched over some of the broken supplies, and she bent down to pick up a flat iron that had been broken in two. "Someone broke in here and destroyed only my things."

"I already called security," Carson offered, going forward to hold her hand.

Zoey turned toward her best friend. "This was years of supplies. Cultivated through experience and need." Carson nodded emphatically. "Thousands of dollars," she echoed, glancing down at everything. "Some of this was limited edition and can't be replaced…"

Carson hugged her. "A makeup artist's kit is like a limb to the artist. To lose it—"

"Why?" She interrupted. "Why would someone do this?"

The heartbreak in her voice made me angry. Seeing her standing with all of her hard work demolished at her feet like this brought out a primal desire to hunt down whoever did this.

Laura stepped forward. Her usually indifferent or even frosty attitude toward Zoey was subdued. Even she was horrified by this kind of betrayal. "Could it be a fan?"

Zoey released a strangled sound. "I don't have any fans."

Laura made a face, turning toward me. "I meant one of Nick's."

"What do you mean?"

"Well, you two have been in the headlines a lot. People are angry… Maybe one of your fans is jealous and taking it out on her?"

Pinching the bridge of my nose, I motioned to one of the guards. He was at my side in seconds. "Go check all the security footage on the lot. Check the gates. I want to know who did this."

He rushed off, and I glanced around at Zoey. She was still staring at the mess.

"How am I supposed to work?"

The director, head of security, and a few other key production people rushed in. As everyone looked around, tossed out theories, and pretty much gossiped about the newest set disaster, I watched Zoey.

Kneeling in the middle of the mess, she began to scoop up some of it, her hands instantly covered.

Seeing a tube of lipstick she thought survived, she lunged at it, hope sparking in her eyes. I watched her tug off the top and twist the bottom… only for a snapped and smashed nub of product to appear. It slid from her hands and rolled across the floor, bouncing into a broken brush.

I thought about how she woke up screaming last night. How brave she'd been when she let me look into her face. I thought about her playful mood this morning and then heard her whispered confession float through the back of my head.

She didn't deserve this.

Hadn't she been through enough?

Kneeling beside her, I wrapped a hand around hers. She tried to pull back, saying, "My hands are mess," but I refused to let go.

What could I say to make this better?

Nothing. Again, words felt like tokens when action would be more meaningful.

"Make a list of everything you lost. Get a projected cost of it all too." I glanced up at her friend. "Carson will help."

He nodded enthusiastically.

"Once it's done, you can submit it to the producers and get reimbursed." Spinning around to stand, I faced the director. "The studio will cover this, right? Because it happened on the lot."

He looked as if he'd swallowed a case of lemons, but he knew there was only one answer. "Of course. We have insurance for things like this." He looked at Zoey. "Do what Nick said. Get a list together."

"What about work?"

"We have a packed schedule 'til we finish." Someone holding a clipboard spoke up.

"We can get someone else in here to replace—"

Zoey gasped.

"No!" I said at the same time.

"It's the reasonable thing to do," the director refuted.

"Are you fucking kidding me right now?" I spat. "You want to fire her for something she wasn't responsible for? Punish her—the victim?"

"Of course not, Nick."

"Mr. Preston." I cut in, my voice unbending.

The director swallowed.

"Maybe I should call in Blair." I pulled out the big guns. "I think this qualifies as harassment in the workplace."

"We aren't the ones harassing her. We are just trying to—" One of the other clipboard holders jumped in.

The director held up his hand. "No one is getting fired. We can handle this. Zoey, see what you can salvage here, if anything. Then you can take the afternoon to go get the supplies you need for the next few days. Whatever you're missing, I'm sure some of the other artists here will be happy to share."

Carson agreed instantly, and then to my surprise, Laura agreed too.

"Thank you," Zoey said, her shoulders slumping with relief.

"Do it fast," he said, avoiding my gaze. "We can't afford any lost time on set."

"We'll step in and handle everything until she gets back," Carson asserted, tucking his arm around Laura.

Zoey turned toward the other artists. "Thank you both so much."

"Anything for you, girl," Carson told her.

"Deal with this," the director ordered a few staff and then turned to me. "Mr. Preston, I hope this makes you feel better about the working environment here."

I wasn't about to kiss his ass.

"Thanks for your cooperation." I agreed.

"I hope you will concur there is no reason to call in Blair."

"I won't call her," I said, giving him relief. "But since she's my mother, there's no telling when she might drop in."

Alarm filled his eyes, but he banked it quickly. "Sure. Sure." He cleared his throat. "Back to work!" he yelled.

Yep. I, a grown-ass man, just threatened another grown-ass man with my momma.

It worked.

Nobody messed with Blair Preston.

When most of the crowd went back to their jobs, Zoey sidled up to me. "Who's Blair?"

"My mother."

Her mouth fell open. I used the opportunity to touch her chin and snap her mouth shut. "Can you cover the cost of all the stuff you lost until they cut you a check?"

Pursing her lips, I watched her consider. She nodded once. "For the necessities to finish the shoot, I can. I'll just get the extras later."

"Get what you want. I'll cover it."

She made a face. "No way."

"Why not?"

"Because I can take care of myself."

"I know that."

"Then this conversation is over."

She started to spin away, but I caught the back of her T-shirt, towing her back. "You okay?" I asked against her ear.

She turned, eyes probing mine. "Do you really think this was one of your fans? The press hasn't died down at all?"

I frowned. I hadn't looked yesterday. Clearly, I should have. I made a mental note to have Callie check in with my manager.

Wait. Where the hell was Callie? Quickly, I took out my phone and sent her a text.

Where are you?

"It's still a hot topic," Carson said, coming in with all the info we needed about the press. "There is still a lot of speculation."

My phone buzzed with a reply from my wayward assistant. *Sorry! Busted pipe in my kitchen. Will be there as soon as the repair guy gets here!*

No worries, I texted back.

Zoey sighed, gazing at all her ruined supplies. I reached for her, but she slipped away. "You should have Carson get you ready for set. You're going to be late."

I wanted to stay with her, but I couldn't. Rumors were already rampant. I'd basically just threatened the director to protect her. I couldn't be late to set.

Before heading off to Carson's station, I moved up close behind her again. "The bodyguards will drive you. Don't go anywhere without them. If anything happens, call me."

"I'll be fine." She assured me, her voice much softer and relenting than I expected.

"Thank you."

Her eyes lifted to mine, a question clearly in her gaze.

"For not making me worry about you this afternoon."

"I'll be fine." She assured me.

She didn't realize how closely I paid attention to her. If she did, she might have tried to be more convincing.

I didn't know what was worse: the heat or the pain.

It seemed they worked together to make me as miserable as humanly possible. I was losing hope. Likely soon, my fate would match that of the dead body not too far from where I lay.

The back of my arm hurt so bad that sometimes I would black out. Or perhaps it was the dehydration, hunger, or overheating I was also inflicted with.

The cause didn't really matter, because I actually started to enjoy blacking out, because at least then there was nothing.

I wasn't sure what his plan was. The more time that passed, the more confused I became. I was weak and grower weaker, not even possessing the energy to mark the passage of time on the wall. Time was irrelevant anyway because time was not on my side.

Sometimes I would hear the faint ring of a school bell, which made me wonder where I was.

The long nightgown he forced me to put on stuck to my sweaty legs and tangled around the shackle at my ankle. Pushing up off the grungy floor, a wave of nausea rolled over me. My body heaved, spewing up nothing but making me feel like my soul was being ripped from my spine.

Collapsing back against the grimy, flaking pool floor, pain made me writhe. The long sleeves on the gown, though cotton, rubbed against the burn he'd inflicted on the back of my arm, and I would nearly black out from the friction.

Infused with the spirit of anger and hate, I pushed up, gripping the fabric near my shoulder and ripping the seams. Air brushed over the wound when the fabric was gone, and a tear slid over my cheek. I'd rather have this soiled oxygen rub it than the fabric.

Using the torn material to mop the sweat and blood from my face, I leaned back into the cracked wall. My cheek felt tight and throbbed, so I dabbed at it again, noting the white fabric was now red. When he'd forced me down and burned me, I'd cut my cheek on the bottom of the pool. I'd fought him when he ripped my clothes, and he'd hit me.

I tried to get away when he'd tugged this stupid gown over my head, and he took out a knife.

The body across from me was beginning to decay. The heat coupled with the conditions of this place seemed to rot her flesh faster every day. The odor had burned my nostrils until the smell no longer bothered me.

The rat came back, and I stared, unshocked, while it made a feast of her decomposing flesh.

The clanking sound of an old elevator way overdue for a repair echoed through the giant room, making my body shake uncontrollably. The doors creaked open, and the sound of the man's whistling floated through the otherwise stagnant room.

He always whistled the same song. It was a melody I would never forget.

I listened as he moved around, making more noise than he normally did. It sounded like he was moving things around or unpacking something he'd brought.

Fear slammed into me so hard my head snapped back against the wall. Dizziness washed over me, and I closed my eyes, listening.

Had he brought another girl?

When he'd brought me here, the other girl had still been alive... but she didn't stay that way for long.

I wouldn't beg and scream like she did for her life. No matter how much I wanted to live.

How many of us were there? How many more would there be?

Why was someone this sick? What could possibly incite this kind of behavior?

A wall of icy water slapped down from above. Shocked, I looked up, and another wave smacked me right in the face. Water surged up my nose, into my mouth, and burned the back of my throat. I started to choke and cough, raising my arms to protect my face.

The spray stung. The wounds on my face burned. The cuts and scrapes on my hands felt like they were being ripped open anew.

Skittering as far back as the chain allowed, I glanced up. He was standing on the edge of the pool, legs planted apart, those awful hiking boots gripping the ground. Clutched in his hand was a hose, which he was aiming right at me.

Water shot out again, blasting me right in the center of my body. The white cotton gown plastered to my body, offering a full view of everything beneath it.

As horrifying as it was, the cold water was welcome. It offered a surge of clarity I hadn't known in days. Some of the filth and sweat adhering to every part of me blissfully rinsed away.

Even though I wanted nothing from him, my arms lowered and I opened my mouth. I was so incredibly thirsty, the need for water outweighing any pride I had left.

I drank and drank until I coughed and spewed. Then I drank some more.

The water shut off as abruptly as it began, and he lumbered away, disappearing out of my line of vision. The weight of the wet fabric dragged at my weak body, but I lifted the long hem and used the drenched cotton to clean off my face and hands.

The man without a face stepped back to the edge, towering over the cage he kept me in. In his hand was a giant toolbox, and the horror nearly made me sink to my knees.

He stared at me for a long time. I felt his eyes roaming my body as he took in every detail. He hated me. He desired me. Above all else, he thought he owned me.

A tsking sound floated through the mouth hole of the inside-out mask, and he raised his hand to point at me.

He was unhappy. I'd done something to piss him off.

Even though I'd just been damn near dying of heat, I was cold now. Frigid, actually. The icy water he'd blasted me with coupled with the horror of whatever he was up to now made me numb.

He turned and walked away. Once again out of sight.

The sounds of scuffling, banging, and a host of other noises I didn't understand filled the space. I couldn't see any of what he was doing. All I could do was listen.

And then he climbed down into the pool. The crinkle of plastic accompanied him, and I watched wide-eyed as he went to the body lying close by.

He rolled what was left of her in a giant sheet of plastic. Rolling, rolling… until all I could see was the smears of red and brown streaking the inside of the plastic.

After tying some rope around her wrapped-up body, he hefted her over his shoulder. I stared at the stain her body left behind as he hauled her up out of the pool, leaving me down here completely alone.

More noise.

The crinkle of plastic.

A short while later, I felt him staring. Tilting my head up, I saw him looking down from above.

Holding up a bag, he dropped it beside me. It was another nightgown. A replica of the one I had on.

"Change. It's almost time."

He left. I knew if I didn't do something before he came back, I'd never have the chance again.

* * *

Phantom pain. Eighty percent of amputee's experience this at some point. As if the pain of losing a limb wasn't enough, a person had to experience painful sensations radiating from a part of them that was no longer there.

I experienced phantom limb pain quite a bit during the first few years after having my lower leg amputated. Eventually, it went away.

As I walked through the aisles of the beauty supply store, it haunted me once more. I felt the first twinge and brushed it off. The second twinge made me glance down at my sneaker.

The third twinge made me stumble into a rack and nearly brought me to my knees.

The guard closest to me rushed over, catching me around the waist to keep me upright.

"I'm okay." I gasped, reacquainting myself with the pain I thought I wouldn't have to feel again.

"What's happened?" The guard seemed concerned.

He snapped to the other man with us, and he rushed over, pulling out a phone.

"No!" I said, reaching out to stop him. "Don't call anyone."

"You need medical attention."

"No," I insisted, standing up to support myself. The guard was reluctant to release me, so I pushed his arm away. "I just stumbled. I'm completely fine."

I had to make a valiant effort to keep my throbbing foot flat on the floor. The urge to reach down and massage the ankle screaming at me was real.

It would do no good. I couldn't massage an ankle that wasn't even there. Rubbing the prosthetic would result in absolutely nothing.

The pain was something I had to feel. To live with. To remember.

It seemed fair I had to lose the leg yet have my body remember the pain.

I wouldn't mind the pain if I'd been able to keep the limb.

It didn't work like that, though, at least not for me.

"I'll call Mr. Preston." The guard decided.

I snatched the phone out of his hand. "You will not!"

"But he said—"

"I don't care what he said!"

"He's paying us, ma'am."

"He's not paying you to interrupt his workday for no reason at all. I'm fine!" I insisted, then walked down the aisle, turned, and came back. "See?"

Reluctantly, they nodded. I handed him the phone. "I'm almost done here. Then we head back to set."

They returned to guarding, and I went back to throwing things in the basket I was carrying.

Why now? Why was this happening now?

The dreams were more frequent; the panic was harder to control. I'd felt like I was being watched before, and now this.

It almost seemed as if my body was warning me, as if deep inside, I sensed something... *someone*.

My leg buckled under my own weight, and sharp stabbing pain shot into my hip. Biting down on my lip and gripping the end of the aisle, I bent my head, trying to breathe through the pain.

It's not really there. It's just a memory. Your body is playing tricks on you. Your brain is just confused.

The mantra was nice, but it didn't make the pain any less real.

"Ma'am?"

Taking a deep breath, I spun, shoving the basket with all my supplies at the bodyguard. "I need to use the restroom."

His arms closed around the basket, and he signaled to his partner to follow me.

Quickly, I limped to the bathroom with the man scurrying behind me. His body brushed against mine, making me yelp.

"I'm sorry," he said, pulling open the door to hold it open.

A shuddering breath left my lips. "It's okay. I'm just jumpy from earlier."

"Understandable," he said, an unreadable expression on his face.

I started ahead, and he grabbed my arm, stopping me. "Wait."

He went into the bathroom, checking to make sure I could pee in peace. I couldn't help but wonder how much one was paid to check the toilet before his client used it.

"I'll wait right here," the guard said, appearing again.

"I hope Nick pays you well," I muttered.

I was pretty sure I heard him laugh the second I stepped through the door. Once I was alone, I let the pain twist my face and nearly dragged the prosthetic across the room until I could lean against the sink.

Even though I knew I would see nothing, I lifted the pant leg and stared at the foot and pylon (the parts of my prosthetic that made up my "ankle").

I had no way of knowing when the pain would stop. It could be moments. It could be days.

I turned on the faucet, allowing cool water to run through my fingers. I wanted so badly to splash it over my face, but that would ruin the makeup I had in place.

Instead, I drank from the palm of my hand, hoping the feeling of the cool water sliding down my throat would be enough. It wasn't. In fact, the drink didn't slide anywhere at all. It lodged in my closing throat like it wanted to choke me.

Panic clenched my chest and my hand flew up to my neck, grabbing like I could somehow push the water down.

Struggling to swallow, struggling to drag in even a small breath of air, the attack slammed into me, making my knees buckle. I slid to the floor, where I sat shivering and shaking as phantom pain and dread took control of my body… and my mind.

* * *

He'd brought a ladder.

A rickety wooden one that rose toward the exposed rafters. Sitting at the very top was the toolbox I'd seen him carrying.

I can use whatever's inside.

It didn't even matter what it was. Anything was better than nothing. I could find something to maybe free me from this chain.

Of course, the ladder was in sight but out of reach. As if he'd put it there to taunt me, to show me how close yet how very far away escape really was.

I'd all but given up before, but now my will was reignited. The frigid water, the way he'd taunted me… Glancing over my shoulder, I looked at the dark stain marring the pool floor across the way.

If I didn't do something, the next stain down here would be mine.

Even though I knew it was probably useless, I began fighting with the shackle around my ankle. I tried before to get my foot out, going as far as breaking the skin and using my own blood as lubrication.

All that resulted in was pain and blood loss.

As I fought again, more blood welled from the unhealed wounds. Wiping my red fingers on the ruined gown, I got up, dragging the pained foot toward the wall and staring up at the ladder.

I just needed something… My eyes focused on the crumbling wall nearby. Some sections still had broken tile, even though most of the pool was crumbling plaster. The chain tugged me backward as I ran forward, ignoring the pain in my leg from overextending it. Using my bare hands, I began clawing at the wall, drawing blood, reinjuring wounds as I picked and pulled.

Pieces of tile and chunks of wall came off, landing in a mess at my bare feet.

Eventually, one whole tile broke off, landing in my palms. Victorious, I rushed over and steadied myself, throwing the tile up at the toolbox.

It missed.

I heard it break when it hit the floor above.

Rushing back I pulled another chunk of tile free and threw it above. Again and again, I repeated this, sometimes hitting the underside of the box, sometimes missing completely.

With trembling arms and legs, I collapsed into a heap, weeping in frustration.

"Why?" I yelled, my voice echoing.

The bag with the clean gown caught my attention. There was something else inside. Lunging for it, my dirty hands snatched up a plastic water bottle.

I tested the weight of it in my hand and smiled.

This was it. My last chance. If I didn't do it this time, I might as well slit my wrists with the tiles.

Closing my eyes, I took a steadying breath.

"Please…" I whispered. Then using the last bit of strength I had, I tossed the bottle up.

It crashed against the bottom of the toolbox, knocking it off the ladder. The loud banging sound it made as it tumbled down made me crouch and cover my head.

I heard the contents spill out everywhere. Ping! Pang! Thump!

When everything fell quiet, I uncovered my head.

The toolbox was still somewhere above… but a few tools had fallen down to me.

A surge of hope gave me energy as I scuttled around, gathering my treasure. A screwdriver, a few nails…

Over there!

I had to stretch and claw at the ground to reach it. My bones felt like they were separating from their sockets, but when my hand closed around the handle of that hammer, triumph soothed the worst of my pain.

Using one of the nails and then the screwdriver, I tried to pick the lock keeping the steel around my ankle.

"Ahh!" I screamed when the screwdriver slipped, stabbing into the already damaged flesh. Pitching to the side, I vomited the water I'd drunk from the hose.

Feeling hollow and wrung out, I sat back, convincing myself not to give up.

Next, I tried beating the chain with the hammer, hoping it would break and I could run free. The chain was stronger than the hammer, and my entire foot was bathed in red. The constant struggle to get free had taken its toll.

My strangled cry bounced up to the rafters, and I lay back, staring up into the shadows. The chain tugged, making me wince, but it gave me an idea.

Rising on shaking legs, my arms hanging limply at my sides, I shuffled to the wall where the chain was bolted in.

Bolted into the crumbling, weakened wall.

The iron and chain were too strong to break… but the plaster it was anchored in was not.

Gripping the hammer, I brought it down against the wall. Plaster and dust exploded everywhere, particles slapping my cheeks and going into my eyes. Satisfied, I hit the wall again.

Again.

Again.

Each time, it crumbled a little more. With each hit, I grew weaker but even more determined.

I hammered until I collapsed, shaking and dizzy. The metal plate anchoring the chain to the wall was wobbling, hanging crookedly from the crumbling plaster.

One. More. Hit.

Raising the hammer above my head, swaying on my feet, I summoned the very last bit of will I had inside me and brought it down as hard as my body would allow.

The hit vibrated my arms and legs, stinging my hands and making the hammer fall to the floor. I fell back, my arms flailing at my sides, grappling at thin air. My bloody heel slipped as I stumbled, propelling me back even more.

I slammed into the ground so hard I was momentarily stunned. When reality seeped back in, I felt the splashing of water against my ear.

Horrified, I sat up, shuddering.

I landed in the puddle of stagnant water. Oh God, the way it smelled.

Wait…

How did I get over here? This filthy water had been something I couldn't reach. Scrambling up, I braced all the weight I had on my right leg because my left foot could no longer bear anything but pain.

That's when I realized. Staring in disbelief, I started to sob.

That last hit… the force of my fall… It pulled the anchor out of the wall.

I was free.

Traffic in L.A. was a bitch, but there were ways around it. My entire body leaned with the turn as I pulled into the parking lot, driving right up onto the sidewalk near the doors.

Shutting down the engine with one hand and ripping off the helmet with the other, I didn't even think about the possibility of the press being around.

A rush of conditioned air blasted me when I dashed inside, a bell on the door signaling my arrival.

One of the bodyguards I'd hired stepped around the corner, glancing in the direction of the sound. Surprise flickered over his features when he saw it was me. "That was fast."

"Where is she?" I demanded, stalking through the store.

One of the employees appeared and gave me one of those gaping shocked looks. "Nick Preston?"

"Please don't tell anyone I'm here until after I leave," I pleaded, rushing by.

"She's in the bathroom." The bodyguard continued our conversation as if we hadn't been interrupted. As he spoke, he pointed in the direction I needed to go.

The second man I'd hired stood outside the door, blocking anyone else from going inside.

"She's been in there a while," he reported. "I yelled through the door. She said she was fine."

I didn't have to tell him to move. The look on my face said it for me. He stepped aside, and I yanked the ladies' room door open and barged inside. "Zoey!"

She was sitting in the middle of the floor, dark head bowed, hands clutched in the center of her lap. Her eyes, which were bloodshot and slightly unfocused, widened. "Nick?"

Dropping into a low crouch, I reached for her hand, which was unnaturally cold. "What happened? Why are you on the floor?"

"What are you doing here?" She wondered, staring at our linked hands.

The sound of rushing water made me look up and around. The middle sink was turned on, a stream of water rushing down the drain. Without releasing her hand, I leaned up to shut it off.

"Did you fall? Why didn't you call out for help?" I worried, giving her fingers a squeeze.

"I told them not to call you."

"Calling me is their job."

"I don't want bodyguards." She grumped, and I had to fight the urge to smile.

"Are you hurt?" I demanded.

Her eyes lowered. "I had a panic attack," she mumbled.

Letting out a relieved breath, I grasped her around the arms to help tow her upright. "Did you take your meds?"

She nodded. "I was waiting for them to kick in before I went back out there."

Nodding, I pushed her head down onto my shoulder, surrounding her with my arms. To my surprise, she cuddled in, letting out a quiet sigh.

My stomach flipped, and a surge of adrenaline shot through me. Such a small thing, but the impact it had was enormous.

Sure, I'd held her before. Hell, last night, she slept in my arms. But this was a first. She came to me almost willingly, as though she'd been waiting or craving the comfort I could provide.

Usually, she was hesitant and reaching out seemed to cost her something. Right now, she took, willingly soaking in something she needed, and what she needed was me.

Ah, fuck. I was so gone.

She owned me now. My heart was bought and paid for by a woman I'd only kissed twice.

"I'm glad you're here," she whispered.

My fingers curled into my palms. I really didn't think I'd ever heard sweeter words. I was winning her over. Little by little.

"What happened earlier, is that what caused the panic attack?"

She was quiet for a moment. Then I felt her head shake. "Sometimes I have flashbacks."

"Flashbacks," I echoed, wrinkling my nose.

"I was at a place like this the day of my accident…" Her voice trailed away, arms withdrawing.

As she pulled away, my body tightened, ready to keep her near.

Turns out I didn't have to fight for her because she stayed close on her own, tucking her arms between us, resting her palms on the width of my chest.

Without thought, I kissed the top of her head. "From now on, when you need to come here, I'll come with you."

"We should go," she said, slipping away.

Turning her back, she adjusted her shirt, then pulled her hair into a ponytail, holding it for a moment before letting it fall back into place. When she turned back, a few strands already clung to her cheek and neck.

"Do you want to pull your hair back?"

"Always," she quipped. "But I only ever do that when I'm alone."

Ah, her hair was just another shield she wore.

How exhausting.

"C'mon." I held out my hand. "Let's finish getting what you need so we can go."

Her hesitation didn't deter me. I just grasped her hand and towed her along behind me. The guards didn't even glance down at our clasped hands when we came out of the bathroom. One stood alert, gazing around the shop, and the other stood dutifully holding her shopping basket.

"Thank you," she said, reaching for it.

Clearing his throat, he gripped it harder. "It's my pleasure to carry it."

I saw a protest forming on her lips, so I squeezed her hand.

"Thank you." She relented. "I think I have everything I need for right now. I'll just pay. Then we can go."

The cashier stared at me the entire time she rang up Zoey's stuff.

"You didn't call the press, did you?" I asked, leaning on the counter.

She hit some button, and the computer made a weird sound. Alarmed, she quickly corrected what she did and then giggled. "Of course not."

There was a stack of paper sacks on the counter. I snatched one up and then leaned farther over the counter toward the girl.

"Can I borrow your pen?" I asked, pointing to the ballpoint stuck behind her ear.

She nodded.

I plucked it from its place and went back to my side of the counter. Zoey stared between me and the cashier with wide eyes.

I glanced at her and winked.

"What's your name?" I asked the girl.

"Sophie."

"Well, Soph," I said, scrawling a personalized message across the paper. "Can I call you Soph?"

She nodded emphatically.

"Thank you for keeping this little visit between us. I'm sure I'll be back from time to time."

The girl blinked. "You shop for makeup?"

I laughed. "No. But my girl does."

"Y-your girl…"

Zoey kicked me. I didn't even flinch.

Flashing a smile, I handed the pen and autograph over. "Maybe don't tell the press about that either."

"Can I take a selfie with you?"

I hopped over the counter and leaned close to her, throwing up two fingers. Once the photo was taken, I pulled out some cash, but Zoey made a sound and handed over her card instead.

I let it slide because I was already getting away with a shit ton of shenanigans today.

It was a good day, huh?

The guards went outside first, then held the door open when they deemed it safe for us to leave the store.

"What the hell was that?" Zoey asked, turning on me the second we were on the sidewalk.

"I take selfies with fans a lot."

"I wasn't talking about the selfie."

"The autograph, then? Figured she earned it since she didn't call all her friends."

"*Nick*," she growled.

"I kinda like it when you growl like that."

Bright pink bloomed on her cheeks, her lips snapping shut.

Chuckling, I pulled the keys out of my pocket and tossed them to the closest bodyguard. "Can you drive a bike?"

He glanced between the keys and the motorcycle parked beside us. "Yes."

"Good. Follow us back to the studio. I'll ride with Zoey in the SUV."

"You have a motorcycle?" she exclaimed.

"It's not mine. It's one of the producers'."

"What are you doing with it?"

"I needed to get here fast. The traffic would have slowed me down in the Viper."

Her mouth dropped open. "You—"

I stepped closer to her. "Yep. I violated my contract just to come see you."

She frowned. "It says in your contract you can't drive a motorcycle?"

"I'm worth a lot of money. They don't want me doing shit that could wreck this face." I quipped, pointing to myself. "Sexiest man alive, remember?"

Something akin to hurt flashed behind her eyes. It was there and gone so fast I almost missed it. Almost.

Too late, I realized what I said.

"Zoey."

Her chin tilted up. Serious brown eyes zeroed in on mine. "Why would you violate your contract like that?"

I took a step forward. "Because you needed me."

Surprise crossed her face once more. "We should go." Spinning around toward the parking lot, she nearly pitched sideways off the sidewalk.

"Whoa," I said, catching her around the waist.

Her breathing was uneven when our eyes connected. For long electric moments, attraction and chemistry zinged between us.

Scrambling back, she tugged anxiously at her hair.

Feeling like I wanted to get away with even more than I already had, I slid my hand around hers. She jolted, glancing down in shock.

"What are you doing?" she demanded, her voice breathless.

"Helping you to the car," I answered casually. "You seem a little unsteady on your feet."

"Am not!" she shot back.

But she didn't pull her hand from mine.

The paper clutched in my hands crumbled beneath my anger. The way it crushed and wrinkled was like a surge of oxygen right into my lungs.

Slanting my attention back to the headlines on the screen, I realized.

At first, I thought these were just rumors. I thought it was promotion for a film.

Until I saw them that day on set. I noted the way he looked at what was mine.

He'd shielded her with his body. Ushered her into his car. They disappeared behind the gates of his property and didn't reappear until morning.

She had protection. Two men shadowing her every move. He hired bodyguards. Trying to keep me from what was mine!

And now this! The entire dashboard vibrated beneath the force of my fist. How dare he show up here—at our meeting place!

The edge of the paper sliced into my finger, and the prick of pain brought me back.

After today, she'd understand that I was the one in charge. She couldn't hide behind makeup, behind the gates of the set, especially not behind him.

Smiling, I uncrumpled the paper, smoothing out the wrinkles to stare down at the words.

Soon, everyone would know exactly where she belonged.

"Where's the beef?" Carson asked, motioning to my one shopping bag filled with new supplies.

"In your pants?" I quipped without even thinking.

He didn't miss a beat. "Well, *obviously,* I'm well equipped, but you seem to be lacking." Shuffling over in his rainbow sequin Converse, he peered in the bag like there might be a lizard there and not makeup. "Honey, I thought you went shopping?"

"I'm tired," I said, sinking into my chair. There was still a powdery residue clinging to it from earlier.

A sympathetic sound floated over my head. "I'll take care of it. Leave all the supplies to me."

An unexpected weight lifted off me, and I perked up. "Really?"

Waving his hand, he said, "What are besties for?"

"I'll give you my card before we leave later."

"Shopping with someone else's money. My favorite thing. Besides beef that is."

I made a gagging sound.

"Girl, you brought it up." He gave me the side eye. "Dirty ho."

I laughed. It felt good. It seemed like forever since I'd last laughed. Since I'd last felt relaxed and carefree. More and more unfortunate things were happening. My grip on reality was starting to shake. I felt my insides beginning to crumble.

I had a bad feeling. A feeling I couldn't seem to make go away.

"So," Carson whispered, perching on the arm of my chair, "was that Nick I saw speeding out of the lot on someone's motorcycle just a bit ago and then returning inside the SUV you left in?"

My cheeks heated. Shyness and also maybe a little bit of excitement bloomed within me. "Maybe," I answered, picking at a loose string on my jeans.

"One minute, he was sitting in my chair, getting did, and the next, he was answering his phone and running out the door."

"I told them not to call him," I murmured to myself.

"I, for one, enjoy seeing that sexy specimen of a man running around after you." Sighing, he put a hand over his heart. Today, he was dressed in a powder-blue button-up dress shirt with the top few buttons undone and the collar turned up around his jaws. "You lucky bitch."

"He just feels responsible because of the press," I said, not wanting him to make too much out of it.

Or maybe it was myself I was reminding.

Thinking back to last night when he peeled away the hood and saw the truth of who I really was… Since that moment, I'd been struggling.

Struggling not to fall. Struggling not to think of him, rely on him… *want* him.

Someone like him could never actually want someone like me. We were incompatible. A modern day Beauty and the Beast. We might be thrown together right now, but that would shift and change… Who I was never would.

Remember that, Zoey.

"Don't make me smack those falsies right off your face," Carson scolded.

Offended, I reached up to gently feel the false lashes lining my eyes. "You wouldn't dare."

"Girl, no. That's a cardinal sin." Pursing his lips, he pointed a manicured finger at me. Yep. He got manicures. "You shouldn't sell yourself short."

"I'm not. I just know my place."

He raised a sculpted brow.

I sighed. "I'm behind the scenes in the makeup trailer. He's in front of the camera, made for the spotlight."

"The way he acts says the only spotlight he sees shines right down on you."

Butterflies floated around in my belly. "Ugh, enough," I said, pushing out of the chair, making him stumble off the arm. "I need to try and organize this."

"Make a list as you go of all the stuff you didn't buy."

Hefting the smaller kit I often carried around onto the counter, I frowned down at how light it felt now. My frown deepened when I noticed the lock on it was broken. "Great," I muttered.

"Look here." Carson beckoned, right beside me again.

I turned, and he started dabbing my face with blotting papers.

"What are you doing?" I asked, flinching away.

"You've been sparkling. And Lord knows that look isn't for anyone. Not even Edward Cullen."

FYI: Carson was obsessed with *Twilight*.

His joke was funny, but I didn't laugh. I was too busy feeling my stomach twist because his hands were on my face. Close to my scars. Close to all the work I did to cover them. I had broken out in a clammy sweat when I'd been freaking out in the bathroom. I had gulped down a few handfuls of water from the faucet when I took my pills…

Jerking away from Carson, I spun toward the giant mirror behind us to make sure all the coverage was still in place.

"You're still covered."

My eyes met his in the mirror. A knowing look passed between us.

"You saw the photo online," I practically mouthed.

"Briefly."

"Carson, I—" For once, I felt absolutely guilty for hiding my face. I'd never experienced this feeling before. I never, not even for a brief second, felt like I was deceiving anyone by hiding the way I looked. To me, it was about survival.

He held up his hand. "Stop there."

"What?"

He tugged me around, guiding me into the chair. "You don't owe me an explanation. I understand."

"How could you?"

Patting a fluffy brush into the lid of some loose powder, he changed his words. "Maybe I don't. But we're friends, so it doesn't matter."

"Most people would feel betrayed."

"I am not most people."

"Hashtag fact."

"Mm-hmm." He agreed. The brush moved over my face as he fixed my makeup. "But I do hope you know I'm not the type to judge a person. I know all too well what judgement feels like."

My hand covered his, stopping his movements. "You are the best person I know. You're the only friend I have. I didn't say anything because I just wanted to keep you all to myself. You're the only thing in my life that doesn't have baggage."

He handed the powder and brush to me so he could reach into his fanny pack (white today) to pull out the hot-pink fan he always carried. "You're going to ruin my makeup," he blubbered, fanning his face while tilting it up toward the ceiling.

I started tearing up too. My God, I was an emotional wreck.

When he was sufficiently fanned, he went back to fixing my face. "No pressure, but if you ever want to talk, I'll listen. I won't even give you my opinion."

I laughed. "Liar."

"My opinions are very wise."

"They are." I agreed. After another moment, he lowered the powder and reached for a lipstick. "Thank you," I said, meeting his eyes. "Someday, I'll tell you everything, okay?"

He waved away my words like it was no big deal, but I knew he was touched. "I'd rather you tell me every detail about how good Mr. Sexiest Man Alive is in bed."

I gasped, making the lipstick he was applying smear.

He looked at the mess, pursing his lips. "You probably looked like that after he kissed you senseless. *Amirite?*"

"Carson! Oh my God!"

"You ain't denying it."

"I have *not* slept with him!"

"But you kissed."

My gaze slid away, and I was pretty sure my face turned fifteen shades of red.

"I better be maid of honor at the wedding."

I smacked him. "Stop!"

"I'm not wearing green."

"Fix my lipstick," I demanded.

He heckled, and I tried not to smile. A little best friend time was exactly what I needed.

I knew Nick entered the trailer before I even laid eyes on him. As I mentioned before, the air in every room changed when he walked in. Something about his presence altered everything around him. And now his presence altered everything *inside* me.

I am in trouble.

"Has anyone seen or talked to Callie today?" he asked the room.

Peeking around Carson, I saw him frowning at his phone.

Everyone shook their heads.

Josh, who was across the room in Laura's chair, spun around to look at Nick. "You haven't seen her at all today?"

"No," he muttered. "She texted this morning that she would be late because of a busted pipe, but that was hours ago. She hasn't called or answered any of the messages I've left since."

"Maybe she lost her phone. Seems like something she would do," Laura offered.

"But she would still be here," Nick insisted.

"Maybe she's sick?" Carson suggested.

Nick thought about it, then shook his head. "Something doesn't feel right."

"Do you have any contact information for her friends or family?" Josh asked, concern clear on his handsome face.

"No."

"Do you have her address?" I asked.

Nick glanced up at me, and damn, if I couldn't help but notice the way his green eyes softened just a little. "Of course."

"Maybe you should go check on her."

With a decisive nod, he tucked the cell into his jeans while his long legs ate up the distance between us. Carson moved aside as he reached for my hand, tugging me out of the chair. "Good idea. Let's go."

"Me?" I gaped.

"It was your suggestion." He countered.

"But she's your secretary."

"And I already left you alone once today. How did that go?"

I gasped.

Carson snickered, and I shot him an evil eye. He didn't look threatened at all. *Brat.*

Twisting my arm out of his grasp, I skittered away. "I have to work."

"Bring it. You can organize that at home," he refuted, gesturing to all my stuff.

"I already offered to do it." Carson cut in.

I was going to kill him. No. I was going to shave off one of his eyebrows. People in New York would hear him shriek.

"Good man." Nick grabbed my hand again, gripping my fingers like a vise. He turned to go but stopped abruptly, making me slam into his back.

"Ow," I said, rubbing my forehead and scowling.

He turned, coming so close we bumped together and the toe of one shoe covered mine. "Let me see," he murmured quietly, brushing at my bangs.

"It's fine," I muttered, trying to push away his hand.

He didn't allow it, and I was incredibly aware of all the eyes watching us. In fact, it was making my skin crawl. I didn't like attention like this. And right now, we were the focus of all of it.

Staying still, I let him look at my forehead, which was perfectly fine. His eyes caressed mine when he was done, and his fingers brushed the bangs back into place.

The way he stared made my mouth run dry, and my fingers curl into my palms. My tongue pressed against the roof of my mouth, practically anticipating meeting his.

He wanted to kiss me. If we'd been alone, he already would have.

I wanted him to.

Clearing his throat, he moved so I was blocked by his wide shoulders.

"Jessica," he said, deflating all the eagerness rushing through my limbs.

"Are you living together?" she demanded.

My entire body stiffened, panic washing over me.

"Why would you think that?" Nick replied mildly, crossing his arms over his chest like he was bored.

"You said *at home*."

"Which she has." Nick led.

Jessica made a rude sound. "We all know someone broke into her place and took pictures of her." Leaning around Nick, she gave me an appraising glare. Nick shifted, cutting her off. "And you two have been arriving in the same car every morning. She's being followed around by your bodyguards."

"They aren't mine." Nick denied.

"They're from the company you use."

Nick seemed tired of the questions. "What's your point, Jessica?"

"Are you involved?"

"I don't really think that's your business."

"I'm your leading lady!"

"In a movie," he replied, "not in real life."

I sucked in a breath. His words were like a pointy stick aimed at an already riled-up bear.

Jessica made a sound that I imagined a volcano also made before it erupted. My hand brushed over the small of Nick's back, fingers curling into the shirt he wore. It was a white dress shirt, the material stiff and ironed.

It wasn't what I wanted, and before I even thought about it, I was tugging the tucked ends up so I could slip my fingers beneath to find the warmth of his skin.

He didn't even react.

But I did.

The second his heat seeped into my cold fingers, it was like being zapped by electricity. Like being woken from some kind of trance.

Horrified, I looked down. My hand was definitely doing that. Definitely pushed up under the shirt I'd just pulled loose, my skin definitely touching his.

I pulled back so violently I lost my balance and tumbled. My side hit the chair, making it spin and allowing me to fall farther.

Distressed, Carson knelt beside me as I winced at the pain in my side. "Today is not your day," he said, reaching down to help me.

My attention automatically shifted as someone much larger than my best friend loomed behind him. Nick's eyes were stormy, and I could tell he was running out of patience.

I am a lot of trouble. More trouble than I'm worth.

"I'm fine," I insisted, allowing Carson to pull me to my feet. My body was freaking exhausted. Between the sandbag, the nightmare, the panic attack, and now this, I felt like I could sleep for an entire week and still need more rest.

Nick's hand clapped down on Carson's shoulder, making his brown eyes round in surprise. He moved aside, and Nick stepped close.

He didn't touch me. He didn't say anything. He stared at me with those thundery eyes. As he did, he tugged the rest of his shirt out of his waistband, letting it fall against his hips.

I swallowed thickly, sure everyone heard the sound.

"Get your bag," he intoned quietly.

It was an order, and I obeyed.

The second it was in my hand, he took the other one, pulling me into his side. Jessica was standing there gaping… and so was everyone else.

"I'm going to check on my assistant, and I'm taking Zoey with me," he announced like he dared anyone to even breathe.

I scrambled to keep up with his long strides, making me feel like I was not as tall as I actually was.

"What about filming?" Jessica called.

He didn't even stop or look back. "My scenes for the day are shot. I'll be here for my call time tomorrow."

The bodyguards fell into step behind us as we went across the lot. Tugging me around the passenger side of the Viper, Nick flung open the door and pinned me with a look.

I climbed in, not even considering defying him. Danger simmered around him, and that smolder everyone loved so much was burning a hole through everything it touched.

I waited for the door to slam, anticipating the loud bang, but it never came.

Instead, I found myself surrounded. Like a lion closing in on his prey, he leaned into the car, caging me against the leather with his muscular arms.

"I-I'm sorry." I apologized, not even knowing what I was sorry for.

His intensity was making me jittery. It was also making me melt. My thighs squeezed together, and my hands gripped the edge of the seat.

Eyes flaring, he dove forward, lips claiming mine like he owned them and didn't have to ask. He kissed me deeply without even penetrating my mouth. The power with which he sucked made my cheeks collapse and my chest puff out. The sound of him inhaling through his nose rang in my ears, and it felt like he wasn't breathing, but devouring everything I was.

Even as he pulled away, his lips clung to mine like Velcro refusing to release. The sound of us breaking apart was clear, and I collapsed back into the seat, still confined by his arms.

Our stares locked and held. I wouldn't have been able to look away if a bomb went off a yard away. Even when his hand took hold of mine, my eyes stayed on his.

Shifting just enough, Nick raised my fingers beneath the hem of his shirt, pressing them against his sculpted abs. I tried to pull away, but his hand covered mine, pinning it in place.

"You can touch me whenever you want," he told me.

"I-I… I—" Oh, I was nervous. My tongue wasn't the only thing stuttering just then. My heart was too. "I d-didn't realize what I was doing."

Again, he said, "You can touch me whenever you want."

"Everyone probably saw," I whispered, dismayed.

"A room full of people or one with just us, I'll never deny you."

Oh, holy shit. I was no match for this. For him.

I stopped breathing altogether when he tugged my hand from beneath his shirt to press a kiss against my knuckles.

"Take the rest of the day off," he called to the guards just before he closed the car door.

I realized then it didn't matter how I tried to shield my heart from Nick. He was powerful enough just to take it.

44

moth

The sound of someone falling over on the other side of the door was followed by a muffled cry of pain.

This is going to be so easy.

Seconds later, the door swung open. "Oh, thank God!" she exclaimed.

Her blond hair and blue eyes were perfect. Her place next to him was also perfection.

Two birds. One stone.

I smiled from under the baseball hat I wore. "Got yourself an emergency?"

"The pipe burst in my kitchen, and I can't find the shutoff valve. My entire apartment is turning into a swimming pool."

The corners around my eyes crinkled with my laugh. "Good thing I got here before you floated away."

Waving me in, she stepped back. "Hurry, come in!"

The tools in the toolbox I carried rattled when I stepped inside. Water was indeed spewing all over the kitchen. Exclaiming about the mess, I rushed to the sink, climbing beneath it to shut off the water.

"It was under there this whole time!" She gasped, standing nearby, peering under the cabinet where I lay.

Chuckling, I said, "It'd be hard to find if you didn't know what you were looking for."

"Well, thank goodness you do! Thanks for getting here so quickly."

"Just doing my job," I replied, coming out from under the cabinet. The coveralls I wore were already wet from the knees down, my chest splattered with water drops.

Shifting from foot to foot, the small blond chewed her lower lip. A rush of adrenaline I hadn't felt in seven long years surged through my veins, making me feel alive.

"How long do you think this will take to fix?"

"Shouldn't be too long. Just need to replace the section of pipe."

"I'm already late for work." She worried.

Opening the toolbox, I reached inside. "I'll get started right away so you can get on with your day."

"Ugh, thank you so much!"

I smiled.

"Can I get you anything?" she asked, going to the refrigerator. "How about a water or some juice while you work?"

"Juice sounds refreshing."

Leaning inside, she shuffled a few things around to find the juice. She had on a long dress that skimmed the floor when she moved.

It was like a nightgown.

Finding a small bottle of juice, she pulled up out of the icebox. "Ah!" she yelped when her body collided with mine.

"Oh," she said, her blue eyes widening. "I didn't see you there."

Nervous energy skittered around her, and I breathed in deep.

"Here's the juice," she said, holding it out while backing away. She couldn't go far, though, because the appliance was at her back.

Ignoring the juice, I took in all her features. *She will do. She will do nicely.*

"Did you change your mind?" she asked, her voice turning wary. Still extending the juice between us, she asked, "Would you like something else instead?"

Behind my back, my hand gripped tighter around the hammer.

I smiled.

"Actually, I would."

Knock, knock.

No answer.

Knock, knock!

Nothing.

Dropping my closed fist from the red door, I spun around, looking to see if anything seemed amiss.

Everything appeared fine, but the sense of foreboding inside me continued to grow. "Why isn't she answering?" I muttered, running a hand through my hair.

"Try calling her," Zoey suggested.

The ringing on the other end of the line was echoed by a simultaneous muffled ring. Zoey's hand grabbed my forearm. "I can hear her cell ringing inside."

Banging my fist on the door again, I yelled. "Callie! Callie, it's Nick. Open the door!"

The sound of the ringing phone stopped, and against my ear, her voicemail came on.

"Callie!" I yelled, banging again.

"Didn't you say she had a busted pipe?"

I nodded.

A worried look crossed her features. "You don't think she slipped and fell, do you?"

Grasping her sides carefully, I nudged her backward. "Stand back."

"What are you—"

Crraaack! The sound of splintering wood filled the air. The door sagged on its hinges. Glancing around to make sure Zoey was still in the clear, I brought my foot down on the door again. It burst inward, hitting against the wall and springing back.

"Wait here," I ordered, pushing the door wide and stepping inside.

"Callie?" I called, roaming around the empty apartment for my assistant. "Callie, it's Nick!"

Stepping farther inside, I saw her phone on the counter dividing the kitchen from the rest of the space. The bag she always carried lay right beside it.

I yelled her name again, rushing into the bedroom and the adjoining bath.

"She's not here?" Zoey was standing in the center of the living room, her features drawn and pale.

"No. But all her stuff is," I said, gesturing to the counter.

Grabbing her bag, Zoey dumped the contents out on the counter. Holding up a set of keys, she frowned. "Her car keys are still here."

Cursing low, I went into the kitchen. The cabinet beneath the kitchen sink was wide open, water all over the floor. Leaning down, I looked inside, but all I saw was a broken pipe.

"She said she was waiting for the repair man…" I thought out loud.

"Nick." The tone in which Zoey called my name made the hair on the back of my neck rise.

She was standing inside the kitchen, back to me, body rigid. "What is it?" I asked, immediately concerned.

Even though I gazed down at her, she stared straight ahead.

"Angel?" I prompted, laying my palm against the back of her neck.

Reaching between us, she grabbed my shirt, giving it a tug. "Look." Her voice was hollow, and the finger she pointed with was unsteady.

Following her direction, I shifted my gaze.

Splatters of red marred the front of the white fridge door.

"I-is that blood?" Zoey asked.

Using an arm to tuck her behind me, I moved closer to investigate. It definitely looked like blood. And it was fresh.

Spinning away from the gruesome sight didn't stop the horrible thoughts assaulting my brain. Fear for Callie pounded at my temples and made my stomach twist. Gently Taking Zoey's ashen face between my palms, I told her, "Go wait outside."

She tried to shift, to look behind me.

"Eyes on me," I instructed. I didn't like that vacant look taking over. I didn't like the colorless sheen to her skin.

"What happened here?" she whispered, swaying a little.

Pulling her into my body, I hugged her as tight as I dared. "I don't know." Drawing back, I said, "Go wait for me outside. I'm going to call the police."

Slowly, she nodded and turned away.

Calling her name, I tugged her back. When her chin didn't lift, I lifted it for her. The kiss was soft and quick, but in that moment, it seemed necessary. "Stay right by the door. If you need me, yell."

When she was out of the kitchen, I glanced back at the blood. *What the hell happened to you, Callie?*

Pulling out my phone, I started to dial for help.

A low keening sound drifted from across the room. My head snapped up.

Zoey stood rigid with her back turned. Her head was angled down, arms in front of her body like she was holding something.

"No," she whimpered. A sound I hadn't ever heard before rumbled from her throat. "Please, no…"

"Zoey?" I started around the island. My heart was pounding, body already reacting to a threat I couldn't see.

A sob seemed to rip through her body, making her sag.

I yelled her name again. She turned just enough for me to see the look on her face. It stopped me in my tracks.

She'd turned haggard, ghostlike, and… *broken* in a matter of seconds.

"Nick," she whispered.

The sound of my name was like a jagged dagger right to my chest. Swaying on her feet, her eyes rolled back in her head. I ran forward as she crumpled to the ground.

Somewhere far away, my name was being called.

I liked the sound of the voice beckoning me, but something held back my reply. I liked it here better. The veil of unconsciousness was the strongest shield I'd ever known. So strong and capable, I thought vaguely of staying here forever.

"Zoey!" he yelled again. My peaceful existence was disturbed by rough hands shaking me. "Don't do this to me." He worried, and I learned something.

The strongest shield I'd ever known wasn't impenetrable. Not even its density could keep him from reaching me.

I thought I was alone here.

I will never be alone if Nick is at my side.

As much as I wanted to stay here, I wanted to be with him more.

Lashes fluttering, harsh sunlight chased away what was left of the veil. A small sound escaped from my lips, and a shadow cast over me, blocking the worst of the light.

"Zoey?"

Fingers patted my cheek, and my unfocused gaze cleared for Nick to fill my sight. I'd never seen him look so pale. The golden-haired California boy who forever looked kissed by the sun was suddenly robbed of the warm hue and was replaced by monochrome dullness not even makeup could conceal.

"Say something," he pleaded.

"You make a really beautiful ghost."

Frowning, the backs of his knuckles stroked over my cheek. "Something that makes sense."

"You're scared," I whispered.

"Christ," he swore. "You've taken more years off my life in the last few weeks than anything else ever."

"I'm sorry."

Gathering me close, he pressed his lips against my forehead. I was lying on the floor, but he held most of me in his arms. "What happened?"

"You passed out."

It all came back in a single rush. The blood. Callie… the paper. Gasping as if I hadn't breathed in minutes, my body jolted upright out of Nick's lap.

"Easy." He encouraged, pulling me back. "What's the matter? Are you sick?"

Beside me, I saw the picture frame lying facedown, the edge of paper sticking out from beneath it. Shuddering, I turned into the circle of Nick's body. He didn't question my actions; he didn't hesitate to offer comfort.

"I'll have them send an ambulance with the police." He decided, reaching for his phone.

"Wait," I said, placing my hand over his. "You haven't called the police?"

"You passed out before I could."

"That's good."

A strange look crossed his features. "I have to call them. Callie—"

"We definitely have to call them. But there's something I need to tell you first."

"It can't wait?"

Lowering my gaze, I said, "I wish it could. I wish I didn't ever have to tell you."

"What's this about?"

Pulling out of his arms, I picked up the frame, hugging it against my chest. I wasn't even sure how to say it. How to begin. This was a story I'd never told anyone before... only it wasn't a story; it was my past.

And now the past I tried so hard to cover up, to pretend never happened, was bursting into the present and threatening my future.

"Angel," he prompted, keeping his voice gentle despite the impatience shimmering around him.

Pulling the frame from my body, I turned it around, sliding it into his waiting hands.

The paper taped to it was folded in half, and he lifted it out of the way to see the photo. The glass covering the picture was cracked now. A few slivers had already fallen somewhere onto the floor. Beneath the shattered barrier was a headshot of Callie, her blond-haired, blue-eyed beauty on full display.

"This is what made you pass out?" Nick asked, confused.

Not answering in words, I flipped the paper over the image and pulled it open so he could read the note that was pieced together letter by letter with magazine and newspaper clippings.

The words made me shudder, but it wasn't the words I feared the most. The bottom corner of the wrinkled, abused-looking sheet was burned as if someone lit it on fire, then changed their mind and snuffed it out. The singed, uneven edge brought back vivid memories of what it felt like when fire tried to eat you alive.

Just looking at it again made me lightheaded and sick with fear.

They were all wrong. He isn't dead. He's out there. Waiting.

"What is this?" Nick wondered, his fingers turning white around the edges of the frame.

"It's a warning. A promise." I couldn't help but shiver. *God, it's happening again.* My voice was hoarse when I spoke again. "He's back."

"Who's back?"

I felt myself slipping into that hole of despair, back into the darkness I'd barely escaped the first time.

"Zoey!" Nick's voice was sharp, the fingers grasping my chin tight. "What are you saying?" he demanded. "You know who this note is from?"

I nodded, numb.

"Who?"

When I didn't answer, he gave me a shake. My body flopped like a rag doll, then, slowly, I fingered the left side of my face.

Holding my scars, I met his stare. *"Him,"* I rasped. "The man who did this to me."

She had my attention. One thousand percent of it.

Not even the niggling, familiar feeling gnawing at my gut and making my spine tingle was enough to overpower the look on this angel's face.

It was the look of an angel who'd fallen into hell.

A look of innocence stolen.

Her voice the sound of a woman haunted.

Lifting her from the floor, I carried her over to the couch, letting the soft cushions cradle her body.

Him, she'd said, fingering her scars. *The man who did this to me.*

What. The. Fuck?

"You said you were in a car accident." I began, lowering beside her, trying to understand.

Clutching the frame, she stared off into space. I couldn't help but wonder where she was right now, because mentally, it wasn't here with me.

"I wasn't in a car accident." Her voice was raspy and foreign. "I know that's what you think, and I never corrected you."

"It's okay." I soothed. I had no idea what to say, what to do. But damn, I was willing to try. "You're ready to tell me now?"

She shook her head. When her eyes focused on me, some of the tightness in my shoulders eased just a bit. I felt as if when her eyes were on me, she would be safe, that she would be anchored here instead of that dark place inside her.

"I've never told anyone. I don't want to tell you." Tears filled her eyes. "But now I don't have a choice."

"You can tell me anything." Laying my hand palm up on the cushion between us, I wiggled my fingers, inviting her touch. "Anything at all."

She stared at my offering sadly and stayed exactly how she was.

Unoffended, I left my hand there. Her rebuff didn't sting because I hadn't expected her to come to me. I wouldn't pull back, though. I would stay this way in case she changed her mind. So she could see that no matter what she said, I would still be here.

"Did you ever hear about the Bloodlust Killer?"

I frowned. "The serial killer?"

She nodded, eyes encouraging me to continue.

"I think everyone in California has heard of him."

"It's been a while… I wasn't sure if you would remember the case."

"He's the most infamous serial killer on the West Coast. He killed, what, ten people?

"Eleven," she whispered. "Almost twelve."

An odd feeling overwhelmed me. It was uncomfortable and ominous. "He died before the police could haul him to jail." I recalled. "A lot of people were angry because his victims never got the justice they deserved."

"He didn't die."

No sarcasm. Not a guess. Just a quiet statement. A bold, unwavering truth.

Tilting my head, I tried to comprehend what was happening. "What?"

Her eyes remained downcast. I saw them occasionally drift to my still-offered hand. I had to fight to keep from reaching for her. "They all said he died, but it was never actually confirmed." Her face lifted, and even though there was obvious fear in her eyes, they were steady on mine. "I'm telling you that killer isn't dead. He's still alive."

"How could you possibly know that?"

The sound of her lungs shuddering as she sucked in a deep breath made me feel like I was walking through a haunted house, anticipating ghouls to jump out.

Lowering the frame, Zoey pointed to the eerie, pieced-together letter with a single quivering finger. "This is from him. This is his way of telling me he's back."

Leaning forward, I stared between her and the note. "Telling *you*?"

She nodded.

I shook my head, trying to clear the cobwebs, trying to understand. "If this note was for you, why would it be here in Callie's apartment?"

"He knew I would find it…" Her voice was hollow. Paranoid, she glanced around, searching all the corners of the room. "He's been watching me."

"Zoey," I demanded, irritation and fear making me angry. "What the hell are you saying? Why would you think this?"

Releasing her lower lip from the abuse of her teeth, she blew my world apart.

"Because I was number twelve," she confessed. "Seven years ago, the Bloodlust Killer kidnapped me, held me hostage, and almost killed me."

Shock reverberated through my body. It was impossible to stay still. Bolting up off the sofa, I paced the living room, trying to wrap my head around the bomb she'd just set off.

Stopping abruptly, I turned, pleading with my eyes and my voice. "Please tell me that's not true."

Her lower lip quivered, and my heart dropped. "I'm sorry," she whispered. "Everyone thinks he's dead, even the police. But I know he isn't… and this," she said, tapping her finger against the grotesque note. "This is proof. He's come back. He's come back to finish what he started."

The pace in which I rushed to her matched the pace of my pounding heart. The sofa slid crookedly on the floor when I practically jumped onto it, my knee bumping against hers. Without permission, without the caution I always used with her, my fingers reached for her face. Despite the makeup covering all her scars, I caressed all the places I knew it hid, including tracing over her eyebrow with the pad of my thumb.

Lowering my hand, I shifted attention to her leg. Leaning down, grasping the hem of her pants, I tugged the fabric upward, revealing the prosthetic she wore in place of her missing leg.

"He did this to you?" I demanded, my voice harsh. "You're telling me that some animal inflicted all this pain on you, and you've lived for seven years all alone… in hiding?"

She nodded, a tear trickling down her cheek.

Anger unlike anything I'd ever felt before assaulted me. It was so powerful tears rushed my vision and vomit clogged my throat.

When I said I wanted to see all the times she needed me and I hadn't been there, I meant it. But this… Never in a million years did I imagine this.

Grabbing her face, I implored. "Tell me. Tell me everything."

And so she did.

The weight of the chain tried to drag me back down. Down into the depths of the abandoned pool, down into what I considered an open grave.

I wouldn't go back down there…

"Ahh!"

My body hit the ground with a sickening thud. Stars swam behind my eyelids, lighting up the darkness with a dizzying glow. I knew I was alive because being dead could never hurt this much.

That was the benefit of death, right? No pain. No fear.

Nothing.

I hadn't endured this long to succumb to nothing. Even if the appeal of nothing was great.

Sitting up was daunting, but I did it all the same. Glancing up at the ladder I'd just slipped off, I noted how the dirty rungs were streaked with red.

The weight of the shackle and chain dragged me down. The slick substance of my own blood made me lose my grip.

Get up. Try again.

Balancing on my right foot, hunching in like a woman with a broken spine, I stared through matted, half-wet clumps of hair at my newest opponent.

I would get up that ladder. I would get out of this grave. Once at the top, I would climb into that elevator and rise to safety.

Dragging the chain up, I wound it loosely around my neck like a fashionable scarf. The next scarf I wore would be designer. It would be cashmere and monogrammed with my new initials. It didn't matter how much it cost, because no matter the price, it would be cheaper than what I was paying now.

With the chain out of the way, I used the clean gown that psycho had brought me to wipe away the blood and sweat from my hands and feet. Beneath the shackle, my ankle was still bleeding. The flesh was gnarled and raw. It seemed what little skin I had left was swollen and oozing with more than just blood. Ripping off a section of the gown, I tied the fabric around the wound, crying out in pain. That scrap of fabric would hold off the blood at least until I was up the ladder.

It took longer than I expected to get out of the deep end of that pool. My limbs were weak, my vision a little faulty. My left foot was numb, so I had to stare down to make sure it was actually on each step as I climbed.

How could something be numb yet so painful at the same time?

The back of my arm felt raw and irritated. At times, my only thought was to lie down.

I fought my way to the top of that ladder, and when I got there, I sprawled on the floor as if I'd made a journey to the moon. Allowing myself a few moments to cry and catch my breath, I stared up into the rafters, wondering just how high the ceiling in this place rose.

The hollow sound of a noise somewhere in the distance made me lurch up. I had to hurry! If I didn't move fast, he would come back. He would find me.

He would be angry.

I would die.

Wincing at the pain, I levered up until I was standing, balancing on my right leg. The chain felt as though it weighed a thousand pounds. Concentrating on each step I took, I stared down at the dirt-crusted floor. Some of the patches my toes met were green. Mildew and mold… maybe moss?

Where was I?

Another noise brought my head up. Pressing a hand against my palpitating heart, I looked toward the elevator, praying to God he wasn't here.

I forgot all about my captor, though… when I saw the bodies.

My screams bounced from rafter to rafter, echoing like sound effects in a made-for-TV movie. The only way I could silence them was to shove my fist in my mouth. Even then, whimpering and cries burst around, making me sound like a mewling kitten lost in the woods.

Now I knew why he'd brought the ladder.

Now I understood why he'd made so much noise.

They were hanging from the ceiling. Suspended by chain identical to the one around my neck.

Have you ever seen a human cocoon?

I have.

I was looking at them now.

Them = more than one. Seven to be exact. Seven corpses wrapped up in clear tarps like they were merely caterpillars waiting to become butterflies. Blood didn't create butterflies, and the inside of those tarps were most definitely stained with red.

And other colors that I tried not to focus on. I knew from the body I'd lived across from that blood wasn't the only thing that leaked from a corpse.

Shuddering, I averted my gaze. But like a heinous car wreck, I could only glance away before I looked again.

This was sick. So freaking sick.

He'd killed so many people. He'd kept their bodies and strung them up. Was this what he was planning to do to me?

Would I be rolled up in plastic, hung from the ceiling like some kind of trophy?

Falling to my knees, I vomited the rest of the water I'd drank. It burned coming up, and the retching sounds I made hurt my ears just as the action hurt my insides.

Shaking, weak, and almost delirious, I got up. Dragging my injured foot, I passed a cocoon, the eyes of the woman inside watching me.

The second body I fell into, landing on my back. I stared up as it swayed over me like a pendulum counting the last seconds of my life.

The elevator hummed to life, and the broken, screeching sounds of the gears nearly made me jump out of my skin. The chain rattled when I ran off, crouching behind some old pool equipment that was literally growing weeds.

He was whistling again. That same tune he always did. I put my wrist in my mouth to stop the chattering of my teeth as he stepped out of the car and into the abandoned space. From my vantage point, I watched him stare lovingly at his handiwork, eyes resting on each body for long moments.

He was proud of what he did. I could see it right there in his face.

Surely, this man had been born in hell and clawed his way to earth. There was no explanation for such depravity.

I shrank back against the wall as he walked forward, his face twisting when he saw the upset ladder and knocked-over toolbox. Instead of running over to see, he strolled, whistling again like he didn't have a care in the world.

Crouching, he stared at the mess I'd made. Reaching for the bottle of water, he lifted it, staring silently before setting it aside.

Rising, he went to the edge of the pool and gazed down.

"Agghhh!" he roared, suddenly bursting to life like a rabid beast set free from a cage.

The scream I held in burned the back of my throat, and tears streamed down my face.

"Where are you?" he thundered, stomping around the pool, knocking into the cocoons and making them sway.

Shivering, I thought over my options.

He was on the other side of the pool. I could make it to the elevator and close myself in.

I had to try.

Lurching up, I started to run, my bare feet slapping against the cold floor as I went. I didn't look back, though I know he saw me the second I moved. I focused on rushing for that elevator and hit the button for the doors as many times as I could.

The small light above the button lit up, and I nearly peed myself with fear. He was coming… running, breathing.

A quick glance over my shoulder showed him stepping around the last body between us.

I hit the button again. My knees started to give out.

When he was almost in reach, I threw my back against the wall and unwound the chain from around my neck. Holding it like a weapon, I dared him to come close.

The inside-out mask he wore made his skin look plastic and shiny smooth. It was a stark contrast to his dirty clothes, stained hiking boots, and heavy breathing.

He lunged closer, and I swung the chain. It smacked into him, making him stumble back.

The elevator door dragged open with a bone-chilling sound. Sobbing, I hobbled through the doors, nearly to safety.

A hand grabbed the back of the stupid gown and dragged me back. I screamed, grabbing at the doors, clawing and fighting to get into the car.

A vise-like arm snaked around my waist, and I threw my head back, smashing it against his. His grip slacked for a moment, and I fell onto the ground. Crawling forward, I made it into the car, and the doors began to grind closed.

That god-awful hiking boot shoved its way between them. All I saw was the blood-stained brown toe with frayed brown laces blocking my way to safety.

I cried, and he pried open the doors.

His large frame filled the doorway, standing in the center as though he dared the rickety doors to close on him.

Lifting a finger, he waved it in the air, back and forth. No, no, no, he said without words. Bending down, he grabbed the end of the chain and began to tug.

"No!" I wailed, scrambling back as he towed me forward. Grabbing the shackle around my ankle, I began to fight. Hitting my already damaged foot, I tried to break it so I could yank it free. If I'd had a saw in that moment, I'd have cut through the bone.

"Noooo!" I wailed again, my voice giving up its fight.

He didn't touch me. Instead, he dragged me out of the elevator and across the floor like a dead animal on a leash. My fingers left a trail of blood as I tried to claw the ground.

Giving the chain some kind of tug, I found myself on my back, staring up at a cocoon that was previously across the room. The body in this one was more decayed, but I could still make out the eyes staring at me from the bottom.

I couldn't scream. I couldn't cry.

All I could do was glower at those eyes.

Another tug and he was standing over me, a shiny blade grasped in one hand. Without a word, he bent down and removed the shackle from my ankle. Without even considering why, I skittered back and shoved up to my feet.

Teetering on unsteady legs, I stared at him.

"Run," he rasped.

I did. I ran, not realizing at first this was all just part of his game. He stood and watched me weave through the bodies. The sounds of the chains squeaking as they swung would haunt me forever.

I went for the elevator again, but before I got there, he grabbed me, spinning me around.

I dodged the first swipe of the blade.

The second caught my shoulder.

The pain barely registered because I was so used to the feeling now. All I felt in that moment was adrenaline and the pure desire to escape.

Suddenly, I changed direction. Instead of going for the elevator, I rushed him. Sinking low, I caught him around the waist, plowing him down. Landing on top of him, our eyes connected, and what I saw was terrifying.

Nothing. Nothing at all.

He was completely empty. Void of life.

Maybe that was why he wanted to take so many.

It wouldn't matter! *I wanted to yell.* You could kill a thousand people, and you would still be dead inside!

He didn't try to fight me off. Instead, he lay under me and stared. It was like he forgot the knife in his hand. He forgot he wanted me dead.

I didn't forget I wanted to live. Shoving up, I ran.

The blow to the back of my head brought me down. Drowsy and barely lucid, I stared through unfocused eyes. Everything seemed upside down, sideways.

I felt him drag me somewhere, but where, I didn't know.

In the distance, I heard sirens, and I started to cry. Sounds of splashing and splattering made me confused. The familiar putrid smell of something burned my nostrils.

All I could focus on was the sound of those sirens.

Not the strike of the match.

Not the whoosh of the flame.

"I'm The Moth, and you're the flame," he said from somewhere. "Bye-bye."

Orange and red became the only colors I saw. Heat unlike anything I felt before robbed me of breath.

The sound of the sirens suddenly disappeared, and searing pain so vile took over. It was so wicked, fighting to live no longer mattered.

This was the end.

This was death.

"I woke up in the hospital. An entire month had passed." Her voice was hoarse and smoky, almost like her body remembered what it was like to almost be burned alive. "If the police had been just five minutes longer, I would have burned to death."

I reached for her.

She pulled away.

I didn't try again.

It was taking everything for her to relive this, for her to tell me her truth.

"My left side suffered burns. A few of the scars are from other injuries while I was there." Her eyes lifted to mine, and I felt like she was seeing me for the first time in a while. "You saw my back that day, right?"

I nodded.

"It's from the fire. The scar is from the knife."

I opened my mouth, but she sat up, cutting me off. "Did you see the other mark?"

I frowned. "Other mark?"

Her hand slid around, holding herself. "On the back of my arm."

I shook my head. "I'd only been trying to cover you. I didn't see."

A very faint smile tugged her lips, and I wanted to weep. She was still in there somewhere, my angel… my angel who literally walked through hell.

Scooting forward, she put her back to me and tugged off her shirt.

"Zoey, you don't have—"

"I want to."

I fell silent as she tossed the shirt aside. Turning more, she showed me her back. The left side indeed had scarring from burns. Lifting her arm out, she reached around and pointed.

"There."

Cautiously, I reached out. "May I?"

Her head bobbed. Grasping her arm, I held it up to see the mark she gestured to.

A strangled sound ripped out of my throat. "H-he… did this to you?"

"He branded me. He said I was his."

Now I knew. Now I knew what a murderous rage felt like. What it meant to be so angry it tainted your logical thought.

Leaning in, I blinked, trying to gain enough composure to see. "Is that… a moth?"

"He's the moth, and I'm the flame…" Her voice trailed away. "Maybe that's why he tried to burn me in the end."

Releasing her arm, I jumped up and began to pace. Overcome with rage and despair, I did the only thing I could.

My fist plowed right through the drywall, giving way under my rage like butter against a hot knife. Burning pain seared my knuckles and was sickly satisfactory. Yanking my hand free of the wall, bits of drywall and debris rained around my feet. The slick sensation of blood dripping over my knuckles was also something I enjoyed.

Zoey was on her feet when I turned back around, rocking from side to side as far away from me as she could get.

"I won't ever hurt you," I told her. "But the rage…" My voice trailed away, and I lifted my bleeding fist. "I had to put it somewhere."

Her eyes were three sizes bigger than before. They were the wrong color. They should have been blue. I didn't want to see her hidden face anymore. After hearing everything she survived, I wanted to see the real her.

"You cover yourself up that way because you're hiding," I finally said, realizing it wasn't only because of the scars themselves.

"They told me he died in the fire. That he didn't make it out. They said they found his burned body, but they never actually confirmed the corpse was his."

What the fuck did a man say? No words existed that could ever offer comfort, sorrow, or even understanding.

She cleared her throat, still shifting from foot to foot. "While I was in a coma, they amputated my leg from the knee down. The damage from the shackle, the damage I inflicted on myself trying to get free, was all too much. Gangrene apparently set in. So while I was out, they took the leg.”

The words “please stop” were on the tip of my tongue. I wanted to say them so desperately. I couldn’t hear anymore. I couldn’t listen to everything this woman survived without breaking down.

I said nothing.

I endured because if she could live through what she did, the very least I could do was listen to the harrowing tale. I knew she’d suffered trauma, and I knew she trusted no one.

I knew, *but damn*, I hadn’t known.

“Zoey.”

The second I said her name, she moved. Going into the water-logged kitchen, she searched around. Not finding whatever it was she wanted, she came forward, hesitating for a moment when she drew close.

I held still, afraid to even breathe. Her eyes strayed down to my bleeding hand, and then she moved past me without issue. Listening to the sounds she made in bathroom, I wondered what she was doing, but I didn’t dare ask. She reappeared a moment later, carrying a large white kit with a red cross on the front.

Perching on the sofa, she turned toward me. “Come here.”

I went but didn’t sit down. Zoey patted the cushion beside her.

“You sure?”

“I trust you.”

I blew out a shaky breath. “I swear to God those words mean more to me than if you’d said I love you.”

Lifting the lid off the kit, she made herself busy, looking for what she wanted. “Those words are more important to me than I love you," she told me as she searched.

My ass hit the cushion.

I felt like a weak son of a bitch, but this woman was robbing me of every ounce of strength I had.

I loved her.

She just told me the most heinous, tormenting tale of abuse I seriously had ever heard. But I loved her.

"I love you," I said, unable to keep in the words.

Pausing, she glanced up. "Tell me that after the shock wears off."

"I mean it."

"I won't hold you to it."

Her reaction didn't offend me. It just made me love her more.

"Give me your hand," she said, holding out her palm.

I surrendered my bloody, scraped-up fist.

I couldn't tear my eyes away from her as she carefully cleaned the stinging cuts on my hand.

"I cut myself off from everyone and everything," she said quietly, ripping open a few bandages. "The PTSD was so severe it took me over a year just to function normally. I had to relearn how to walk, how to live with a prosthetic. The burns took so long to heal. I had a few skin grafts, but they were so painful I stopped. It seemed like he was causing me even more pain because I was trying to get rid of the pain he'd already caused, you know?"

I made a sound, eyes still eating up her face.

"After a few years, I was able to get back to some kind of life. Because of my background in makeup, I was able to teach myself how to cover up all my scars. It was good practice for movie sets, and eventually, I was able to get a job on a small crew."

"What about your family? Your friends?" I asked.

"I never reached back out. Even though I hadn't died… I kind of did. They were part of my old life, a life that no longer existed. I changed my name, the way I looked. I changed everything but the city I lived in."

"Why didn't you move far away?"

"Because working in Hollywood was basically the perfect cover. If he was still out there, he wouldn't think I would stick around here. I like the security of the movie sets, the privacy they afford. And I traveled around for movie locations, which meant I was never in one place very long."

I didn't want to ask. I had to. "Haven't you been lonely?"

"Every day," she whispered. "All done," she announced, sitting back and picking up the mess she made.

I glanced down at my neatly bandaged hand.

Closing the lid of the kit, she started to stand. My hand shot out, grabbing her, pulling her into my lap. She fell softly, her arms looping around my neck like she'd just been waiting for me to seize her.

Saying nothing, I buried my face into the side of her neck. Her fingers delved into the hair at the base of my skull. Tightening my arms around her, breathing in the scent of her skin, I allowed just one tear leak out, letting the softness of her hair drink it in.

After a while, the crushing weight on my chest loosened and I pulled back, still keeping my arms around her. "You're never going to be lonely ever again."

"We need to call the police."

Once the call was made, I set aside the phone, looping my arms around her waist once more. "Aren't I heavy?" she asked, starting to rise.

"No." I pulled her back down.

"I can't stop thinking about Callie," she whispered.

"Me either," I confessed. If Zoey was right about this, then Callie was in the hands of a monster. "But why her?" I murmured. "If he came back for you... why her?"

"He couldn't get to me." I felt her fingers in my hair, tugging so I would meet her gaze. "He couldn't get to me because of you."

I wasn't glad that deviant had Callie, but I also wasn't regretful I'd managed to protect Zoey.

My brow furrowed. "So he was angry at me, so he took my assistant?"

Grabbing her phone, Zoey did a few things on the screen, then glanced up.

"What is it?" I asked, wary of the look in her eye.

Turning the phone around, she showed me an image.

She had blond, shoulder-length hair, blue eyes, flawless skin, and a bright smile. Something was so familiar about her. Something...

"This was me," Zoey told me. "This is what I looked like... *before*."

It started to click into place. My gut started to scream. Grabbing the photo the note was taped to, I held the old pic of Zoey beside it.

They looked similar. Blond hair. Blue eyes. Innocent...

What am I missing here?

"I think it was him that destroyed my makeup. He's angry because I changed the way I look..."

"He took Callie because she looks the way he wants you to," I murmured.

"I think so," she hypothesized.

I shook my head briefly. There was something else. *Something…*

Flipping the note over, the photo of Callie, I stared down at the crudely cut out letters, at the way they were all taped together.

Blond hair. Blue eyes. Moth to a Flame…

A hundred images flashed behind my eyes. The past came roaring to the present. Puzzle pieces clicked into place, revealing a staggering, grisly realization.

Holy shit.

"I don't understand," I said, staring out the window of the Viper at a house that was easily the size of a small country.

Nick shut off the engine. The interior lights went out.

Turning in the shadowy interior, I sought out his face. "Why are we here? And why were you so anxious to get away from the cops?"

"We told the cops everything we could to help Callie," he answered, pocketing the keys.

"There's something more going on here."

"Yes, there is."

I stared at his vacated seat as he jogged around the sports car to wrench open my door.

He called my name. I looked over my shoulder. Offering his hand, he asked, "Do you trust me?"

"What is this, *Aladdin*?"

He chuckled but pushed his hand closer. "Do you?"

Smacking his hand away, I said, "You know I do."

Leaning in, he unbuckled my seat belt, pulling back only slightly. Despite the day and night we'd had, he still took my breath away. His presence was still enough to make me forget even for a moment that everything had gone to hell.

He whispered. "Can I kiss you?"

I closed my eyes.

Sensation after sensation rolled over me as his lips nibbled mine before grasping the back of my head and settling firmly against my mouth. Parting my lips, his tongue danced with mine, and pleasure flushed my skin.

Before pulling away completely, he kissed my forehead. The tenderness in the action made my heart thump unevenly.

"You shocked the shit out of me earlier. You know that, right?" he asked, helping me out of the car.

"You're the first person I've ever told," I confessed, shy. "Except the police, of course."

Taking me around the waist, he moved in front of me, blocking the giant mansion his parents called home.

His forehead pressed against mine. "You can tell me anything. Can I tell you anything?"

I made a sound of agreement.

"Good," he said, taking my hand and starting toward the house. "Because now it's my turn to shock the shit out of you."

Shocking me was going to be pretty hard considering all the surprise I'd already lived through. "What is this about?" I asked as he pulled open the ultra-wide front door, guiding me inside a foyer that literally took my breath away.

A double winding staircase, stairs that literally lit up from within. Iron railings, tile floor with intricate inlays, and a chandelier that would put a castle to shame.

"Mom!" Nick yelled, pulling me inside like he didn't even see the splendor in front of us. "Mom, I'm home!"

Gaping, I stared at him. He was acting like a teenager home from school, the kind who would drop his bag and kick off his shoes while bellowing for attention.

And… yep, he was kicking off his shoes, letting them litter the perfectly pristine floor.

His hand slid over the small of my back, his lips brushing against my ear. "Relax, angel," he whispered. "It's just home."

Easy for him to say!

A blond woman appeared at the top of one of the staircases, looking like she belonged on the big screen.

"Nick!" she exclaimed, joy on her face. "I didn't know you were coming tonight."

"Hey, Mom," he said, sounding just like the kid I'd imagined before.

His mom, who didn't look old enough to have a son Nick's age, floated down the stairs like her feet weighed nothing at all. She was wearing a white flowy top with sleeves that floated out behind her as she descended. Her bright-blond hair was cut into a stylish pixie, with long bangs falling over her forehead.

I understood why Nick's family was considered Hollywood royalty, because this woman looked like a queen.

When her feet cleared the bottom step, she rushed over, and I nearly gaped because she was so much shorter than her very tall son. She just came to his shoulder. Nick smiled and wrapped her in a hug.

Patting his back, she laughed, then pulled away to look at me. "Ah, the wonton makeup artist who cast a spell over my son and moved in with him?"

My mouth fell open.

"Mom!" Nick scolded, but then he laughed. "How the hell did you know we're living together?"

She didn't even miss a beat. "Haven't you checked the headlines today? It's trending."

I gasped.

Nick made a face.

Fumbling around, I grabbed my cell and pulled up the latest gossip headlines… which we were once again dominating. Groaning, I lowered the phone and looked at Nick. "The press knows I'm staying at your house."

"Jessica," he spat.

My mouth fell open yet again. Strolling over, Nick snapped it shut.

"Tell Zoey you were just kidding."

His mom stepped forward and took my hand. Reflexively, I almost snatched it away, but thankfully, I caught myself. The way Nick palmed my lower back told me he noticed.

"Mrs. Preston," I rushed to say. "I promise you I'm not wonton, and I haven't cast any spells."

She laughed. "Call me Blair, and of course you haven't."

I glanced at Nick. He winked. "Mom knows all about the press and what a pack of liars they are."

She nodded. "They've definitely been having a field day with you." She stroked the side of my head. This time, I did pull away.

"I am staying at his house." I burst out. What the hell had possessed me to say that?

"She knows," Nick whispered loudly.

I made a face. He could have told me all of this before we walked in.

"Are you hungry?" Blair asked her son. "I won't tell your trainer I fed you."

"This isn't a social visit, Mom."

Whatever she heard in his voice made her concerned.

He told her, "I need to see the box."

Her face paled. Clearly, she knew what "box" Nick was referring to, and clearly, it wasn't something pleasant.

"Why would you—"

"It's important." He cut her off. "Please."

Blair's eyes slid to me, then back to Nick. "I'll get it."

She went back up the stairs, and Nick took my hand to lead me into a large dining room with a table that could easily seat twenty people.

One wall had floor-to-ceiling drapes, and I imagined when they were open in the daytime, the fabric would frame a magnificent view.

Pulling out a chair, Nick guided me into it, then sat down in one right beside me.

"Ever since I met you, I couldn't stay away," he told me, stretching his arm out over the back of my chair. "I felt connected to you... drawn to you."

I shuddered, thinking of the note we'd surrendered to the police just a short while ago. "Not a good choice of words."

"I couldn't understand what it was about you."

"Fascination?" I tried, thinking of all my scars.

He shook his head. "I stopped caring after a while because it didn't matter anymore." He leaned in, and my stomach flipped. "All that matters is that you stay by my side."

"Nick." I began, feeling jittery and shy. He was so very good with words. Turns out my heart was so very good at being swayed by them.

It scared me.

"I realized tonight there is a reason I felt so connected to you."

"There is?"

He nodded. "Because we are connected. Through the past… through tragedy."

"I don't understand."

Blair came into the room, carrying a large white box with a matching lid. "Here it is," she said, a lot of the earlier warmth in her voice lacking.

Taking the box from his mom, Nick placed it on the table and pulled off the lid. A moment later, he pulled out a large envelope, opening the flap.

Taking out a sheet of paper, he slid it across the glossy tabletop in front of me.

I looked down.

My blood ran cold.

"What is that?" Abruptly, I stood from the chair, nearly falling over it in my attempt to get away from that sheet of paper.

Nick caught me, using his body to support mine. I melted into him, unable to tear my eyes away from the pieced-together note.

Pieced together with magazine and newspaper clippings.

"Where did you get that?" I whispered, horrified.

His arm slid around my waist from behind like he knew I was about to need him to hold me up.

"This was sent to my grandmother… a couple weeks before she was killed on set."

He took my weight readily when my knees gave out.

I pointed at the paper. My voice shook. "That looks exactly like the one we just gave to the police."

"I know," Nick replied.

Still holding me, he leaned around and pulled something else from inside the box, laying it on the table beside the note.

A whimper passed through my lips. It was a photograph. A headshot of the late Deborah Ascott. Blond hair. Blue eyes. Bright smile.

"My grandmother was killed on the set of her movie, *Moth to a Flame 2.*"

"You think the man who tried to kill me is The Moth… a-a-and," I stuttered, no longer able to form words.

His arms slipped back around me. "And if he is The Moth, then my grandmother was the original flame."

By now, she'd gotten my note. All the pieces would fit together, revealing the truth of everything I'd done. Sequels cannot be rushed, but I'd been waiting a very long time for mine.

Our climax was coming, and my only regret was that I couldn't be there to see the look on my flame's face when she fully understood I'd found her.

I had work to do.

A walk to take down memory lane.

It was like coming home after a long trip abroad. Memories lingered, even if they were coated in dust. Everywhere I looked, I was re-energized by how it all began, by the pure love of horror and the rush of first kill.

Dropping my bait onto the floor, I stared down, disgusted. So bothersome but a means to an end. Placing my boot flat against the cocoon, I pushed, unrolling until the unconscious stand-in lay atop the blood-smeared plastic.

Dragging her to the center of the tarp, I checked to see if she was breathing. I didn't really care either way, but live bait usually worked better than dead.

Oh, good. She was still alive.

Taking out a metal shackle, I fastened it around her ankle. I doubted she would wake up for a while, but still, she had to play her part.

Leaving her chained in the corner of the room, I went to prepare the rest of the scene.

"No. No way." Zoey refused, flat denial in her voice.

Her body pushed against mine as she backed away from the items on the table. I went backward with her, allowing her the distance from the evidence but keeping my arms tightly wrapped around her as she went.

"It's too much." Her voice wobbled. Turning in the circle of my arms, her chin lifted. "It's just a coincidence. A creepy… tragic coincidence."

I knew she wanted to believe it. Hell, I think I probably did too. Why else would it have taken me so long to piece this together? Why else did it take so long to comprehend?

Because shit like this is unbelievable. Shit like this only happens in the movies.

My life was like a movie, though. My family was "old Hollywood" and my grandmother literally died on film.

Film.

Releasing Zoey, I hurried to the box, digging around until I found the slim case. Clutching it, I spun around.

Without me, her body slumped. Hunched over on herself, her hand pressed to her chest. She looked wrung out, hollow, and about to fall down.

Cursing, I put aside the case and went to her.

"Nick," my mother said. Honestly, I'd forgotten she was here. "What's going on? What's happening?"

"I think I might have some new information about Grandmother's murder."

She gasped, dropping into a dining chair. "How?"

"No." Zoey refused. "There's no way."

"Angel," I said gently, guiding her down into a chair, kneeling before her and taking her hands in mine. "This is too coincidental to be a coincidence. There's too much to just explain it all away."

"Son," Mom intoned. "You can't just bring this up and then not explain. Your grandmother…"

"I know, Mom. Please. Let me explain."

Searching Zoey's eyes, I implored her to listen, to not shut down.

Cautiously, she nodded, her fingers like vises around mine. I wanted to get up and pace, to work through all the jumbled thoughts and pieces I felt coming together, but it seemed the comfort of my presence was needed by the woman clutching my hand.

Rotating, I sat on the floor between her legs, resting our joined hands on my shoulder.

"Zoey is the sole survivor of the Bloodlust Killer," I told my mother, who gasped and put a hand against her mouth. "She was there the day he died… She was the victim they managed to save from the fire."

"Oh my God," Mom exclaimed. "That was you?"

Behind me, Zoey nodded. "They never released my identity to the press because I was too traumatized to deal with the attention."

"Well, of course," Mom murmured. "That man… he killed so many people."

"Eleven," Zoey echoed. It was like the number was burned in her brain. As if she carried the weight of eleven deaths around with her every day of her life.

She'd almost been the twelfth victim. How close I'd come to never meeting her.

"Is it possible Grandmother wasn't killed by an obsessive fan?" I asked.

Mom frowned. "That's what all the evidence points to. Someone who was obsessed with her and the huge success of *Moth to a Flame*. The notes prove it." She gestured toward the note I showed Zoey.

Zoey perked up. "There's more than one?"

I nodded. "She got three."

"Two are exactly the same," Mom informed her, getting up to reach inside the box. "This one is the only different one."

Zoey reached over my shoulder to take it with trembling fingers. Brushing her aside, I took the letter and held it out for her to see.

I'm coming for you in the sequel. Killers don't die. Victims do.

Zoey shuddered. "I don't understand. If people knew she was being harassed, how could he get onto set to kill her?"

Mom answered, regret and sorrow making her voice low. "No one knew. We found these letters after she was gone."

Zoey made a sound. "She didn't tell anyone?"

"Actors get letters and threats almost on a daily basis. She was a huge slasher film star. She got stuff like this a lot. She probably didn't realize this was a real threat," I explained.

"But it was real. She died."

"The police concluded it was someone obsessed with the movie." Mom continued. "But after he jumped out the window on set, he disappeared."

"What if he didn't? What if he became the Bloodlust Killer and continued to kill?"

"What makes you think they're the same person?"

I ticked off the reasons crowding around in my head:

1. Grandmother was killed on the set of *Moth to a Flame 2*. He sent her letters using the movie title. *I'm drawn to you like a moth to a flame.*

2. Zoey got the same letter.

3. The killer was angry when he realized Zoey changed her appearance. She used to be blond and blue-eyed just like Grandmother. She looked like his original victim.

"That could be a coincidence," Mom refuted.

"Actually, all the victims had the same physical features," Zoey echoed.

I shot a look over my shoulder. "Really?"

Biting her lip, she nodded miserably.

"He couldn't get to you, so he took Callie instead," I added.

"Callie?" Mom burst out, standing from her chair.

Quickly, I explained about my assistant, all the color leeching from Mom's face.

"Dear God." Her voice quaked. "Will this never be over?"

"He calls himself The Moth," Zoey said. "All his victims are the flames…"

"Just like in Grandmother's movie."

"Then why is he known as the Bloodlust Killer? Why did the press never report about this?"

"It was kept confidential to avoid copycat crimes. And because the police were afraid that it would incite statewide panic. They thought it was best to keep many details of the investigation private to not compromise the case. The press dubbed him the Bloodlust Killer because they said he killed eleven women because of his own personal bloodlust."

"But that man died!"

"I think that's what they wanted the public to believe. But obviously, he didn't," Zoey whispered as she rubbed at the brand on her arm. Her eyes widened. "She wasn't branded!"

"What?" Mom questioned.

"The Bloodlust Killer branded all his victims. He burned a moth into their arms."

"Deborah definitely didn't have that." Mom agreed.

I made a sound. "He didn't have time to brand her. There were too many people around. That's why I think she was his first victim… After that, he took on the role of The Moth and used fire on all his victims."

My mother put a hand to her throat. "You think killing your grandmother gave him a taste for murder?"

"He said it in his note. Killers don't die. Victims do."

"It's too much," Zoey said again. "It can't possibly all be connected."

"When was the Bloodlust Killer's first kill that the police know of?" I asked the room, lifting my phone to search for the information.

Turns out I didn't need to search. Zoey had all the answers… like every detail about that sick fuck was branded in her brain.

On her skin. In her brain.

I myself was experiencing bloodlust. I wanted to kill that son of a bitch ten times over.

"The first body of a woman with a moth burned into the back of her arm was discovered in 1985. Two more were found, one in 1987 and then again in 1990. There were eight bodies discovered the night I was saved. All of them had moths burned into them. That makes a total of eleven, me being number twelve. He was presumed dead seven years ago… and no bodies with a brand have been found since."

"Deborah was killed in 1984, a year before the first victim was found with a moth," Mom surmised. Her brow furrowed, and she went on. "So between 1990 and 2011, there were no branded bodies found?" she asked. "That's a long gap for a serial killer."

"Several women who meet his profile went missing and were never found," Zoey said quietly. "Well, one was, but her body was burned beyond recognition, which made seeing any kind of brand impossible."

"So he could have other victims out there that were never found." Mom concluded.

Zoey made a noise.

"If everyone thought he was dead, why start killing again? Why not just stay in hiding…?" My mother continued to think out loud.

"Because of me," I confessed.

Zoey's eyes flashed to me, and Mom gasped. "What?"

"Because of the accident on set. Because the press became obsessed with Zoey. She was exposed, and he must have seen."

"It all started up again after that picture was posted online." Zoey reluctantly agreed. "He realized I'd been hiding and covering up my appearance. He destroyed all my makeup… I think he's been watching me." A distressed sound made me turn toward her. Her hands clasped the front of my shirt. "The sandbag on set… Could that have been him?"

"I don't know," I answered, thinking back to that day, recalling the way her scars were exposed. Could he have wanted to see if she was branded? Could he have set her up?

I didn't voice those thoughts out loud. It was speculation, and everyone was already scared enough.

"And now Callie…" Zoey's voice wavered.

Reaching for her hand, I gave it a reassuring squeeze. "Callie is going to be fine."

"How can you be so sure?"

I couldn't. In fact, I was worried as fuck about my assistant. She didn't deserve this. No one did.

Mom jumped up. "Do you think he knows who you are, Nick? That you are the grandson of Deborah Ascott?"

Zoey also leapt from her chair, eyes wild with panic. "No! He can't!"

When I reaching for her, she shoved away, face crumpling.

"First Callie and now you, Nick! I won't let him do this!" Chin wobbling, voice breaking, she raced to the door with an uneven gait. "Call off your bodyguards!" she demanded. "I'm going back home. I'll wait for him to get me, and once he does, the rest of you will be safe."

I ran after her, hugging her from behind. "Are you crazy?" I demanded.

She fought and wiggled, trying to get out of my hold. I wouldn't let her go. There was no way in hell I would allow her to sacrifice her own safety for mine.

"Nick!" she cried, stomping down on my foot.

Cursing, I refused release her. "I'm not letting you go."

"You have to!" she wailed. "Please! Let me go. Let me fix this!" A sound of pain dropped from her lips, and her body sagged against mine. "Ow," she whimpered.

"Angel?" I worried, looking down. "What happened? What hurts?"

"It's just my leg," she answered, reaching around to the back of her thigh.

Swinging her up, I pinpointed my mother, who was watching the scene with an astonished face. "I'm taking her up to one of the guest rooms."

She nodded. "I won't disturb you."

"Thanks."

"Nick," she called when I started out.

"We'll finish this talk soon." I promised without stopping.

Taking the stairs two at a time, I went up to the wing of the house my parents used solely for guests. It was a quiet part of the house that the servants only ever went into clean or when there were people staying here.

Throwing open the first door I came to, I strode inside, placing her on a giant, downy bed.

Tears streaked her face, and dark circles bruised under her eyes. "Let me see," I crooned, wrapping my hands around the contracting leg muscle, beginning to massage.

"Don't." She fussed, pushing at my hands, but not very effectively.

"Sit still," I demanded, not letting go.

She said my name, her voice unsteady. Tenderness filled me, and I lowered on the edge of the mattress close by, still working the muscles of her leg.

"Feeling any better?"

She nodded.

I let go of her leg long enough to guide her shoulders down onto the mattress. "Lie down," I urged. "You look like you're ready to fall over."

Sighing, she sank into the blankets, and I went back to massaging her leg. "This bed is really soft," she whispered.

"You like it?"

"Mmm."

The silence surrounding us felt like an indulgence because the noise of the past few days had been almost off the charts. I watched her lashes flutter against her cheeks before her eyes would reopen and stare up at the ceiling.

"Nick?"

I made a sound, acknowledging her.

"Do you really think the man who killed your grandmother is the same man who tried to kill me?"

"And now he has Callie." I agreed.

"Connected by death…" she murmured.

My hands paused in their ministrations. Moving so I was over her, my hands on either side of her body, I waited until her eyelids lifted and our stares met.

Her breathing caught, and awareness lit up her eyes.

"Connected by death, yes," I told her. "But fused together by love."

She looked off to the side. "I told you to stop saying that."

"I won't stop. I do love you."

"I can't say it back."

"You don't have to. I love you enough for the both of us."

"Nick—"

I covered her mouth with my hand.

"I didn't say you had to love me, so you aren't allowed to say I can't love you."

We stared at each other for the span of several heartbeats, electricity crackling through the room, so strong I could almost hear it. The softness of her lips puckered and pressed a kiss to the palm of my hand.

My stomach flipped over.

Slowly, I lifted my hand away. Her lips were still pursed.

All my attention went down to her mouth. Need and desire made my fingers curl into the sheets.

"Your mom is waiting for us," she whispered.

The corner of my lips turned up. "Is that really what you're thinking about right now?"

Her throat worked against the force of her swallow. The smirk tugging at my mouth disappeared.

Slowly. So achingly slow, I lowered toward her, gauging her reaction with every centimeter.

I felt rather than saw her hands fist in the blankets, and her anticipation sent my heart into a gallop.

Just before our lips connected, I rubbed my tongue over mine, giving them a little bit of slip. Her body arched up, and I used the opportunity to slide my arm under her, holding her body firmly along mine.

I fell into her kiss, into her taste. Time froze, and nothing else existed except for the way our lips caressed.

Changing the angle, I dove into her deeper, grinding my mouth over hers again and again until a growl vibrated my chest.

Her hands grasped my waist, tugging at the hem of my shirt until her fingertips dragged over bare skin and my entire body turned hot.

God, I wanted her. I wanted her in a way I'd never wanted anything or anyone ever before. I hadn't been lying. We might be connected by death, but to my heart, she was life.

My heart only saw her, only felt her. The connection that drew us together no longer mattered because it was nothing compared to what would keep us from drifting apart.

When our mouths separated, the sweet, low suckling sounds of our making out ceased, and immediately, I missed the noise.

Her cheeks were flushed when I pulled back. Seeing the bright spots of color suffuse her skin made me feel like I'd finally done something right. "I think we should go home."

"Our homes are in two different places," she told me.

I shook my head. "Oh no, angel. Your home is with me."

She looked away. "I can't stay with you anymore."

"Then I'll stay with you."

"We should talk to the police again."

I nodded, glancing at the clock. "First thing in the morning. It's late now. You look like you're about to fall over."

Abruptly, tears filled her eyes. "I'm so scared for Callie. I know exactly what she's living…"

"Hey now," I crooned, trying to hush some of her worry. Picking her up off the bed, I cradled her close. "We're going to find her. She's going to be okay. That girl has about a thousand lives. If she didn't, her own clumsiness would have already killed her."

Zoey made a sound—a cross between a laugh and a cry.

I didn't put her down again until I buckled her into the Viper. I had no clue what tomorrow was going to bring, but for tonight, I felt like all I could do was hold on tight.

The hour was late. The day had long turned dark, and the moon, large and heavy, hung low in the starless sky.

The press didn't care. They were waiting anyway, as if their sole purpose in life was to get photos confirming that Mr. Hollywood Royalty himself really was living with a beastly makeup artist.

The second the red Viper slowed for the gate blocking off his community, we were surrounded. Despite the tint on the windows, the flashing of the cameras was still piercing. Our names were being yelled over the purr of the expensive engine, along with question after question and requests for a statement.

"Son of a bitch," Nick swore, slowing even more because the vultures were practically throwing themselves in the path of the car.

"This is exactly why I should have gone home."

"They would be here regardless," he spat. "And they're probably at your place too."

Slap! Slap! Slap! The sharp, abrupt sound made me shriek and cower in my seat.

Nick said a few foul words, but when his hand slid over my arms, which were covering my head, his touch was gentle. "Don't be scared, angel. We'll be through the gate in seconds."

"Zoey!" a reporter yelled. "Zoey, roll down your window!"

Slap! Slap! Slap!

Every hard bang on the side of the car made me jump, despite the fact I knew what it was.

I was on edge. No. I was teetering on a cliff. *He is back. He never actually left. He's coming for me.*

Nick's palm slammed down on the horn, blasting out a warning that did nothing but fray my nerves more. Revving the engine of the sports car, he jerked forward, forcing back some of the crowd.

One of his hands settled on the back of my head, his fingers playing lightly with the strands of hair. I thought it would make the chaos inside me worse, but it didn't.

Knowing he was there helped.

The yelling grew duller, and the banging on our doors stopped as the car slid through the gates into the private community.

"What If they sneak through?" I worried, peering out the back window at the disappearing crowd.

"They'll get arrested," he deadpanned.

"Really?"

"Why do you think I pay so much to live behind these gates?"

"If those gates are so great, then why do you have another set in front of your house?" I muttered, glancing back once more.

He shrugged, his wide shoulders seeming even wider in the small interior of his fancy car. "I'm a cautious guy."

I didn't comment further as we waited for the gate blocking off his property to swing wide enough to drive through. A moment later, the garage door was lowering behind us, and he switched off the engine.

Instead of getting out, his arm reached for the back of my seat and his big body leaned close. "Look, I'm not going to sit here and tell you those gates out there mean nothing could get through. We both know bad shit happens."

"Sometimes unbelievable shit."

His lips tugged up in a quick smile. "Right." He agreed, running the pad of his pointer finger down the bridge of my nose. "But I can promise I'll do everything in my capability to try and keep you safe."

I looked away, uncomfortable because of the way his words made me feel.

"Zoey?"

"Why?" I asked, abrupt.

"What?"

"Why do you care this much?"

I could see his reflection in the passenger window, which I thought was sorely unfair because I was looking away to avoid seeing him. Despite a gallant effort not to look, every time he even moved an inch, my eyes focused in on the reflection. On him.

It was as if he knew I was looking because he kept his eyes straight ahead. It almost felt like he was staring at me, inviting me to look directly at his face and his answer.

"Because I love you."

How could he just say that? How could he feel it?

There wasn't a hint of hesitation in his tone. He didn't look away when he said it, *any* of the times those words crossed his lips. Even now, when he knew I was turned away, he stared straight ahead, looking right into the glass.

Pressing my forehead against the cool surface of the window, I shut my eyes. "What even is love?" I wondered.

"I think it probably means different things to different people."

"That was a rhetorical question," I muttered. Did the man have an answer for everything?

"So you don't want to know what it is to me?"

Damn him! Of course I want to know! I didn't answer.

"Okay then," he said, climbing out of the Viper and shutting the door behind him.

Glancing around, I watched his long legs carry him past the windshield. He didn't seem bothered in the least that I rebuffed him.

He could at least try!

Making a sour face, I scooped up my bag from between my feet and reached for the handle to get out. The door opened before I could grasp it, Nick towering in the open space.

As I pushed up to exit, he crouched down. We would have bumped heads if he hadn't grasped my shoulders, gently keeping me back.

"What are you doing?" I asked, suddenly breathless.

His hands dropped from my shoulders to rest on my knees. I couldn't enjoy the touch because insecurity took over. Glancing down to where his hand covered my left knee, I wondered.

Can he feel the top of the prosthetic? Is he weirded out by the end of my leg and the beginning of the socket? Is he sitting there right now trying not to react when what he really wants is to pull his hand away?

I was different. Not in a good way.

Following my gaze, he looked down, then back up. He didn't remove his hand. Instead, his fingers splayed so he could touch more.

Stiffening, about to pull away, I was stilled by his voice.

"You're different."

My eyes shot up. *That's what I just said!*

"But in a good way."

Wait—what?

"Nick." Pulling my foot in, I tried to slip out of his hold.

His body moved with mine like we were magnets with the exact same pull and where I went, he followed as though it were the law of physics.

Settling his palm more firmly over my knee, he refused to let go.

"That day when you fell into the water…" He began. "And you clung to me like I was all you had in the world."

"I-I was scared." I excused myself, embarrassed.

"A piece of me fell right then."

Surprise drew me up.

"The next day, when you came to work and told everyone about your leg…"

I blew out a shaky laugh. "God, I was so scared that day."

"You were brave and stubborn." The pride in his voice made my heart beat faster. When he smiled, all his face lit up. "Another piece of me chipped away."

What was he doing right now? What was this he was saying?

"The night your place was broken into, I literally broke every speed law to get there. All I could think was, *Not her. Anyone but her.*"

"Nick…"

"When I filmed that kissing scene with Jessica and you had to stand there and watch…" He recalled. "I didn't like it."

I didn't like it either. "It was just work."

He repeated, "I didn't like it."

I looked into his jewel-toned eyes, almost challenging all his pretty words. "Jessica is very beautiful."

"Jessica isn't you."

I looked away first. It was me who couldn't take the challenge.

Nudging my chin with the backs of his fingers, he drew my eyes back to his. "You asked me what love is, and this is my answer. It's piece by piece. Moment by moment. Including what's happening right now."

My brows drew together. "What's happening right now?"

"You haven't made me move my hand."

We both glanced down.

His hand still covered my left knee. Proving his point, Nick flexed his fingers and rubbed his palm gently over the area. I knew he could feel it. The distinction between my body and the device.

"This is love to me, Zoey," he whispered. "It's you."

My heart tumbled, crashing into my stomach. Honestly, I kind of wanted to puke. But not because I felt sick.

Oh. So that's what he's been doing.

He'd been fitting himself inside my heart.

She couldn't say it.

She didn't have to.

The fact Zoey felt it was more than enough for me. Not that she would admit that either, but again, she didn't have to.

It was adorable the way she'd run off to her room as though she could hide herself away. Zoey was good at hiding, but I wouldn't let her hide from me. Not anymore.

Fuck, life was short. It was unpredictable. It was hard.

One had to tread carefully with Zoey, understandably so. But if I let her set the pace completely, my arms would wear out from treading and I'd drown.

Discovering the man who killed my grandmother was still out there, still killing, and had set his sights on Zoey should have given me a sense of panicked urgency, an unstoppable drive to hurry the hell up and catch the bastard before he destroyed any more lives.

I did feel that way… but there was something else.

The desire to slow down.

The need to steal moments with Zoey away from all the chaos and danger. The urge to wrap her up in my arms and make certain she understood that even though we were brought together by death, I needed her in my life.

If I didn't take these moments with her, all we'd have was trauma.

I wanted more. I wanted to be the one to give her more.

Maybe it was selfish. But if a man wasn't selfish with his own life, was it really his? Who else could I live for? The Moth? Allowing that psycho to dictate every moment we spent was power I refused to relinquish.

I took a shower, made sure the bodyguards were in position around the property, and set the security alarm as added precaution. Then I shut off my phone and let myself in her room.

The sound of running water from the adjoining bath floated around the partially closed door. Light spilled out, stretching across the carpet in a wide beam. The only other light in the room was from a small lamp clicked on by the bed.

"Zo," I called out, pushing open the door.

"Agh!" she exclaimed, jolting in surprise. Leaning against the counter, pressing a hand against her chest, she leveled me with a scolding stare.

I laughed.

She was wearing a fluffy headband with bunny ears. It was a complete mismatch to the scowl on her face. Shaking her finger at me, she blubbered, "You think that's funny?" around the toothbrush hanging from between her lips. Toothpaste made a ring around her mouth and started to drip down her chin.

Still chuckling, I came forward, swiping at the mess with my thumb.

Her eyes widened so big I thought they might fall right out of her face. Shrieking again, she spun, ducking her head.

"Get out!" she demanded, pulling the toothbrush out of her mouth.

"No."

Her back stiffened, and she spit the water from her mouth into the sink, aggressively grabbing the hand towel beside her. Even after she was finished, she stayed rooted in place, back turned, face down, body so stiff it probably hurt.

Guilt pricked at me, weakening some of the resolve I had when I first walked in.

But then she shifted. Just enough that the ponytail she had her hair in swayed, the end of it brushing the back of her neck.

Tenderness washed over me like a tidal wave in a surging sea.

She was dressed all in pink. I never realized how girly it was until I saw it on her body. Her tank top was cotton and a racerback style. The burns to her left arm and the brand she always kept hidden were fully exposed.

Sensing I was looking, she reached around to lay a hand over what she could.

Shifting my eyes downward, I looked at the pink shorts hugging her tiny ass. She was tall and slender, barely any meat on her bones at all. But she still had a shape, a shape those running shorts accentuated right down to the white stripes down the sides.

Her skin was creamy and pale, untouched by the sun and outside world. It was the first time I'd ever seen her prosthetic entirely, the first time she wasn't covered up.

It was mechanical and looked to be mostly made of metal. The foot surprised me the most I think because there wasn't one at all. It kind of looked like… a paddle. No, like the insert of a shoe that had been created out of metal instead of something padded. Another similar-size paddle layered over it but arched up to give support to the metal rod making up the ankle. The skin above the prosthetic was covered by what looked like the top of a sock.

"You're staring."

"Because you're letting me look at you."

"I'm not letting you. You barged in."

"I knocked."

She made a rude sound.

"Turn around, angel."

"No. Go to bed."

The grip she had on her arm was turning her fingers white.

Sighing, I scooped her up. She was so surprised she fell backward, right into my arms.

"What are you doing?" she shrieked, smacking me on the shoulder. "Where is your shirt?" she hollered when her hand met bare skin.

"You told me to go to bed. I'm not going without you."

She hit me again. "Put me down!"

I sat her on the bathroom counter, moving in so I was between her legs. Instantly, her forehead fell onto my shoulder, her arms remaining at her sides.

"What are you doing, Nick?"

"Pushing you out of your comfort zone."

"My whole life is out of my comfort zone."

I made a sound, tugging on her ponytail. "No. You're scared as hell, and that keeps you from grabbing things that could make you happy."

A scoffing sound filled the bathroom. "Like you?"

"Yes. Like me."

Her body was completely still, but her voice was shaky. "Now isn't the time."

"If not now, when?"

She fell silent.

"The Moth is out there—" She fretted, but I cut her off.

"Yes, he is. He's been out there since nineteen eighty-four. Since before we were even born. How long will you give him, Zo? How long will you let him rule your world?"

"That's not fair."

"I know it's not." I agreed. I wasn't being fair. I was pushing. But I was doing it with a sincere heart. "You know what else isn't fair?"

She made a rude sound that made me smile.

"That you're sitting here hiding that beautiful face from me."

"I thought I was going to be alone the rest of the night," she grumped.

I'd never thought grumpiness was charming until now.

"Ahh," I mused. "That explains the cute ponytail."

She made a sound.

"And the bunny ears," I teased.

Gasping, she slapped a hand against the fuzzy headband and groaned.

Pulling her hand away, I kissed the backs of her fingers. "Are your eyes blue right now?"

She nodded.

"Show me."

She didn't say no, but she didn't lift her face either.

Placing my hands on either side of her neck, using the pads of my thumbs at her throat, I applied very minimal pressure, just enough to get her to tip back her head.

Shifting back a little, I gazed down into her fully exposed face.

The startling blue of her eyes made my heart gallop unevenly. Her eyelashes were naturally light, making me think of sunshine in a cloudless sapphire sky. Her nose was perky and cute, decorated with a small spattering of light freckles. The tone of her skin was pink and smooth, her lips naturally rosy.

She looked younger this way, with all her hair swept away from her face. Without makeup hiding many of her features. There was an innocence and freshness about her that inspired an even greater sense of protectiveness within me.

My silence unnerved her, as did my undivided attention. The tips of the bunny ears smacked me in the chin when she ducked her face.

"Let's make a deal," I suggested.

She looked up, nose wrinkling. "What?"

Unable to stop myself, I grabbed one of her cheeks and pinched it lightly. "You look even more like a bunny when you do your nose like that."

She smacked my hand away. "What deal?"

The teasing left my eyes and my voice. Grasping her sides, I shifted closer. "That you'll always let me see you like this."

Maybe it was too much. Or maybe I didn't want to see doubt in her eyes right now. Tonight.

Tilting my head to the side, I reconsidered. "How about for tonight, then?"

"What about tomorrow?" she whispered.

"I'll ask you again tomorrow. And the day after that. And the day after that. I'll take it one day at a time until you can give me more than that."

She blew out a shaky breath, ducking her face into my shoulder once more. "You're really good at this."

"No. I just know what I want."

"And you want me?"

"Yes."

She fell quiet. Not exactly the kind of response a guy wants when he basically lays it all out on the line. But hey, she didn't kick me out of the room. Progress. Right?

"You done in here?"

She nodded.

When I lifted her off the counter, she squealed, hands grasping my shoulders. Her legs wound around my waist, and she pulled back, wide blue eyes surprised. "What are you doing?"

"Taking you to bed."

Flipping off the light as I went, I went back through the bedroom to the door.

"The bed is over there," she said, pointing over my shoulder.

"You're sleeping in my bed tonight."

"When did you get so bossy?" she muttered.

I grinned. "I've always been this bossy, angel. I just always give in to you." Stopping halfway through the house, I put my face close to hers. "It's your turn to give in to me."

She stiffened, and I continued carrying her through the dark house.

"Where's all the bodyguards?" she asked, gazing around, timid.

"Outside. No one's in here but us tonight."

The only light in my room was from a small lamp near the bed, and it illuminated the room just enough without being overly bright.

All the bedding was black, with the exception of the sheets, which were white with black pinstripes.

After sitting Zoey on the bed, I sat close, angling to face her. "Show me how this thing works." I motioned to her leg.

Her hand went to it defensively. Or maybe protectively. Maybe both.

"What? Why?"

"Because I want to know about it."

Her eyes were wary like she was trying to decide what exactly I wanted.

"You don't normally sleep with it, right?"

She made a sound of agreement. "Not at home."

"All right, show me how it comes off."

She gaped.

"Didn't you already agree to let me see you tonight?"

"I thought you meant my face." She pointed at her scars, her ponytail, and that doggone cute headband.

"I meant all of you, Zo."

Again, her hand went to her knee. I understood her guard. I respected it. But fuck, it was exhausting. Perhaps pushing wasn't the best course of action. Or maybe my patience was wearing out. Even though I didn't want it, disappointment made my heart heavy. I wasn't sure what else I could do to get closer to her.

There wasn't anything. Anything but time.

Rising from the bed, I told her, "I'll take you back to your room so you can take it off and sleep comfortably."

"Wait." The touch against my wrist was light, but it was more than enough to make me turn back.

I half smiled. "Want me to carry you again?" Bending, I reached for her, but she grabbed my hands, stopping me.

I looked up. Our faces were almost level, our noses close to touching. The second our eyes met and held, currents of electricity passed between us. The air turned thick, and a knot of desire formed solidly in the center of my throat.

She didn't say anything, instead pulling me down onto the mattress beside her.

"To take it off, you have to push this pin down here near the ankle," she said, leaning down to show me the small button.

"Zoey."

Her hands paused, but she didn't look up.

"I pushed too hard. I'll wait 'til you're ready."

"I want to grab onto something that will make me happy."

I wasn't expecting that answer, and in the moments it took to recover, she started moving again. Pressing the pin down, she pulled off the prosthetic in a single motion. "It weighs about four pounds," she explained, lifting it up for me to see. "This part here is made of fiberglass." She pointed to the part that her leg slid down inside. "If you look in there at the bottom, there is a hole. That's where the pin clicks into place."

Setting it aside, she snuck a glance out of the corner of her eye before clearing her throat and turning toward the leg.

"This is my amputated leg," she introduced, rubbing her hand along the small part of leg that remained below her knee. It was actually more than I expected, not that I really expected anything.

There was definitely what looked like a white sock over the leg and a metal rod (or pin as she called it) sticking out of the end. Seeing it there made my stomach tumble.

"It's not very attractive," she said, obviously looking at my face.

Which I clearly did not control well. *Fuck.*

"No." I hurried to explain. "It's just… Does that hurt?" I pointed to the pin. "I don't want you to hurt."

When she didn't say anything, I glanced up. She was staring at me, her eyes tender.

"What?"

"You're worried it hurts me?" she whispered.

I nodded.

She sniffled lightly, then leaned in, pressing her lips to my cheek. "No one's ever asked me if it hurts."

A strand of hair was sticking out from under the headband, so I reached out and tucked it away.

Pulling back, she went back to explaining. "The pin isn't in my leg." Tugging off the sock, she set it aside, then reached down for something else. "This is called a liner." She went on, tugging off what looked like yet another sock. This one was grey and wasn't made of cotton. But when she pulled it off, the pin came with it. "It's made of silicon. This is what the pin is attached to, and that's what goes into the socket."

I nodded.

Turning the liner inside out, she went on. "See? The inside is made of a silicon material. This thing here that the pin is attached to?" She pointed to a white disk-shape thing on the end. "Is called an umbrella. To put it on your leg, you hold the umbrella section so it's flat and then you place it against the leg, then roll on the liner."

"And then you put the sock on it, then the socket?" I asked.

She nodded. "The pin clicks into place when you stand up, and that is what basically locks the prosthetic in place."

"Seems pretty simple."

A current of tension surrounded her. Then she cleared her throat. I didn't understand why until she set aside the liner and gazed down at her fully exposed leg.

Ah.

"So." She began nervously. "This is my leg." Rubbing her hands over the skin, she trailed down to where it was rounded on the end. "It's actually called a stump."

I frowned. "Really?"

She nodded.

"I don't like that," I grumbled, suddenly irritated.

"Why not?"

"It seems like a bad thing to say." I hesitated. "Like an insult."

She giggled. "It's just a technical term. It's what it called. It's not meant to be anything insulting."

I nodded, stealing a glance back down.

"It's gets thinner down here because it has shrunk. Loss of muscle mass, things like that."

The skin was smooth and clean. There wasn't any terrible scaring or anything like that. Maybe I expected it to look more… rough? But it didn't. It just looked like a leg with a section missing.

"When I sleep at night, I wear a shrinker in case the limb swells. That way I still fit into the socket in the morning."

"A shrinker?" I asked. "Is that like a sock?" I remembered seeing her with something like that on the night her place was broken into.

She nodded. "Yep."

"And that's it?"

She seemed mildly amused. "Well, for the prosthetic, yes."

"What about in the shower?"

"No, this one isn't made for water. Plus, it's important to keep the stump—" I made a sound. She patted me on the shoulder and cleared her throat. "The end of the leg clean so I don't get sores."

I realized something. "Isn't it hard to shower with one leg?"

"I have handles and a bench in my shower at home."

Anger made me jump up off the bed. "Not here. Why the hell didn't you say anything to me? How hard has it been for you in the mornings?"

Her eyes widened. "I've managed."

I let about five curse words loose and rubbed a hand over my hair.

"Nick." She gasped. "That was really dirty."

"I'm pissed off," I muttered. How could I be so stupid to not think about how she would be affected living here? My house was not really handicap friendly.

I stopped pacing. "I never thought of you as handicapped."

"What?"

I turned. "You aren't handicapped to me, so I never thought of it. Because of that, you've had to live with difficulty."

Pushing up off the bed, she wobbled a little, trying to maintain her balance. Rushing over, I grasped her waist.

"I hardly call staying in this mansion difficult."

"I'm sorry. Tell me everything you need. I'll get contractors out here tomorrow."

"Don't be ridiculous." She half snorted, pushing me away.

Without my balance, she lost hers and fell backward.

I caught her around the waist, but it was too late. The momentum was already there, and both of us fell back on the bed with me landing firmly on top of her.

"Fuck me in the goat ass," I muttered, pushing up so I didn't crush her.

"What?" she exclaimed, slapping her palms on my biceps.

"Did I hurt you?"

"No, but that poor goat." She worried.

I threw back my head and laughed.

She joined me, and the sound of our laughter mingling brought a rush of emotion so strong all sound stalled in my throat.

Our eyes connected. Humor turned to desire, and desire gave way to something else. Something I wasn't expecting.

Emotion. Tenderness. Love.

"Thank you for showing me," I whispered, dragging the backs of my fingers across her cheekbone.

"You don't think…" Her lips rolled in, stopping her words.

"Don't think what?"

The tip of her pink tongue stroked over her mouth, and her eyes left mine. "That it's ugly?"

Grasping her chin a little rougher than I intended, I forced her face back to mine. I hoped my green eyes seared her with sincerity. I hoped the truth of my words could be felt all the way to her bones. "There is not one thing about you that's ugly. Not one damn thing."

I punctuated the words with a demanding kiss, as if I could shove the words into her soul by fusing my mouth with hers. A small moan vibrated her chest, and I kissed deeper, encouraged by her reaction.

She melted into the mattress, and I forgot about supporting my own weight, instead pressing her deeper into the blankets until every inch of her was pressed against every inch of me. When at last my lungs screamed for air, I ripped my mouth away, sucking in great gulps before delving into her neck to suck at the skin.

"Nick." She gasped, tensing. "Wait."

Startled, I pulled back immediately, scouring her face for the answer to what I did wrong.

Her eyes were unfocused, her lips swollen and red. Her cheeks were spotted with pink, and the bunny headband was falling off her head.

I was proud of my handiwork. I was proud that she looked so thoroughly fucked when all I'd done was kiss her.

"What?" I gasped, still not comprehending what I'd done wrong.

Her eyes flashed with insecurity as her hand slid between us to cup the side of her neck. Eyes narrowing, I grasped her chin. "Did I hurt you?" I demanded, turning her face so I could see. "I have a tendency to use my teeth," I muttered, pissed at myself.

Her hand was in the way. I couldn't see what I'd done.

"Move your hand, angel."

"Nick."

"Angel," I growled.

Reluctantly, her hand fell aside.

Realization dawned. It was her left side. I'd grazed the scar on her jawline… probably kissed the scarring on her neck.

Horror washed through me. "Did it hurt? Is your skin sensitive there?" When she didn't answer, I glared down. "Zoey."

She blinked, shocked. "You didn't notice where you were kissing?"

"What? No. All I was doing was feeling—" My words ended abruptly. "Is that what this is about?" I asked, fucking relieved. "Because I touched them?"

She nodded.

Rolling off her, my back hit the mattress. "You almost gave me a fucking coronary." I moaned. "I thought I hurt you."

"You cuss a lot."

"I'm horny," I blurted out.

The second I did, I froze. *What the fuck is wrong with me tonight?* "Zoey, I—"

She started laughing.

Leaning up on one elbow, I glowered down at her. "What's so funny?"

"You," she answered, dissolving into a fit of giggles. The giggling was more insulting than the laughter.

"Explain yourself."

"You burst in the bathroom and try to be all bossy and forceful, but you're just as nervous as I am."

"I am not," I declared.

"Are too." She giggled again.

"Take that back."

"No!"

I leapt on her again, straddling her hips and pinning her down. Burying my fingers in her ribs, I started to tickle her.

She bucked and giggled. "Ow!"

I leapt off her again. "Zoey!" Grabbing the tank top, I yanked it up, looking down at her ribs. While my face was buried beneath the pink tank, she started laughing again.

Pulling my face out, I pinned her with a glare. "Are you joking with me right now?"

"Your face!" She pointed.

"I thought I hurt you!"

She kept right on giggling.

Damn her, the sound was incredibly cute.

Her body still shaking with amusement, I crawled over her, resting my elbows on either side of her and lowering so I was lying atop her.

Once there was full contact between us, her humor died away, and we were left watching each other in the dim bedroom light.

The sound of her swallowing gave me immense satisfaction. Yeah, maybe I was a little nervous with her. But she was nervous too.

"I'm so afraid I'll do something wrong with you," I confided. "I want to push, but I'm so anxious I'll scare you away."

"No one's ever cared this much," she returned. "I'm not sure I'm worth it…" Her voice wobbled, her eyes straying away. But then they came back, settling on mine like the blue sky over a green forest. "But please keep pushing. It's hard for me, but I don't mind it when it's you doing it."

Butterflies went wild in my middle, excitement twisted me up inside, and my heart swelled so much it pressed against my ribs.

Slowly, I reached up to tug the headband off her head, tossing it somewhere into the room. Smoothing the stray hair away from her face, I gazed down, taking in every inch of her.

"All the other pieces of me that hadn't fallen for you yet? They all just crumbled. I'm completely and totally in love with you."

Tears gathered in her eyes, shimmering like sunlight on the Caribbean. Holding her face in place, I closed the distance between us, my nose brushing against her cheek first.

Her breath caught, but she didn't push me away and I held still, giving her ample time to do it.

Granted permission, I brushed my lips over her cheek, slowly, lovingly kissing all the burns, all the scars… all the pain.

Yes, the texture was uneven against my lips, and yes, when I kissed the raised scar in the center of her brow, my heart ached a little for everything she'd been through… but that wasn't what I focused on.

It wasn't what I wanted her to focus on.

I made love her to face, to her old injuries and the pain they still caused. I tried to soothe away any insecurity she felt by letting me this close. I wanted her to know that even though the skin was damaged, it could still feel my lips, it was still worthy of caress.

When the flavor of salt passed over my tongue, I pulled back, blinking down at her with half-closed eyes.

She was crying.

Silent tears leaked from her eyes, sliding down the sides of her face and dripping onto the bed.

"Do you want me to stop?" I whispered.

She shook her head.

"Can you feel it now?" I asked her. "How much I love you?"

Another tear slipped free, I leaned down and licked it away.

"I think I can," she confessed.

"Do you want more?"

She nodded.

There was no hesitation in Nick Preston. Not a single, solitary drop. The confidence in which he touched me, the sincerity in his gaze, left no room for doubt.

In eight years, no one had even come close to this.
In eight years, no one even tried.
Until him.
Until now.

Right now in this bed, under the dim light of the lamp, I wasn't a beast and he wasn't a beauty. Though, he was beautiful. There would never be anyone as beautiful as him.

I wasn't a woman with scars and a missing limb. I didn't live in hiding, and my heart wasn't walled off by grief. He wasn't a celebrity adored by everyone, royalty that could have anything and anyone he wanted.

This room wasn't crowded by jealous fans, bitter rivals, or people wanting to pull us apart.

I was a girl. He was a boy.

Our hearts beat in sync, and our bodies melted into one.

His breath was hot against my skin, his lips smooth and damp. Every stroke of his tongue made me cry out, and the way his wide frame blocked out the entire world above me offered peace I'd truly never felt before.

When he pushed away, I grabbed to pull him back. His eyes were darker than usual, his face flushed with desire. Instead of pulling him down, I allowed him to pull me up, tugging off the tank top as I sat up.

Air brushed over my sensitive breasts, my nipples already puckered. He kissed me again before climbing off my lap and moving around behind me, positioning me so I was sitting between his spread legs.

Goose bumps rose along my arms when he brushed the ponytail out of the way, fastening his lips on my shoulder. Suckling his way down, he kissed over the back of my arm… over the scars marring the skin. I tensed for the first time when he drew close to the brand, unsure how I would feel if he touched the mark that sicko forced me to wear.

Again, Nick didn't hesitate, as if he didn't give a flying fuck some other man branded me, some other man tried to claim me as his.

The thickness of his tongue licked over it, as if it wasn't the mark of a psycho, but a dessert he couldn't wait to eat.

I gasped, feeling the dampness of his tongue, the texture of it rubbing over that stain.

Curling his hands around my shoulders, he did it again, and literally everything inside me loosened.

Moaning, I reached around, burying my fingers in his hair as he kissed and sucked across my back, going up to use his teeth on the back of my neck.

My body rocked impatiently, moving against him, feeling his erection against my lower back.

Oh, he was good. So good.

I'd gone from timid and unsure to writhing against him, practically begging for me.

Wrapping an arm around me from behind, he pulled me down, slipping around and pulling off the rest of my clothes.

His body looked like a masterpiece created by a sculptor, not a flesh-and-blood man. The definition of his chest made my hands itch to run over it, and the way his abs rippled all the way down beneath the waistband of his shorts gave me a dry mouth.

Emboldened by the fiery look in his eyes, I reached up, grasping the white string on the front of his shorts, and tugged. His pants sagged, revealing that V-shape muscle that was kryptonite for everyone with ovaries.

"You sure?" he asked, even though his chest was heaving, even though his pupils were dilated and the cock under his shorts was straining to get free.

"I'm sure."

Diving on me again, his mouth devoured mine, and the cock I'd been ogling seconds before pushed against my drenched center, making me moan.

While I tugged at his waistband, an impatient sound ripped from my throat as he kissed over my collarbone.

Chuckling, he leaned up, reaching into his nightstand and coming back with a row of condoms.

I arched a brow at the amount in his grip, and he offered a roguish grin. "I told you I'm a horny bastard."

Tossing them down, he pulled his pants free, finally revealing the part of him I'd only felt and not yet seen.

It was beautiful. Did you expect anything less? Rising out of a neat patch of golden hair, skin smooth and shiny, head swollen and thick.

He reached for the condom, and my teeth sank into my lower lip.

Sensing a change, he glanced up, pausing as he rolled on the protection. "What's wrong?"

I swallowed.

"I'll stop."

I caught his hand before he could pull off the rubber, stroking his fingers with a reassuring hand. "I want to." I promised. "I just… It's been eight years."

A slow smile spread over his face, lighting up his eyes. "Really?"

"Like you didn't know," I muttered.

Finished with his task, our bodies brushed together, my legs automatically opening to accept him.

Brushing my hair away from my face, he gazed down with loving eyes. He didn't say anything for a long time, just stared at me… his eyes saying so much without him whispering a word.

"I'll take care of you, angel."

All the nerves blew away, and my hand curled around his back.

Our lips fused the moment he pushed into my body. A sound ripped from my throat, but he caught it, swallowing it down. I felt his arms and legs shake as he held himself still, allowing my body time to adjust to his size.

Tugging my lips free, I kissed his shoulder, and he started to move.

Sensation after sensation rocked my body. Currents of pleasure shot like lightning beneath my skin. He moved with care but with strength, and my body succumbed to his completely.

Nick had earned my trust, knowing exactly when to hold back and now knowing exactly when to push. All the fear and stress fell away. For the first time in as long as I can remember, I was present solely in the moment, feeling nothing but the way he filled me.

There was nothing more precious than what he was giving to me, and though I didn't say the words, my heart whispered, *I love you,* over and over.

"What are you doing?" she shrieked, delighting my heart.

I was beginning to think this woman could do no wrong.

"Taking a shower," I replied mildly as the sheets covering her fine, naked body slowly stripped away.

"Then why are you yanking me out of bed?" she asked, covering her naked chest with her arms.

A laugh rumbled out of me. "It's a little late to be covering that now, sweetheart. I've already seen it."

She smacked me.

I liked it.

Reaching into the shower, I turned on the sprays, stepping back out with her still in my arms.

"Nick!" she demanded.

Her hair was half out of the ponytail it had been in last night, and the strands were all wild about her head.

Her blue eyes were fuzzy from sleep, and she had whisker burns on her cheeks from me.

"Guess I need to shave," I said, frowning at the marks.

"Huh?"

Gently kissing the rash, I stepped into the shower, backing in so the water didn't hit her all at once.

"All my stuff is in the other shower!"

"Use mine." I shrugged. Leaning into her ear, I whispered, "So you'll smell like me all day."

She made a rude sound, but the corners of her lips turned up.

"From now on, you will shower with me," I declared, setting her down but anchoring an arm around her waist.

"And why is that?"

"I've been a bad boyfriend. I should have fixed the shower right away. So I'll help you until the problem is rectified."

"B-boyfriend!" she exclaimed. "Who said you were my boyfriend?"

"Boyfriend or husband, angel. Pick one."

"What?" The shock on her face was pretty enjoyable.

Ah, I was in a good mood today.

"Boyfriend it is." I agreed.

"You can't just declare something like that."

"Rinse your hair," I said, turning her into the spray.

She gave me a dirty look, but she started rinsing her hair. Popping the top on the shampoo, I held it out for her. "You don't want to be my girlfriend?"

"I didn't say that." She hedged, soaping up her head.

"What would the press say if they knew I was denied by a woman?"

"I didn't deny you," she insisted.

Reaching around, I patted her bare ass. "Be a good girlfriend and give me a kiss."

Her eyes narrowed. I kissed her anyway. She kissed me back.

That meant she agreed.

Conditioner in her hair, I was washing her body when she said, "My future isn't certain."

As I lowered the loofah, suds dripped down my fingers, landing on the shower floor. "What?"

She spun in the circle of my arm, lifting somber blue eyes. "I can't be your girlfriend because I might not be here much longer." In a much quieter voice, she added, "He's coming for me."

The loofah hit the wall with a loud smack. Suds splattered everything, including us. Grabbing her shoulders, I yanked her back to glare down at her.

"You're saying you can't be mine because you're already his?"

Her eyes widened. "N-n-no, I—"

"We're going to get one thing straight right here, right now." I fumed. Water from the multiple showerheads and wall-mounted jets sprayed around us. The waterfall from the ceiling rained over our heads, and I brought us backward to pin her against the wall.

"That animal has no claim on you whatsoever. No hold on your life… no right to your death. You saying you won't be mine because he's coming for you is bullshit! I know you're scared. Fuck, I am too. But that's not going to stop me from holding on to you, loving you."

Her chin wobbled. Under my hold, she trembled. "What happens if he kills me?" She burst out, a sob ripping from her throat. "It would have been better to not have me at all. Then you wouldn't have to lose me."

Her words pierced my heart. The thought of her suddenly disappearing from my life was so awful my chest ached.

I pulled her close, pressing my cheek against her head, cradling her in my arms. "It's too late for that, angel. Girlfriend or not, you're already mine. Mine. Not his." That sicko thinking he had some claim on her made me want to kill. Pulling her back, I stared intently. "I won't let him hurt you. Your future is not uncertain. It's here with me."

"I'm so afraid you're going to get hurt," she confessed, the words rushing out and full of despair. "What if something happens to you? What if he takes you away from me?"

Ahh. Here it was. The real issue. Zoey wasn't afraid that I might lose her. She was afraid that she was going to lose me.

She couldn't say I love you. She couldn't put a label on our relationship. She was afraid if she did, it would all be taken away. Like her entire life ended seven years ago.

She'd lost everything, even her own identity. Frankly, it was a miracle she'd opened up to me this much.

Sliding my hands beneath her arms, I lifted. Automatically, her legs wound around my waist. Pinning her against the wall with my body, I brushed the wet hair from her face.

The anguish in her eyes shackled me like armor. There was nothing in this world that could protect me better than the love of this woman, knowing just how devastated she would be if I was suddenly gone. Her fear made me strong. Strong enough to fight everything—even her demons—so I could remain at her side.

Kissing the corner of her mouth, I whispered that I loved her. "You can love me, angel. You can think about next week, next month, even next year. I'm not going anywhere, and neither are you. You're stuck with me now, and no one, not even that deranged psychopath, will keep us apart."

"You don't know that," she whispered, cuddling into my shoulder.

"I do know. I've known from the minute I first laid eyes on you that we're connected. It's the kind of connection that's strong enough to keep both our hearts beating."

"Nick," she whispered.

"We're going to meet with the cops in a bit. We're going to find Callie and put that animal in a cage. And then you and me… we're going to have a long, happy life."

"I don't know how you do it. But you make me feel strong."

"You *are* strong."

"I'm not used to… having someone."

Most of the thunder churning inside me quieted. The calm in her eyes was greater than the panic, and for her to admit she "had someone" was something I considered a win. "You have time to get used to it. All the time you need."

She nodded, going back in to hug me fiercely.

"So," I said, injecting some playfulness back into my tone. "You gonna wash my back?"

She laughed. "Get me the soap."

"So bossy," I murmured, pulling away.

When I turned to give her my back, I felt the mask I used to cover my dark mood fall away. As her hands slid over my skin, I made a silent promise to myself.

That psychopath took my grandmother… There was no way in hell I'd let him take anyone else I loved.

It was surreal.

I went from a shower with the sexiest man alive to a meeting with the police about the serial killer who was after me, and now I was supposed go to the set like it was just some ordinary workday and everything wasn't burning down around me.

Wait.

That fire analogy was in *really* poor taste.

Standing in the window, I watched the detectives' unmarked car head down the long driveway toward the gate guarding Nick's property.

Callie.

Thoughts of Nick's assistant plagued me, creating a sense of urgency beneath my skin and tightness in my chest. The meeting with the police left me with lackluster confidence they would be able to find her. Callie's whereabouts were still unknown, and the more minutes that passed, the more anxious I became because I—above anyone else—knew exactly what she could be suffering through. The longer that monster had her, the worse it would be.

I didn't want Callie to end up like me. Or worse… dead.

Guilt overwhelmed me, adding another layer to the panic threatening to bring me down. While she was out there frightened and held captive, I'd spent the night in Nick's arms, grabbing hold of something I truly wanted but never allowed myself to have.

I knew it was wrong, but I was weak to Nick. To the way he made me feel.

Meeting him changed everything for me. In such a short time, he shattered the wall I kept around my heart, bulldozed in, and took control.

I felt stronger. More confident. Alive.

Funny, it wasn't staring into the face of death that made me feel alive. It was staring into Nick's eyes.

It was love.

If I lost that, if I lost him, then The Moth wouldn't have to kill me because I'd already be walking around lifeless.

It was selfish, though. I couldn't sacrifice Callie so I could have happiness. I wouldn't truly have happiness anyway if it was at the expense of someone else.

The Moth took Callie because of me, and it was me who was going to get her back.

The cops were still piecing together all the evidence, all the information we'd dumped on them since yesterday. This morning added even more to get through. The possibility that the man who'd killed

Deborah Ascott was also the Bloodlust Killer, aka The Moth, was a lot to digest. It would take time to build a case, to put together evidence and clues.

Callie didn't have time.

And honestly, neither did I. He was coming for me. The note he left was proof. The Moth wasn't the kind of man who would sit back and wait. He'd been playing with me too long.

I knew him better than anyone else because I was literally the only person to ever meet him and live.

This was up to me.

Callie's life, my life, even Nick's life and his grandmother's justice all rested in my hands.

Where could he be? Think!

Something brushed against my side, making me jump. I would have fallen into the window if Nick's arm didn't pull me back.

"I didn't mean to scare you." He apologized against my ear. I liked the way his hand rubbed soothingly against my waist, punctuating the apology.

Remnants from the way he made me feel last night poured over me, excitement mixing with the panic already tumbling around.

Overwhelmed with emotions, I turned in his arm, his other one slipping around me as well. Burrowing close, I cuddled against his chest, inhaling his familiar scent.

I never knew the scent of someone could make me feel safe.

The thought made me still. My heart began to pound erratically, and my hands began to tremble. Nausea hit me like a tidal wave, making me clutch tighter to Nick.

"Zo?" He started to pull back, concern dripping from his voice.

I followed, clutching harder, just wanting to be against him.

"Okay," he whispered, folding himself around me. "It's okay."

My whole body was trembling now, and it was an effort to keep my teeth from chattering.

Sweeping me off my feet, Nick carried me through the house into my bedroom, sitting down on the bed with me in his lap, and I remained stuck to him like an octopus.

"I'm getting in your bag," he said, his voice seemingly far away.

The distance I heard panicked me more, and a sob vibrated my throat. Curling a hand around the back of his neck, I pressed even closer, assuring myself he was actually still right here.

With his palm against the back of my head, he gently nudged me back. I looked up at him, eyes drinking in his face like I was dehydrated.

"Open your mouth," he instructed. His fingers brushed against my lips, and I opened for him. My anxiety medication slid across my tongue, leaving that nasty flavor all melting pills created.

I made a face but swallowed it down.

Nick produced a glass of water from the nightstand, but when I reached up to take it, he made a tsking sound and held it to my lips himself.

After a few swallows, I collapsed against his chest again, utterly drained.

Moving us back on the bed, Nick settled against the headboard and pillows, tucking me along his side. Draped partly over him, I let my eyes drift closed, focusing on the feel of his fingers dragging up and down my back.

I don't know how long he held me like that, but eventually, the worst of the panic faded away and rational thought returned. My body no longer shuddered and trembled, and the storm in my stomach was calm.

"I had a panic attack," I told him, keeping my arm tucked tightly around his middle.

"Yeah."

"I've brought a lot of trouble to your life. A lot of baggage."

His fingers pulled through the length of my hair. "You've brought more happiness than anything."

"We can't be happy until Callie is safe. Until this is over."

"The police—"

"They didn't catch him when he killed your grandmother. They didn't catch him as the Bloodlust Killer… They aren't going to be able to catch him now."

"They have a lot more to go on now."

"Callie doesn't have that kind of time. Neither do I."

He paused. "What are you thinking?"

Taking a deep breath, I sat up. "The police said they already checked the school where he'd kept me before."

Nick nodded. "No one is there. The fire destroyed a lot of the building. You can't even get down into that old basement where the original pool was now."

"Why there?" I murmured. "Why would he take his victims to an abandoned underground pool at a high school?"

"Because it was abandoned and forgotten about. Because it was perfectly covered by the brand-new pool and gym on the floor above it and all the classrooms above that. No one would ever think a serial killer was keeping his victims literally underneath a bunch of kids."

"But there has to be a reason, right? A personal connection or something."

"The police are already searching every pool, open and closed down, within a hundred-mile radius. If he's using another pool, they'll find him."

I shook my head. He wouldn't be stupid enough to use the same kind of pool again.

Think!

"It all started with Deborah, though… with *Moth to a Flame*," I murmured.

Nick made a sound of agreement. "On the set of the sequel."

I jerked back. "The movie was never released."

He shook his head. "Of course not."

"Her murder was filmed, right?"

Nodding, he said, "They thought she was acting, that they had gone off script… until it was too late."

"Does your family have a copy of that movie? Of what happened?"

Nick frowned. "Yes. They made a cut with my grandmother's death as the actual end of the sequel. But my family prevented it from being released."

"That DVD you had last night at your mom's…"

He nodded. "That was it. I was going to show you, but I don't think—"

I grabbed his forearm, cutting off his words. "Show me!"

Concern darkened his features. "I don't think that's a good idea."

"I need to see it, Nick! It might have some clues."

"Then the police—"

"I know him!" I yelled. "I know how his mind works. I might see something that could help Callie."

"You just had a panic attack." His voice was gentle, as was the hand cupping the side of my face.

"I'll keep having them as long as he's out there. And they'll only get worse if Callie dies because of me."

The gentleness left his tone. "This is not your fault."

"Do you have the DVD?"

His eyes cut away.

"Nick!"

"I brought it last night."

Scrambling off the bed, I held out my hand for him. "I need to watch it. Right now."

Reluctantly, he nodded. "If it's too much," he said, grabbing my shoulders, "you'll tell me?"

I agreed readily, tugging him from the room so he could fetch the movie. Pacing in front of the large, thin flat-screen mounted on the wall, I waited impatiently for him to appear.

The second he did, all my attention went to the slim case in his hand, and my mind began to reel. The calm I'd managed to regain thanks to Nick's arms and my medication was being endangered by what I was about to see.

It didn't matter. It couldn't matter.

All that mattered was getting Callie back.

I paced more while Nick slid the DVD into the side of the flat-screen and picked up a thin remote. My quick movements were a direct contrast to his stillness as he called up the picture.

"Skip to the end," I told him.

Once he was there, the picture paused, and he turned, stepping into my line of vision and blocking out everything else.

"Play it," I urged, trying to go around him.

Catching my hand, he guided me to the couch, pulling me down beside him. "Are you sure about this? We already know there are similarities between his killings. This could…"

My eyes met his when he faltered.

He sighed. "I miss your blue eyes," he murmured.

"This could trigger another panic attack. Is that what you're worried about?"

He nodded.

"But if it helps, then that's all that matters."

"*You* matter."

"Then do this for me," I pleaded.

One of his hands lifted mine, linking our fingers together, and the other raised the remote and hit play.

My melodic whistling was interrupted by the sound of pathetic whimpering. I would have been angry at the ruination of my song, but I'd been waiting for this. For her.

She was weaker than my flame, her resolve more like a spark. The hit on the head knocked her out the entire night, which made it hard to play.

I looked forward to the lead of this movie showing up because this stand-in was rather lame.

But finally, she was awake.

This movie could begin.

"Hello?" she called out, her voice timid and afraid.

My whistling continued because the song wasn't finished. She started crying, her pathetic, meek whining disturbing the song I was singing just for her.

"Shut up!" I screamed, burying the toe of my boot in her side to punctuate the command.

"*Ungh.*" She gasped, falling over and curling in on herself.

I continued to whistle, finishing out the melody. When the song was over, I stared down at the quaking woman who was crying silently.

No fight in this one.

Not many had the kind of fight inside them strong enough to ignite a flame. Only few were enough to draw in The Moth and make him dance by the fire, risking his wings.

Horror movies were only good when the killer had a worthy opponent, someone who was capable of matching his wickedness with their own.

In the end, evil wicked would always win out over the pure hearted because death always won over life.

Grabbing a fistful of the blond hair on my captive's head, I yanked her up. She cried out, grabbing at the hand pulling at her roots, smacking my wrists.

Ignoring her lowly attempts, I ripped the covering off her eyes. She cried out, her hand moving to her bleeding skull. Head wounds always bled so much, but plastic was good at keeping things tidy.

"I already picked out your spot," I told her, pointing at a length of chain suspended from the ceiling.

Her eyes were shell-shocked and slightly foggy, but her blue stare followed my direction.

She stared as if she didn't understand, so I kicked the plastic she was sitting on, giving her a clue.

The stand-in looked down, horrified at the blood smeared around and soaking her clothes. Adrenaline must have made it through her veins because she perked up, looking back at the chain and then near it to a chain that was not empty.

Covering her hand with her mouth, she screamed as she flung backward, forcing me to rip out some of her hair as she went. Her eyes were wide like saucers, and the fear permeating the air around us was a beautiful perfume.

Her stare bounced between all the cocoons hanging from the ceiling before looking back down at the plastic I would use to create hers.

"Your turn is coming."

She started to scream, scrambling up to run away. Tilting my head, I watched as the chain shackled around her ankle halted her retreat.

Horrified, she grabbed at the metal, tugging and screaming.

"Let me go!" she begged. "Please!"

I stared at her. She would look better in a white gown that wasn't stained with blood.

When I started to walk away, she called out, "Wait!"

I stopped. No one had ever asked me to stay with them before. I turned back.

"Please, don't leave me here."

The spark I saw in her grew a little brighter.

"Please," she pleaded. "Tell me what you want."

The sound of her calling me back made me hurry. The second I came into view, she fell back on her butt, weeping.

"Thank you for coming back." Her voice was desperate. Like she needed me. "Why are you doing this?" she whimpered.

Tossing the folded gown beside her, I pointed to it.

When she reached for it with red-stained hands, I lunged, smacking them away. Cringing back, she folded in on herself. I snatched her hand, she screamed, but I held it out, showing her how filthy she was.

Staring between me and her hand, eventually, she nodded.

I let go, and she used the end of her dress to wipe off the blood. This time, when she reached for the gown, I didn't stop her.

When I didn't move or turn away, she peered up at me. "My head hurts."

The chain slapped against the floor when I dragged her over. Her shouts and cries of pain echoed around the room as I ripped off the filthy clothing covering her body.

"No!" she cried, fighting. "No!"

I backhanded her across the face, making her fall silent.

After that, I dressed her in the nightgown, allowing it to fall into place over her legs.

When I was done, she scuttled back, wrapping her hands around her knees. "Th-thank y-you," she said, not looking at me.

My head tilted. No one had ever thanked me before either.

Her eyes strayed to the hanging bundles of plastic around the room. Then she winced, putting a hand to her forehead.

Squatting, in front of her, I stared at the wound on her head.

Her movements stilled. Slowly, her hand lowered from her head, and her eyes met mine. She stared directly at my mask, not shrinking away, eyes traveling down to the hoodie, then back up again to my face. "Why do you seem so familiar? Why did you put on that mask? I've already seen your face."

She gasped.

"*Moth to a Flame*," she whispered, glancing down at the gown and then back up. "You killed Deborah Ascott… You killed Nick's grandmother!"

Jolting upright, I paced away. *Nick's grandmother? Nick Preston… the same Nick who was keeping me from my flame?*

"Who?" I demanded.

Cowering, she shook her head. "Nothing. I-it was just a g-guess."

I pulled my leg back to kick her, and she fell over onto the floor. "No, please!"

"Explain!" I demanded again, holding my foot poised for attack.

"That's why you're doing this, right? Because I'm Nick's assistant? I don't know what kind of vendetta you have against his family, but haven't they suffered enough? You killed his grandmother, his grandfather killed himself, and his mother has never had peace!"

My heart sped up, beating excitedly.

How poetic. I was drawn back to my flame because she was fatefully connected to my very first kill.

A horror film connected through decades… a sequel that was actually a saga. The opportunity for an epic conclusion.

She screamed and called out to me as I left the room, desperately trying to call me back. At first, I was slightly charmed that she wanted my company, but now I was busy.

If I made the connection, then my flame would too.

It wouldn't be long now. She would be here soon.

Her nightgown brushed against her ankles, either urging her on or warning her to run away.

She couldn't run anymore.

Out in the hallway, the creaking of the stairs proved she was right. Her heart accelerated to the point of pain. Her feet quickened farther into the bedroom until she bounced off one of the hanging bundles.

"He made me wear a nightgown like that," Zoey whispered, eyes fastened to the screen, hand gripping mine like we might be ripped apart. "Long, white… the fabric was so heavy when it got wet, when he hosed me down. It felt like I was wearing a weighted vest, like my weak legs and injured body couldn't possibly withhold the burden."

My stomach flipped. The breakfast I'd eaten earlier sloshed around, but that wasn't what made me queasy. It was the sound of her voice. The hollow way she spoke like she was possessed by demonic memories that no exorcism could purge.

"There were bodies like that where I was. Wrapped up in plastic, not opaque enough to hide the majority of his victims. Some of them had been cocooned for so long the state of their bodies was only contained by the material he wrapped them in."

I didn't look at the screen, and she didn't look away. She was imprisoned by the horror in front of her, just as I was by the woman beside me.

Her feet pounded over the sound of her whimper as she weaved through the other dead bodies, rushing for the door. Out in the hall, she stopped, coming face to face with the killer who was obsessively drawn to her.

"It was just like that," she murmured, hand squeezing me even tighter. "I ran through the bodies… but he was there."

On the screen, my grandmother screamed as the knife drove into her body. It was a sound that haunted my nightmares. Even though I'd never known her, it didn't matter. Her murder haunted me like a ghost with unfinished business, and now I understood why.

Zoey made a sound, her hand going to her shoulder where she had been stabbed.

"That's enough," I said, lifting the remote to shut off the TV.

"Wait!" she insisted, pushing my hand down. "I need to see."

Bloodcurdling screams filled the room, and Zoey cowered into my side, her body shaking like a newborn calf.

Enough.

Muting the sound instantly, the shrieks of murder cut off, but the clingy feeling of death permeated the room anyway.

Curling my arm around her, I tugged Zoey into my lap, pushing her head against my chest. She let me hold her, but her eyes strained to still see the TV.

"He just jumped right through the window," she echoed, watching as he crashed through the glass. "That was for real?"

I made a sound of agreement.

Finally, her eyes came to me. "What happened after that?"

Gesturing, we both watched the final moments of *Moth to a Flame's* sequel.

Red and blue lights flashed around a darkened yard. Broken glass glittered under the moonlight, and emergency responders milled around.

The camera focused from above, spanning down over the empty, bloodstained place where a body should have been. The murder weapon's silvery blade was darkened with blood and abandoned amongst shards of glass.

Zooming in farther, a moth with irregular-shaped wings in tan and brown fluttered down, landing in the thick, sticky blood.

The echo of sirens and a fruitless search for a killer punctuated every flap of its dirty wings.

Then up it flew, dipping and rising against the dark sky, red staining it's body as it escaped into the night just like the illusive killer.

"It was the same. But different," she echoed, collapsing into me.

"Different how?" I murmured, stroking the side of her head and all the way down the length of her hair.

Zoey leaned her head against my chest and breathed deep. "In the movie, he stabbed her to death and then escaped into thin air. In real life, he stabbed me, knocked me out, then lit the place on fire, leaving me to burn to death."

I made a sound. The picture she painted was horrifying. And it made the murder my grandmother suffered seem preferable.

"Why do you think he did that?" I murmured, trying to be solid and reasonable when I really wanted to be unstable and irrational.

"One of the school janitors grew suspicious of a van they often saw around the campus. He would drive around but never drop off or pick up a child. So the janitor wrote down the plate number and called it in. The van was registered to a man who coincidentally went to the high school many years before."

"So the police were on to him."

"I don't think anyone thought he was the Bloodlust Killer, but the call from the police freaked him out."

"He wanted to burn the place to get rid of all the evidence." I concluded.

Zoey nodded. "And all the bodies. The night of the fire, someone saw him carrying something large and wrapped up into the school. School was out for the day and it was dark, so the witness called the police."

"And they got there just in time to save you," I said, hugging her close and kissing the top of her head. "Thank God."

"I think what he was carrying in that night was a body he wanted everyone to assume was his. The media coverage and public outcry that a serial killer was using a school as his den was so out of control the police released a statement saying it was his body in the fire. That he was dead."

"They wanted to calm everyone down."

"And they wanted to believe a monster like that was dead."

"But he wasn't." I shook my head.

"No. And now he's back. Wanting to finish what he started."

"Like filming a sequel all over again." I pondered out loud.

Zoey pulled back, looking at me with wide eyes. "What did you say?"

"Deborah lived in the first *Moth to a Flame* movie… Maybe he thought she shouldn't have. And then he sees you in the media, figures out you didn't die the first time either…" The look on her face made my heart constrict. "It's okay. I was just talking out loud. I'm an actor. My brain automatically goes to movies and sequels."

When I tried to pull her back into me, she resisted.

Her finger stabbed in the direction of the TV. "Where was this movie filmed?"

I frowned. "Here in L.A. Actually, it's on the lot next to the set we're working on now." Annoyance flashed over me when I remembered. "They actually never tore it down. After what happened there, no one wanted to be around it. They just sectioned off the house it was filmed in and forgot it. The execs trying to convince me to be part of movie about my grandmother are hinting around at using the set for the production."

She lurched off my lap so fast she would have fallen if I hadn't caught her. Standing up with her this time, I kept a steadying hand on her to ask, "What's wrong?"

Spinning toward the TV, still wobbly on her legs, she said, "That's where he is. That's where he took Callie."

"He couldn't have. It's all gated off, and there's security."

"But you just said that house was abandoned."

"It is, but the large lot it's located on is not. Movies still film there."

"But not close to that house." She led.

I frowned. "You really think he could be there?"

"If a gaggle of nosy reporters can get onto our lot to harass me, then one man who's eluded the police since the eighties can get into that house."

Grabbing my phone, I started to dial. "I'll call the cops."

Zoey took off, rushing in the direction of the garage. "I need to borrow your car."

Ripping the phone from my ear, I ran after her. "Zoey!"

"I'm going!"

"The hell you are!" I roared, catching up to her, yanking her around.

She stumbled into my chest but bounced right back up, fire in her eyes. "I am. You can't stop me."

"I'm not letting you anywhere near that psycho," I growled.

Yanking her body from mine, she said, "You don't have a choice."

Fleeing into the garage, she snatched the keys for my Viper off the wall.

"Zoey, stop!" I yelled. "You can't drive like this."

Her chest was heaving when she spun, her hair flying around her like a cape. "Then you drive."

I thought about Callie. About the fact that I was closer to the lot than the police. I had the clearance to get through security…

Tearing my eyes off her, I finished dialing the detective who'd just left us not even an hour before. The second he answered, I started to talk. "We think he could be at the old *Moth to a Flame* set," I told him. Rattling off the address, I asked him to meet us there.

"You can't go there, Preston," the man asserted. "Under no circumstances are you allowed to visit the potential scene of the crime."

I looked back up at Zoey, who made an impatient sound and went around to the driver's side of the red sports car.

"Then you'd better get there first," I said and cut off the call.

The engine purred to life as I stalked around, wrenching open the door to lean in and shut it off.

"Nick!" Zoey yelled, reaching to start it up again.

Grabbing her wrist, I yanked her out of the car.

"Stop!" she screamed, hysteria in her voice. "I have to do this! I can't let Callie die because of me!"

Her fist hammered into my chest, pushing me back. My hand tightened around her wrist, trying to pull her close.

"Let go!"

"Stop!" I said, trying not to hurt her as she hit me again. "Zoey!" I roared, the sound of my anger breaking through her panic.

Her body stilled, and she looked up.

"There's too much traffic for the Viper. Let's take my bike."

Confusion clouded her eyes. "What?"

Towing her along with me, I went to the corner of the garage where I kept the motorcycle I wasn't supposed to have covered in the corner.

Ripping off the cover, I picked up a helmet and handed it to her before reaching for another.

The keys were already in the ignition, so I straddled the machine and started her up. The motor purred to life with ease. Just because I wasn't contractually allowed to drive it didn't mean I didn't make sure it was drivable.

With the helmet strapped on her head, all I could see was her tearstained eyes through the shield, watching me.

When I thumbed at the seat behind me, her head bobbed and she climbed on. Her arms felt like small vises sliding around my waist, and their fragility made a fierce wave of doubt crash over me.

I shouldn't be doing this. I shouldn't just drive her into a potential disaster.

One of my hands left the handle bar, covering hers at my waist.

Her fingers gave mine a squeeze, and she leaned up next to my helmet. "Callie needs us!"

Fuck.

Taking my hand, she lifted it back to the handle, hers returning to my waist.

The crotch rocket glided out of the garage, down the driveway, and weaved through the press who were still camped out before I punched the engine and drove through the heavy L.A. traffic without any interruption at all.

The second Nick showed his face in the helmet, the guards waved him onto the lot without a passing glance.

I felt dizzy from the speed at which we traveled to get here, and my legs were numb from the vibration of the engine.

Nick drove through the lot, past the active sets and current productions, until everything became more desolate and we reached a section where it seemed mainly equipment and large props were stored.

Going beyond that, my skin started to crawl and goose bumps rose along my arms and legs with an eerie feeling of déjà vu. If I'd been hoping this was where Callie was before, I was now certain.

The very air that blew around us, squeezing inside the helmet I wore, filled my senses with the same kind of fear and dread I'd lived in when I was chained up like an animal waiting for slaughter.

This kind of air was hard to breathe. It filled your lungs and clogged them, not refreshing your body, but instead weighing it down.

The motorcycle downshifted, and though our speed slowed, my arms around Nick tightened. As he drove, I glanced over my shoulder, hoping to see flashing blue and red lights, instead seeing nothing but a cloud of dust drifting in our wake.

We'd made it here very fast, much faster than the police would be able to arrive.

Our bodies tilted when Nick took a turn, angling the bike into a paved lot filled with cracks and weeds. The building beside it was in no better shape, certainly empty.

When he shut off the bike and tugged off the helmet, I flipped up the face shield. "This isn't the house."

"Driving up to the front door isn't the best plan."

He was right. My thinking was becoming muddied with fear and urgency. Fumbling around with the strap, I tried to get the helmet off.

Brushing my fingers away, Nick undid the clasp and pulled it off on the first try. Wind blew through my hair, and I squinted against the sun.

Gentle fingers brushed my bangs down into place, and worried, green eyes caressed my face. "We can wait right here for the police."

"I can't," I said, even though I wanted to do just that. "That monster took so much from me. He's been terrorizing me, toying with me, and he's torturing Callie right now. I can't leave this up to the police this time. This has to end."

His voice was hesitant and quiet. "What do you want to do?"

"Find Callie," I said, climbing off the bike and starting off on unsteady legs.

Nick caught my hand. "He's probably expecting you." Shifting closer, he ordered, "Stay here. I'll go see if she's there."

He probably was expecting me, which was why I had to be the one to go. He wouldn't give Callie up to Nick… but me? I could trade myself for her.

"I'm going," was all I said.

His fingers laced through mine. "Then I'm coming too."

"Which way is the house?" I asked.

He pointed, and we started off, walking through an abandoned section of land that felt haunted the farther in we got.

When the house loomed into view, my footsteps faltered and panic constricted my chest. Clutching my shirt, I breathed shallowly, trying to get control of the emotions taking over.

"Angel," Nick said, sliding around in front of me, blocking the house from sight. "Eyes on me," he urged, tipping up my chin.

I was still breathing erratically and the center of my torso burned, but his face was beautiful and looking at his emerald eyes did offer some relief. "I'm good," I said, shaking him off and starting forward.

An air of loneliness clouded around the home. The weeds crowding the wraparound porch and front steps did nothing to help. One of the shutters was missing on the second story, a few shingles had long since been blown away, and the front door handle was rusting.

Nick tugged my hand, and we started around the back, my foot crunching over brittle glass buried deep beneath overgrown grass. Looking up, I saw a large half-circle window with jagged pieces of dirty glass lining the edges. The boarded windowpane was long gone, and a tattered, dirty curtain flapped behind it.

Staring back down underfoot, I realized this was the place the killer likely fell. This was the place his life should have ended twenty years ago, but instead, he'd managed to get up and run away.

Not too far from the backyard was a line of trees, and I imagined him slipping into the coverage and then somehow escaping so he could come back many years later and kidnap me.

So many lives would have been saved if he'd died that day, if the police had managed to catch him.

Instead, here I was. Creeping around this abandoned, creepy house that no one ever lived in but where someone had been brutally murdered.

Putting his finger against his lips, Nick urged me to be silent, and we tiptoed the rest of the way alongside of the house in case there was more broken glass we couldn't see.

At the corner, he pushed me against the wall, covering my body with his and then peering around to the back. Seconds later, his face was inches from mine, and the smell of his skin brought back a wave of what we'd done last night.

I love you, my heart whispered.

Pointing, I followed his finger to the tree line where a van of some kind was parked.

Adrenaline spiked in my body, making thought almost impossible and the urge to act imperative. *He's here.*

Sensing what I was about to do, Nick pinned me against the house, covering my mouth with his palm. Putting his lips beside my ear, he said, "Now that we know he's here, we'll wait for the cops."

My eyes widened, and I started to shake my head.

The body pinning mine went taut, threatening to use the strength I didn't have against me.

Moaning low in the back of my throat, I let my body slump sideways. Grabbing at the back of my thigh, I massaged the area as I started sliding down the side of the house.

"Ah, angel," he swore low, pulling back so he could lean down and pick me up.

Regaining my center of gravity, I thrust up, catching him by surprise and shoving with all the strength I could muster.

Shock flared in his eyes as he stumbled back, and a sick sense of guilt came like a kick in the gut. But I kept going, rushing from between him and the house and breaking toward the back door.

He cursed low, but I didn't look back. Instead, I rushed up the back stairs, which creaked in warning with every step I took.

Ignoring the alarm bells, the fear, and the stark warning from the house itself, I ripped open the back door, not even flinching when it fell off two of its hinges.

There was no use in being quiet right now. I wanted him to know I was coming.

I wanted him to know I was here.

"I got your note!" Her voice echoed from the first floor, making my heart flutter like a pair of wings.

"They all told me I didn't have to hide. I didn't have to change my name or the way I looked… They all tried to convince me that you were dead!" she yelled. Her heavy footfalls on the hollow floor below told me exactly where she was.

She was coming.

Soon, she would be close enough to touch.

Close enough to kill.

"I knew better. I knew you were out there somewhere!"

So much like the original flame. So much spunk. So much fight in her.

"Help!" the stand-in yelled from inside the bedroom. "Is anyone there? Help me!"

"Callie!"

"Zoey! Up here! Help!"

Footsteps pounded on the stairs. The rotting wood moaned and creaked, the perfect soundtrack for a horror film.

I slid back into the shadows, listening to my little stand-in say her lines on cue.

"Zoey," she wailed, fear and panic perfectly balanced in her cry. "Please help me!"

She was the perfect bait. The perfect ignitor for the flame I'd been waiting for.

"Zoey!" I roared, running into the house as she put her foot on the first stair leading to the second floor.

She paused, glancing up, apology flashing in her eyes. But then she turned back and started up, the sound of the weak wood draining about ten years off my life.

She was almost to the top when I caught up to her. Slipping an arm around her waist, I lifted her, carrying her the rest of the way.

"Nick!" Callie screamed from the down the hall.

Zoey started running even though her feet weren't even on the floor. Hitting at my arm still around her waist, she tried to make me put her down.

"We stay together," I ordered, knowing I couldn't stop her but absolutely refusing to let her do this alone.

I heard her start to speak, but my ears stopped working when something heavy and hard rammed into the back of my head. Unfocused and with pain radiating through me, I pushed Zoey away, knowing she probably cried out, but not being able to find the sound of her voice.

I fell hard onto the floor, the boards rattling under my body as though I'd caused an earthquake. Rolling onto my side, I reached up, covering the back of my head, feeling the slickness of blood.

Hands grabbed my face, and the image of an angel loomed over, her dark hair tumbling over her shoulders. I started to smile, but piercing pain reminded me of the situation, and alarm overruled everything else.

I have to protect this angel. I have to, above everything else, keep her safe.

Her lips were moving, calling out my name. Tears streaked her very pale face, and worry filled her eyes.

I reached for her hand, missing it the first time but able to grab it the second. "I'm okay," I told her. "Hit my head."

How the fuck did I hit my head? I'd been standing at the top of the stairs.

A shadow moved behind Zoey, looming into view. The inside-out mask he wore appeared to be nothing but smooth, shiny skin. No lips. No nose. No hair. Just a faceless head with vacant eyes.

Zoey was so focused on me she didn't even see him. She didn't even feel his evil presence.

Our eyes connected. The glint of a large knife mirrored his heinous image, making it look like there were two of him.

"Run," I said, grabbing at Zoey, trying to push her away. "Run!"

He brought the knife up, his lipless mouth pulling into a twisted smile. His arm slashed down, and I forced back the nausea and dizziness assaulting me to pull Zoey down as I rolled over her.

Searing pain shot through me like lightning, igniting all my senses and making them scream. The blade slid into my skin like butter, going right through me to lodge into the wood on the floor.

"No!" Zoey screamed. *"No!"*

He ripped the knife up, the sound of my flesh tearing loud in my ears. Zoey tried to push me off, she tried to slip from under me, but even injured, I wouldn't let her go.

I would take a hundred stabs of that knife before I gave up shielding her.

Adrenaline and sheer will to keep her safe gave me the strength to push up off the floor, hauling her with me. I stumbled but stayed upright and spun, holding her behind me with my uninjured side.

The man lunged at me again. I threw out a roundhouse kick, knocking the knife out of his hand and into a room off the hallway.

He went after it, and we ran toward the sounds of Callie's pleas.

Closing the bedroom door behind us, I turned the lock, knowing it would only buy us a few seconds but using all the time we could.

Zoey grabbed my arm, sobs falling mercilessly from her lips. "He stabbed you!" she wailed. "Oh my God, you're bleeding."

"It's a flesh wound." I tried to reassure her, feeling the blood flowing like a river down my arm. "C'mon, we gotta move."

"Nick!" Callie yelled, drawing our attention.

My assistant was across the room in the corner, her hunched form lit up by the long white nightgown covering her body.

Rushing to a window, I pulled back the blackout curtains, allowing sunlight to filter into the room.

Zoey whimpered, and everything in me went on high alert. When I turned back, I saw her standing in the center of a few cocoons swaying from the ceiling.

Behind us, there was a knock on the bedroom door.

Callie started to cry.

Rushing forward, I put an arm around my girl, covering her eyes. "Don't look at them," I instructed, dragging her toward Callie.

"I'm chained up!" Callie wailed, lifting the god-awful gown and showing us a metal shackle.

Zoey went limp against me, staring down at the cuff around Callie's leg.

"I can't get free."

The door burst in. The sound of wood splintering made us all look around. The Moth walked in, dressed exactly the way he'd dressed the night he killed my grandmother.

Sudden uncontrollable rage rose inside me. Despite the stab wound, the head wound, and the fact we were cornered, unadulterated anger took over.

"You son of a bitch!" I roared and lunged.

He swiped with the knife already coated in my blood, and I evaded. Throwing out another kick, I hit him dead center in his chest, which made him stumble backward. Not letting him recover, I lunged forward, delivering a swift punch to the side of the head, which made him hit the floor.

Blood dripped down the back of my neck, streaking my skin and curling around my forearm like ribbons.

Using the bloodied hand, I grabbed a handful of his hoodie, hauling half his body up off the floor.

Sudden pain made me drop him and stumble back.

Zoey screamed, and I looked down, noting a smaller blade sticking out of the side of my leg.

Grabbing the knife, I pulled it out and plunged it into his thigh. He yelled, the first sound I'd heard him make, and fuck yeah, it was a satisfying noise.

Standing, I put the heel of my foot on the handle and pushed it deeper, making him writhe on the floor. "Where're the keys?" I asked, motioning toward Callie.

Zoey flung her arms around me from behind, towing me away from him. Dizzy and unfocused, I turned, grabbing her by the face and surveying her blurred features. "You okay, angel?"

"Stop getting stabbed."

I started to smile, but she screamed and shoved me aside. I fell, and she stepped forward right into the fist of The Moth.

Her body hit the floor, and I roared. Lunging after him, I tackled the man, burying my fist into his gut. One of his hands went for the knife wound in my leg, and the other reached around my arm and poked at the jagged hole.

I yelled, and he rolled, pinning me beneath him, raising the knife over my chest.

"No!" Zoey screamed. "No, please, no!"

Still holding the knife over me, the faceless man tilted his head.

"Take me! Take me instead," she wailed.

"No!" I said, struggling to get up. He punched me in the arm wound again, making me recoil.

"If you kill him right now, I'll run. Our sequel will never be finished. It's him or me, okay? You can't have us both. If you let them go, I swear I'll stay. You can do whatever you want to me."

"Zoey! No!" I bellowed, throwing a punch. It connected with The Moth, and he fell off me.

I went for Zoey, but she moved away, running over to that animal's side. "Please," she begged. "Please let them go."

He reached into the pocket of his hoodie and held out a key.

A desperate sound ripped out of her, and she threw the key to me. "Unchain her!"

I hesitated for a second, but Callie started crying again, so I rushed to get her free. Once my assistant was standing on her own, I ran toward Zoey.

The Moth grabbed her, holding the knife at her throat.

My footsteps faltered. Holding my hands out, palms up, I said, "Just let her go. Come at me."

"No!" she insisted. "Get out of here, Nick. Go!"

"I'm not leaving you here."

Zoey cried out when the blade pricked her neck and a rivulet of red oozed down.

I moved forward, but the blade pressed harder.

"Stop!" I exclaimed. "I won't come closer. Just… stop."

"Take her and get out," The Moth said, his voice sounding scarily normal compared to the way he looked and behaved. "Take her and get out right now, or I'll slice her head off in front of you."

"Go," Zoey pleaded.

I shook my head.

She winced when the knife pricked her again.

Pain unlike anything I'd ever experienced before gripped my heart. "I'm going!" I declared. "We're going."

Grabbing Callie and shielding her with my body, we moved toward the door as I kept my eyes on Zoey and that knife the entire way. "Go!" I told my assistant, pushing her into the hallway. "Go!"

"You too!" The Moth yelled, sounding a little less stable than before.

"You killed my grandmother," I said, pointing out into the hallway. "Right over there. Deborah Ascott. And now here I am, her flesh and blood... Forget the sequel with her." I gestured to Zoey. "Finish what you started with my family."

Instead of cutting her a third time, the fucker squeezed her neck, making blood gush from the cut and a choking sound gargle from her lips.

"Stop!" I begged, my voice breaking. Seeing her blood was my kryptonite. If I walked out of here, if I let him think I was really leaving, he would let her go. I would buy her a few minutes. "I'm going," I announced.

Zoey's eyes collided with mine.

"I love you," I told her, the words like sandpaper ripping across an uneven board.

She nodded.

Walking out of that room was the hardest thing I'd ever done.

Callie was at the top of the stairs, shivering and crying in that fucking sick gown.

The entire way down the stairs, I fought the urge to run back up. The entire way downstairs, I prayed to God I wouldn't live to regret this moment.

There was no noise at all from upstairs as I led Callie out the front door.

No sound of death.
No sound of life.
Just nothing.

And then there were two.

A moth and his flame.

A killer and a woman who refused to be his victim for a single second longer.

He shoved me away the moment the front door shut with a definitive sound. My knees hit the floor, and pain radiated up my left thigh.

It didn't matter, though. I could deal with a little pain. With the stinging cuts from his blade against my flesh. Nick and Callie were safe. Gone from this house. And even if I died five minutes from now, at least I would die alone.

I didn't plan to die, though.

Not today. Not by his hand.

"The police are on their way," I told him. "I called them before I even arrived."

Carrying the knife stained with my and Nick's blood, he picked up a folded white square of fabric.

I didn't flinch away when he came close and extended the gown.

I took it.

He left through the busted in door, leaving me alone with the cocoons hanging from the ceiling.

Heart hammering, neck stinging, I ran to the window to look out, hoping for a glimpse of Nick or the sound of police sirens in the distance.

All I heard was silence.

I knew Nick wasn't going to leave me here. As much as I wanted him to, that man was just not built that way. I only had a limited amount of time before he came back, before he was in danger once more.

I pulled on the gown over my clothes, letting it fall all the way down until it brushed the floor. A strong sense of panic and the past washed over me, momentarily rendering me paralyzed.

I couldn't stop. If I stopped to think about this, about him, I might never start moving again.

The gown swished around my shoes as I went around the room, looking for some kind of weapon, finding nothing except a length of chain.

Wrapping it around my hand, I made a fist, figuring it was better than nothing.

My heart was erratic, my breathing labored, and every step I took made me feel like I might collapse. I kept going anyway.

I thought of all the years I'd hidden. All the nightmares I'd suffered through. I thought about Nick… about how he made me want to live again. About how strong he made me realize I really was.

One foot after another. One step and then another.

I paused only briefly at the bedroom door before stepping through splintered, busted wood into the hallway.

She couldn't run anymore.

Too many people had died. He would keep coming to her, just as he promised. Like a moth drawn to a flame—until the moth was burned up or the flame went out.

Out in the hallway, the creaking of the stairs proved she was right.

Lifting my chin, I looked into the shadows for him, but he wasn't there. Sunlight did filter in through the broken window at the end of the hall. Ripped, dirty drapes flapped like tattered ghosts in a haunted house. Even though there was sun, there were even more shadows. Everything was draped in a filter of death and gore.

Playing my part, I started toward the window.

A noise from somewhere in the house made her pause. She tilted her head, listening. Heavy footfalls coming up the stairs whisked her back toward the window, to the sheer white curtains draping the panes.

He was taking his time. He knew she would wait.

There was no escaping him. If she ran tonight, he'd come back tomorrow.

She was tired of running. Exhausted from being chased.

Someone would die tonight, whether it was him or her.

I couldn't hide behind the curtains. They were too battered for that, and there was too much light for me to be concealed. I did back up against them, though, watching as the shiny-masked man topped the stairs.

We stared at each other, the knife at his side still bathed in blood.

In the distance, sirens finally cut through the day, telling me to hold on just a little bit longer.

His eyes flared, and I smiled.

When he lunged toward me, I punched out with my chain-wrapped fist, but he shoved it away and grabbed my neck. He lifted me off my feet like I weighed nothing at all, like my body was floating off the floor.

Flashbacks of the movie I'd just watched assailed me, making me wonder if this was real or a dream.

"Zoey!" Nick's yell floated up the stairs, firmly planting me in reality.

I kicked out, burying the toe of my shoe into his balls. Grunting, his grip slackened, and I fell out of his hold. Before I could get up, he swung the knife down, and I lunged to the side, just barely avoiding a stab.

Nick appeared at the top of the steps, eyes wild and drenched in blood. All I could think about was his safety, about how I would rather die than lose him.

Grabbing The Moth by the back of the neck, Nick pulled him around, burying a fist in his middle. The grip he had on the knife loosened, and I reached up, ripping it from his grasp.

The Moth turned around, coming for me, but I slammed the knife down into his bloodstained hiking boot, the blade breaking bone as I forced it down.

He howled in pain, grappling for me, but his foot was now pinned to the floor.

"Thank God, Zoey!" Nick called, reaching around to tow me up, eyes roaming every inch of me.

Over his shoulder, I saw The Moth lunge. Screaming, I shoved Nick out of the way and barreled forward. My body slammed into his, and he fell backward, grappling for the only support he could find... the old, brittle curtain.

The rod it hung on ripped from the wall, and he rocked back, arms flailing. I reached out and shoved him again, the force breaking the knife off in his foot and sending him flailing out the broken window.

What was left of the glass shattered as he fell. Right before he disappeared, his hand clamped around my wrist, and my body started to go with him.

He began to laugh. A chilling, bone-numbing sound.

Closing my eyes, I felt weightless as I started to fall.

I guessed it wasn't him or me that would die tonight... Instead, it would be both.

Her body tipped out the window. That fucking madman tried to drag her down to hell with him.

Angels didn't belong in hell. Zoey belonged with me.

"I got you." I wrapped my arms around her from behind, anchoring her before she fell out the window completely.

"Don't let go," she pleaded, a definite strain in her voice.

"Never." I swore.

The sicko still clinging to her arm swung his body, trying to dislodge the hold I had on her. Zoey winced when jagged glass cut into her middle, but she didn't cry out.

My teeth gnashed together with the force of my grit when I stretched out the arm with the stab wound. My hands and forearms were slick with blood, making me fear the grip I had on Zoey would be lost. Ignoring the throbbing pain and dizziness trying to disorient me, I leaned down, pressing my chest firmly against her back.

Seeing that I now had an even better hold, The Moth began flailing erratically and frankly pissing me the fuck off.

A distressed sound ripped from her throat when The Moth slapped his other hand around her wrist. Now he hung off her, pulling her down with both hands.

He didn't look at her, though. Instead, he looked at me.

Daring me. Challenging me.

If I pulled her the rest of the way in, then he would come too. If I saved my girl, then I would be saving him.

As if I cared.

There was no choice here.

Both bodies heaved upward as I towed her into the house.

"No!" she wailed. "Wait!"

I stopped because I was worried the uneven glass pierced her again. "Are you hurt?"

"Nick might be willing to save you." Zoey spoke, her voice dark and pitched downward. "But I sure as hell won't."

"Zoey, no!" I yelled, afraid of what she was going to do. Sticking it to that psycho wasn't as important as her safety.

Her voice directed at me was so much gentler than the one she'd used to taunt the killer. "Trust me."

Trust was an easy thing to give until you were in a situation where it could literally mean life or death. It didn't matter. Zoey had my trust. All of it. Even in a situation as dire as this.

"I do trust you, angel."

Swiping her free hand over my slick arm, she reached down to where the maniac gripped her. Using the blood coating her fingers like a lubricant, she pried his hand off her wrist. All three of us jolted toward the ground when his grip loosened, but I held strong.

The Moth made a strangled sound, the first inkling of fear I'd ever noticed from his pompous, murderous ass.

Zoey wrenched his remaining hand off her, and when he was dangling over the ground, basically at her mercy, she spoke with strength ringing in her voice. "Victims survive and killers *do* die."

She let go.

He plummeted toward the ground, and I pulled her to safety.

"Nick." She gasped, both of us falling back into the hall.

I hit the wall, pain radiating from my leg to my skull, but I didn't let go of her. I made sure I took the brunt of the collision.

She yelled my name again, hands grabbing my face and pulling it down. "Stop taking hits for me!"

I scoffed. "Never."

Her face crumpled, and a floodgate of fear and grief opened wide. Wrapping my arms around her, I held her while she sobbed and shook.

Police stormed the house, and relief poured over me.

"Hey," I murmured as the officers' shouts reached us from all directions. "Hey." I tried again, peeling her off my chest so I could see her face. "How bad are you hurt?"

She shook her head and tried to burrow into me once more.

"Let me see your neck." I started tilting her head up, but she pushed my hand away.

"You were stabbed twice." She fumed, but the anger seemed diluted because of the tears still streaking her cheeks. "And your head!"

"Good thing you were here to shove him out a window."

Her eyes grew about three sizes, and she nearly pitched sideways while shoving to her feet.

"Easy." I warned, grabbing ahold of her and using the wall as leverage for us both.

A strangled sound floated behind her when she rushed over to the window to peer out. Her whole body stiffened, and I went to her instantly. She spun into me, burying her face in my chest.

Rubbing her back, I looked below and felt satisfaction soothe some of the injuries paining me.

He was still down there. Broken and twisted.

Dead.

"It's okay now, angel," I murmured. "He can't hurt you anymore."

"I killed him."

"You saved yourself." I corrected.

That got her to lift her head. "I did?"

I nodded. "And me too."

That earned me a small smile.

Tenderness swelled up inside me. Tucking a strand of hair behind her ear, I glanced down at the nightgown swallowing her whole. Everything that piece of fabric represented made my skin crawl.

The sentiment must have shown on my face because Zoey glanced down. Horror changed her features, and panic flared in her eyes.

Suddenly, she seemed short of breath as she ripped at the high neck and billowing fabric. "Get it off me!" she shrieked. "Get it off!"

Her hands were rough but too shaky to be useful. The panic seizing her didn't allow her to stop and think. All she could do was frantically tug at the gown.

Out of the corner of my eye, I noted the officers who were coming up the stairs paused, warily assessing the situation.

Angling myself between her and their prying eyes, I grabbed the lace trying to choke her.

"Eyes on me, angel," I implored.

Her chest was still heaving when her eyes met mine. A hard tug tore the fabric, and I ripped it right down the center, then peeled it off her body.

When it was off her, she tossed it on the ground and stepped on it, shuddering.

The officers behind me continued on, passing by on their way down the hall. The second they stepped into the room where Callie had been, I heard one of them swear emphatically.

A part of me was mildly amused (though I didn't show it) because those fuckers had just been watching Zoey like she was overreacting because of a cotton gown. Guess seeing those giant plastic cocoons hanging from the ceiling changed their perspective.

Turning back to my girl, I wrapped an arm (the uninjured one) around her waist, tugging her close. "I know a lot of strong women, but I honestly think you are the strongest I've ever met."

She gasped, straightening away from me. "Callie!"

"Callie's fine." I assured her. "I got her out of the house and made sure she was safe. She's with the paramedics by now."

"Thank God." The relief in her voice was unmistakable. But that relief quickly turned into a scowl. Planting her fists on her hips, she glared. "You never should have come back into the house for me."

I felt my eyes narrow, and I took a step closer to her, practically bringing us nose to nose. "You never should have traded my safety for yours."

She made a rude sound and pointed at the knife wound in my arm, then at the one in my leg.

"That's different." I snarled.

Suddenly, her eyes welled up and fresh tears spilled over. "You could have been k-killed." Her voice shook. "I've never been so scared," she whispered, swiping at her cheeks. "Not even when I was alone with him."

My pounding heart fumbled when those words wrapped around it. Butterflies lifted off in my stomach, and deep affection erased any anger I might have felt. Cupping the back of her neck, I pulled her in. I was woozy from blood loss, but it didn't matter.

Her shoulders shook as she cried some more, and all I wanted to do was soothe her. "I'm not going anywhere, angel. I don't want to be anywhere you aren't."

Her fingers tightened against my back, and I kissed the top of her head.

"Mr. Preston, Miss Halston?" the detective on the case called as he came up the stairs. "Are you ready to give a statement?"

Lifting my lips from her hair, I gazed around. "Maybe give us a minute."

"No," Zoey asserted, pulling away. As she spoke, her hand reached for mine and our fingers laced together. "I'm ready."

The second the detective topped the steps, his eyes widened and a low whistle cut through his pursed lips. "That's a hell of a lot of blood, Mr. Preston."

"Nick." I corrected.

He nodded and gestured for us to accompany him. "The statement can wait. Let's get you seen by the medics first."

Outside, police were everywhere, and two ambulances were parked close by. Callie was in the back of one, getting treated for a head wound and some minor injuries. She'd been through hell, and I felt partially responsible for that. But she was alive, and that was most important.

"There's something I need to do," Zoey said, trying to slip out of my hold.

"Not without me," I said, pulling her close once more.

"I... I have to see him. I want to make sure he's dead." Her eyes were fearful and wary as she looked off in The Moth's direction.

I didn't try and talk her out of it. She needed this closure, and I understood why. And yeah, I wanted to look the dead bastard in the face too. I wanted the closure my grandmother and mother never got.

We leaned on each other as we approached the surrounded body. Officers parted when they saw us. Conversations dropped to whispers.

Zoey hesitated before stepping close, and I waited patiently, allowing her to set the pace.

Nodding, she moved forward, her hand gripping mine where I held her waist.

We stood over the dead body of a man who'd terrorized people for over twenty years.

"I want to see his face," Zoey said.

"Are you sure?" I asked, uncertain it was a good idea.

She nodded. "I want to see him as a regular man… not this faceless creature."

I glanced at the detective standing close by, and he nodded once.

"I'll do it," I said, releasing her.

"No." She stopped me. "I will."

Stepping back, I watched my girl squat and reach out with shaking hands. Grasping the edge of the mask, she pulled it up over his chin, peeling it back to reveal his face.

It was just as she said. He was just a man in his fifties with graying hair and wrinkles around his eyes. There was nothing especially striking about him, which I supposed made him scarier. If I were to see a man like this on the street, I would think of him as a neighbor or even perhaps a friend.

The detective cleared his throat and stepped forward, shuffling some papers in his hands. "The information came in before you called this morning. Name is Ronald Valve. He was born in nineteen sixty-four and went to Weston High School…"

"The place where I was held captive," Zoey whispered, staring down at the man.

"Yes. Turns out he was in some kind of horror movie club in high school, and that's where he first watched *Moth to a Flame*. We were able to track down a fellow club member who told us that Ron here was obsessed with the movie. The teacher who ran the club knew someone in Hollywood and told him that The

Moth would be killed off in the sequel." The detective cleared his throat. "He was very angry because he said killers don't die. Victims do."

"All this because he didn't like the end of a movie?" I spat.

"Killers don't die. Victims do," Zoey echoed.

I didn't like the tone in her voice. "Hey," I murmured, taking her hand. "It's over. He can't hurt you ever again."

Nodding, Zoey sank into my side a little more firmly. I took that as my cue to lead her away. As we turned, a strangled cry burst out from the ground, and the bloody hand of the man who was supposed to be dead shot out, grabbing Zoey's ankle.

She screamed and jolted back. The Moth turned his head, viewing at her with empty eyes.

I stomped on his arm, breaking his hold on her leg, and wrapped her against my chest, whirling her away from the man.

What was it with this bastard? He really did belong in a horror film because he freaking refused to die.

Seconds later, a gunshot rang out. Zoey forced herself closer against me, and I pressed a hand over her ear, buffering any more chaos that might erupt.

"He's dead this time," one of the officers announced.

Still shielding Zoey, I glanced. *Yep*. He was dead. Unless, of course, he didn't need half his head to live.

Around us, everyone clapped.

No, probably not very respectful, but dude had it coming.

I picked up Zoey and started toward the ambulance.

"Nick!" She gasped. "Put me down! You have stab wounds!"

"You want to add another to my heart?" I drawled.

She wrinkled her nose. Then panic filled her eyes. "You're heart! What's wrong with your heart?"

She was kind of adorable when she worried about me.

"Nothing as long as you let me hold you."

She smacked me in the chest.

"Oww," I whined, playing it up a little.

"I'm sorry!" She fretted. "Are you hurt more? What can I do?"

"Kiss me," I said, not missing a beat.

Realization dawned, and her eyes narrowed. "That's not funny, Nick Preston! I don't care if you're a movie star or not, pretending to be hurt after the day we've had is cruel."

"My arm really does hurt," I confessed. Not to mention, I knew I was rocking a concussion.

"Stop!" she commanded.

I stopped.

Taking my face in her hands, she guided it down, pressing her lips firmly against mine. Bleeding or not, I took full advantage of her sweet lips, letting the knowledge that we were both safe wrap around us while we kissed.

A few months later…

My hair was in a ponytail; no makeup graced my face. My eyes were as blue as the day I was born, and more importantly… I was happy.

I didn't have to hide anymore.

I didn't have to pretend.

I was free.

I was no longer a prisoner of the bad things that happened. I wasn't ashamed of everything I'd been through.

"Where's my blue-eyed angel?" Nick called from the bedroom.

My heart still skipped a beat when I heard his voice. I wondered how many years it would take for that to stop. I kind of hoped it never did.

He appeared in the bathroom door as I turned to meet him, his golden hair plastered to his forehead and his shirt damp with sweat. Still, when he pulled me in, I went to him. I was done denying the way I felt. I was done being afraid.

"You're smelly!" I laughed, wrapping my arms around his torso.

"It takes work to be this buff," he said, flexing an impressive bicep for me to check out. As if I hadn't seen it a hundred times before.

I smiled, rubbing a palm over his defined arm. "Buff or not, I'd love you the same."

The teasing glint disappeared from his face. Slowly, his arm lowered to his side. The change in the atmosphere was instantaneous, going from playful to electrified in one second flat.

He whispered, "What did you just say?"

It slipped right out without me thinking. And now that it was said, I couldn't grab it back. Groaning, I let my forehead fall against his chest.

"It just came out. I know—"

His hands closed around my shoulders, carefully but firmly drawing me back. The look in his eyes was so intense that a knot instantly formed in my throat. "Did you mean it?"

Why did that question break my heart and make me ache? The answer was happy.

Because it took so much to get here. And I went and ruined it by blurting it out in the bathroom. He'd waited so patiently for those three words… words I knew he wanted so much to hear.

I felt bad for ruining something so important, for not making it as special as I could. "I planned to tell you in a much better way."

Nick gave me a small shake. "Zoey. Did you mean it?"

The expression in his eyes dragged me in, wrapped around me, and made everything else slip away. "Of course I mean it. I've felt it for a long time, but I finally trust myself enough to give those words." Lowering my eyes, I frowned. "I wanted to find the perfect way to tell you, but I ruined it."

"You ruined it?" he echoed.

A thought came to me. I looked up, hopeful. "Forget you heard me. I'll plan something special and—"

His kiss stopped the words and seared me to the core. My toes curled against the floor, and my hands anchored onto those well-formed biceps for support. As he kissed, one hand wrapped around my ponytail, tugging my head back for him to deepen the kiss.

Our tongues tangled, dancing to a rhythm only they knew, and I pushed closer, plastering myself against his body.

Breaking off the kiss abruptly, I swayed forward, but his body was solid and kept me up. "I will not forget. I'll never unhear those words, no matter what."

"But we're in the bathroom," I whined.

"It doesn't matter where we are or who we're with. The fact that it just slipped out in regular conversation is better than any moment you could ever plan. That means you feel it without thinking, that I'm in here"—he pointed to my chest—"and you're okay with it."

Tears prickled the back of my eyes, but I held them at bay. "I'm more than okay with it."

Taking my face in his hands, he held me in a stare. "Yeah?"

I nodded.

"Say it again."

"I love you." No hesitation. No fear. "I love you, Nick."

His lips were on mine again, kissing me fiercely. Picking me up, he backtracked into our bedroom, and we fell on the bed.

His broad body caged me in, eyes roaming over me possessively like he was reclaiming what he already owned. Reaching around with one hand, he tugged the shirt over his head, tossing it aside, revealing a chiseled body still glistening with sweat.

Barely a minute later, we were both completely naked and his lips were devouring mine once more, our bodies moving in perfect sync.

Abruptly, he pushed up, skin flushed, lips damp, and eyes filled with wild desire. "Again, angel."

I smiled.

"I love you." The confession was punctuated by my moan when he thrust deep. I arched off the bed, giving in to every physical and emotion sensation he brought down.

The frenzy in which we went at each other brought us crashing down in a hurry, leaving us both breathing heavy and boneless against the bed.

"You make me so fucking happy," he said, rolling onto his side and throwing a leg over my body.

Reaching up, I dragged my fingers through his hair as he pressed a kiss against my bare shoulder. "Thank you for being so patient with me. Thank you for never giving up."

"I'll always be here for you, angel. Always."

When I turned my head, our noses bumped together, making me giggle. He swallowed it down with another sweet kiss.

"Let's go away together. Somewhere tropical where the cabanas float over the water and the only thing I have to share you with is the incredible view."

"The movie about Deborah starts production next week." I reminded him. After everything that happened, he signed on to be part of it. He wanted to make sure his family was portrayed truthfully and that our connection to the murder was revealed.

"Guess we'll have to leave tonight."

I sat up, propping on one elbow to stare down at him incredulously. "Tonight?"

"We're going to be busy the next few months with this production. There are going to be a lot of hard moments…" he said, his eyes softening. Carefully brushing my bangs to the side, he smiled. "I want to give you some happy memories to fall back on."

"I wouldn't have agreed to work on this production with you if I didn't think I could handle it." Yes, it was going to be hard, but as I said before, I was free. Doing this movie, adding in my connection to The Moth, and being a voice for all the women he murdered after Deborah was a way to acknowledge all the trauma and move on.

"I know you can handle it. You can handle anything. So how about handling a trip to the Maldives?"

"Seriously?" I asked, biting down on my lower lip.

Plucking it free with his fingers, he rubbed the pad of his thumb along it. "I already booked the flight."

I couldn't help it. I smiled.

"Whoop!" he hollered, knowing I was totally going to surrender. Rolling on top of me, he grinned down. "Does this mean I finally get to call you my girlfriend?"

I nodded. "If that's what you want."

"Oh, I want." He nuzzled the side of my neck. "And someday in the not so distant future, I'm going to upgrade you to wife."

My stomach fluttered with a thousand butterflies. "How about we pack first?"

"Throw some stuff in a bag for me, will ya, angel? I need to take a shower."

"You a tell a man you love him, and he instantly thinks you're his housekeeper," I muttered, adjusting the blankets on the bed. "Eeep!" I squealed when his bare arms wound around me from behind, lifting me off the ground and spinning us around.

"I could never think of you like that," he whispered in my ear. "You're my everything."

Leaning back, I kissed his cheek.

"I don't need much," he muttered. "Just some shorts, a couple T-shirts… and you."

"Go take a shower." I gave in, totally charmed by him.

"Plane leaves in three hours!" he hollered from the bathroom.

I gasped. "You didn't even know if I would agree to come with you!"

He peeked around the door, all messy hair, ornery green eyes, and naked torso. "Ah, angel, I knew."

I lifted my chin. "Yeah? And just how did you know?"

His smile was quick and sure. "Because you, my love, are just as drawn to me as I am to you."

I didn't bother arguing… He was right.

THE END

I started this book in 2017. I wrote about six thousand words and started to struggle with it. I'm not really sure why. Then another book took over my brain, and I put this one aside. Fast-forward to now (2019), and it's been a rough writing year for me. It's been hard to get into a book and write, write, write. Truthfully, I've often been discouraged by this job and everything that comes with writing. It's easy to let all those things take over and suck out my creativity and motivation to write.

I pulled this book out because I really wanted to write something about a serial killer.

Side note: Is wanting to write about serial killer the same thing as like craving chips or ice cream? I mean, who wakes up and thinks, *I want to spend some time with a serial killer today?*

Anywho, I thought of this book and decided to expand on my original ideas and add in The Moth. I also decided to add some flashbacks to the past that both Zoey and Nick experienced. Well, really, it was Deborah, but we saw it all through Nick's eyes.

I really enjoyed plotting out this book. I feel like there were a lot of moving parts and details. I actually had to do MATH—which is my mortal enemy—to figure out dates and ages, etc. I have a lot of notes and scribbled details that I used to keep track of things to help complete this story arc. Also, my friend, Adrienne, was a great help in bouncing ideas around and plotting serial killer things, so without her, the plot wouldn't be as rich as it is now.

All that being said, this book was a difficult write. It left my brain tired at the end of most writing sessions. Getting into The Moth's head was challenging, and sometimes when I would write his POV, I would wonder if I did him justice.

I still wonder that about all three characters—if I did them justice. I really tried hard to connect with them and bring their personalities to life. I wanted Zoey to be vulnerable and closed off but also strong and willing to persevere. Sometimes I found it hard to balance the PTSD she experienced with her strength. I've also never written about an amputee, so I did a lot of research online about prosthetics. I sincerely hope I wrote about that part of her with truth. If I made any errors, I meant no offense or disrespect.

For Nick, I wanted to portray that he was more than the sexiest man alive and that he wanted more out of life than just the perks of being a celebrity. I wanted to show how his life was also impacted by The Moth and how Zoey and Nick were connected by the past. I liked his confidence and how he accepted the strong feelings he had for Zoey almost right away. I think someone like her needed someone like him, because if it was anyone with less strength, they might have given up on her.

Though this was a challenging book to write, I'm proud of how it came out. Even when it was tough, I kept going (like Zoey!) and tried to bring out the best story I could. So while this book was two years in the making, I hope you all will find the wait was worth it and get wrapped up in the story of Zoey and Nick.

Thank you all for reading and for all the support you've shown me. It keeps me going even in seasons when writing is discouraging and I'd rather be a barista (lol).

Until next book!

XOXO,
Cambria

Cambria Hebert is an award-winning, bestselling novelist of more than forty books. She went to college for a bachelor's degree, couldn't pick a major, and ended up with a degree in cosmetology. So rest assured her characters will always have good hair.

Besides writing, Cambria loves a caramel latte, staying up late, sleeping in, and watching movies. She considers math human torture and has an irrational fear of birds (including chickens). You can often find her painting her toenails (because she bites her fingernails) or walking her Chihuahuas (the real rulers of the house).

Cambria has written within the young adult and new adult genres, penning many paranormal and contemporary titles. She has also written romantic suspense, science fiction, and male/male romance. Her favorite genre to read and write is contemporary romance. A few of her most recognized titles are: *The Hashtag Series, GearShark Series, Text, Amnesia,* and *Butterfly.*

Recent awards include: Author of the Year, Best Contemporary Series (*The Hashtag Series*), Best Contemporary Book of the Year, Best Book Trailer of the Year, Best Contemporary Lead, Best Contemporary Book Cover of the Year. In addition, her most recognized title, *#Nerd,* was listed at Buzzfeed.com as a top fifty summer romance read.

Cambria Hebert owns and operates Cambria Hebert Books, LLC.

You can find out more about Cambria and her titles by visiting her website: http://www.cambriahebert.com.

Please sign up for her newsletter to stay in the know about all her cover reveals, releases, and more: http://eepurl.com/bUL5_5

452